BROKEN

BLESSED SERIES * BOOK ONE

TONI JACKSON LAMPLEY

TABLE OF CONTENTS

Broken

Blessed Series, Book 1

© 2026 Toni Jackson Lampley

All rights reserved. No portion of this publication may be reproduced, stored in a retrieval system, or transmitted in any form or by any means—electronic, mechanical, photocopying, recording, scanning, or other—except for brief quotations in critical reviews or articles, without the prior written permission of the publisher.

Blessed Series

Book 1: *Broken*

Book 2: *Made* (forthcoming)

Published in Hampton, VA, by Fruition Publishing Concierge Services®. Fruition Publishing Concierge Services® is a division of Alesha Brown, LLC.

Fruition Publishing Concierge Services® can bring authors to your live event. For more information or to book an event, visit Fruition Publishing Concierge Services® at:

www.FruitionPublishing.com

Library Of Congress Control Number: 2026902379

ISBN: 978-1-954486-71-3 paperback

ISBN: 978-1-954486-72-0 eBook

Printed in the United States of America

10 9 8 7 6 5 4 3 2 1

Second Edition

PREFACE

As a young girl, I just felt different. Awkward. I cannot explain it, even today.

I was fun and outgoing, but quietly in my room, writing, sketching, and creating brought my spirit to life. For a long time, I didn't share any of those creations with anyone, although they were hiding in plain sight. I was afraid of what others would think if they knew my true self.

I got the impression that what I had to offer the world was not important. Everyone else's offering seemed better. I was bound by a posture of perfection, telling myself I had to be twice as good at everything. That self-talk and overthinking paralyzed me from time to time. I would have moments of consciousness, but being my true self was now more uncomfortable than the perfection.

I perfected going through the motions. I forgot I loved to create. Like the woman in the Bible with a disabling spirit (Luke 13:10-17, ESV), I was bent over, unable to see myself. This is a sad place for the soul.

With time, I grew in my faith. I realized that I was free to be me through Jesus Christ.

In my twenties, I joined a solid church family, where I grew stronger in the Word of God and met my husband. This is where I rested. I expected that my husband and I would grow in our faith together, remain firm in God's promises, and help other married couples strengthen their spiritual bonds.

None of this happened. I felt pressure and strain on our marriage. I appreciated and loved my husband, my children, and my job. I could not understand what was happening. Later, the truth was revealed.

I was breaking trying to sustain them by myself, without God. I allowed them to define me. **The blessings from God overshadow the blessing of God.**

I was in pain emotionally, and it was the pain of pride. I saw us as Christians who were simply going through the motions of life. In reality, we were self-reliant, exhausted, and defeated because we were trying to build a life without a true, deep connection with God. Our Bible, the Word of God on which we were to stand on, was left on the shelf, far from the forefront of our minds, nor in our hearts. Once I was aware of this truth, I prayed and repented.

God gave me the opportunity to work as a design consultant for a home builder. As I was going in and out of homes under construction, I saw how God's relationship with me was much like the design process. My desire to construct my life in Christ and strengthen my relationship with Him grew stronger.

After the home construction company dissolved, I met people who provided me with emotional and spiritual guidance and support. I became a business counselor, advising people on how to start, grow, and enhance their small businesses. All of this was God's design to help me recognize that my purpose was not just to build my life, but also to help others design theirs.

In my personal life, I had plates spinning, and my posture was still off balance. I'd get up early to love my husband and feed and dress our kids for daycare and preschool. After long days at work, I would prepare dinner, clean up afterward, then bathe the kids, dress them for bed, and read them a story before putting them to sleep.

I'd start a load of laundry, try to do something I enjoyed, but all too often I was too tired. During this time, my dad was diagnosed with dementia. To aid my mom, I had my dad stay with us every other weekend. It was painful to watch my dad slowly slip away from awareness and forget my name. Often, I secretly cried myself to sleep. It was painful to do these things alone.

I was doing everything I knew to do. I was being faithful to God. I was serving and giving to my family. I couldn't do any more than what I was already doing.

Once again, I was like the woman bent over. I slumped back into the hurtful posture of negative self-talk and overthinking. Though I could look up, it was emotionally painful and difficult. Our third child was seven months old when my aunt died. My dad needed assisted living, and God told me to quit my job. In the marriage, I felt abandoned, unloved, and lost. I couldn't spin those plates any longer, and I couldn't hold it all in any longer. I broke, and not just in half; I was shattered into pieces.

These were dark times. I was depressed, and this was not the life I wanted to live. I thought of suicide, but I knew better. How awful it would be for my children to find me dead. I remember praying to God not to wake me up. I knew it would be horrible if I took my life, but if He took it, I'd be relieved of my suffering. Today, I'm so grateful He ignored me.

The depression deepened with hopelessness, despair, and abandonment all around. It was during these times that God was the most tender. One night as I got up to pray, God whispered, "You're beautiful." As I would spend my Friday nights alone after work and grocery shopping, I wondered if I was doing something wrong. I begged God for a word to guide me through this difficult time. My Heavenly Father answered, "Stand."

In my broken state, I stood, and God provided sound advice. My spiritual mom reminded me that God, through Jesus Christ, had made me a postured woman. The agony of my circumstances was making it uncomfortable to be upright, yet I was being molded by His design. I could stop examining myself to the point of exhaustion. In Jesus' name, I was enough.

I prayed to God to direct my steps, and He did. Sadly, I divorced, and my dad died, but God provided. He comforted me, restored my mind, called me, touched me, and healed me. Today, I use my creativity to honor Him, praise Him, and help others in their walk with God.

According to Jacob Nordby's book, *The Creative Cure*, socialization combined with trauma can lead to perfection. Socialization is a part of our everyday life, from wearing clothes and brushing our teeth to learning to drive. But socialization can also be oppressive when it keeps us from dreaming, being curious, and taking healthy risks that lead to our gifting. Socialization can say, "Don't dream of being an actress; that's not a viable career choice," or "You're too old to be a dancer now." Nordby shares that statements like these stunt our creative selves. I say it harms our living posture, leading us to adopt an unhealthy, frail, and insecure position. It can break us.

While I had a beautiful childhood, I must admit that primary school was difficult. In school, I was bullied and faced discrimination because of my skin color, resulting in the assumption that I would be average, not apply myself, or strive for excellence. My parents had a different set of expectations.

My sister and I were expected to be the best versions of ourselves. In my young mind, I knew my parents' view was better, but school was stressful. To be recognized, not dismissed or teased, meant maintaining perfect posture. I couldn't be myself in this stance.

The stance suppressed my writing, sketching, and creativity. The Christian life gave me permission to be me. Jesus came and offered an abundant life. I understood, and still do today, that I am a creative soul. The creative design process is how God built me. However, the hurt in my marriage, the pain of divorce, and the loss of my dad put me back in a deformed posture. Before I knew it, I was bent over, not seeing myself, having the wrong perspective on life, depressed, and not being able to see things clearly. I broke.

The woman with the disabling spirit was in her debilitating posture for eighteen years. Despite her posture, she was going to church to hear Jesus.

She was faithful to God (Jesus called her a daughter of Abraham). Jesus revealed her affliction was because of a demon. I believe a spirit caused her suffering through no fault of her own. I can relate.

What society deems appropriate, someone else's sin or sin done to you, can traumatize you, break you, bind you, cripple you, and have you hunched over, unable to see your true self for years. Jesus noticed she belonged to Him and called her, touched her, and healed her on the Sabbath. When the religious leaders of the synagogue challenged his healing, he called them hypocrites, for Jesus knew that they would free their livestock anytime if they were bound, needing care. How much more would the Son of God free his daughter of her infirmity immediately?!!

She left glorifying and praising God, ready to honor and praise the one who healed her. She was grateful, hopeful, and her past was behind her.

In this season of my life, my living posture is healthy, but is always being refined. I am learning to let go, forgive, and move forward. The creative process and getting to know my true creative self-enabled me to do all of this. I developed her through God's Word. This gift of writing, sketching, and designing brings a joy I cannot put into words. I have a new perspective.

I share about my posture and how creativity is giving me life and hope, and is one way I glorify and praise God. I recognize that life events can trigger that disabling posture, but my creative gift from God calms me. The thought of writing a book has always been within me. The good people in my life pushed me to achieve this dream/goal.

When I sat down to write, socialization came forth. *If you want to write a book about your life, write an autobiography.* That voice didn't excite me. I didn't want you, my audience, to think about or focus on me.

I still wanted to write a book for you, so I thought about a self-help book. A self-help book would allow me to share the steps I took to grow during my difficult times and perhaps be an inspiration to you. But with so many self-help books available. I decided against it. I kept thinking of the Holy Bible itself. For me, it is the only book that is truly the blueprint for living and the compass for all the directions life takes us.

After a creative exercise where I had to write a short story using items on my dining room table, I thought about fiction. It was clear right away that this was my voice. I decided to create a book series based on posture.

Fiction is a wonderful, empathetic genre in writing. We enjoy getting lost in a good novel, stepping inside the characters' lives and imagining we are there. We become enamored with the characters and become engrossed in their stories and adventures. We find ourselves cheering them on or getting upset at their decisions. I like how fiction novels linger in our minds. It can be an example of what to do and what not to do, foster ideas, answer questions, and unlock doors we didn't know existed.

As you read *Broken,* the first book in the four-book series of *Blessed,* I wish you all of these things. This is a work of fiction, love, romance, sex, loss, corruption, and adventure. I write about what I've learned, felt, and what God has said to me. It is my sincere prayer that God allows every person who comes across this series to see the characters' posture. I pray the series touches you, moves you, and convicts you to develop and deepen your relationship with God through Jesus Christ.

A word for the broken is STAND. Standing while broken is a sweet endurance, uncomfortable, humbling, and yet required if we want a blessed life. In brokenness, if you allow Jesus into your life, you get the best seat in the house of God. It is true: "He is near to the brokenhearted and saves the crushed in spirit (Psalm 34:18)."

In this posture, you get to know Him, trust Him, and realize He is not just collecting your broken pieces; He's helping you create your story.

In Him,

Toni

CHAPTER 1

$\mathcal{A}$manda shut herself inside her walk-in closet to access her full-length mirror. The outfit—basic black pants with a white sleeveless silk shirt and a bolero jacket—would have to do. She was running late for work, and one more minute with her boys eating breakfast downstairs unattended would warrant a mess she didn't have time to clean.

"Boys!" she yelled from the top of the stairs, turning lights off and shutting bedroom doors. She had her open-toe slingback heels hanging off her right middle finger, her right earring in the palm of her hand. She stopped for a few seconds to put on her earring and hurried down the stairs.

"How are we doing?" She asked as she got to the end of the stairs, dropped her shoes to the floor, and slid her feet into them one at a time.

"Are we ready to go?"

"Yeah, Mom," Matthew said from the kitchen table, putting the plastic cereal bowl up to his lips to slurp down the last of its sugary milk contents.

"Mom, could you please tell Mason to put on his shoes?" Matthew looked at his younger brother in disgust. "I've told him twice," he said, holding up two fingers.

Before Amanda could answer, Mason whined. "I can't find them. I've been looking."

Amanda couldn't help but smile at her boys. Where had the time gone? Matthew, a third-grader, in his navy-blue t-shirt, gym shorts, and tennis shoes, headed to the mudroom for his backpack. He was the responsible one, serious more often than not, and had a smile that warmed her insides. A handsome boy with brown eyes, dark hair that he never wanted to comb, but today was not bad. Matthew always begged for a Mohawk when in the barber chair. He was lean and tall for an eight-year-old.

Then there was Mason, a first grader. If it weren't for his emotions, he would be in the third grade. So smart, Amanda thought, and looked the part with his glasses and that sweet dimple on his right cheek when he smiled. He stood in front of her in his red polo shirt and khaki shorts, like he was ready for college prep, not elementary school. His arms stretched out, and his shoulders were by his ears for a moment.

"Really, Mom, I can't find my shoes."

Amanda sighed for a moment as she thought. She opened the kitchen sliding glass door, saw Mason's shoes on the deck, grabbed them, and gave them to him with directives as she closed the door and locked it back.

"Put your shoes on, grab your backpack, and get in the car."

Mason obeyed.

With rapid speed, Amanda cleared the kitchen table by putting cereal bowls, spoons, and cups in the sink, cereal back in the pantry, and milk in the refrigerator, while double-checking that no one had left a backpack or school project. She grabbed her purse, keys, phone, and sunglasses. She shut the door behind her.

The boys had already lifted the garage door and buckled themselves in the back seat of the SUV. She got in, put on her sunglasses, started the engine, put the SUV in reverse, and hit the button on top of the sun visor. With the garage door down, Amanda looked at the vehicle clock. She had twenty minutes to drop off the boys and make it to work. Doable, she thought.

She pushed her phone to connect to the SUV, saying, "Call Bruce." The boys in the back cheered as the phone rang.

"Hey!" the voice answered.

"Hi Bruce!" Mason raced to say before Matthew.

"Hey, little man, what's up?" Bruce replied. "How are my nephews this mornin'?"

"We're good!" Matthew interjected with excitement.

"The gang's all here and headed to school," Amanda said with a smile. "Are you good? Still picking the boys up after school?"

Amanda could hear drilling, saws, hammers, and nail guns going off in the background.

Bruce stepped closer to his truck to hear Amanda better.

"Yeah. We will finish up here early. I'll pick'em up at three with video games ready to go."

With the boys grinning in the back, Amanda rolled her eyes and agreed.

"David comin' home today?" Bruce asked.

"Yes," Amanda confirmed, "and I'm glad. His new promotion is wearing me out."

"I hear yah." Bruce said. "I'm happy to help."

"Thanks."

"Love you, sis."

They exchanged goodbyes. Bruce hung up; Amanda disconnected. Bruce was her husband David's brother, but Bruce respected and loved Amanda like she were his actual sister. The Lloyd family was a close, loving, and devoted unit, something Amanda was grateful for because her family was gone.

If it weren't for the double glass doors with Augusta Retail etched on the front, the retail brokerage firm could be mistaken for a hotel. The office was modern and clean. The lobby was furnished with two cherry wood coffee tables displayed with smoky gray chairs. Each vignette rested on the side of a 20-foot decorative rug that led to the semicircle reception desk. Behind the desk was a gray stone wall displaying the four time zones in the United States. As Amanda approached the desk, she noticed Vanessa Prescott at her post.

"Good morning, Ms. Prescott," Amanda said with a smile.

Vanessa had a good morning look on her face, but said, "You've been in your position for over a year now, Mrs. Lloyd," she mocked.

"You can call me Vanessa." But Amanda wanted to give Vanessa the proper respect. Vanessa Prescott was the cornerstone of the office. She knew when remodels and resets were happening, which team to send, and made sure the products got there. She handled the damages, returns, the missed shipments, and everything in between. Her salt and pepper hair in a bun was the only thing that could define her age. She had a thin face, ivory-smooth skin, glasses on the edge of her nose, and she was kind but not sweet. She was matter-of-fact, spoke her mind, and loved her job.

Vanessa handed Amanda a stack of pink slips. "You're the popular one this morning before 9 am."

Amanda grabbed the messages and sighed as she headed to her office. The Augusta Retail office was just one semicircle. Behind the stone wall, in the middle, was the copy/mailroom. That area opened onto the company break room.

The semicircle started with a conference room and ended with another, with the staff offices in between. Amanda's office was on the back right of Norah Livingstone, the senior office director. Nathan Montgomery, the office director, was on the back left of Norah. Amanda was recently named the assistant director. The remaining four offices were for the retail sales representatives and the executive administrative assistant to Norah Laura Marshall.

Norah, Nathan, and Amanda worked well together. They started in Augusta as retail sales reps and worked their way through the company ranks, and landed in Brookview together in one of the five offices around the country. Between the three of them, they managed the comings and goings of over 5,000 brand names for a variety of national product companies. They made sure their clients' products were among the best in their category and had superior shelf placement in the retail chains in their tri-state territory.

As he was sitting at his desk, Nathan could see Amanda walking into her office through the glass window next to his office door. He took a deep breath of pleasure, smiled, and allowed his stomach to do its somersault. It was all business on her face, but he found her breathtakingly beautiful. With brown hair that rested on her shoulders and produced natural curls around her face, her skin was the color of salted caramel. Those brown eyes had golden highlights when she smiled.

Her body was perfect in his eyes. If he had to guess, she was probably a size 8. She wasn't tall, but with the heels she wore every day, she looked directly into his eyes.

She had soft curves. Today's black pants today hit her in all the right places; her waist not too small, but the right proportion to complement her hips. Even though the pants didn't show the outline of her legs, he had her thigh-knee-calf curve memorized when she sat down in their staff meetings in her heels. He closed his eyes to find the picture in his memory.

Amanda made him think of his college days when he listened to soulful R&B love songs. The soft piano with the distinct bass, the slow, sultry voice of the man sharing how much he wanted the woman...her beauty, singing how much he desired her. Nathan remembered how much he loved those songs. He let a melody play in his head and enjoyed the fact that those songs came to mind when he thought of her. He took another breath. Just like that, the song in his head skipped and then stopped. He remembered she was married, and he honored that. Back to work.

Amanda turned on her office lights and sat in her white leather office chair. She made it just in time for the weekly conference call with Insel Cosmetic Group. She listened; nothing new. Talking about Christmas now was necessary for work, but she was thinking about summer. The boys were heading to camp for a couple of weeks. She hoped her world would slow down for a moment, and David would travel less.

After the call, she had a few urgent matters, but she took a moment and stopped. With her head reclined back, she took several deep breaths and let her body sink into her chair. She emptied her mind. With the rushing around of the morning, she needed to do this. She calmed herself and prayed. She thought of three things she was grateful for: David, her two boys, and how independent they were becoming, and feeling safe.

David sent Amanda a text saying he was leaving his hotel at noon and had a little over a three-hour drive ahead of him, and needed time in the office to return his company car. This was a first for him: to be out of town over a weekend, heading home on a Monday. Normally, it was work all week, followed by a Friday at home, but the new store in Prairie Heights, Illinois, had many grand opening events over the weekend, and as the new vice president of the territory, he had to be there.

He was excited about his new post. It was a chance to make the grocery store chain more convenient for the modern family and not lose its hometown feel. He thought of the legacy he would leave his sons, being able to support their avenues to college. And then there was Amanda.

Amanda was a good woman, and he was proud of her. Their sons were growing up well because of her guidance and her instruction; he just supported them. Amanda understood the stress of retail. The overseeing of 25 stores now—their sales or lack thereof, the personnel, the building itself, the partners and vendors—she lived part of that with him. Perhaps now she could relax.

She was a super wife. He could have hobbies and go out with the guys, and she supported it. But as he drove in the company car in silence, he wished she hadn't given him so much freedom. He went out without her and was gone too long.

"Shit," he said to himself out loud. Before he could complete the thought, his phone interrupted. He pressed the talk button on the steering wheel to answer. The office. And on it goes, he thought.

Amanda thought about David. She ordered their favorites from Lloyd's. Michael Lloyd, David's father, owned the deli-style gourmet restaurant bearing their last name. After he divorced their mother, Meredith, Michael threw all his emotions and heart into cooking. Two years of food truck success birthed the restaurant, now celebrating 15 years.

Her standard order? Caprese salad with chicken for her; apricot-braised pork loin with coleslaw for David. Lloyd's would even deliver it to their home. She didn't bother her father-in-law about her order, wanting to be treated like any other customer. She realized owning a business was hard work, and family didn't always need to be an interruption or ask for a free meal.

She was ready to go home; it was three o'clock. Bruce had the boys, and David would be home around 4:30. She was calling it quits.

"Vanessa?" Amanda rested her arms on the reception desk.

"Yes, ma'am?" Vanessa responded.

"I'm gonna call it a day, but why is there a big box in my office? Something new from a company?"

"I'm not sure what that is all about. But the packing slips say it's essential oils, eye pillows, neck wraps, and bath teas."

Amanda grew excited. "Nice. Who from? We don't represent the home and gift category."

"I know, and it was sent directly to you." Vanessa looked at the packing slip and put it in her stack of to-dos.

"It says Snowflake Ranch somewhere in Texas. I'll check and see if it is on the new product manifest. I'll figure it out. You go home."

"You don't have to tell me twice. Tell Nathan I'll catch up with him tomorrow on the new downtown drugstore project."

Amanda headed out the door as Vanessa waved goodbye and continued to stare at her computer screen.

When David got home, he found Amanda with her back to him at the kitchen sink. She was washing the breakfast dishes with the water running and garbage disposal on; she didn't hear him. He took that moment to look at her. She was wearing a turquoise spaghetti-strapped sundress, her hair in a messy ponytail. That hourglass silhouette—her waist, hips, and ass—was perfection.

"Honey?" he smiled.

Amanda turned off the disposal and water, turning around to see David.

"Hey, babe." She smiled and tilted her head sweetly.

David saw her bright creamed-coffee complexion, those brown eyes dancing, full lips with gloss, and the front of her dress exposed her neck and chest. No bra needed, the dress just covered the bottom of her breasts, giving her cleavage and him an instant erection.

"Wow, I don't remember this dress." He slid his hands around her waist and pulled her close to him.

"Just wear this for me!"

She blushed. He smelled her. She was fresh from the shower, and he kissed her behind her ear. Then he whispered, "I missed you."

Her stomach quivered, and she felt wet between her legs. That place behind her ear was a pleasure spot, and he knew it. He took a deep breath and held her.

She put her arms around him and leaned into his white shirt that smelled of aftershave and starch. David was tall. With Amanda's head resting on his chest, he looked at her, cupped her chin and slowly kissed her lips, tasting cotton candy and true love.

"I missed you, too," she answered. She looked up at him. She loved his warm ivory skin, high cheekbones, brown hair, brown eyes, and smile with perfect teeth. His lips were narrow and his nose refined and pointed. She kissed him back. He wanted her, and he started unbuttoning his shirt. David wasn't built like a bodybuilder; no ripples or six-pack, but he was muscular and lean. He liked to run and did so on most mornings before doing anything else.

He kissed her lips again, softly. Then, he looked at her. David wanted to say he was sorry, but he couldn't. He wanted to explain, but he didn't know how. He wanted to satisfy himself and displace his consciousness, so he kissed her lips again, this time requesting tongue. Amanda granted it to him. The kisses they shared now were more rapid and heated.

Amanda placed her hands on David's chest. He grabbed one of her hands and brought it to his lips. He kissed her fingertips and placed her hand inside his. With his chest exposed and wet lips, he led his wife up the stairs to their bedroom, and they had sex.

CHAPTER 2

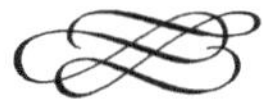

$\mathcal{A}$manda felt bittersweet. She walked out of church feeling renewed and refreshed, but she was alone. David had stopped going with her for almost a year now. His excuse was work or needing to rest. The boys were in the children's ministry and begged to go out to the farm with their grandparents afterwards.

Amanda and David would join them in an hour, but what once was a joyful time in church with her husband now felt like abandonment. When Amanda returned home, she heard David in the den, but she went upstairs to change clothes. David heard Amanda come through the door and head upstairs.

He closed his spreadsheets and shut down his computer. Was it time to go already? The morning went by fast. He was dressed in his jeans and a t-shirt and had loaded the SUV with fishing gear. He headed to the kitchen, took two bottles of water from the refrigerator, took out the salad Amanda had prepared, and saw a bag of potatoes and wondered if they were for dinner.

"Amanda, honey?" he raised his voice from the bottom of the stairs.

"These potatoes. Are they going?"

"No, babe." Within minutes, Amanda was headed down the stairs in her jeans, red V-neck t-shirt, and stylish tennis shoes.

"Dad has potatoes from the garden; they are so much better." She greeted him at the bottom of the stairs with a kiss.

David saw his wife and put his hands on her waist, looking into her eyes and checking out her figure.

"You look amazing. How was church?"

"I missed you," Amanda answered kindly.

"Don't start," he shot back and smacked her butt.

"I'm not." Amanda whined, smiled, then added, "You asked me a question, and I answered with the truth."

David couldn't argue and didn't want to, so he changed the subject.

"Let me guess, the boys are already with Mom and Bill."

Amanda nodded yes. They continued to pack the SUV and headed to the farm.

Wellsberg Farm was an acreage fifteen minutes out of town owned by Bill Wellsberg, David's stepfather. After Meredith and Michael divorced, Meredith met Bill three years later. He came with a house, Meredith said, that had been in Bill's family for at least three generations.

It was more than a house; it sat on five acres. Even though Bill worked at the community college as an English professor and Meredith was a nurse at one of the local clinics, they managed to do the basics like keeping chickens for fresh farm eggs. The lake was a full acre, fully stocked with largemouth bass, catfish, and crappie, and a garden loaded with vegetables. Bill had planted blackberries, raspberries and blueberries in the early spring and looked forward to jams and preserves in seasons to come.

For David, it was the fresh air he loved. The trees swaying, the birds chirping, insects humming and buzzing, and yet, he would tell people it was so quiet and peaceful out at the farm. Amanda enjoyed having a family. This was her greeting card moment, driving up to the large farmhouse with the wrap-around porch and homemade swing under the old oak tree. Brandie, the chocolate lab, too mature to bark with excitement and run up to the SUV these days, was stretched out on the front lawn, enjoying Mason stroking her coat. She stood up as they pulled up in the driveway.

"Mom," Mason acknowledged Amanda first. "Brandie, such a good girl, helped put the chickens in the barn." He continued to stroke the dog. Amanda smiled at Mason as she exited the SUV with her purse on her shoulder and the salad bowl in her hands.

Meredith came out from the side door that led to the kitchen and onto the porch. Just three years ago, Bill had contracted Bruce and team to make some renovations to the house, like the side door that led to the kitchen. Now they didn't have to walk all the way around the house to get to the garden.

"Hey there," Meredith said as she came out with her apron on. Meredith's hair was short and blonde. Her skin cream color and the dark brown eyes that David inherited. She smiled.

Meredith was a pretty woman who was aging slowly. She had no laugh lines, but little highlights of gray around her hairline.

"Can I help with anything?"

"Oh no, Mom, we got it." David had parked, got out, walked in front of the SUV, placed a kiss on his mom's cheek, and proceeded towards Mason, picking him up and giving him a kiss.

"Mason," Amanda looked affectionately at her son now, next to David. "I'm so happy you are helping Papa Bill with the chickens."

"Amanda, let me help you with that salad. I'll bring it in the house. Mason is dyin' to show you the new baby chicks."

Just as Amanda gave Meredith the salad and said thank you, an old red pickup truck came up the driveway and parked behind Amanda's SUV. It was Bruce. In the backseat, Amanda could see the head of a small boy.

It was Matthew. Amanda waited for the truck to stop. David stopped in the yard.

"Mom," Matthew said as he unbuckled his seatbelt and opened the back-cab door. "We went to get stuff to start Papa Bill's herb garden, and Mr. Taylor had some old pallets we could use. They're in the back." Matthew was excited as he jumped out of the truck.

Amanda gave Matthew a hug and noted that she was equally enthusiastic about his adventure.

"Sounds like a fun project. Where is Papa Bill?"

Matthew pointed to the metal building.

"He's in the shop. I'll tell him we're back."

Matthew was ready to head to the metal building, but he saw David and gave him a long hug.

"Dad, I'm so happy to see you. Going fishin' later, right?"

David enjoyed the hug from his oldest son and put his hand on top of his dark brown, wavy hair.

"Got the poles in the back of the SUV. Go on, tell Papa Bill you're back."

With Amanda headed to see chickens with Mason, Meredith headed to the house with the salad, and Matthew headed towards the shop. There stood David and Bruce, smiling at each other, and they hugged and headed towards the porch. Bruce, who was the same height as David, was fit and muscular. He was handsome and sported a beige-ivory skin tone from working in the sun. Women loved his physique, and he had a smile with a dimple. He always had girlfriends ever since high school.

They knew Bill kept a cooler on the porch filled with beer next to his favorite lawn chair. Out of respect, the men never sat in Bill's chair, but David took two beers out of the cooler, and they sat around the outdoor coffee table. They each cracked open their beers and said nothing for several minutes, just enjoying the quiet view of green grass, blue sky, and the smell of summer coming.

"What is it like being a vice president of store operations for 25 stores? You now have that corner office, an executive administrative assistant, an expense account, a company car…"

"…and a whole lot of headaches and bullshit," David replied, interrupting his brother and giving him a dose of reality.

"I'm grateful, and yes, I have a nice office, and Vikki is one of the best, but there are challenges, and I'm feeling them. Nothing I can't handle, but there is a learning curve. I'm stressed."

David was overwhelmed in dealing with the stress of work and its politics. His guard was down, and there was Sam.

"Well, hang in there. Amanda called me a few times to help. Glad to do that, but the boys miss you." Bruce saw Mason across the barnyard, showing Amanda the chicks as David put his beer on the table.

"I miss them too." David looked at Mason and Amanda together. From the look on her face, David saw she loved being a mom. She took an interest in being with Mason, especially her facial expressions when he did something well, and her ability to understand his frustration of being six but sensitive and taking many things too personally.

"Amanda is doing well, David," Bruce said. "You're good."

"Look at her. She is losing weight, or maybe being in her thirties agrees with her. After all she has been through, never once has she denied my needs as a man, you know." David looked at his brother with a smirk.

"She's sweet and caring."

"Lucky man," Bruce said, holding up his beer in acknowledgment and taking a drink. "Single life isn't what it once was."

David looked at his brother for the rest of the story.

"These girls—I call them girls—flirt, drink, and want what they want. Sex, money, and then after the partying is over, they couldn't care less. They're too young, at least, to be at the bar. I can't do the bar scene anymore."

"So glad to hear you say that. How's Candice?" David asked and raised an eyebrow.

"Oh, the friend with benefits." Bruce took a breath in, then out.

"She was at my place last month. Gave me a massage with a happy ending." David was more stirred than Bruce.

"That shit is so much hotter when the person you're with really cares about you. I ended Candice. I couldn't do it anymore."

David didn't dare mention Chloe. He knew something had gone wrong in that relationship, but Bruce really cared for her. He knew Amanda knew more than she led on, but with the sister-brother relationship they have, he respected her.

"Bruce, every relationship has its challenges. Amanda and I...sometimes sex and intimacy can be a challenge. I love her so much. With all the things she's been through, having been in and out of the foster care system, I can't even imagine all the things she has seen and heard that she brings to the bed every night."

"Yes, we've done counseling, and Amanda is well. After surviving postpartum depression with Mason, she's better. She went back to work, of course, thriving and now with a promotion."

David stared at his wife until she disappeared into the barn with their son.

"She looks stunning, but sexually and emotionally, I don't push her. I know she loves me, but she is not sure of herself. I don't want to trigger thoughts of the past, even though she doesn't remember the rape."

"Ask her about it," Bruce said matter-of-factly. He handed his brother his beer from the table.

"Amanda is so devoted to you that if you asked her about being more forward in the bedroom, she would try to please you."

"And that's just it. How much of that would be because I asked or because she wants to?"

Bruce rolled his eyes. "She loves you. She wants you. Don't worry about Amanda. If you talk to her, she…"

"…she will tell me her past is in the past, she's over the trauma and whatever I want, right down to the way she makes my coffee, I shall have it because she's grateful." David knew the answer.

"We've been married ten years, not ten months. I just want her to be happy loving me, not obligated to love me."

With that explanation, Bruce did not push. David was strong-minded and stubborn. When he had his mind set on the way something was, it was hard to change his mind.

Bruce knew a mere conversation would not change his mind. It was a Lloyd thing. Reactive, never proactive: hit the wall, realize that hurt, and hopefully learn the lesson.

The day couldn't have been more perfect. Bill had smoked a few pork tenderloins; Amanda made her famous salad the family loved with corn, avocados, and bacon; and Meredith made mashed potatoes, corn on the cob, and green beans, all from the garden. They told old stories and laughed at each other's jokes.

Bill was a tall man, thick in stature, able to move around the farm with no sign of being tired. He was rough and stern with Matthew and Mason, especially when it concerned their safety. But when he spoke, it was poetry. He had a way with words.

Amanda could listen to him for hours; he encouraged her. "Now, I don't know about the rest of you, but I believe it is time for us gentlemen to go fishing," Bill said at the table, and that was the sign dinner was over.

The Lloyds were well on their way to late afternoon. The boys cheered, and Amanda and Meredith rose to clear the table, David and Bruce following. Amanda and David met at the kitchen sink. He approached her from behind. She turned, and his arms wrapped around her as he rested his hands on the counter.

Their eyes met; she saw concern but desire in his eyes. He kissed her politely, smiled, and winked. The combination of that movement always made her want to kiss him, but then he felt his phone buzzing in his pocket. David's words saddened her.

"I have to get that."

The moment was gone.

David reached for his phone and disappeared onto the porch, holding the phone. Amanda had a face of loss. The entire family felt the joy leave the room.

"Dad can be such a jerk," Matthew blurted out. "I hate that phone."

With the scene before them, the family knew the story. Matthew put his empty plate on the counter and went out the front door with a temper.

"I'll go." Bruce gave the salad bowl to his mom and went after Matthew. Mason said nothing. He took Meredith's hand and leaned against her leg, touching the hem of her apron. Amanda had her eyes closed to fight tears of embarrassment and sadness.

"Meri, could you get Mason ready to fish? I will take care of the dishes. I just need a minute." Amanda left the house, passing David, who didn't notice, and headed towards the garden.

She sat on the bench facing the garden for several minutes before Bill came out and sat next to her. He said nothing at first, then touched her hand.

"You know, I don't know how you do it." He was pleasant. "You work, you keep a household, you keep the children, you keep a husband, but who keeps Amanda? Huh?"

She loved his words and leaned against his arm, taking his hand. "I'm sorry, Dad. Back there shouldn't have been a big deal, but it happens so much, I cannot hide my reaction, and neither can the boys."

There were no words from Bill for a moment. He listened to Amanda talk about David and his late Monday nights, and the distance he has created from church and friends outside of work. His temper was short sometimes; his affection selfish.

Bill finally spoke. "He's got that corporate sickness. Don't worry, he loves you. He'll figure it out."

"You're a praying woman. Tell God what you want; He will fix it."

It sounded so simple, but Amanda knew it to be true. She had prayed for another mom, and God gave her Janice Williams. She was fourteen by then, but Janice taught her all about God, who He was, and what He could do in her life if she would allow Him. When Bill left her side, she sat there a few more minutes and quietly prayed for her family.

Bill and Bruce talked to David before the boys joined them for fishing. David reassured them he was just working hard, and he needed a certain project to go well. He knew it was more than that; his relationship with Sam was showing up in his behavior.

After they came in from fishing, it was time to load the SUV for the drive home. It was getting late: the boys had school in the morning, and it was back to work for David and Amanda. Meri and Bill hugged their children and grandchildren and watched them leave the farm. Matthew and Mason didn't make it to the blacktop road before they were in the backseat sleeping.

Amanda turned to the backseat to see the boys with their heads hanging low, trying to find comfortable positions against each other. She looked at them fondly and then looked at David as he drove. He was deeply focused on something as he drove. She wondered what it was.

Amanda remembered when they would talk about life and the upcoming week on this stretch of road. Now there was nothing but silence. Amanda looked out the passenger window as he drove.

"Amanda?" David finally broke the silence.

She turned to him.

"I'm doing this all for us. I'm trying to figure all this out. I'm not balancing this well."

Amanda sighed and went back to looking out the window.

"I know you are working hard. I appreciate all you do for us as a family…"

David was waiting for his wife to finish her sentence.

"… but at what cost?" She turned to him, "You are not home. And when you are, you're not. God has given us such a beautiful life, and you've just left Him on the side of the road."

"Honey, don't start that again. Just because I can't go to church right now doesn't mean I've left God altogether. Getting this promotion was hard enough. I'm tired, and I need you to understand."

David kept his eyes on the road.

Amanda hated it when David got defensive. What happened to the humble man she married? She was tired too. She was working and managing the household. When David came at her in this way, she shut down and didn't want to talk to him.

"I understand," she uttered quietly.

David could tell he hurt some part of her, but he didn't know what to say without all his wrongdoings spilling out.

"I love you." He reached for her hand.

She gave it to him, and he kissed it.

Amanda fought back tears. Her disappointment stemmed from her husband's use of love to mask his actions. She saw right through him and chose to show him love calmly.

"I love you, too." She found a smile.

"Just know I am here, David. I support you, and I care for you."

In her mind, she thought, even if you can't see me or you don't care.

CHAPTER 3

*H*e took advantage of the coolness of late spring, slipped out of the house, and went for a run. David left his earbuds on purpose. He needed to hear himself breathing, thinking he had found his pace. He ran for minutes with no thought.

The rhythm of his shoes hitting the blacktop trail, birds speaking, and wind whispering, just his breath, and now his thoughts emerged. *Do I even want the damn promotion? All the drama and politics after years with the company, this happens? I know I did the right thing, but how do I tell the family, especially Amanda?*

Breathe. Senior vice presidents, the other vice presidents. Ugh! I don't care about winning or losing their respect; I'm pissed. How do you work with people who are jealous, racist, and flat out don't want you to succeed?!

David had no thoughts for several more minutes. Admiring the sunrise, the dew on the grass, and the deer grazing in the distance. *Sam...I shouldn't have done it. Done it? I'm doing it now! Using her. Both of us are using each other. And then Amanda...I don't deserve her. I'm being cold and distant, which is not fair to her.*

I'm messing it all up here. I'm taking advantage of Amanda's kindness, faithfulness, and loyalty. Breathe. Who does this? I'm an ass! After the Acuff Academy launch, I'll tell her.

He ran for five more minutes. He decided he was better off single, and the boys would be better with her. By then, he had reached the end of his route. He stopped running and walked up the driveway.

David came into the house through the garage. Immediately, he smelled the scent of freshly brewed coffee. Amanda was awake and at her desk in the den, reading her devotional with her favorite mug in her hand. She remained seated as he entered and the garage door closed.

"Honey?" he whispered, standing in the doorway of the den. "I've got plenty of errands to run today before I make it to the office. Got that meeting tonight, remember? Let me take the boys to school."

"Ok. You sure?" She asked, wondering if he thought about how much time he missed with Matthew and Mason.

He entered the room, kissed the top of her head, and closed his eyes, thinking of his morning run.

"Yes, I got it. Enjoy your morning."

He left her and headed upstairs to the shower.

Amanda got to the office early and worked on a shampoo and conditioner reset scheduled for next week in Mount Vernon. The office was quiet when she first walked in, but she saw sales representatives coming and going outside her office glass window. Norah was in the office today, which always meant more activity and visitors. It was time. She rose from her chair, opened her office door, and headed to the mailroom. She checked her mailbox, greeted a few employees, and headed to Nathan's office.

"Good morning," she said as she knocked on his open door.

"Hi!" Nathan smiled at Amanda warmly. Nathan Montgomery was a good director, Amanda thought. He was down-to-earth and thoughtful. Out of the three of them, he was the one who thought about the retail sales representatives and their families, and put thought into every gathering, gift, and public relations/marketing activity. Blonde hair with gray, hazel eyes, and a no-teeth smile that was sincere. If she had to describe him in two words, they would be genuine and private.

He was single; that's all she knew. He didn't talk about himself or his life much. Nathan was always the one asking questions and encouraging others.

"Meeting in your office this morning?" She asked.

"We can." He rose from his office chair behind the desk, came around, pulled out a chair from the meeting table in his office, and invited Amanda to sit.

Amanda had on a pink, floral-printed skirt with a solid, matching blouse. Nathan noticed. She sat with her legs crossed at her ankles, and there was that leg curve. He left the back of her chair just as Norah walked in.

"Morning," Norah Livingstone smiled. "I love how we just find each other when it's time to meet." Amanda loved how Norah came in family-friendly. She also found her to be dynamic. In Amanda's eyes, she was the sales queen. This woman couldn't be 52 years old, as the local women's magazine BVM Woman (Brookview Metro) stated last month when it named her businesswoman of the year.

Norah was of Puerto Rican descent, with dark, straight, short, and stylish hair. A full-figured woman with striking features, she always came to work in full makeup, jewelry, and high heels, ready to talk retail management. She was a master negotiator and knew the players in the industry.

Today's meeting was centered on Brookview's new downtown drugstore. After the closure of two major retail stores in the town square, business leaders and developers in the county were raising funds to create a downtown drugstore, fully equipped with a hometown pharmacy and a much-desired health and beauty care section.

"What do you think?" Norah asked, rolling the blueprint out on the meeting table. "Does it look good? We are at least three years out. A service designation, no?"

"Yes," Nathan agreed. "The major players in health and beauty want in. Organic foods and wellness brands would be a good fit here. Amanda, cosmetics are your wheelhouse. Is everyone on board?"

"Yes. I need a youth cosmetic line. I'll do the research. But I still think we need another thing... an experience. This drugstore needs an ice cream parlor, a soda fountain, the experience of a good 'ole fashion drugstore with a modern twist."

Amanda stared at the print. "This is too much beverage. Will the county allow alcohol sales after a certain time? Would it be too accessible to minors? If we go before the city council, we need to be ready for that scrutiny," Amanda explained.

"Good things to think about, which is why we are doing this early. Scott Acuff hasn't made it to the table yet," Norah said. "Do you think David will say something?"

"David has his own territory now. I don't think he knows anything. I need to tell him and talk to my father-in-law. I don't think this project will be major competition for them," Amanda interjected.

"Well, keep me posted on your findings. I'm going to Ohio, leaving on Friday. Hindley Corp. is visiting early next week, so I'm visiting my girls and grandbabies. See you both in a week."

Norah had two grown daughters who live in Cincinnati and Dayton, Ohio. She enjoyed the luxury of spending the weekend with them when she had to be at Hindley Corp., a health and beauty care company, for meetings and training.

They discussed the new product manifest, resets, and remodels. Nathan set the date for the fall staff gathering, and Amanda told them about the essential oils and accessories in her office, and wondered if it was a category worth pursuing. She updated them on missed shipments and warehouse issues.

When Amanda returned to her office, she noticed the large floral bouquet in a glass vase on her desk. Beautiful blue hydrangeas arranged with white roses and baby's breath. She thought of David as she smiled and pulled out the card.

The envelope was addressed to LLOYD. When she opened the envelope and read the card, her heart stopped. Was this a joke? Amanda felt all the color leave her face. It read:

Sam, our time together was amazing… thinking about you. D.

It was her husband's handwriting. She felt sick. *David?* She thought. Suddenly, the room was spinning. She quickly closed her door, locked it, and sat down in her chair.

A copper penny taste formed in her mouth. She grabbed her trash can and bent down to put her face in it.

Breathe, Amanda, breathe. Amanda started breathing slowly from her diaphragm. As she was coming to herself, the questions flowed.

Who the hell is Sam? How did these flowers end up here? There was no mistake about the *D.* That was how David signed all his notes. *Why? How? WHEN? For how long?* Once again, Amanda felt herself getting upset, so she resumed her breathing exercises.

Amanda, think. You must figure this out. Give yourself a minute. What do you want to do? She did the breathing exercises for another minute. For the first time in years, she thought about her therapist.

This is my husband. Lord, what should I do? Guide my steps. With tears in her eyes, she sat in silence. She wasn't supposed to know this information. This was a mistake. She decided to buy herself some time.

Amanda picked up the phone and hit the Do Not Disturb button. She rescheduled her 11:00 am meeting quickly to 2:00 pm. As she reread the card, everything became clear. It explained his behavioral changes, his just-sex attitude, the distant selfishness of it all, the phone calls, late meetings, etc. David was having an affair.

Her husband was not the one-night stand type. He was sending this woman flowers and personalizing the card. Amanda took a deep breath, found the florist's name on the card, looked up their phone number online, and called before she realized it. A distressed young girl answered the phone.

"Swanson's .... ah yeah...this is Poppy."

"Poppy, I'm calling about a floral arrangement sent to me by mistake?" Amanda sounded professional.

"Oh MY God! Not another one!" she whined. "I'm SO sorry."

Amanda closed her eyes for a moment.

"Listen, it is not a big deal yet. I will keep the flowers but pay for the exact same floral bouquet to go to the correct address."

"Oh wow! That is SO cool." Poppy was excited and relieved.

"You're saving my ass. I've only been here a week, and our computer database is fuc... I mean, messing up."

"Oh, I understand. I think Mr. David Lloyd came in this morning and probably gave you the correct address?"

"Yeah, the businessman. He has an account here," Poppy said as she looked at David's information on her computer screen.

"Wrote out the card himself."

Amanda's heart hurt at the sound of the words.

"The computer must've generated a delivery ticket to Augusta Retail by mistake, but I have it right here." Amanda heard Poppy shuffling through papers.

"Here we go. The Waters Square Hotel and a Samantha Coleman."

Amanda felt a tear fall from her face. Sam is Samantha. David intended to send the flowers to her.

"Yes, Augusta will keep the flowers. Can you send her the exact same flowers as soon as possible?" Amanda gave Poppy her credit card information.

"It is important this doesn't show up on Mr. Lloyd's account. I don't want him charged twice."

Amanda lied, saying she was Mr. Lloyd's personal assistant and didn't want to get in trouble. Poppy understood that completely. Amanda hung up the phone with her hands cold, moist, and shaking.

She settled herself and returned to her computer. With a quick search of Waters Square Hotel, she saw the hotel was on the edge of town in a district called the Water's Edge. Water's Edge was being developed with old money, named after Douglas Waters, a builder in the area generations ago. The hotel housed college guests, out-of-town professors, and dignitaries, and was owned by Brookview Community College. Hotel, restaurant, and hospitality management majors managed the property.

The staff website page had a picture of Samantha Coleman, program sales director. She was pretty, with long blonde hair and blue eyes. Amanda's body stung all over.

Was that what he wanted now? Based on her graduation date, she was two years younger than Amanda. She couldn't read anymore. Her eyes became blurred with tears. Amanda hid herself in her office, stayed away from the glass window, and allowed herself to cry.

"We do that well," Sam said breathlessly as she straddled him, kissed his cheek, and removed herself from on top of him.

"I agree," David said, breathing hard as he kissed her back. She snuggled next to him with her head on his shoulder and her bare leg draped across his leg.

"The flowers were beautiful today." She put her hand on his chest. "Don't worry, I didn't say anything to anyone…"

"Sam, I'm sorry for all the secrecy, but I want to be honest with you. Our relationship has caught me by surprise, and my wife…"

Sam stopped him by placing her index finger on his lips.

"I know, a lot of people can't know about this. I really want to help you and to make this program successful. I care about you."

David closed his eyes with guilt resting on his mind. All of this wasn't planned. At a young professional event in Carbondale, David was stressed that night and thought about how much simpler his life would be if he were single. At the time, Amanda had no time for him. She was in her first season of managing resets and remodels. Being a candidate for promotion was challenging for him; he now wished he had told Amanda everything he was feeling. But that night, he met Sam, a beautiful blonde, friendly, and single.

He couldn't believe they were from the same town and had never met. Of course, Sam knew the Lloyd family but had never met anyone in it. They talked about high school—she was a couple of grades lower than him.

They talked all night about retail and life. She told him about Brookview Community College and how she ended up back home after her mom died, and helped to clear the family home. He told her about the stress of being on the promotion track, having a wife and two boys, and the challenges of making everything work.

They spent all night talking to each other until the event was over. She invited him for a drink at the hotel where she was staying. David didn't say no. She flirted, he flirted, and before they even realized, they were in Sam's hotel room, stripping off clothes and in the bed, with release and regret. Her voice interrupted his thoughts.

"Listen, David, we are adults here, and I'm happy we met. Let's be whatever we need to be for each other right now. Let's get through this mess together. You understand…"

"I do," David said as he stroked her hair. "I'm overwhelmed right now. You help me leave it behind, even if only for a moment."

"I get it," Sam said. She moved her leg from his, turned around with her back facing him, and said, "Hold me."

He got behind her, wrapped his arm around her, and kissed her shoulder. "Ok."

David smiled as he smelled sweat in her hair, but positioned himself in a way that if she fell asleep, he could slip away and not wake her.

Sam found David to be handsome, smart, and successful. He was the full package for her, except he was married and shouldn't be there. He loved his wife, and Sam knew it. The attraction snuck up on them both. After Carbondale, they tried to keep their distance, but David asked for her help. They tried to keep it professional, but it grew harder and harder to do with the emotions they both shared.

"Sam," he whispered.

"David," she whispered with her eyes closed, smiling. Knowing their parting ritual was coming.

"Thank you," he said.

"You're welcome," she replied. "I know how this ends."

With that, Sam fell asleep satisfied.

For the rest of the week, Amanda pretended. She got dressed, found a smile, got the boys to school, went to the office, came home, and made dinner. David was always home by six. She wondered if he knew something, but didn't say anything.

When he saw distance in her eyes, Amanda redirected and told him how tired she was. She wasn't lying. She had barely slept since finding out. When everyone was asleep, she would go to the lower-level bathroom, shut the door, and let her back slide down the back of the door, her head between her knees, and cry. Broken. Amanda would stay there until her butt got cold on the tile floor or she nodded off to sleep for a minute and took herself back to bed.

One night, as she thought of David's actions—his excuses of working late, getting up earlier for the run, and going straight *to work*—she wondered what else David was hiding. She snuck out to the garage while everyone slept. She searched his car, and that's where she found them. In the console between the driver and passenger seat, under the peppermints and travel-sized tissues at the bottom of the console, hidden were condoms.

David, what are you doing to us? Amanda asked as she closed her eyes and rested her head on the steering wheel. After another crying session, she slipped back into the house and slid back into the bed next to David, thinking he didn't know she had left. But he knew. David thought her nightmares had returned.

"Honey, are you okay?"

He rolled over and spooned her. She didn't answer him. She appreciated his warmth and fell asleep.

~

It was Friday. The morning was busy. Several sales representatives turned in their reports of completed resets to Amanda. Norah came in briefly to manage email, set appointments for late summer concerning the downtown project, and left to catch her flight to Ohio. Nathan was in his office dealing with personnel issues and annual reviews.

After lunch, it was quiet. Vanessa took the afternoon off (sales reps used this time to travel and head home for the weekend). Amanda was in the far conference room on days like this to spread out the completed reset drawings and look at the upcoming resets and remodels spreadsheets. It was almost 4:00 pm when Amanda cleared out of the conference room and shut down her computer in her office. She went back to the conference room to shut down the audio-visual system and turn off the lights, but she sat on the conference table with her legs dangling off the floor, feet crossed, and the television remote in her hand. She was distracted by her thoughts.

What do I say this weekend? Do I tell him I know? What if he lies to me? Tell me I'm the crazy one? Do I know who David is anymore? The last time we made love...it was different... I'm not satisfying him anymore. Silent tears left her eyes. She had more thoughts about David, just not engaged with the children, and was always in the den working.

"Amanda?" Nathan said, surprised, looking at his watch, walking into the room.

"What are you still doing here?"

Amanda didn't respond right away.

"Amanda?" Nathan repeated.

Startled, she looked at him and presented a smile, but had forgotten tears still lived on her face.

"Hey, hey," Nathan said, taking the remote from her hand as he looked at her. "What's wrong? Are you okay?"

"Currently, no," Amanda wiped her tears. "But I will be." She took her purse and pulled out her cell phone. 4:24 pm.

"Stay here." Nathan briefly touched her hand; went to the end of the conference room, to the back counter, put the remote down, and took the box of tissues.

Amanda texted David that she'd be home in an hour and not to worry. Nathan came back to her, put one of his hands on top of hers, and then gave her a tissue with the other.

"Take your time, Amanda." Nathan sat in a conference chair, looking up at her as she remained sitting on the conference room table with her hands down by her sides, gripping the table. Her shoulders were up to her ears, and her head was down.

She took a deep breath in and let out a large sigh. As her shoulders went down, she went into her purse again and pulled out the florist's card. She read it to herself silently this time, without tears. She handed the card to Nathan.

"The flowers that came on Monday were not for me, but that is my husband's handwriting."

Nathan read the card as Amanda told him what she thought and what she had done. She put the card back in her purse.

Silence filled the room. But it was noisy inside Nathan's mind. He was hot with anger as he thought to himself: *What?! What is David thinking?! Okay, he wasn't thinking, or he was thinking with something else. This woman is beautiful, your boys? Amanda is devoted to you and your family. What the hell?!*

But then Nathan remembered where his mind had been years ago.

"Are you going to confront him?" Nathan asked, breaking the silence in the room.

"And hear a lie?" Amanda began to cry again.

"For what? For him to tell me she is just a friend, a business acquaintance who helped him out? No, lies will just make it worse. It won't fix my heart, and I'm broken."

"I want to process this and... Nathan, I'm sorry to dump all of this on you. I'm just realizing I haven't spoken a word to anyone about this 'til right now. Not the best thing."

She grabbed tissues to catch her tears. Without hesitation, Nathan stood up and opened his arms to her. She slid off the table and accepted his invitation. She rested her head on his left chest and let her tears flow, often shaking. Nathan rubbed her back softly.

To Amanda, it felt like she was in Nathan's arms for a while, but it was only for five minutes. She stopped crying for three of those minutes, blew her nose, and rested in his arms in silence. Then she realized his shirt was wet with tears.

"I'm sorry," she chuckled. "Your shirt is a mess."

Raising her head, she felt wet and saw her makeup on his company white polo shirt.

Nathan smiled back, looking down at himself. "There are plenty more of these shirts around here."

She put her head back on his chest. "Thank you, Nathan, for just being here."

Nathan closed his eyes and savored this time, taking it in. Her hair was like chocolate silk, soft and luxurious, smelling of the tropics. To hold her was a privilege, like holding a precious, expensive stone; exclusive, delicate, but strong.

Before he could stop himself, he kissed her hair. "You are so beautiful."

When the words left him, he wanted them back. Maybe she didn't hear him, but she did.

Amanda gently raised her head and looked into Nathan's eyes, searching for the source of the compliment. When she found it, what she saw beyond his hazel eyes was interest. Amanda thought Nathan was good-looking, with an air of mystery. He had a five o'clock shadow that was blonde with gray. His skin was fair and cool, his hair styled like someone in their twenties, but tiny crow's feet at the edges of his eyes revealed his true age. He had perfectly proportioned lips

As she searched for the meaning of this encounter, Nathan leaned in and barely kissed her lips. Amanda closed her eyes to feel Nathan's emotions transfer to her.

"Amanda, please don't say anything," Nathan said, embarrassed at first. Then, he stepped away from her and took her hand. "Follow me."

He led her to the end of the conference room, where, in the corner, he unfolded the three-way full-length mirrors.

"I want you to see who you are."

Standing face to face, Nathan and Amanda locked eyes deeply. "Can I touch you?"

Amanda took a deep breath; she was full of emotion. She was curious.

"Amanda..." Nathan whispered.

"... okay," Amanda interrupted. "Touch me."

Those words came from a place of neglect inside. David wasn't really touching her, satisfying her. She wanted someone who she felt cared for her to touch her.

Nathan calmed himself and then stared into her eyes. He untucked her white blouse from her skirt, slowly unbuttoning it, exposing her white laced bra. He turned Amanda to the three-way mirror so she could see herself. He stood behind her, so close she could feel him.

"Look at you, you're beautiful," he whispered in her ear. "You're sexy."

In that moment, she saw herself. The contrast of tan skin and her bra, her blouse open and cascading down her right shoulder. Nathan placed his left hand on her chest and moved his hand down, touching each breast over her bra. He kissed the back of her neck. She saw her nipples stand at attention and took a deep breath.

His fingers circled around each nipple, never removing the bra or going underneath it. With his right hand, he slowly raised her skirt to her waist.

"Look at yourself."

Nathan saw Amanda's chest rise and fall, her lips apart slightly, her eyes desiring, wanting; her hair halfway in her face. He continued to control himself, but the anticipation of what he was going to do next made Amanda want more. Nathan put his right hand over her white lace panties and walked his fingers between her legs. It was there he touched the spot that gave her pleasure. He kept his hand there for seconds and felt moist.

She quickly turned around and faced him. She looked at him aroused, lusting as she stared at his belt buckle and then touched it. Nathan touched her hand. "No."

He was soft and gentle. He closed his eyes for a second, thinking of his past mistake with his ex-wife.

"You...you're hot, making me want to lay you on this conference table and have my way with you." He spoke softly and searched her with his eyes.

"Your legs in these heels, this bra, your body..." Nathan continued to hold her close.

"Sweetheart, you are the picture in my dreams." He winked. "And your ass?" He rubbed her behind and pressed his lips together, enjoying the view and the touch.

"David's a fool."

Amanda half-smiled.

"I'm going home and taking the coldest shower imaginable," Nathan said in a teasing way, but was serious. He began re-buttoning Amanda's blouse and lowering her skirt.

"What just happened?!" Amanda felt like she was now coming back to reality. She blushed, taking over adjusting her clothing, running her fingers through her hair, now ashamed.

"You just happened. Confident, beautiful Amanda just happened." Nathan said.

Amanda started to cry.

"Please stop crying. Perhaps David has forgotten what he has. Is he stressed? Whatever it is, I wanted to show you that you still have the power to turn his head. David should be having an amazing time with you, not some Sam woman."

Nathan took her hand and looked at her.

"Don't stop having sex with him; it makes it worse. Make him want you and desire you." He told her this wasn't her fault.

Amanda listened, but couldn't help but want to know more about Nathan.

"Is this wisdom coming from a place?"

He sighed. "Amanda, I wasn't always a nice guy. I lost my wife because I was more than foolish; I was selfish and prideful."

Amanda waited, but that was all Nathan disclosed.

"Allow me to walk you to your car." He smiled and kissed her forehead.

Amanda called David while driving home. She was disappointed; it was going to be a typical Friday. The boys were already with Meri and Bill at the farm, preparing for dinner and roasting marshmallows afterwards. David hung out with some old store managers, drinking. She would be home alone or join her in-laws.

Tonight, Amanda needed her friends. Everyone in her friend circle had their own lives now, complete with their jobs, children, and husbands. With all the family activities, finding time to get together was hard, but she knew she could call Regina.

"Hey girl! What's going on?" Just hearing the familiar voice of her dear friend drove Amanda to tears.

"Regina, I'm in over my head. Operation Girlfriend needed."

"Oh, baby girl, come over to the spa. I'm here. We're closing early for a big day tomorrow. What's wrong?"

"David is having an affair, I'm pretty certain of it..." Regina interrupted Amanda.

"Oh, hell naw!" Regina exclaimed. "David Lloyd? Your husband?!"

Amanda kept driving, looking at the car display screen occasionally.

"Listen, get over here. You need to explain this to me."

Amanda told Regina that she was on her way. She hung up and called Meri and Bill and talked to the boys for a moment. When she got to Regina's parking lot, she texted David and told him she was out with the girls.

Regina owned Renew, a full spa equipped with massage therapists, hair stylists, nail technicians, and wellness coaches. Her husband, Greg, complimented her vision by having his fitness center on campus. Together, they had a 3,000-square-foot facility with half an acre of green space for outdoor classes and meditation.

Amanda was so proud of them. Their dream from college was right there, west of town. Regina and Greg were college lovers, meeting in kinesiology class. Regina was a pretty African-American woman with milk chocolate skin, brown eyes, and dark, straight, long hair. Her complexion was flawless, and she was never without eyeliner and lip gloss. She greeted Amanda at the front door.

"Hey, you!" Regina hugged Amanda for several seconds, and Amanda cried again.

"Aw, girl, get in here." She consoled her longtime friend for a few more seconds and locked the glass doors.

Amanda took in the walnut wood floors, the white walls, gray curtains from floor to ceiling, and the oversized white leather chaise lounge chairs.

"This place is great. I know I should have come here more often."

"Girl, we all have various things we are doing. I should come to you sometime. Before you say anything, go back there." Regina pointed to a frosted glass door with a *W* on it.

"Take a shower. Everything you need is in there. Put on a robe. Just get yourself together and relax."

Regina and Amanda exchanged hugs again, and then Regina saw Amanda disappear behind the door.

Regina remembered how she met Amanda in college and instantly took her in as a sister-friend. Amanda was alone, waking up, eating in the dining hall, going to class, studying, doing life alone. She was always in jeans and a t-shirt. Regina really noticed her when she didn't leave for Thanksgiving or Christmas and wondered if she had family.

Regina recalled the day she discovered Amanda was a foster kid going to college on her own. Their English class united them as they had to edit each other's papers. Amanda wrote a paper about her life without her parents. Regina couldn't imagine it. Amanda was so smart and beautiful.

Her paper was well-written but sad. Amanda was quiet and kind despite her situation, Regina remembered with a smile. When she asked her to sit with them for dinner, Amanda agreed but said nothing the first few times. Only when Jeff Coffman, the party animal of the group, came to Saturday morning breakfast with a hangover, did she speak. She left the table first and came back with a glass of tomato juice with ice and put it in front of him.

"Drink it. You'll feel better."

The table was silent. Jeff put it up to his nose and smelled it first.

"Whoa! What's in this?"

"Now, you're gonna get picky after the night you had?" Amanda smiled.

There it was—her smile, beautiful and lively. The table laughed.

"It's tomato juice, olives, and black pepper. It should detox you."

Jeff drank the drink. After one dry pancake and a large belch, Jeff replied, "Oh thank you, God."

Amanda said, "Call on someone who knows you." The table laughed again.

Throughout the rest of college, Amanda was the person people came to for help. She was nice, but Regina remembered the group wanting to take care of her, giving her the nickname White Chocolate. The name wasn't just because her mom was white and her dad was black, but because she was kind, sweet, and smooth with her sense of humor. She could sneak up on you with humor wrapped in truth.

"Is she here?" Greg asked, interrupting Regina's memory.

"Yes, she's taking a shower," Regina said while making tea in the kitchen. "Now, babe, she may not want you here. Operation Girlfriend doesn't come with an overprotective girlfriend's husband."

She gave him a peck on the cheek.

"Now you know I'm more than that," Greg said, leaning up against the counter.

"I wanna know if I gotta invite David over for a little one-on-one. You know, handle things man-to-man on the court."

"Well, I'm just ready to put all his shit outside!" A loud female voice came from behind them. It was Leslie. She had been friends with Regina and Greg Phillips since their first business venture, which was just a fitness club. She had met Amanda at many of Regina's gatherings and loved her. Amanda loved her too.

Greg rolled his eyes jokingly, saying, "Who let you in?" He finally saw Leslie in her black jumpsuit, large handbag on her shoulder, rhinestones on her flip-flops.

"I have a key." She smiled, waving it in the air on her keychain.

"Regina, we've gotta talk about your bad business decisions," Greg continued to joke.

"I thought you all said David was so in love with Amanda." Leslie looked at the couple. "What in the world happened? My Amanda can take any more heartbreak."

Leslie truly loved Amanda. Although their friendship was not as long as Greg and Regina's, it was no less meaningful.

"David does love Amanda." Regina wanted to defend David because she loved him too. "Please don't tell that sweet girl in there to throw her husband's clothes outside…"

Regina knew Leslie was teasing, but wanted to make sure, just in case.

"We are not in some movie where the police won't come, and God won't care."

"Amen," Leslie said. She knew her sister-friend was speaking the truth.

"See? You can't come in here talking crazy," Greg continued to banter with Leslie. "My wife will set you straight."

"Whatever, Greg," Leslie said, waving her hand at him. "What are you still doing here? This is Operation Girlfriend."

"Well, I love Amanda too, and I'm sure if Stan weren't at the hospital, he'd be here too."

Leslie rolled her eyes, but knew her husband would be equally concerned about Amanda. "You're right."

"Ah, what was that? Say that again?" Greg said with his ear out. He laughed self-righteously. "I'm right."

All three of them laughed at the exchange. Leslie finally got her brotherly hug from Greg.

"Amanda's in the shower. I'm making her tea," Regina said.

"I bought something a little stronger," Leslie said, opening her bag and pulling out two bottles of wine.

"Red or white, my friend?" But Leslie already knew the answer. She put the white wine in the refrigerator and opened the red, Amanda's favorite.

Amanda was grateful. As she exited the shower in a white cotton bathrobe, she saw her friends sitting on one of the large chaise lounge chairs, and Greg standing with hot tea, fruit, cheese, and wine on a table in front of them. She was so happy to see Leslie and Greg, too. Her mind flashed back to college and her beginnings as an Ana cosmetic representative when she met Leslie.

Leslie acted strong, with a quick wit and smartass answer for everything, but honestly, she was a faithful friend. After hearing her story, Leslie asked, "What are you afraid of the most?" Such a powerful question that Amanda had to think for a moment.

"Not feeling safe, I guess, and doing life all alone again." She remembered Leslie expressing that it would never happen again with her and Stan around. Regina and Greg agreed. Then it was back to Leslie being her fun-loving self, hosting dinner parties, barbecues, and calling at the last minute to go to the movies, while their families went to bed. One thing Leslie said once to Amanda that she never forgot: *You're a beautiful, gracious warrior.* Amanda didn't feel that way right then, especially as her friends looked at her with concern.

"You lie down here." Regina pointed to another identical chaise lounge chair across from them. Amanda sat where she was told. The girls looked at Greg.

"Yeah, I know; I'm not invited to *Operation Girlfriend.* I'm gonna wash the towels and get things set up for tomorrow." Greg gave Amanda a hug.

"I know David loves you, so whatever this is, it has to be an accident." Amanda loved Greg's reassurance.

"Yeah, don't go defending the male species now," Leslie said as Greg headed to the laundry room. Greg waved his hand at Leslie.

Regina looked at Amanda, waiting. Amanda showed her friends the florist's card she had taken from her purse, shared what she had done and why she believed David was having an affair.

"Okay, Amanda, let me get this straight. The flowers came to Augusta for you with the mistress's name on the damn card?" Regina asked, trying to grasp the information.

"Yeah, the floral shop messed up the order. David personally went into the floral shop, filled out the card, that's his handwriting, I know that. There was a mix-up with the information he gave them and the information in their system," Amanda explained.

"And then you kept the flowers, sent the mistress identical flowers with a card with the same message, and David doesn't have a clue?" Leslie chimed in.

"Regina, do you still want to start out with some tea? I'm going straight for the wine," Leslie said, pouring a glass of wine for Amanda first and then one for herself.

Amanda took the wine. "I wanted to buy myself some time to process things. Maybe I was overreacting, trying to find an innocent explanation. But *Sam, our time together was amazing* doesn't sound innocent. What amazing time are you having with another woman?"

"Exactly," Regina said. "Tell me again who this heifer is."

"Oh no, I got it right here online. Samantha Coleman, program sales director at Waters Square Hotel..." Leslie looked at her phone.

"She's pretty," Amanda stated. "Blonde..."

"She's not Amanda. That's my problem." Regina interrupted as she sipped her wine.

"A white girl? Really? Well, he'll regret that eventually. We are much better in bed," Leslie joked, but she was angry at David.

"Maybe that's what he wants now," Amanda started innocently.

Regina looked at her friend. "Sweetie, that is NOT what he wants. He wants you. You are gorgeous; you're more than pretty. David has lost his damn mind, is all."

"Yeah, things are different now. He sees her on Monday nights, his scheduled *meeting time*. I found the box of condoms in his car. He takes a shower immediately when he gets home, and his cell phone stays locked."

At that moment, Greg walked back in. He stood at Amanda's feet. She moved them so he could sit.

"Amanda, why haven't you spoken to David? Told him you know?"

Greg took her hand. Of course, he had been listening to the conversation from the back.

"At first, denial. Now, I'm scared of his answers. Now, I'm no better than he is."

Her friends all looked at her with curious faces, waiting in suspense for an explanation.

"Nathan made a pass at me tonight, and I allowed it to happen," Amanda said, shaking her head and placing a hand on her forehead.

"Sweet Jesus, who the hell is Nathan?" Leslie asked. "Damn. This wine might not be strong enough."

Regina gave Leslie a look to stop her antics, then she looked at Amanda. "Nathan from your job?!"

"Yes. He was consoling me." Amanda told them about the encounter. She was embarrassed as she was still sitting next to Greg.

"Damn," Greg said. "I'm not sure whether I would punch the guy or buy him a drink."

"Greg!" the women said, frowning at him.

"What? I mean it. Nathan meant well, kinda. Sure, he was crushing on a married woman and lost control. Yeah, that's bad. But he stopped it from going all the way. That's good. He respects you and your marriage. Good. But can you still work with him now that emotions are high? Bad. I like that he told you to go home to David and gave you sound advice."

"Yes," Amanda agreed with Greg. "Nathan is not going to pursue me, and I'm not going to pursue him."

"Amanda, what do you want?" Regina asked.

Amanda took a deep breath. "I love David. I'm in love with David. I love my boys, my in-laws, and mostly I want to love myself."

"Baby girl, you don't love yourself?" Regina asked. "What's going on? You are beautiful inside and out."

"I need to be mature about all of this," Amanda spoke.

"Then I'm the wrong person to get advice from." Leslie smiled, joking. "I'm ready to do bodily harm."

They all laughed, knowing Leslie was the spiritual one, but trying to lighten the mood.

"Seriously, you are lovely. You are the best mother and the best wife," Leslie said.

"Yes," Regina exclaimed with added emotion. "You see after those boys every day. You make sure their needs are met, and you make sure they get quality time with their grandparents in equal portions. Uncle Bruce is in the mix when you and David need quality time. You still clean your own house, and the boys have chores. We know all your business. David told us one night in secret, you give Saturday morning blow jobs and make Sunday morning cinnamon rolls."

Amanda blushed, laughed, and told Regina to stop.

"Now you know, when we all get together as married couples, we talk." Greg laughed. "David told us how good he has it."

"Well, I love him. But what kind of environment have I created at home that made him go to Samantha?"

"Only David can answer that," Greg said. "I'd wanna know that you know."

"And the moment he slept with *Sam*, he should've said something. Why does she have to say something?" Regina snapped back.

"Greg, as a man, what am I missing here?" Amanda finally asked.

"Oh, baby girl, I don't know. You all have a lot going on—your promotion, David's new promotion. I imagine David still worries about you and your emotions; whether he's providing and meeting your needs as a safe place..."

"See, I'm not confident with David, nor do I expect him to protect me all the time." Amanda said.

"Amanda, it's a man's job to protect his family and cover his wife. If he's tired of doing that, then I have a problem with David," Greg said.

Regina finally understood what Amanda was saying.

Regina stared at her husband. "Greg, please, dear, fold the towels."

He rolled his eyes at his wife, knowing she was right. He gave Amanda a hug. "For what it's worth, fight for him on your knees. God knows what David needs."

Regina watched her husband head toward the laundry room. "He is right about praying."

"Yes," Amanda acknowledged.

"Amanda, do you mean you are not confident with David sexually?" Regina finally said softly.

"C'mon, who am I kidding? David was so tender with me as we dated because of my past. We waited until our wedding night to have sex. That...was amazing."

"He used to satisfy me, but now that has stopped. I knew something was wrong, but what did I do?" Amanda started crying again. The woman got her tissue, and Amanda continued.

"What if it isn't what I am doing? Is it what I'm not doing? After having children, the day-to-day routine, are we having *married couple sex* because we are so tired?"

The women agreed and shared stories of falling asleep before sex, and Leslie shared how Stan once fell asleep during sex because she was that boring. They all laughed.

"So, are you afraid to initiate sex? Is something holding you back from asking David to give you lovin'?" Leslie asked, looking at Amanda. "He doesn't always have to be the one to ask. Your name is on the marriage license too, you know what I mean?" Leslie asked, raising an eyebrow.

"I'm afraid of rejection. I'm already neglected. With the way we have sex now, it's all about him," Amanda admitted.

Regina's face showed disappointment, but then she asked, "Amanda, why do you think Nathan is attracted to you?"

"Regina, we are trying to get Nathan out of her mind and David home," Leslie said.

"I know," Regina said, speaking softly. "I'm going somewhere with this."

"Regina, I don't know. He sees me at work, doing my job." Amanda said.

"Exactly. I bet you are confident, bold, taking charge, smiling, and laughing. And your posture at home?"

Amanda was convicted. "It's definitely not that. I'm tired and dragging. The kids challenge me."

"Me too," Regina said. "This is a lesson for us all."

Amanda saw what Regina was saying. She thought for a moment, just to be sure. Her past didn't have anything to do with how she felt about David. She loved him and found him attractive. Did he know that? She wasn't sure if he knew.

"Amanda, draw David in," Leslie said, interrupting her thought. "You're the wife."

"And to help with that draw, let me do your hair," Regina requested. "Quick highlights?"

Amanda loved the idea and nodded yes. As Leslie gave her a manicure and a pedicure, and Regina started her hair, Amanda thought about what Nathan told her, *This is not your fault.*

But was it?

CHAPTER 4

*A*manda woke up in the guest bedroom on the lower level. Last night, she decided that she wanted the morning to herself. David didn't come in until well after midnight; 2:00 am to be exact. She heard the garage door and his familiar walk across the kitchen floor.

She didn't tell her friends that those Saturday morning blowjobs were just a memory. David got up to run most mornings while she prepared the boys' breakfast, and on went the day.

She got dressed and walked out of the house to a little coffeehouse close to their neighborhood. The doorbell signaled her arrival. Inside, the grinder was on, jazz music played, and, as the first customer, Amanda had her pick of seats. She picked her beloved corner.

You could see the street one way from the coffeehouse, and the mural on the wall that depicted artistic coffee mugs and uplifting words. Right away, a young man with dark hair in a man bun addressed her. Out of habit, she smiled and said, *A tall café latte with vanilla*. She sat at the small round table where she put her purse on one chair and sat in the other.

Amanda took in the smell of coffee and the fact that she was alone. No boys, no husband, no work, no household chores in front of her, just Amanda. She remembered what Bill had asked her: *Who takes care of Amanda?* She whispered to herself, *Amanda takes care of Amanda.*

When the latte came, Amanda had her phone out, checking email and the morning news. She allowed the drink to sit and cool a bit, her phone turned down on its face. She needed to think and make some decisions.

Stay married, she thought. Nathan and Greg were right. Not having sex with her husband creates more neglect for her. Nathan gets a foothold, and for David, he wouldn't get his needs met at home. Not getting his needs met at home would make Samantha a necessity versus a want.

Amanda agreed with Regina. *Needs met at home.* Did David like having sex with me? Had our sex life become boring? He was so careful and gentle, not triggering her past. She had to get confident.

Amanda agreed with Leslie. *What if she started initiating sex?* The worst thing that could happen was rejection. She already felt that, so maybe she should give it a try. New bras and panties, new outfits, and ways to relieve his stress so David felt more comfortable at home.

Amanda prayed for God to help her, guide her, and protect her. With that prayer, she felt a fight coming on. She thought the enemy wanted her marriage to fall apart to create division and cause trouble. *Am I prepared to fight?* She prayed again and decided she was. Amanda heard a buzz, and her phone danced on the table. She turned the phone over and looked. It was Nathan. She swiped to answer.

"Nathan."

"Amanda. I'm sorry to bother you on a Saturday. I was just hoping to leave a message. I wanted to apologize for my behavior last night. It crossed a line personally and professionally. Since I was out of line, I would completely understand if you wanted to report…"

"Nathan, I'm not going to report anything," Amanda interrupted. "I gave you permission to touch me. Right about now, I'm grateful you insisted on a cold shower."

"Yeah," Nathan recalled, he did stop them from going further.

"Listen, I want you to save your marriage. I'm praying that is possible."

"Thank you. Me too." Amanda wanted this conversation to be brief; she couldn't be emotional with Nathan anymore. There was an attraction, and she needed to cool it down. However, part of her wanted to get closer to Nathan. He was divorced, and he obviously regretted it.

"I appreciate you calling me; rest easy. I'm not going to say a word." Nathan could tell by Amanda's tone that she was done being emotional, and he thought of it as a good thing.

"Well, thank you, Amanda."

He was relieved. He closed his eyes, grateful he didn't completely mess up his life, again.

"Enjoy your day. See you on Monday."

"I will. You do the same."

Amanda finished her latte, texted Leslie to say she hadn't seen David, and she was headed to go shopping for sexy clothes. Leslie wished she could come along, but she promised the day to Stan and his parents.

Amanda was happy to go alone. She felt that with no one to influence her, she would find what she really liked.

Amanda now saw the text from David.

> Honey, are you okay? You didn't have to
> sleep downstairs. I'm fine. With Dad and
> Bruce, the usual routine.

Amanda texted back.

> Babe, I love you. I'm fine. Got up early;
> didn't want to disturb you. I'm going
> shopping!

David texted back that he noticed she had lost weight; she looked great. Told her to transfer money from savings to checking and enjoy herself.

Amanda noticed her clothes were not as tight. She felt good, but she decided right then and there that she should set an appointment with her doctor.

Yeah, David was using condoms, but did he use them every time? She couldn't get pregnant anymore; Mason's emergency C-section ended the possibilities. But sexually transmitted diseases were still possible. She put the doctor's visit on her to-do list on her phone. She transferred the money from the account, as David said, and went up to pay for her latte.

"Already paid for," the barista told her, then slipped her a piece of paper with the name Mark and a phone number. "You can thank the gentleman in the corner here," he said in a low voice, pointing to him.

There sat a white, middle-aged man with dark hair and light eyes. He nodded in Amanda's direction. She gave him a kind look and showed him her wedding ring.

"I'm flattered. Thank you for the coffee."

He gave her a look of disappointment, but of respect. She left the coffeehouse.

Saturdays for Amanda always involved groceries. Of course, she shopped at her neighborhood Acuff's. Today, if she were going to shop for herself, grocery shopping would have to wait, but it definitely had to occur before getting the boys from the farm. What couldn't wait was her stop to Sarah's Farm at the downtown farmer's market.

She parked her SUV, took her wallet, and walked up the street to a booth with rows and rows of fresh lavender, sage, and wildflowers. As she approached, she could see the tables of fresh produce and handmade crafts. It wasn't long before Clyde saw her.

"Mrs. Amanda. No boys today?" Clyde, in his early seventies with white hair in a ponytail, a big belly, light eyes, and a worn white apron labeled *for Sarah* engraved in green with a red strawberry next to it.

"No boys today, Clyde," Amanda said with her smile. "What's good?"

"Well, from the farm, these blueberries are sweet right now." He gave Amanda one on a toothpick. She took the toothpick and tasted it.

"Great. Two pints of those." Amanda looked around and gathered strawberries, grapes, and pineapple rings. She handed Clyde a hundred-dollar bill. He knew she didn't want change.

"Now, Mrs. Amanda," he said, blushing as always.

Amanda gave him a look and pointed, as always, to his apron's *for Sarah* label. Clyde always took her hand and held it for a moment to say thank you. Amanda would say a quick prayer for Clyde's family and then allow him to assist other customers. Amanda took the extra time to go home, put her finds from Sarah's Farm in the refrigerator, and then went to shop for clothes.

She went to the outlet mall between Brookview and Lindale. Amanda enjoyed the time to herself and was excited about the clothes she was finding that fit her style and purpose. She found the bras and panties, sundresses, jumpsuits, tops, jeans, and her favorite wedged high heels. The thicker heel was perfect for giving her height, support, and comfort.

As she stopped to get a salad with a lemonade, she sat at the outdoor patio food court when an African American man sat at the table next to her. He was nice looking, sunglasses on, and by his stature, Amanda could tell he visited the gym at least twice a week. He was wearing an orange t-shirt that said, *mind over matter*, athletic shorts, and running shoes. The gentleman gave her a smile and said hello.

"Hi," Amanda responded.

"I don't see very many of us in this area," he said.

Amanda knew exactly what he meant. The closest three towns— Brookview, Lindale, and Galesboro—had a four percent population of African American people.

"No, you won't see very many of us. Where are you from?"

The man was excited that Amanda wanted to make conversation.

"Carbondale. Just came up here for a change of scenery." He held out his hand. "I'm glad I did. I'm Aaron."

"I'm Amanda." She took his hand and shook it.

"Do you mind?" Aaron wanted to sit with her.

Amanda nodded with approval.

"Mr. ...?" Amanda was searching for his last name.

"Homes," he said. "Like a house."

He took a seat across from her, noticing her shopping bags for a moment, then returning to her beauty.

"Mr. Homes, I'm married."

"Yes," Aaron said, noticing the ring. "All the pretty ones are." He paused to sip his drink.

Amanda blushed.

"Listen, there is no harm in having lunch with a pretty woman, is there?" Aaron was giving Amanda permission to enjoy her salad, and he was happy to talk to her.

"No, there isn't," she said, smiling and blushing.

"Amanda, you are holding out on me. I'm sure that smile alone has stopped traffic."

"Mr. Homes, you're charming." Amanda started eating her salad.

"Please call me Aaron."

Aaron was a nice man. He was forty years old, a business owner, but Amanda got the feeling he was more than that. He had a deep, smooth voice, and she noticed that when he laughed, his brown eyes exuded happiness and security. While allowing her to enjoy her salad, he revealed he was looking for simple, inexpensive pictures to decorate the business he had just acquired.

"It was nice to meet you," Amanda said, looking at her watch. She knew she needed to keep moving.

"The pleasure was all mine, truly," Aaron said as he rose from the table. Amanda rose from the table, attempting to gather her shopping bags. Aaron wanted to help her.

"Let me help you to your car," he said. "I promise you, I am not crazy."

Amanda laughed. She felt safe and allowed him to walk her to her SUV.

When they approached, Aaron could tell by her black Acura RDX that she was a well-kept woman, but was far from flashy.

"Your husband keeps you well."

"Thanks," Amanda said, lifting the back of the SUV with her key remote as Aaron put the bags in.

"Does he make you happy?" Aaron asked, facing her as the hatchback closed.

Amanda didn't answer right away. She passed him to get into the driver's seat.

"Yes," she finally said as she sat in the seat.

"Well, I'm sure there is a story there," Aaron said, standing next to Amanda and holding the driver door.

Amanda found her sunglasses in her purse and put them on. Aaron asked if he could use her pen, which he noticed on the top of her console. She gave it to him. He then took her left hand and kissed it.

"I'm glad I met you," he said, opening her hand and writing his phone number on her palm.

Before Amanda could say anything, Aaron spoke.

"I know; you're married. Whatever is going on, I hope your husband starts paying attention. I hope he sees my number and you tell him about our lunch. I'm an intentional man."

Amanda smiled at him. "I will do that."

Aaron gave Amanda her pen back, told her to drive safely, and closed her door.

Amanda drove off with a smile. She had to admit that the enemy was really tempting her today.

When Amanda drove into the garage, David's car was still gone. Good news, she thought. She could put her new outfits away, try a few on, and get her strategy together. She was excited and couldn't wait to see what David would say about her hair and her new attitude. Then, she got nervous.

What if he wasn't interested anymore? She thought about the man at the coffeehouse, Mark, and then Aaron. She decided to believe in her actions and that her husband had not lost interest and still loved her. Amanda raced upstairs with her bags.

Amanda came down the stairs in her new skinny bootleg jeans with her new wedged heels. She paired it with a short-sleeved black top that had to be zipped up like a jacket. The bra she wore accentuated her breasts. She made sure the zipper was low enough to show cleavage, just for David. It was still cool outside, so she put on her long black sweater duster just to cover her arms. When David saw her, she knew he was interested.

"Amanda. Honey, look at you?!" He took one of her hands, raised it up, and he spun her around as if they were dancing. He pulled her in close, and she planted a passionate kiss on his lips.

"Thank you! Yes, I love this." She looked at David. He was in his muscle shirt and athletic shorts, wearing that perfect smile as his eyes searched her. He wanted her and she knew it. David didn't let her go.

"Coming upstairs with me?" He asked.

"Babe, I don't have time for that now," she said, pouting.

"I need to go to the grocery store, pick up the boys from the farm, and they wanted to go to the movies tonight."

David saw something different in his wife's eyes. It was good, bright, and sure.

"Okay," he said, looking at her cleavage. "But these are mine. I need no assistant store director, or anyone else at Acuff, for that matter, having wild thoughts."

He zipped the top all the way up to her neck.

Amanda zipped it back down to a modest position. "There. This is comfortable."

David searched her again. "Your hair is nice. The highlights complement everything about your face," he said. "Regina?"

Amanda shook her hair. "Yes, she's so good."

It was then that David noticed the phone number in her hand. "Really?"

Amanda looked at the number. Her face was flushed and hot.

"Listen, I'm innocent. I wasn't dressed like this. This is for your eyes only."

David believed her. He knew Amanda was an attractive woman. Any man seeing her alone would ask her out.

"And how did this man get this close to you?" David raised his eyebrow. Amanda told him about her lunch.

David shook his head. "Honey, be careful."

"I am." Amanda truly did feel secure with Aaron.

"Listen," David said, still holding her close. "I'm paying attention, and I'm being intentional right now." He kissed her.

"You sure you don't have a few minutes?" Amanda knew if she stood one more minute next to her husband, he would have her naked.

"Babe, go up and shower." She rubbed his arms, and he gently released her.

"I'll be home before you know it," she said, heading to the kitchen and exiting via the garage door.

On the way to the grocery store, Amanda was smiling so brightly. She had done it! She knew David was thinking about her, wondering what was going on. What she didn't account for was how wonderful she would feel.

Amanda looked and felt great, and she realized she had so much to be grateful for. She was right; David was thinking about her. In the shower, he was confused, thinking something new was going on. Was all this for him or someone else?

CHAPTER 5

The Acuff corporate offices were on a three-acre campus. It had two large corporate parking lots—one for employees and company cars, the other for visitors—in front of its conference center. A courtyard right beside the cafeteria/restaurant offered employees an outdoor lunch space.

There were several entrances to the building. David parked his car in the company parking lot and entered the building from the employee entrance. After going through two double doors, he was in the lobby.

Acuff was shaped in a square with three floors, with the lobby on the first floor. The lobby displayed a water feature that took up the center, with tropical plants and flowers. David made it a point to go around to the front of the lobby—fully furnished with chairs, sofas, tables with magazines—and greet Colette and Diane, who were like permanent fixtures behind the reception desk.

"Good morning, ladies." David nodded with his travel mug in one hand, computer bag with laptop in the other. They acknowledged him with a smile and polite conversation most days, but it was Monday. The lobby was full of what looked like sales representatives and directors from corporations. Diane just waved, marked David as "in" on her clipboard, and kept assisting guests.

David never took the elevator. He went up the open spiral staircase, and at the top was Vikki Dalton holding a cup of coffee. Behind her were a set of sofas and a coffee table. David half smiled when he saw her. Vikki had short strawberry-blonde hair—he was sure she dyed it—green eyes, and thin lips which did not smile back. He was certain she and his mom were drinking from the same fountain of youth because Vikki was in her mid-fifties, but she looked years younger. Her skin was smooth.

"Good morning, David."

"Vikki, are you going to do this every morning I'm here?" He said as they walked to his office.

"I hope that coffee is for yourself."

He took a drink from his travel mug. "Amanda takes care of me."

"Yes, I see that," Vikki stated, and decided to sip the coffee.

"So when do I get to meet your wife? I'm surprised she still wants to work the way she does with your new salary and bonuses."

"I haven't told her the exact amount of my increase," David admitted.

"Oh, that's not gonna end well, David. Plan on telling her sometime soon?" Vikki asked.

"Don't give me that tone. She recently got promoted and endured the stress surrounding my promotion. I'd like to get this academy off the ground before I tell her."

Vikki sighed. "You young people. I knew what Maxwell had for lunch by the skid marks in his drawers." Now, her southern accent was more pronounced.

David choked on his coffee, then laughed as they continued to walk. Vikki kept fussing.

"I'm gonna tell you right now, I don't support crazy vice presidents who upset their wives. You're on your own. I'm in the wives' club. If she comes up here to cuss you out, I'm likely to join in."

Vikki was smiling, but they both knew she was serious. Vikki didn't get to be an executive administrative assistant by not sharing her opinion. She was loyal, didn't share secrets, and didn't spend time with the other assistants talking about the corporate gossip of the day. She was a widow and lived with her daughter, Susan, in the neighboring town of Galesboro.

"So what's so crazy that you had to meet me at the top of the stairs?"

"Crazy isn't the word I would use. Old man Acuff just increased your academy budget by giving you five percent from the retention/turnover fund."

"This is awesome!" David grinned as he walked into his office. "He's in the office today?"

"No, but he wants lunch with you today at Lakeford Country Club," Vikki stated.

"Classy; off campus. What can I expect?" Even though David had been with Acuff since he was fourteen, he learned early to get everyone's take on a situation. He sat down at his desk, turned on his computer, and Vikki sat in the chair across from him.

"Lunch. A check never comes to the table ever. Don't order a cocktail even though he'll ask you to join him in one. After the salad, he'll start the conversation. Say thank you. He'll tell you his concerns, but I don't think he has any. He trusts you and just wants to be kept in the loop. Scott doesn't often give him the details he wants."

David looked at her. "How do you know this stuff?"

"Barbara, his admin, likes us," Vikki winked. "She tells me everything."

David started looking at the papers on his desk. "Good to know."

Vikki rose from the chair and told David to look at the course fees for the culinary arts program. He nodded.

After a few phone calls and emails, David sat back in his chair, looking out of his third-story window at the simple Brookview skyline. He closed his eyes for a moment, and there in his memory was Amanda.

She was totally sexy all weekend, he thought. On Saturday night, they took the boys to the movies. She sat next to him. Usually, the boys sat between them, but when Matthew wanted to sit on the end, the parents sat in between the boys. Sitting next to her, she fed him popcorn once, her hand on his upper thigh, and every so often she would whisper in his ear, "Love you," or "Look at Mason's sweet little face." He smiled at the memory.

By last night, he couldn't take it. He had to have her. After the boys had gone to bed, she came downstairs to the kitchen in a white tank top, no bra, and black and white thin-striped boyfriend panties. Her nipples so visible; her ass cheeks hanging out as she hovered over the kitchen island, eating ice cream. She stood at just the right angle for him to see her from the den.

He remembered how she was eating the ice cream; he wanted to be that spoon. He took her upstairs, and they had sex. *She's doing it all on purpose,* he thought. *Why? Did she find out about Sam? No, how could she? And if she did, that would not be her response.*

Then, he remembered the girls' night? He believed something had happened there. He smiled. Whatever contest or bet it was, David hoped Amanda was winning.

When Amanda showed Norah and Nathan the essential oils and accessories in her office, they were impressed. The packaging and how the eye pillows and neck wraps were well made.

"I can see why you're interested in bringing this category to our offices." Norah sniffed the lavender essential oil. "I could see this in the organic/wellness section."

"Me too," Amanda replied. "But it's hard to purchase the eye pillow, neck wraps, and these aloe socks in the aisle. They are so boutique and high-end."

"I think if you kept them in the plastic and had some kind of special shelving, people would buy it." Nathan piped in, but was more interested in the company. "What is the name of this company?"

"Snowflake Ranch," Amanda answered. "I know, weird coming out of Texas, but I couldn't find out any more information. Just that they invited me to their showroom at the Dallas Market."

Amanda rose to put the neck roll and eye pillow back in the box, and Norah spoke. "I think this is worth pursuing."

Norah adjusted herself in the chair. "In fact, the three of us should go to the Dallas Market Center and view this category this summer. We have to go there anyway for our annual meeting at our Dallas office. We might as well take some time and go to the market."

Amanda liked the idea. Nathan agreed. Their leadership staff meeting continued with the summer schedule of resets. Nathan took the liberty of ordering them lunch—a ham and Swiss cheese sandwich for Norah and chicken salad for Amanda. Because they ordered so often from *Lloyd's*, Nathan knew Norah wanted her bread toasted, and Amanda had to have extra crackers and iceberg lettuce on the side. They didn't have to tell him; Nathan knew. With the way he paid attention and cared, Amanda began to appreciate him more after the soft kiss they shared.

There was no tension between them. He didn't ask her about David, nor did she tell him what happened. But he noticed her new look and confidence level, and he was proud. He thought it just complemented what he already knew about her. He wouldn't lie to himself; he cared for Amanda.

If she weren't married, he would pursue her, not only because she was beautiful, but because she was smart, intelligent, and devoted herself to the things that mattered most in life.

~

Amanda got caught up in her new store set for Quinn's drugstore in Lindale; she completely forgot about her doctor's appointment. She quickly left work and made it to the clinic just in time. Dr. Marion Shaw was a nice man, just busy like all doctors Amanda knew. He was straight to the point, but really wasn't going to leave the conversation without knowing the patient completely understood the situation. He was bald with blue eyes and had a caring disposition. Dr. Marion performed a thorough exam on Amanda. He asked all the uncomfortable questions like: *Did she change sexual partners?*

She was honest. She stated she hadn't changed sexual partners but had doubts about her husband. It landed so awkwardly in her mouth; she felt sad, betrayed, and Dr. Shaw didn't show any emotion, even though he knew David and all the visits he attended during Amanda's pregnancies.

He told her he would call her with the test results. He assured her the weight loss was not enough to cause concern, but she needed to watch her stress levels, eating habits, and sleeping habits.

Brookview Clinic was a tight community. Even though the nurses in OBGYN kept things confidential, she knew her mother-in-law would somehow find out she was in the clinic, so Amanda went down to Orthopedics to see Meri. Meri was with a patient. Since it was Monday night, Amanda knew David would not be home. She left her mother-in-law a note to join her and the boys for dinner. Amanda then went to pick up the boys from school.

When she got to the school, as usual, parents were lined up in their cars to pick up their children. The boys told their mom never to get in the *take forever drop-off* and *pick-up line*. They would come out of the school building together and cross the street. Matthew insisted he was a *big kid* now and didn't need Mom to pick him up directly in front of the school. *Lame* was the word he used.

Amanda stepped out of her SUV, shut the door, and leaned against the driver's door, waiting for the boys. She looked model-like in her high heels and slate-blue pantsuit with her hair in the breeze.

"Amanda?" A brunette-haired woman came up to her in her denim capris and t-shirt.

Amanda smiled and recognized the woman. "Lisa! How are you?"

"I'm well, but not as good as you!" Lisa said, looking at Amanda. "You look great! The 9 to 5 looks good on you, and I heard David is now a vice president."

Amanda took off her sunglasses and gave Lisa a look. Lisa Reynolds, a stay-at-home mom who knew everything about everybody. She was friendly, sweet, and pretty. She was flawless with bone-colored skin, manicured nails, and a figure that communicated she worked out daily. Her husband was a dermatologist, and they lived in the gated community of Brentwood, which was north of town.

"Thank you, Lisa, but look at you! You're gorgeous in just a simple t-shirt. I have to work at this; I haven't changed. David and I are the same." Amanda told her sincerely.

"Sure. I'll give it six months, and David won't come home like he used to, and some younger version of you will come around, and you'll be just like the rest of us." Lisa was blunt.

Amanda's heart flopped. She put her glasses back on to hide the truth of Lisa's statement. Yet, she was concerned about Lisa.

"No, Lisa. Don't tell me Bryon…" Amanda looked at her, and Lisa began to speak.

"We should start a club." Lisa had pain in her eyes. "Bryon and I will work it out. It is so much cheaper to keep me. Melissa, Allison, and Pamela all have loveless marriages. They are living single but married. Crazy, huh?"

Amanda took a deep breath and expressed how sorry she was to hear about her friends. When Mason was in daycare and preschool, these ladies were in her life every day with fish crackers, fruit snacks, strollers, and sneaking margaritas to drink as they walked to the park on Friday afternoons.

"Lisa, I will be praying for you both," Amanda said, taking off her glasses.

"Thanks," Lisa said. "You're blessed, Amanda. I could always tell that David loves you for real."

Lisa put on a smile and gave Matthew and Mason hugs as they made it to the car. Lisa saw her children coming up the hill in the distance.

"Hey, Amanda. What's the story of your brother-in-law?" She winked.

"What about him?" Amanda said.

"When he picks the boys up from school, you should see the single moms." Lisa laughed. "Lips glossed and hair flipped. I wonder if he even notices these women falling all over themselves."

Amanda laughed as she helped the boys into the car.

"He is easy on the eyes; always has been. What can I say? You never know with Bruce. He has a heart of gold and loves kids," Amanda replied. The women laughed and said their goodbyes.

Matthew and Mason quickly communicated that they had no extra work from school and begged to play video games in the lower level. Amanda didn't have the energy to argue, so she gave in. She had just put the lasagna in the oven and was ready to relax when the doorbell rang. To her surprise, it was Nathan.

He was in the same outfit she remembered from work. Dark pants, a V-neck burgundy sweater vest with a button-down printed dress shirt underneath. His face was full of concern; his eyes relieved when he saw her.

"Oh, thank God!" he said with a deep exhale. "Could you answer your phone? Call a person back or somethin'."

"What?" Amanda frowned for a moment and began looking around for her phone. Nathan stood at the door. He wasn't interested in coming into her home.

There was an awkward moment before she said, "Wait here."

Amanda grabbed her phone from her purse, which was resting on the kitchen island, and then she met Nathan again at her front door. She sat on the front porch swing, and he leaned against her front porch post with his arms folded.

"I'm sorry." Amanda realized she hadn't turned her phone back on from her doctor's visit. She now noticed Nathan and Vanessa's messages.

"I was running late for my doctor's appointment. It was on my calendar."

"Amanda," Nathan reached into his back pocket. "You left your office keys in your office door. Your computer was left on, phone misplaced, blueprints left out on your meeting table, and none of us saw you leave."

She took her office keys from him and sighed. "I'm sorry; I've been so preoccupied. As you can see, I'm fine." Amanda texted Vanessa that she was home and safe.

"Amanda, what did your doctor say?" Nathan relaxed his arms. "I bet you it was to rest. Take the rest of the week off. You look wonderful, but your mind...it's completely somewhere else."

Amanda closed her eyes and relaxed her shoulders. There was quiet.

"I know you are trying to save your marriage," Nathan said in an almost whisper.

Amanda opened her eyes. There were tears in them. "Yeah."

Nathan was now serious. "As the director of the office, I don't want to see you for the rest of the week. Personal leave, vacation, whichever; you have plenty of both."

"Okay," Amanda said just to please Nathan. "Thank you for checking on me and bringing me my keys."

"Sure," he said. "Have a good night." He took a step off the porch. "I didn't mean to come here unannounced; I hope I haven't..."

Amanda didn't allow him to finish. "He's not here." She began to move the swing a little as her feet shifted. "He's with her."

Amanda hated that she had said it aloud. "Did you do this?"

Nathan didn't understand what she was asking. "Do what?"

"Did you leave your wife at home alone while you…"

Nathan didn't allow her to finish, and he sat on the top step of the porch.

"… while I allowed drugs and alcohol to take over my life. Yes. I abandoned her. I regret it every day." He looked down at his hands.

"What happened?" Amanda asked softly.

Nathan hesitated. He promised himself that if Amanda ever asked anything about his life, he would be honest but unemotional.

"I wasn't always in the brokerage business. At my last job, I got hurt and had to have back surgery. The pain is how it happened. Before I knew it, I was an addict. It had me neglecting my son, cheating on my wife, and angry at myself because I couldn't do my job anymore."

Amanda gave him a look of sympathy and compassion, then asked, "You have a son?"

Nathan smiled at the thought. "Yes, I'm older than you. Christopher is 17 and a senior in high school. He just left here; we went fishing yesterday. Back there, I wasn't a good dad. Up here, I'm grateful to Jesus for the second chance."

Amanda's eyes grew bright as she looked at him. "You are a believer?"

Nathan looked at her and couldn't help but smile back. "Absolutely. Amanda, the Lord saved my life. It took a bar fight, being knocked unconscious, and being left to die in the cold next to a dumpster. Instead of going to jail, I went to the hospital. Let's just say, Jesus met me there and now I'm here."

"Amen," Amanda replied.

Nathan rose from the step, and Amanda got up from the swing.

"I gotta get ready for dinner." She looked at him and saw his hazel eyes were content. In her mind, she guessed he was about forty years old. She had to admit to herself that he was handsome.

"See you next week. I'll take your appointments." Nathan was serious.

Amanda rolled her eyes, still planning to come to work tomorrow, so she changed the subject as he headed to his car, and she remained on the porch. "Your ex-wife..."

"I see what you're doin' here, shifting the focus." He sighed. "We co-parent. She's kind after all the crap I put her through. Next year, she's planning on marrying her boyfriend of two years."

Amanda saw his closed smile of sadness but acceptance. Unexpectedly, she said, "Apologize to her anyway, the way Jesus would want you to apologize. I wonder whether, when, or how David will ever say sorry to me. The more he pretends, the more of me dies inside, so say it. You wear your regret, and perhaps you'll feel relief."

Nathan wanted to hug her, but he now knew better. "Okay, I will. I will pray for you and your marriage." He got into his car. Amanda watched him drive away.

CHAPTER 6

$\mathcal{N}$athan decided to just grab fast food and then head home to his townhouse. That's when he saw Amanda's text that her lasagna was still uncooked after 15 minutes in the oven because she had failed to turn the oven on. *It is a sign*, she texted.

She agreed she needed to rest and texted she was *taking tomorrow off to rest*. He gave her message a thumbs up and decided he would do what Amanda said. He called Jill on his ride home.

"Hey there." The sound of her voice satisfied him. "Everything okay?"

"Oh yeah, sure," he replied. "Just making sure Christopher made it home this morning. I know it's just an hour and a half to Briton. I can't believe he is driving on his own now. Did he make it to school on time?"

"He did," she said, smiling. "Christopher came home after school happy. He said you all had a *great* time. He used the word *great*."

"Good. I'm glad. Thank you for the suggestion. It was wonderful to see him."

There was silence for a moment. Then, Nathan told her, "I really called to talk to you."

"Really?" she asked, concerned. "Is your job okay? The person you are protecting, are they okay?"

Nathan had to tell Jill as much as he could to make sure she and Christopher were safe, so of course, she would think about his job first.

"She is a beautiful black woman I get the pleasure of working alongside every day. Her sons are elementary-aged and adorable. Her husband is a white, prominent, well-known figure. I thought he was devoted to her, but I found out he is having an affair. She's devastated."

"This is the last thing I need her to go through. I need her to be aware and confident. Things are going to unfold soon enough."

"I see," Jill said. "Well, keep me on a *need-to-know basis*." That was Jill's way of understanding his work and its privacy.

"Jill, I'm sorry. This assignment is not like any of the others I've done. It hits close to home. This woman, Amanda, is broken-hearted about her husband's infidelity. It brought back memories of how I treated you."

"I lied to you, said you weren't good enough, and made you feel less than a woman. I'm sorry for that, and I regret it every day. I regret my lashing out and the substance use to numb the pain of so many hurts. Hurting because I felt I had been dumb to turn my back on a suspect. Angry and hurt at having to leave the force and start over. As a man, I felt I shouldn't ask for help."

"My mom left us when I was young, and my dad taught me to *rely on no one; you can only depend on yourself*, he would say. I shut you out. I'm sorry."

Jill was silent, but Nathan could tell she was listening.

"Catherine was a mistake. I didn't love her; I used her. With her being your friend on top of it all, I knew it would crush you. There is no excuse; I'm just explaining."

"I wanted everyone to hurt like I was hurting. I didn't even realize how much money I had blown and wasted on drugs, alcohol, and clothes until we divorced. What a fool I was! Jill, I don't mean to bring all this up again, but I've never come right out and just owned it."

Nothing was said for a moment.

"Nate, I know I wasn't there for your rehabilitation and recovery. I'm sorry I couldn't face you, but I read the letter you sent. You apologized then."

"I did," Nathan remembered, "and it was about Christopher—how much I missed his pre-teen years, and the burden I put on you. I thanked you for your graciousness in letting me build a relationship with him now. Today, I felt regret, which tells me I haven't said all the truth I need to say. That's why I called you before I lost my nerve or deemed it unimportant."

"Jill, I'm sorry I hurt you. You are an amazing woman. The beauty you have on the outside is even more evident on the inside. Your heart and love for family touches me."

Jill stopped moving about in her kitchen and sat on the sofa in the living room. She heard every word Nathan was saying, and it felt surreal. She had waited years for this conversation of true feelings and thoughts. All she managed to say was thank you.

Before Nathan hung up, he called her by the nickname he had for her.

"No, Cinnamon, thank you for your patience and your forgiveness. I wish you all the happiness and love in your new beginning."

When Meri came to the door for dinner, the boys were excited.

"Momma Meri!" Mason gave the first hug. Matthew followed.

"Boys, allow Momma Meri to get in the house and be comfortable," Amanda told the boys as she was in the kitchen. Meri locked the door behind her and headed towards Amanda.

"Amanda!" Meri hugged her daughter-in love as she called her. "Thank you for leaving the note. Are you okay?"

Amanda knew it was a surprise for her to be at the clinic.

"Yes, Mom. I just needed to see Dr. Shaw," Amanda replied.

"You're not pregnant, are you?" Meri was trying not to be excited.

"No, those days are over, Mom," Amanda smiled. "But I lost weight without trying, and I wanted to make sure it wasn't anything serious. Turns out it was not." She told a partial truth, but she felt better.

"Good." Meri was happy to hear. "You look great. Your hair is gorgeous."

"Thanks, Mom. Sit. Let me get you something to drink." Amanda said and pulled out a bar stool from the kitchen island. "I hope lasagna is okay?"

"Perfect." Meri was simply happy to be invited. "Where's David?"

Amanda purposely put on a kind face. "David has meetings on Monday nights for a special project he is working on. It's just us ladies and two handsome young boys."

Meri smiled, but she didn't like David being out so late. She would mention it to him. Meri took sweet tea from Amanda, and they sat on the couch in the living room talking as the lasagna baked, while the boys went downstairs to watch television.

"Sweetheart, how's work? You look tired."

"It's well. I like it, but David and I need to talk. We are meeting each other coming and going. No time for us, you know?" Amanda was honest.

"Yes," Meri agreed. "David and this new position. I'm not sure this is right."

"Don't worry, we will work it out. I love David."

Meri smiled at Amanda and knew that sentiment to be true. "And David loves you." She pointed out.

"I am so happy we came out to the farm," Amanda said, wanting to shift the conversation. "I hope one day David can invite Michael here."

Meri touched Amanda's hand. "Don't push David. He and his dad have to work that out on their own."

"I know, Mom. At least he and Bruce spend Saturday mornings at the restaurant with him. Matthew and Mason see him at church, but David just never invites him over. Michael doesn't push, just patiently waits for David to talk to him about the past."

"At least they have a relationship," Meri noted.

"And what about you?" Amanda wanted to know. "Do you think about Michael? I know you have Bill, and you love your husband, but…"

"Oh, Amanda," Meri interrupted, shaking her head no. "I love having a daughter like you, and while I thank Michael for the two sons we share, our relationship is history. I love Bill."

Amanda was just like David and Bruce. They loved Bill, but had a hidden desire for their parents to get back together.

"I know, I know. I'm still a little girl when it comes to family."

Meri looked at her with understanding. "I am happy Michael is successful. He is now setting a fine example for you all."

Meri, Amanda, and the boys ate dinner together. The boys shared with their grandmother what they were learning in school and the latest video game levels. Meri loved hearing it all. She helped Amanda clean the kitchen as the boys went upstairs for their showers.

Meri, considering the lateness of the hour, was still concerned David wasn't home. Occasionally, she would see Amanda's face. She recognized it and remembered having that same face years ago. It saddened her.

"Amanda," Meri said, looking at her watch. "I really want to talk to my son."

Amanda gave her mother-in-law a hug. "Please don't worry. God has got this."

"I don't like that he leaves you alone. You take the boys to school, you pick them up from school, you cook dinner, and you get the boys ready for bed. What does he do?" Meri asked indignantly. "I raised him better than that."

"Meri, a lot is going on here." Amanda felt there was no need to keep things private. "David is..."

"... right here, Mom." David came through the garage door entrance wearing a white t-shirt, dress pants, and his white button-down shirt in his hand. He put the white button-down shirt in the laundry room and kissed his mom on the cheek.

Meri looked at him, and right away David knew. "Mom, it's one night a week. I'm glad you came over for dinner to be with my Honey." David went to Amanda and kissed her on the lips.

"Babe, I need to get upstairs and get the boys to bed." Amanda kissed him back, then hugged and kissed Meri good night.

When Amanda disappeared upstairs, Meri gave her son a look that he remembered when he was sixteen and missed his curfew.

"Mom, it's fine," David said, lying. He knew it wasn't fine, but he was going to figure it out.

"David, you're neglecting your wife and family. Stop it!" Meri said under her breath.

"I hear you, Mom," David said and hugged her.

"Please. Amanda is my beautiful daughter-in-law; she has stolen my heart, and I don't want it back." Meri was being selfish. "She loves you; don't give her a reason not to."

David thought about that statement. It landed in a soft place in him, and he felt convicted for the first time in months.

"Okay, Mom. I hear you."

David walked his mom to her car and told her to text him when she got home. He watched her drive off. David brought the duffel bag in from his car.

In the laundry room, he took off his dress pants and put them in the dry-cleaning bag. Standing in his underwear and t-shirt, he began sorting his dry cleaning and other dirty clothes. He smelled sweet perfume from Sam on his dirty clothes and quickly put them in the washing machine and started it.

As he went back out to the garage to take the dry-cleaning bag back to his car for drop-off in the morning, he thought about what his mom said. *She loves you; don't give her a reason not to.* He felt the hurt in his chest at just the thought of losing Amanda's love.

When David made it up to the master bedroom, he saw Amanda was in an eggplant-colored satin nightgown with her hair in a bun. She was applying lotion to her legs in her vanity chair. Her beauty was undeniable.

David immediately felt guilt along with the hurt that was lingering in his chest. She asked about his night, and he replied that it had been uneventful. As he slid into bed next to her, she told him about her day and that Nathan dropped by to return her office keys and insisted she take the rest of the week off. He agreed, saw that his mom texted she got home safely, gave Amanda a peck on the cheek, and turned his back to her to sleep. Amanda turned her back to him and silently prayed for change.

Nathan made it home and sat at his desk in front of his computer. He connected to the company server to see Amanda's calendar. Some appointments seemed simple enough to handle; others he highlighted and thought he would text Amanda in the morning and encourage her to reschedule them. He tried searching the internet for Snowflake Ranch and found little to nothing. The website said it was under construction.

He wasn't surprised. He knew this company wanted to remain a mystery. Nathan knew tomorrow would be a perfect time for him to search Amanda's office without raising suspicion.

As he turned off his computer and headed to watch television in his bedroom, he heard his phone. When he picked it up, he saw Jill's name. She wanted to FaceTime him. He quickly looked at his reflection in the mirror and accepted the call.

"Hey!" Nathan said, giving a pleasant but surprised look.

When he saw her on the screen, he was happy to see her. Her red hair was all one length to her chin. One side of her hair covered her face for a moment until she moved it behind her ear. Nathan saw her brown eyes and thought of his name for her, Cinnamon. Her eyes were shiny, and he could tell she was happy to see him.

"I'm sorry for calling late, but I just..." He saw the tear fall from her left eye. "Nate, I appreciate what you said tonight. I didn't know I needed to hear those words from you, but I guess I did."

Nathan gave a closed smile of compassion. "Well, the truth sets us free." He sat down in the chair at the corner of his bedroom, holding the phone so he could see her.

"Did you want to see my face and make sure it was really me that actually spoke the truth?" He chuckled.

She chuckled back. "Yeah, sort of. I just wanted to look in your eyes and be sincere about my appreciation. I just realized the truth of the past is healing me in the present day. I'm trying to make wise choices."

"Aren't we all?" Nathan thought about his own life and the kiss he shared with Amanda. The thought was a few seconds, then he refocused.

"Can I pray for you and for us?"

Jill nodded yes and closed her eyes. Nathan took a moment to look at her resting face. Her almond milk colored skin displayed a spray of freckles on her cheeks; her lips were narrow at the top and full at the bottom. He noticed her gradual aging; it was showing her appeal and wisdom. He closed his eyes and centered himself.

"Heavenly Father..." Jill felt a touch in her spirit as Nathan prayed. He thanked God for His love and compassion. He praised Him for his tender mercies. Nathan thanked God for humbling him all the way to the floor and allowing him to see how good life could be when he gave God control over his life.

Nathan asked God to continue to heal, reconcile, and redeem Jill. He told God she deserved everything she desired, dreamed, and longed for. He prayed for protection over him, her, and their son, Christopher. Jill felt the Holy Spirit all around her. She now knew Nathan was a different man, a renewed man. She heard it in his voice and felt her inner voice relax with no pretense. Nathan loved God and had a relationship with Him. He sealed the prayer with an amen.

Jill opened her eyes, looked at him with a refreshed face, and thanked him. Nathan gave her a look of *you're welcome* but he didn't say it.

"Enjoy the next chapter of your life. I am sure you and Jeff will be happy."

Jill put her head down for a moment.

"About that...I thought Christopher would've told you by now." Then Jill looked up and thought for a moment.

"Then again, probably not, since I'm always telling him that your life is your life and my life is my life. Jeff and I are no longer together."

Nathan sat up straight in his chair. He was sincerely concerned. "What?" This news interrupted his entire thought process.

"I love Jeff. Our relationship was good. He cares for me; I believe he really does...somewhere." Jill was thinking out loud and recalling the last few years.

"But the moment we got engaged, things changed. He got possessive."

"Oh no. Did he hurt you physically?" Before she could respond, Nathan quickly answered, "I'm sorry, I'm prying. That's none of my business, right? Your life is your life, my life is my life..."

"Until it's not. Nate, we have a son. It's a fair question. And no, he didn't hurt me physically. It's a story, but I'm proud of how our son supported me."

"As it should be," Nathan replied, satisfied.

"Perhaps the next time you're here, we can talk over coffee?"

"I'd love that," Nathan said.

CHAPTER 7

It was Wednesday. Amanda finally agreed with Nathan that staying home for the rest of the week was a good idea. In one day, she got her family's attention. Amanda announced that she needed rest.

Her sleeping in meant David had to not only take the boys to school but also make them breakfast, pack lunches, and pack backpacks. Amanda realized that, being at home or not, she held the power over her attitude. She had a polite and calm composure most of the time, but now Amanda was conscious of it and used it to clear her mind and plan.

David was up early to work on his schedule in the den. Amanda heard him get out of bed. Thirty minutes later, she got out of bed, put on one of David's white button-down shirts, and headed downstairs. It was a bit too early for coffee, so she made herself tea and entered the den. David was sitting at his desk, hovering over papers.

"Honey, I didn't mean to wake you." He looked up at her and noticed her outfit. He gave an endearing look, *but goodness*, he thought to himself, *even straight out of bed, my wife glows.*

"I couldn't sleep." She had her mug in her hand. "What are you working on?" She placed her other hand on his shoulder.

"My schedule. I'm trying to figure out how to manage 25 stores now, not just one. The special project I'm working on will be done soon, so I'll have to travel. The other vice presidents say it will be easy, but I don't want their help." David was still angry.

Amanda looked at her husband's territory map on the paper. After a few minutes of study, she spoke.

"Babe, these stores need your encouragement more than your management." She smiled at him. "You are so good at that. These stores know you and respect you; they just want your expertise. These managers are good."

She took a pencil and drew a cross in his territory, splitting the territory into four quadrants.

"It's not perfect, but if you see about six stores every week, you can make it to most of them in a month. If the stores are doing well, they might see you every other month."

David appreciated Amanda's idea. He loved her soft disposition and her suggestions. She was right.

"Thank you." He looked up at her as he continued. "I like this. Then I could send out a quick sheet telling them my expectations, so they could be prepared for my visit. I didn't like my vice president just popping up like we weren't on the same team, trying to improve sales."

"Exactly," Amanda agreed.

David put his pencil down and focused on Amanda. "Didn't you just buy clothes? What are you doing wearing mine?" He teased.

"Fine," Amanda said, puckering her lips, pretending to pout. She put her tea down on his desk and unbuttoned the shirt. After taking it off, she handed it to him as she stood there in just her panties.

"Here, you can have it back," she said, winking at him.

"Amanda…" David said softly as he searched her with his eyes. She was beautiful. The messy hair, her tantalizing brown eyes, and her body's tan and smooth skin. He knew her breasts would fit perfectly in his hands, and loved her curve from her waist to her hips.

David got up from the chair, and the shirt hit the floor. He went to her and held her close, whispering in her ear, "Now you know I'm a morning lover."

"So what are you going to do about it, Mr. Lloyd?" She whispered back.

"This," David said, kissing Amanda softly on the lips. She felt a chill as their tongues connected slowly.

He led her to the sectional couch with a chaise. She lay there as he took off her panties and continued his kisses on her right ear and neck. Amanda was full of anticipation and desire; David hadn't touched her this way in months.

His hand went between her legs, and he rubbed her slowly. She closed her eyes to enjoy his touch. It didn't take long for her to come. Her climax was so intense that she turned into the pillows on the sectional to release her satisfaction so she wouldn't wake the quiet house. Her legs shook as waves traveled through her body.

David admired her silky tan legs as he stroked her hair and kissed her on the cheek. He could see from the look on her face that she was pleased. As he looked at her, he knew he loved her. David thought, *So, what am I doing with Sam?*

After his morning conference call, Nathan could finally go into Amanda's office and look around. He rolled up the reset blueprints she had left on her meeting table and made sure her computer was off. Nathan noticed she didn't have any new messages, realizing Amanda was retrieving them from home. He thought, *she's kind of resting*. He rolled his eyes with a laugh.

Nathan went through the mail that was stacked at the end of her desk. Everything was in order. He looked around her office to see if he noticed anything out of place before he headed to the Snowflake Ranch box of merchandise. When he pulled out the neck roll and eye pillow, Vanessa walked in and startled him.

"Vanessa." He clutched his chest. "Knock or say somethin'."

Vanessa looked at him as if she owned the office. "Sorry. What are you doing in here, anyway? Amanda forgot something?"

"No, I'm ready to get this box out of her office. This box has a blanket, an essential oil set, candles, a couple of these neck rolls, eye pillows, and socks in here. Stuff I have no clue what to do with." Nathan held up a cloth bag of lavender. "Goodness!"

"Yes, I was going to move the box to the gift closet. It's against company policy for her to keep it." Vanessa put more mail on Amanda's pile.

Nathan gave Vanessa an approving look, then hesitated. "Don't you find it strange they sent all of this product just to invite her to their showroom in Dallas?"

"Sort of..." Vanessa stopped moving. "Then I looked at the packing slip again. This was sent directly to Amanda with just this address; no mention of Augusta Retail. I tried looking them up online, but found nothing but a website under construction. I didn't know what to think or what to do; that's why the box is still here."

Nathan wasn't surprised Vanessa did her own research. He looked in the box one more time for paperwork.

"Hey Vanessa, could you do me a favor? Can you check to see if any of our other offices received a box from Snowflake Ranch?"

He already knew the answer, but if he could get Vanessa concerned, then if anything else came from Snowflake Ranch, she would tell him.

Amanda took the last dish out of the dishwasher and then sat on one of the kitchen barstools as she talked to Regina and Leslie on her cell phone. She shared her days and how things were going with David.

"Amanda!" Regina was happy. "You are a little sexy thing."

"I'd say," Leslie added. "I am certain you are driving David crazy. He's probably wondering what the hell he's doing with Sam or who and what has turned you into this confident, sexy woman."

"Really?" Amanda was still doubtful. Even though he gave her pleasure this morning, David was still preoccupied and hiding.

"See? It is that right there. This humble, soft thing you do." Regina said.

"You are driving your husband right back to you. Just watch and see."

"I have to admit, I love myself," Amanda said proudly as she smiled. "What I thought I was doing to get David's attention off of Sam and onto me is now something altogether greater."

Regina and Leslie were happy to hear their sister-friend's confidence. Amanda shared about Lisa Reynolds and about how there were many women in loveless marriages. They took a moment to pray for those women and their families.

"So how is it with Nathan?" Leslie was direct.

Amanda told them he stopped by the house because she had left her keys. She shared how she was taking the week off and the conversation she had with him.

"Wow...Amanda, please be careful. There is an attraction there," Leslie said.

"I agree," Regina chimed in. "Remember, you love David."

"Remember?" Amanda laughed. "It's all I think about. I am hoping to create a sequel to this morning."

Samantha sat at her desk reviewing the trainee applications David sent her. He made a list of the applicants he felt met the Acuff Academy qualifications and was ready to send them their letters of acceptance outlining the offer and their commitment. He wanted her to know. She was proud of David's idea for a management trainee program at his company and how he was helping the students at Brookview Community College.

She was infatuated with David; he was good-looking and smart. But she knew deep down he was in love with his wife. He was doing this academy for her. Samantha knew she really didn't have a future in his life, except for right now, and she told herself she was fine with it.

David had held her and told her everything was going to work out regarding her mom's property and the expenses to maintain its upkeep. She really lived at the hotel and didn't need the two-story, four-bedroom home, but there it was taking up her time and emotions. She was trying to clear out the house first and then put it up for sale.

Monday said everything. David was just going through the motions, but she wanted to feel good. He had a way of making her forget her troubles.

Sam could tell David was releasing the things he couldn't at home. She closed her eyes and knew their relationship had reached its peak.

"Sam? You have a call on line one." Beth, her student intern, called her out of her thoughts. Samantha picked up the call.

"This is Sam," she replied.

There was silence for a moment. Terrance took in her voice; sweet and professional. He imagined her at a desk with her blonde hair down her back, full lips, and soft blue eyes. In reality, her hair was up, and she was wearing her glasses today instead of her contacts.

"Sam, it's Terrance." Sam sat up in her chair.

～

By lunchtime, David sat comfortably on his office couch, waiting for the pain medication to work for the headache he was nursing. Just not staring at the computer was helping relieve the pressure. He thought about Amanda.

It used to be his thoughts were on Sam and her thin figure standing in the doorway of the hotel bathroom. But now it was his wife. Her physical beauty was stunning; the image of the morning in his dress shirt immediately came to mind. It was more than that; the house felt different.

Amanda wasn't so uptight about everything; she smiled more and was light-hearted. The girls' night was the night it all changed.

He wanted to call Regina, but he talked himself out of it. She would ask him too many questions. Amanda's trip shopping on that Saturday came to mind; the men who made their advances. What really happened? He knew Amanda wasn't cheating; she was not like him. Then it dawned on him.

It was his fault. It was the way he was treating Amanda. This morning was the first time in a while it wasn't just the act of sex—going through the motions and onto the next thing. David sighed at his behavior. He didn't deserve Amanda. He realized his mom was right; to be without her... empty. Abruptly, his cell phone buzzed on the coffee table, drawing his attention.

It was a text from Brad.

On your blindside. I got your back.

David's heart dropped. Brad Frahm was his best friend and had been since the 5th grade. They shared so many memories and stories; there were too many to tell. Both started at Acuff at fourteen and worked their way up to top management. Did Brad find out about Sam and was covering for him? David didn't text back; he just called him.

"Hey man, what's up?" David tried to be calm.

"Hey! First off, I'm sorry I haven't been in touch these last few weeks. Renee and I, Abby in her teens...emotional to say the least."

"I completely understand," David told him. "This job, you know all about the promotion drama. Amanda is busy at work, but sad I work too much. Yet, doing all kinds of things to keep me home...I'm confused."

"Uh-huh," Brad said as he began walking down the aisle with the paper products. "Wanna tell me why Amanda is at the grocery store in the middle of the day?"

David explained how she was taking the week off to rest.

"Uh-huh," Brad said, trying to make sure Amanda didn't see him yet. "Well, she's here at the exact same time the senior vice presidents are here."

David stood up. "Your store?! Why would Amanda come to your store to shop?"

Brad explained he was at the Brookview store helping store director Carl McCallister with his lawn and garden center. It was an exchange they agreed upon. Next week, Carl and some of his assistants will go to Brad's store to assist with their lawn and garden center.

"Brad...I swear to you...don't let that man come within two feet of my wife...I will hurt him." David stayed on the phone, grabbed his suit jacket, and told Vikki he was taking lunch and wasn't sure when he was going to return. He would let her know.

"What is going on? Where is she? Where are they?"

"Listen, I'm going to approach Amanda and stay with her. Can you get here?" Brad had come up with a plan. "But David, promise me you're not gonna start a ruckus in here."

"I'm already headed to my car," David said. "And I promise I will be alright." Brad heard his friend's voice kind of shift.

"Hell, David, that doesn't sound convincing at all. Like the time you shoved Austin McDaniel into the lockers and punched him in eighth grade after I specifically told you to just walk away."

"Listen, he shouldn't have called you a *punk ass albino*, taken your headphones, and broken them. As you can see, I don't like name-calling. I'm calm until someone gets me started. Now what's the plan?"

Brad explained what he was thinking as David got into his car. They ended the call, and Brad made himself known to Amanda.

"Brad!" She gave a warm smile of surprise and then hugged him. "What are you doing here?"

Brad genuinely loved Amanda. There was no other person more perfect for his best friend, David. In his eyes, Amanda was stable, caring, and lovely physically and in personality.

"Amanda," he replied happily. "How are you? I miss you, David, and the boys."

Amanda was excited. "We have to get together this summer. How is Renee? And Abby?"

"All fine," he lied. "Shopping today?"

Amanda explained she was taking some days off and how nice it was to shop without children. She stated she wanted to make a nice dinner tonight and decided on a citrus chicken, which required her a trip to the store. Brad explained why he and his team from his store were working in Brookview.

"Nice that you all can help each other out," Amanda said, then noticed several men walking around the store in suits. She wasn't alarmed; it wasn't uncommon. The Brookview Acuff store was the flagship store, and it was close to the corporate office. What was uncommon was that three of them were headed her way.

"Amanda, please follow my lead," Brad lowered his voice. She gave a nonverbal yes with her eyes. Brad greeted the men with handshakes and casual laughter. He moved to the side and introduced Amanda as the wife of David Lloyd, but Amanda knew by their looks they recognized her from corporate gatherings and knew something she did not know.

One by one, they nodded and gave their congratulations regarding David's promotion and mentioned what an asset David has already been to their team. Amanda sincerely smiled; she knew David worked hard to get the promotion. As Brad walked, she pushed her cart, but accidentally dropped her recipe card. One of the senior vice presidents, Allen Bristol, picked it up and, as he handed it back to her, he covered her hand with his.

Allen was a tall, thin man in his early sixties. Amanda noticed his blue eyes and alabaster aging skin as their hands touched. He said, "It is a pleasure to see you again."

With that comment, Brad gave Allen a stare that prompted him to let go of Amanda's hand sooner than he wanted. The other two senior vice presidents nudged Allen to walk forward with them.

When the vice presidents were down the aisle and turned into the produce section, Brad let out a sigh.

"What was that?" Amanda felt the tension and awkwardness of the exchange.

"The bullshit surrounding David being promoted," Brad commented. Amanda knew she could ask Brad to elaborate, but she didn't. The reason for David's stress was making itself known. She knew it didn't excuse his behavior, especially towards her, yet she understood because she loved him.

"The politics of corporate America," Brad nervously added.

"I guess." Amanda went along with his statement.

Brad asked her if he could show her the new lawn and garden center. She agreed. As they made it there, they entered a beautiful outdoor area with a greenhouse off to the left, but in front of it were lawn ornaments, potted flowers, wind chimes, and colorful Adirondack chairs.

"Brad, this is three times bigger than last year." Amanda was amazed. "I can see why you all are doing the exchange."

"Yes." Brad looked around and saw David sitting on patio furniture in a shaded corner. He stood when he saw them. She noticed him right away as he rose. His suit jacket on the back of the chair, his white button-down shirt still crisp, his dark pants with a few wrinkles from sitting, his smile warm, especially seeing Amanda in her everyday jeans, untucked button-down pink shirt, that showed her gray lace tank top underneath, those wedged heels, and her hair pinned up with loose strands around her face.

Amanda felt a tinge of anger. She knew her husband was lying, keeping secrets, and stressed. And yet, she felt not ready to say anything.

She saw the lemonade and salads on the table of the patio furniture vignette where he was. "Why do I get the feeling I am part of a Lloyd Frahm scheme?" Amanda looked at Brad suspiciously.

"I don't know what you're talking about." Brad folded his arms and looked away from her. "Mrs. Lloyd, allow me to finish your shopping, and I can keep it in the walk-in cooler until you're ready to go."

Amanda shook her head, gave Brad her recipe card with instructions, left the cart, and headed towards her husband.

CHAPTER 8

David woke up in the middle of the night refreshed. Amanda was in a sound sleep. He was glad to see it. Having these days off was what she needed.

He reflected on the past day, got out of bed, put on just his athletic shorts, and traveled down the stairs to the kitchen. He went into the refrigerator, ate the last piece of the citrus chicken right out of the plastic container as he sat on the kitchen barstool.

David stared at the dining table and remembered how hours ago, he and his family were laughing and raving over the chicken and cilantro rice. David thought about what dinner looked like when he was younger; it was silence and spaghetti, which he got tired of eating. As a young man, he ate alone or at the store until Amanda came along. Now that they were married, her meals grounded him. Their home brought peace.

He thought about how earlier she put her bare feet over his sock-footed feet under the table and looked at him lovingly. He loved socks. She hated socks. While he cleaned up the dishes, she put the boys to bed.

They met in the bedroom, where he received an all-over body massage from her. With the citrus chicken before him and his memories, he realized that massage cured the headache he had, off and on, for days. He was grateful and immediately thought about getting some work done.

After he finished in the kitchen, he went to the den. As he turned on the light, his eyes were drawn to last year's family photo that sat on Amanda's desk. Everyone smiling, arms around each other. The truth was, Mason hated pictures. All Matthew wanted to do was make crazy faces and put his two fingers behind Mason's head. He grinned at the thought.

David saw her Bible, her devotion about walking in faith, and he was proud of how Amanda managed to take time every day, if only five minutes, to invite God in her day. Then he saw her journal. He hesitated to open the large black spiral notebook. David looked around. Everyone was asleep. He opened it. What he saw caught him by surprise.

It wasn't what he expected; it was an art journal. How could he have known her for twelve years and not know she was an artist? She used oil pastels and colored pencils. David turned a few pages. Amanda's work was full of beautiful spirals, circles, and words of affirmation. It was evident this was her therapy.

Some drawings seemed happy and vibrant; others were thought-provoking with deep blues, greens, and purples. He stopped at a page towards the front, the lines in the drawing black hashtags like prison bars, and there was one bright yellow circle in the corner of the picture. Amanda's words on the front of the picture were poetry. "Dark lips on me…I don't remember, but I feel darkness. I decided to let the light in." On the back of the art, Amanda's initials and three words. "Remembering rape, healing." David was touched by her words.

He loved the one with yellow, orange, and hot pink fading into each other. The words on the left read, "I'm surrounded by love, goodness, and beautiful things." But the most recent picture was last week. It was light blue and white. Amanda drew eyes, brown and golden like hers, very faint. The bottom right corner read, "Invisible." David closed his eyes; he felt her unhappiness.

He put the journal back where he found it, turned the lights out, left the den, and went back to bed. He didn't feel like working anymore. He knew he had to contact Dr. Nick.

Amanda woke up to David kissing her forehead, stating the boys were in the car, he was taking them to school, and then he was headed to the office. As he shut the bedroom door, she looked up at the ceiling for several minutes, and the idea came to her. She felt good, and it was time to return to work.

"Good morning, Norah. I'm feeling a bit adventurous this morning, and I need a favor," Amanda said on her office phone. Norah was in the California office, due back in on Monday, but Amanda wanted to encourage David at work and knew Norah could help.

"You got me curious, Amanda." Norah loved Amanda's creativity, organization, and attention to detail—something she could use more often. She counted on Amanda to be the forward thinker.

"So, I want to go over to Acuff and show Gerald and Scott the preliminary blueprint for the Brookview downtown project before someone else does, while they are all in the office today."

"Oh, I'm fine with that." Norah chuckled. "I was thinking you wanted something much more challenging."

Amanda laughed. "Well, I promise to take notes on their thoughts, and since I am not going to leave the print with them, shall we allow them to have a copy?"

"Sure, after all, the developers gave it to Hindley Corp., that's how we got our hands on it," Norah spoke frankly. "Tell them your ideas Amanda, like the ice cream parlor. They are the only ones with the resources to pull it off. The developers created this draft blueprint of what the store's structure could be. Please communicate that the possibilities are endless. By the end of the summer, the developers wanted Hindley to submit their ideas."

Amanda understood. As Norah was giving her the final details, Nathan and Vanessa were in the doorway of her office.

"Vikki, is holding on line one," Vanessa informed her. "What is up today? You look...stunning."

Amanda was in a tailored tangerine-colored dress with matching slingback heels and a gray and tangerine bolero jacket. She put her hand up in the air and pushed the line one button on her phone.

"Vikki?"

"Mrs. Lloyd?"

"Call me Amanda, please."

"Listen, you deserve all the respect I can muster for the days and nights you put up with David." She teased and made light conversation. "Come over today about 12:45 to meet with David. Then I can put all of you in the corner conference room at 1:00 pm for a half hour. Does that work?"

"That works for me," Amanda said. "I am looking forward to meeting you."

They exchanged goodbyes. Nathan and Vanessa were still waiting for an answer.

"Do I look okay?" Amanda asked, looking at herself.

"Considering you were supposed to be out this week." Nathan knew she wasn't going to stay away. He wanted to comment on her looks, but allowed Vanessa to answer.

"Yes. What is going on?" Vanessa had her hands on her hips and was actually smiling, which didn't happen often.

"I'm going over to surprise David." She was now blushing. "I get the feeling something is going on at work with him. He keeps talking about a special project and stress, so I'm going over to tell them about the downtown project, blueprint in hand. They'll get to see it before their competition."

"Nice move," Nathan said. "I'm sure Acuff will appreciate the heads up. I get the feeling these developers don't want Acuff to know too much about this project."

"Me too," Amanda acknowledged.

"Well, you will turn heads today," Vanessa acknowledged. "I won't expect you back, right?"

"Oh no, I have a teleconference with a representative from Nickel Cosmetics. If we want to represent a youth cosmetic line, I need to talk to them at 3:00 pm."

After Vanessa left, Nathan watched Amanda proudly. "I don't have words," he said after Vanessa was gone.

"Nathan, I'm trying to get David to turn around," Amanda admitted.

"I'm glad," he said, still standing, ready to leave, and then quickly changed the subject. "Let me know if Meghan from Nickel Cosmetics gives you a hard time. She owes me a favor."

Amanda's eyes grew large. "How do you know Meghan?"

Nathan laughed. "After I divorced, before God got a hold of me for good, I was Meghan's plus one at a family gathering. She was tired of going to events with no one, so…"

Amanda smiled. "Mr. Montgomery, there is a whole side of you that is a complete mystery."

Nathan couldn't lie. "Yes."

When Amanda left Augusta Retail, Vanessa called Nathan up to join her at the front desk. She shared with him that no one from Augusta Retail got a product box from Snowflake Ranch, except for Amanda.

"Now that is strange." Vanessa frowned. "Most companies would send a sample to each of our offices. So this was a personal box for Amanda. It is clear this company doesn't want to do business with

Augusta Retail per se, but wants Amanda to come to their showroom."

This was confirmation for Nathan, "Okay, weird. Anything else from this company? A catalog, even. Did anyone call to see if she got the box? Are there any more boxes at the warehouse?"

"No, but I have my eyes open," Vanessa said. "Nathan, as the HR person, do we have a stalking issue here?"

Nathan encouraged Vanessa not to worry. "The good news is Norah and I are going to the Dallas Market with Amanda. Please don't say anything to Amanda. She has enough on her mind. We don't even handle this category, so it leads me to believe this could be someone from her cosmetic representative days."

Vanessa understood and agreed. Nathan felt his mission was accomplished. Vanessa would be the gatekeeper of any future information that could come from Snowflake Ranch. He could keep his eyes on Amanda and other Augusta Retail employees who were under investigation.

Vikki stepped inside David's office. "Amanda is here."

David put down his spreadsheets and looked up with bright eyes.

"Amanda? My Amanda!?"

"Yes, surprise." Vikki had a pleasant look on her face. "I finally get to meet her. Do you want to greet her, or should I?"

David rose from his desk, straightened his shirt, and put his hands through his hair. Vikki laughed a little. "You are acting like a teenage boy, nervous about your prom date. How long have you been married?"

"What's she doing here? Did you know about this?" David gave Vikki a look, ignoring her question.

"Of course; I know everything. And you look fine." She looked at him.

"David, don't worry. Everyone will be nice to her. We are decent white people."

David gave Vikki a stern look. "Not a word about that incident."

"Never," Vikki had to agree. "No one will mention that."

David walked past Vikki and headed to the top of the stairs. When he got there, his smile met her smile. Her husband was standing there with his lightly starched shirt, no tie, dark pants, clean-shaven, bright eyes, and that smile with perfect teeth. Amanda swooned.

David was speechless. The orange of the dress with her skin tone had him thinking of the beach and her in a bikini with her figure. She looked professional in the tailored dress and was holding a black cardboard tube.

They shared a conservative kiss, but he held her for a minute to say, "I thought you weren't working this week? To what do I owe the pleasure? You smell fantastic."

She blushed and found his hand to hold, then held up the black tube for a moment. "I have something to show you."

David led Amanda back to his office, and there was Vikki. She couldn't help but have a look of contentment. She saw Amanda and just knew she was everything David had communicated. Not only did she give Vikki straight eye contact, but she was warm and inviting. By the looks of her hair, golden eyes, confidence, and her genuine smile, Vikki knew she would be nothing like the other corporate wives. She also knew by the way David said Amanda's name, despite Sam, David loved this woman, Amanda Nicole Lloyd.

"Vikki, the pleasure is all mine. Thank you for setting this up for me. I promise not to take too much of David's, Scott's, and Gerald's time."

"What?" David looked at the women. "What is going on, and why am I the last to know?"

Vikki shot back. "Because you would've asked me a million questions that I could not answer until Amanda got here, so I didn't bother."

Amanda liked their banter and relationship. Vikki would keep David focused, and she appreciated it.

"Babe, is this your office?" David nodded, rolled his eyes at Vikki, and led Amanda into his office, shutting the door behind them. Amanda was so proud.

David's office had large windows with a good view of Brookview, but mostly farmland waiting to be developed, and a large cherry desk with two sofa chairs in front. A conference table with four chairs, and in the corner, a round table in front of a small sofa.

"Wow, David," she said before kissing him. "You have done really well for yourself."

"Oh, honey, I couldn't have done any of this without you." He held her.

"This is us. I have so much to say, but not now, okay?"

Amanda looked in his brown eyes, and there it was. He was afraid to say it, and she was afraid to ask. "Okay."

There was a pause, and she continued. "I really did come here for business."

"I see." He eyed the tube. "What you got there?"

Amanda patted him on the butt. He released her, and she pulled out the blueprint from the tube and rolled it out on the conference table.

"This is the preliminary blueprint for the Brookview downtown project."

"Ah," David said as he helped her spread out the print. "How'd you get this?"

"Well, that is just the thing. The developers, who are from the county here, sent it to Hindley Corp. in Ohio, and of course, they sent it to us at Augusta. We handle all the sets here. They don't do the small-town stuff we do," Amanda explained.

"Amanda," David said, "this is a sizable project. Is this more than one store? What are they doing exactly?"

Amanda pointed out how the gas station/convenience store would be on one corner of the downtown square, with small retail shops in between, and the drugstore on the other corner lot, with a front and back entrance.

"So, what you are looking at is the downtown drugstore. Hindley Corp. wants a sizable section for health and wellness, cosmetics, and a total drugstore feel." Amanda showed him the print.

"But I see minimal grocery stores. Where are you guys? Why haven't the developers asked you to the table?"

"Good question," David thought out loud. "We have the reputation of taking over." He said what Amanda was thinking.

"Exactly. And I'm coming over today to ask you not to, but to offer them something only you can do. You should offer something that the community needs."

Amanda shared her ideas with her husband, and he supported every one of them. She explained she could leave them a copy of the print and shared she didn't want competition for *Lloyd's*.

As she described everything to Scott and Gerald in their meeting, David couldn't have been prouder of his wife. She allowed David to share in the conversation, to bring his expertise of operating a store to the table, and how with Amanda working for Augusta, David at Acuff and their father an entrepreneur of a small operation, that they could all co-exist, respect each other, and revitalize downtown after all the other retail establishments left because they really had nothing invested in Brookview.

"Amanda, it has been a pleasure." Scott shook her hand. "I love the downtown, good 'ole soda fountain shop idea. The young and the old can get behind this idea," he said.

"Don't worry about those developers. Why, I know those old farts; they're scared to ask us, think we may bully them, or ask for our name on the building." Gerald looked at the print one more time with his hands in his pockets.

"David, I think we can manage a produce section in the space, too. We cannot create a food desert in our area. Fresh food is important to our downtown community. There's no place downtown to buy an apple. If they want apartments and condos down there, that has to change."

"I agree, Gerald," David said and extended his hand for a handshake. "You make us proud, David, with all your ideas." He winked. "With this young lady, David, you outkicked your coverage." Gerald went over, took her hand, and cupped it with his other hand.

Amanda smiled. "Gerald, you're too kind."

Scott and Gerald left the conference room, and Amanda and David followed. David gave Vikki the blueprint and asked her to take it to the CAD department to make a copy. David and Amanda sat on the sofa in David's office with the door closed as she waited for the print to be copied.

"Amanda, seriously, thank you." He sat on the sofa, and she leaned against his shoulder with her feet up and shoes off.

"Babe, anything for you." She rubbed his thigh. "I want you to know that I support you in all that you are doing. This year has been challenging. I love you."

David kissed her hair and thought about his actions. What the hell was he doing? He was so confused.

Here he was, thinking being single would be so much easier, but would it? And what about Sam? Was he using her? How did all of this get so twisted? He also thought about Amanda's selflessness. She could've given all this credit and acknowledgment to herself and Augusta. But she thought of him.

After the lunch David had with Gerald, this was a good move for him. A promise was granted that he would keep him in the know about projects and happenings, like the downtown project. His thoughts were interrupted by his cell phone. He grabbed it from the coffee table.

"It's Bruce," he announced.

Amanda looked up and smiled. "Hey, what's going on?"

David said, "I gotcha on speaker, Amanda's here."

"Hey sis. David, I'm just calling to say Pop needs a new two-door commercial refrigerator. The three-door one was a simple fix, but the two-door one is not under warranty anymore. No one can locate the paperwork. Maybe he'll listen to you. It's $2,000; he needs it."

David showed no emotion. "He's being conservative; just order it." David shifted, and Amanda sat up and kissed him on the cheek.

"It's in his budget. I went over the numbers with him two weeks ago, that if you couldn't fix it…"

Bruce interrupted. "I know…" David took him off speaker for a moment and talked to Amanda. "The whole backside of that thing is caked with grease and is rusted out. The motor is on its last leg."

David was no longer interested in his brother's conversation. Amanda was now nibbling on David's ear, and he winked and smiled at her. She moved to his neck. David turned and kissed her.

"Bruce, send me a pic of the new one. I'll talk to him."

"Okay," Bruce said, and then heard Amanda say to David, "I want you. Tonight, undress me, touch me, and I promise to return the favor."

"Oh, my God! I'm so interrupting…" Bruce's voice came through the phone. Weeks ago, Amanda would've been embarrassed, but no longer. She laughed and kissed David one last time before putting her shoes back on. "Promise me?"

David held the phone to his ear, but Amanda had his full attention. "I promise." Vikki knocked on the door, saw David on the cell phone, exchanged goodbyes with Amanda, and handed her back the black cardboard tube.

Amanda bit her lip and looked at her husband with desire. David watched her disappear.

"Did Amanda just initiate?" Bruce was excited. "Told you if you talked to her…"

"Bruce, I did no such thing. Ever since that girls' night, Amanda has been more confident, sexy, and provocative. I'm blown away that just now she asked me to touch her." David was hot inside; he wanted Amanda. Not in the selfish way he used to have sex with her. But now he wanted to touch her, feel her, and satisfy her.

When did that happen? He promised himself he would keep his emotions in check with Sam and Amanda. With Sam, he was single again, no strings. Now Amanda? Who was he fooling? Strings, strings, strings attached.

"I hate you," Bruce said sarcastically. "You are so damn lucky."

"Oh no, I'm blessed. Bruce, she was amazing today." David told his brother about the day.

"Listen, you pick the boys up from school, and I'll take them to baseball practice and feed them. You and Amanda have fun," Bruce said. "Take her to dinner."

David agreed with his brother. He loved Bruce and all his support.

Amanda finished her conference call and was heading home. Nathan was right; Meghan wasn't convinced their high-end youth line needed to be in a small-town drugstore, but wanted to build the relationship because she did owe Nathan a favor. When she mentioned his name, she laughed and called him a *hottie*. Amanda made sure to remember to embarrass him about that someday.

She was the only one home as she parked in the garage and saw her reflection in the car's rearview mirror. There was this confident woman staring back at her. No longer was that woman unsure about being a wife, a mother, or a businesswoman. She looked deeper to see if that nine-year-old girl was there, and she saw her, feeling that the girl was admiring her. Finally, she felt good about herself.

She was upstairs, sitting at her vanity table, when David walked in. He gazed at her for a second, then spoke. "Honey." He went up and kissed her cheek.

"I took the boys to Bruce. He heard you today and insisted. You know, I want him to find someone serious so bad."

Amanda rose from the table and faced him. "Don't worry; in due time. Chloe broke his heart, which takes time."

"I suppose." David looked at his wife and put his hands on her bare arms. "I want you to know something."

Amanda pushed herself into him. "What is that?" Then, she started to unbutton his shirt.

"I love you." David was sincere. "I love the worried Amanda, I love the nagging, whining Amanda, I love the mom Amanda, I love the tired Amanda, and I love this sexy, provocative Amanda." He kissed her upper lip and sucked it. "Whatever has gotten into you, I like it."

He whispered. "You got my attention, especially today. What you did today was far from sexual, but thoughtful and supportive..."

"David, I love you. I just wanted you to know all the ways." She kissed his lower lip and then turned, faced the wall in the small hallway between the *his* and *her* walk-in closets, and with her hands on the wall said, "Unzip me."

He moved her hair out of the way, exposing her neck. Her spot, in full view, begging him to kiss it, below the right ear. He couldn't resist the temptation.

She took a breath when she felt his wet lips there. He unzipped the dress and raised it up, exposing her ass.

"No underwear?!" he whispered, stunned.

She smirked, turned around, completely stepped out of the dress, and there she was in an orange bra, thong, and high heels. She did a runway-model turn. With David's eyes open wide, his vision of the beach stood right in front of him. He was hard but wanted to keep self-control.

"You are killin' me, woman." His breathing became labored.

"David, you're overdressed." She now pushed him against the wall, taking off his shirt.

David kicked off his shoes, unbuckled his pants, and they fell to his feet. He stepped out of them, took her hand, and led her to the bed. He sat on the edge of the bed, taking off his socks. She stood looking down at him. He opened his legs, and she stepped between them.

Amanda carefully took off her shoes, one at a time, and did not lose eye contact with him. She unhooked her bra, allowed it to fall off her shoulders, and threw it on the floor.

"Allow me," David said, as he gently removed her thong and gave her a tender kiss at her C-section scar.

"You're so beautiful." He paused to look at her. Amanda's hair covered one side of her face, but not her brown, wanting eyes. Playfully, she pushed him down on the bed, straddled him, and kissed him passionately on the lips. He kissed her back, and they were both lying on their sides, kissing and fondling one another. David finally took off his underwear, throwing it across the room. Amanda wanted control, but she was now on her back.

David spoke, resting on his right side, facing his wife. "I made you a promise, and I plan on keeping it. The lady comes first."

Amanda sighed with anticipation. "Okay." This is exactly what she wanted, not just the physical. David was into her; she could feel and see it.

"I'm going to kiss you all over," he said as he kissed her forehead and her left cheek. His eyes met hers, and they searched each other before he leaned in and planted one soft kiss on her lips. He loved her lips. He kissed them over and over. His tongue went into her mouth, meeting hers.

David then kissed behind her ear, whispering, "I want you." Her deep breathing turned into a moan that made David hot and his erection stronger.

He took in her scent and instantly started to compare. With his wife, there was no casual scent from a bath shop that Sam would use to hide the smell of sex. No, this was fresh air, exotic flowers, and confidence.

David raised himself so his nose could explore her full neck, shoulders, and chest. His graceful, silent sniffing and his lips left open kisses and her upper body with wet spots where he stopped to just skin. He licked her right between her breasts, and that made her arch her back. Her nipples already tight and firm, he licked and sucked them. Amanda's hands gripped the sheets on the bed as she struggled to hold on.

David took his time, but eventually moved down to her navel. Amanda adjusted herself, no longer lying flat but sitting up slightly and legs open, giving her husband more room at the bottom of the bed. He crawled up between her legs. Amanda, finding a comfortable position lying back on pillows, gave David the opportunity to run his hands across her body, examining every crevice that he desired. He kissed her inner thighs and used his hands to unfold the delicate layers, putting his lips directly in the place that made her call his name. "David," he breathlessly cried out. "Yes, right there."

By using his fingers, lips, and tongue, David found a pattern that satisfied her. He rubbed, licked, and kissed her body until she felt the waves as parts of her body would tense and release. Her final climax was a sweet, gratifying scream, which was music to his ears. He wanted to start all over again, just to hear her song. Her taste was savory; David enjoyed all of her. *Divine wine*, he thought. Wine he had forgotten he loved.

David lay next to her. Amanda was still shaking a little and turned to him. "You, you... Thank you." She kissed him, tasting a remnant of herself.

David saw her satisfaction. "My pleasure." He sincerely meant it. Amanda rested for a minute and then rolled over and straddled him.

David had a surprised look on his face. With her knees on the bed, she kissed him and said in his ear, "I have to have you now." She lifted, felt his hardness, and inserted him into herself.

David closed his eyes, moaning at the insertion. "Oh God." He was amazed; she felt incredible—soft, warm, and firm. Amanda put her ankles under his legs, and she bounced. David opened his eyes to see

Amanda enjoying herself. Even though Sam liked this position, he never felt it like this. He saw her light brown breasts bouncing, her pleasuring herself in the front, making him harder.

"Honey, yes." David took over pleasuring her, and they found a rhythm. David couldn't keep quiet; moans of delight and joy kept coming.

He found the words, "I'm ready." As she bit her bottom lip hard, Amanda felt David rub her faster as the bouncing got faster. He called her name as a loud, breathless release. Amanda came seconds later with a long moan. The only sound after that was their heavy breathing. Amanda slid out gently and collapsed on his right side.

"Amanda Nicole…" David said, lying on his back, completely dumbfounded.

"What has gotten into you?!" he asked, breathing hard.

"Oh, my goodness. I totally did that!" David wasn't sure if she was talking to herself or him.

"Yes, you did." He looked up at the ceiling for a moment, then he rolled onto his side facing her. "That was awesome. Please don't tell me you watched some porn flick and discovered that trick." They both laughed.

"I read an article," she told him, "which was a total turn-on because you have to use your imagination."

There was silence. Amanda felt it in the air, and she wasn't ready for the conversation. She didn't want to hear he was sorry. Sorry wasn't a good enough word for what he was doing. Just the thought of it made her angry. God was doing something here, she felt it. Now wasn't the time, she said to herself.

David held her. As Amanda's head now rested on his chest, he kissed her hair. He closed his eyes, and something inside him shifted. He was emotionally moved and couldn't hold it in any longer.

"Amanda, ever since that girls' night, you've…"

"… changed," Amanda finished. She thought, *It wasn't girls' night, it was Nathan.*

She didn't look at him, but responded, "David, I'm tired of being the victim. I want to be confident and happy. Why not? God loves me. He rescued me from my dark past. I'm beautiful, intelligent, and bright. I have a good, blessed life."

David agreed with her in his head. He thought about his counseling session with Dr. Nick over the phone; he felt pain. He was ready to be honest. He thought about Amanda's artwork. What she was saying was true; she didn't want to be the victim, and she didn't want to be invisible. David touched her jaw tenderly. She looked up at him, into his serious brown eyes. Amanda saw sincerity.

David said, "You are beautiful in so many ways. I see you. I love you."

Amanda kissed his chest. "Thank you."

David felt her exhale. Amanda found comfort in his words.

CHAPTER 9

Matthew and Mason were out of school, and summer officially started. They were in a variety of camps during the day, while David and Amanda worked. Augusta Retail was now on summer hours, so it was 7:00 am to 4:00 pm for Amanda, who often worked much later on Tuesday nights so she could take the boys to the pool on Friday afternoons. She spent her days in the field, visiting stores and managing the warehouse. Norah, Nathan, and she had their trip planned to the Dallas office.

David continued to spend most of his time at the Acuff corporate office in Brookview. The kickoff of the management training program with Brookview Community College was in a week, and he was ready for his participation in the program to take a backseat. The trainees would be placed in his territory soon, so to get the stores ready, he would get up early, drive to the stores three hours away and closer, then come home the same evening.

He would still see Sam on Monday evenings, but it was different now, and they both knew it. Sam was busy with other programs the college was offering students in merchandising and design. Trips were planned to go to Chicago, New York, and Atlanta; her mind was on those things.

After all, she was single. Going to visit fashion houses, major retail chains, and department stores fascinated her. David was enjoying Amanda more and more. Her confidence was not only making him happy but also making him wonder what brought it all on. As the weeks went on, he felt there was more to it than a night out with Regina and Leslie.

David went to *Lloyd's*, like every Saturday morning. With coffee in hand, he walked to the back of the restaurant with his dad. David loved his dad; he just hated his past choices. He chose to have a mistress, leave his family, and thought he loved this other woman until she left him. David was angry for a long time until he built a relationship with his dad as an adult.

Now David was like his dad, but he told himself he was different. He knew he was lying to himself, but he had been so hurt and mad for so long that he wasn't aware of all his emotions regarding his dad. Michael knew David put the past to the side because he loved him as his dad, but their relationship only went so far, and David would shut down and change the subject.

Michael appreciated his sons. He didn't have much to worry about anymore; Bruce loved him deeply, and both made sure he and the business were thriving. With the manager they helped him hire, he could relax a little and think about new adventures like remarrying, he thought.

Perhaps he could find love again. Michael and David could pass for brothers; same height and build. Michael's dark hair was thinning and receding, so he thought of shaving and going bald. He had light eyes and beige-ivory skin. He was proud of what he built and loved that his sons came by every Saturday morning since high school to make sure the store was clean and ready to open.

"Pop, the new two-door looks great." David opened the door of the new refrigerator and examined the door, the lights, and its temperature.

"Yes," Michael said. "I needed a new one. Hate to admit it." He rolled his eyes and got himself a cup of coffee from the carafe in the kitchen.

Employees were bustling about to prepare for the breakfast rush. Maggie rushed past and handed him the weekly produce inventory.

"How's it looking?" David asked.

"Good." He handed the sheet to his son, waiting for the comment.

David looked at the inventory and saw that it was a lot, but remembered the produce budget. "Pop, what's going on? We just looked over the produce budget. How are you getting all of this out of the conservative budget you set?"

Michael looked at David and pointed to the ring on his finger. "What?" David looked at his wedding ring.

Michael nodded his head towards his office. David headed to Dad's office, which was a small room with a door and a window. The only things that could fit comfortably were a desk with a laptop computer, papers everywhere on top of a bookcase, and two steel chairs.

Michael shut the door behind them and began talking.

"Listen. I promised Clyde I wouldn't say anything," Michael said.

"Who is Clyde? Please tell me this is not illegal." David sat in one of the chairs in front of the desk.

"No, it's all about Amanda's donations to Sarah's Farm."

David was still lost. "What?"

"Not a word when you're around here," Michael insisted. "Amanda visits Sarah's Farm every Saturday, just about, at the farmer's market in town. Sarah's Farm started as a fundraiser for Sarah Corbin years ago."

"Remember, she was a young girl, about 12 years old, who went missing, and they later found her body in an abandoned field. They found the guy who did it...a human trafficking ring. It affected Amanda."

"Of course, it did," David said as he listened and remembered.

"So, Clyde Corbin, Sarah's grandfather, and his daughter, Charlotte, bought that abandoned field and created a farm. Starting out with just strawberries, they were Sarah's favorite. People bought strawberries to support the family. But it has grown to a full-blown farm with all kinds of fruits and vegetables, crafts, and now not just *for Sarah* but for all the families who have lost their children in some violent way."

David sat there in silence, now not at all surprised that Amanda was involved. "So, every Saturday, just about, Amanda buys her produce, but never as much as she gives. This week was $100, last week $50, sometimes she only does $30. Whatever is leftover in her personal budget for herself, I don't know. But Clyde came to the back door one day and said Amanda had helped so much that when they have extra, he felt our family should have it."

David couldn't say anything. Lately, Amanda's heart and spirit were capturing him in a way he couldn't explain.

Michael reached for his catering book on the desk. "And Amanda gives to us as well."

David now had his hand on his chin as Michael opened the book. "Do you know how much money a month we get from feeding Augusta Retail? In catering their lunches, retreats, staff meetings?"

David was waiting for the number, and Michael said, "$350-$500 a month, easy. September will be $1,000; they have a retreat. That doesn't count the little lunches/dinners she has delivered to your house or Augusta sales reps who take lunch here."

David smiled. *God*, he said to himself, *thank you for this sweet woman who just loves deeply*. He now felt so unworthy of Amanda.

"Pop, thank you for sharing." David was proud. "She is beautiful, smart, and caring. Just when I think I've got her figured out, there is another beautiful thing or gesture I discover."

They left the office and saw Bruce in the restaurant, sitting in a booth on the phone. Michael saw him and smirked. "Wild child is waiting for us." They both laughed.

"What story will it be today?" Michael asked. "Candice, Brie, Danielle?"

"Nope, Pop," David said. "Candice is gone; Brie is too immature, and Danielle... well, he just didn't like her." David walked towards the table. "Bruce is changing."

Bruce was in the booth in his black Hyatt Construction t-shirt and blue jeans. David watched Bruce wave to Maggie for coffee, and Michael and David sat in front of him.

"Hey Pop," Bruce said, acknowledging his dad and David with a nod. "Nice refrigerator, huh?"

"Yeah," David said. "Almost as nice as the guy who installed it," he laughed.

"You just plug it in." Bruce shook his head, but appreciated his brother noticing. "It was more of a headache to get through the door and set the temperature."

Maggie returned with three large Lloyd coffee mugs and left the carafe of coffee on the table. "Scrambled eggs, bacon, and toast for all three of yah?" She asked with her loud yellow/blonde hair, Lloyd apron, and smile on. All three agreed.

After Maggie left, Bruce looked at his brother. "David should be smiling from ear to ear these days."

David sighed. "Yes." David knew his brother would bring up the latest Amanda story.

"Amanda goes to his office this week..."

David interrupted and realized Bruce was going to tell *that* story. "We are so not talking about my sex life with Pop." His voice lowered.

"What?" Bruce interjected right back. "That's all you two ask me about every Saturday morning. It's so your turn."

"Speaking of...who were you with last night?" David wanted to change the focus.

"If you must know, her name is Serta. I got a new mattress; true story. I love a good night's sleep. Thank you. So what has gotten into Amanda?" Bruce most certainly did not want to change the focus.

David loved his younger brother and their relationship. He did tell him everything about his relationship with Amanda. Ever since high school, Bruce got the girls, and David got the grades. But no one knew about Sam.

"Isn't that the million-dollar question?" David really wanted to know what had sparked this new, confident Amanda. She was focused, driven, initiated sex, and sure of her choices. If she only knew he was with Sam, he thought. All he could think about was the anger and hurt on her face.

He used to be confused about staying married or being single. But as each day went by, David could not imagine having an everyday experience without Amanda. All he knew is she made the household comfortable, lovely, and lively, and now, with what his dad just shared, she loved the family and gave freely.

David looked at Bruce and smiled. "Okay, this week, in the rain, she came to my office. She told Vikki to hold all my calls, locked the door, and closed the window shades. There she was in her raincoat with nothing else on except her panties. We did it right there in my office."

Michael raised an eyebrow and took a sip of coffee, then said, "She got your attention."

"Yeah. The ladies in the office are still teasing me about my *afternoon delight*," David blushed. "Vikki said to me in confidence that she recommends that for me once a month for *her* mental health. I'm much easier to deal with *after Amanda* she says."

The men laughed. Michael said, "I'm willing to bet Amanda is trying to relieve your stress."

"Well, that and who knows how many cocks are trying to get in your henhouse," Bruce stated, and Michael closed his eyes. With his elbow on the table, he put his head in his hand.

"Bruce, does everyone in construction talk like you?"

"Pretty much. We get straight to the point," Bruce said, and continued, moving past Michael's comment.

"In the last several weeks, that happened," David told his dad.

"See?" Bruce threw his hand up for his truth.

"This guy helped her to her car, nice enough. Kissed her hand." David re-told the story. "He wrote his phone number on her hand."

"Really?!" Michael thought of the boldness.

"And told her he hoped I, her husband, noticed and was paying attention because he was an intentional man." David was blown away by Aaron's forwardness.

"Yep." Bruce wasn't surprised. "I've been trying to tell you all, being single today is not what it once was."

"I guess," Michael replied. "So do you think Amanda is loving the attention, but coming home to act it all out?"

"Maybe," David reflected. "But it's more than that, I think. All I know is I'm enjoying my wife. She has given me massages on Thursday nights for weeks. No sex; just her hands touching me is healing. She comes to bed in nightwear that drives me crazy. I can't even call it lingerie because it can be a tight t-shirt and old Daisy Duke cotton shorts, and I'm drooling. She dances when she cleans the kitchen. I'm so in love with this woman. What has happened?"

"You've always been in love with Amanda," Bruce said.

"I have. But life... You get busy with life. In marriage, there is this routine that starts to happen; you become like a factory. Same day, same time, children drop off, children pick up, go to work, come home from work... You stop thinking until time goes by, and you forget the little things that mattered so much."

"Who cares what happened?" Michael said. "Enjoy yourself."

Just then, David wasn't confused anymore. He was half listening when his dad said something about enjoying what you have and not always looking for the next best thing. For a second, he closed his eyes and saw Amanda in his mind. The first time he saw her, the first time he kissed her, and the first time he said he loved her. He thought quickly; every memory in his mind of worth was because of her. No more Sam, he thought. *This is how this ends.*

"All I am saying is, now you are playing a dangerous game." Regina looked at Amanda as their boys played together in Amanda's backyard. "It has been a while, and you haven't told him you know!"

"I know," Amanda confessed and situated herself as she sat in her patio lounge chair on the deck. "Call me crazy, I'm happy."

"How?! You are sharing David with someone else," Regina said, concerned.

"I know. Regina, it is the strangest thing. I have found myself. I like myself. Ever since Nathan, I see this woman in me. She is confident and sure of herself. I know what I want and what I like sexually and everything else in between. If David were to walk out tomorrow, I would cry, but I would be fine. I couldn't say that a month ago. David used to treat me like a fragile flower because of my past. Now, I bet he doesn't think about that because I don't promote it any longer. It is officially in the past."

Regina looked at her friend, and she had to admit she was secure and her esteem was better than she remembered.

"I saw the doctor." Amanda wanted to reassure Regina. "I am healthy. No STDs. I even talked to my therapist and told her everything."

"And?" Regina waited.

"She is glad that I am doing all of this for me, not necessarily to keep David. Although I have to say, it started out that way. She also wants me to confront David when I'm ready. I can't be afraid of his answers because what if David decides he wants a divorce? We talked about the D-word."

"That would break my heart, Amanda." Regina began to get water in her eyes. "You and David have been through hell and back." She shook her head. "No one can tell me that David doesn't love you. I'm sorry. I just know this is a mistake."

"Thank you, Regina. I believe David is torn up inside, confused. I want him to sort it out." Amanda appreciated her friend's concern. "My therapist told me to be ready for the anger."

Regina nodded. "Oh yeah, you are about to get pissed. For most women, that is the first reaction. You are a different breed, Amanda. Greg would feel my heat like a 115-degree day in Arizona before I hit our door."

"I get it," Amanda chuckled. She felt her cell phone vibrate on the patio table. She didn't recognize the number but decided to answer it.

"This is Amanda."

"Amanda?" the voice said.

She recognized the voice. "Vikki?"

"Yes," Vikki replied. "I'm very sorry to call you on a Saturday, but I want to be sure you are planning to attend the Acuff Academy dinner next Saturday with David."

Amanda put her phone on speaker and sat it down on the patio table. "Vikki, I know nothing about it."

Amanda heard a sigh. "I was afraid of that. David is trying to surprise you, I'm sure. It is a project he has been working on since March, which is the reason for my call. You and David need to be at the Acuff Conference Center at 5:30 p.m."

"Okay." Amanda rose to grab her planner and pen, right inside the sliding glass door on the kitchen counter, then returned to the phone and Regina.

"I have it down."

"Great. Could you keep this between us?" Vikki asked. "I'm sure David wants to surprise you."

Regina moved her shoulders as to say *I don't know*. Amanda looked at her phone and decided to go for it. "Okay. I won't say anything, Vikki."

Amanda looked at her phone, then at Regina. "Is Samantha Coleman invited to this event?"

There was silence, then Vikki answered yes. Amanda closed her eyes, and Regina pressed her lips together in anger. Amanda felt Vikki knew about David and Sam. Of course, she did.

"Amanda," Vikki spoke up. "Her plus one is Dr. Terrance Winters."

"I see," Amanda sighed.

"Amanda," Vikki wanted to add. "Thank you, especially for Wednesday." Amanda laughed.

Then, as if Vikki were sending a code, "If there is anything I can ever do for you, please don't hesitate to call me."

Amanda understood. "Okay, I will. Thank you, Vikki." Amanda ended the call.

"That is some shit right there. Vikki clearly knows about this Sam. What happened on Wednesday?"

"Regina, as you can see, I'm not crazy. On Wednesday, I went to David's office in nothing but a raincoat," she winked.

Regina looked at Amanda. "Who are you?!" She gave her friend a high five.

"I'm sure David's mind was blown."

"And so was Vikki's, in a good way."

"Who is Terrance Winters?" Regina asked. "Sam cheating on her man?"

Amanda felt irritated. Her therapist was right. With each turn in this situation, Amanda was getting upset.

When Regina and her son, Derrick, left to pick up her daughter, Kayla, from basketball practice, Amanda did something she had never felt the need to do. David's desk. It was time.

While the boys were downstairs playing with their Lego sets, Amanda went into the den and began searching David's desk. She saw the profit-and-loss statements for the stores David oversaw. Carefully going through them, she noticed David had marked the stores needing help.

She saw David's schedule for travel, and a folder that read Acuff Academy applications with a note posted on the top in David's handwriting:

> *I'm not asking you to lower your standards; I'm asking you to strengthen your reach.*
> *—Dr. J.*

Just as she was about to open the folder, she saw David's planner from last quarter.

She put down the folder and picked up the planner. She turned to March, and there, an Acuff envelope fell out with David's full name on it.

As Amanda opened the pre-opened envelope and read the letter, she said out loud, "Lord, what is going on?!" The letter was from Gerald Acuff, chief executive officer and president of Acuff, Inc.

The letter was one of congratulations on being the vice president of stores in the southern Illinois area. It detailed David's earnings from his old store in Lindale and the bonus he received that quarter, and then the substantial increase he would get as vice president.

Amanda's eyes bulged for a moment as she looked at the amount. David's salary doubled starting in April. He told her about the bonus. They celebrated the promotion, and she knew there was an increase, but *double*? She then noticed his note at the bottom of the letter: "Create savings."

Amanda's mind went in numerous directions as she put everything back where she found it. She looked at her watch; it was 11:30. The bank was still open. She was ready to go when she remembered the boys were downstairs. There was not enough time to get them in the car, so she decided to call. Sure enough, David had created an additional savings account without her.

It wasn't a typical Sunday for the Lloyds. No church, no Sunday dinner. Amanda packed the boys for a two-week camp at Sugar Creek Farms. It was a large estate owned by two churches in the area for Christian children and student ministries. The boys were going to fish, hike, learn survival skills, and learn about who God is in their lives at their age.

Amanda was nervous about them being old enough to be gone for two weeks, but when Bill said he was going to be a group leader for Mason's group, Amanda rested easy. Also, David and Bruce planned to travel up to Sugar Creek to visit the boys on the following Sunday for the parent event. She dropped the boys off with Meri and Bill so they could leave by noon. Amanda got home, and David wasn't around. She was certain he was at the office. He had to travel this week, just overnight, to see three stores in the southwest Illinois area.

Amanda sat on the living room sofa and rested. She had laundry on her mind; she would need to pack for her trip to the Dallas office. At that moment, she decided it was time to confront David, perhaps after the event on Saturday. With the boys gone, they could talk freely, and then she could leave for a few days and clear her head. The doorbell interrupted her thoughts. She went to answer the door. It was Bruce.

"Hey, Sis," Bruce said at the door. "Sorry for the drive-by. I hope I'm not bothering you, but I need to fix Matthew's ceiling fan, and I have a new lamp for Mason's room."

Amanda frowned. "What's wrong with Matthew's ceiling fan, and why does Mason need a new lamp?" Amanda let Bruce in and gave him a hug. She knew a story was coming that she didn't want to hear.

"Well, the other night we were playing," Bruce said, heading upstairs as Amanda followed. "Who knew Matthew would tape *all* his superhero action figures to the ceiling fan and turn it on at high speed when I wasn't looking?"

Amanda rolled her eyes as they opened Matthew's bedroom door to find the ceiling fan hanging crooked. "I don't know who the bigger kid is." Amanda was certain Bruce was somehow the encourager of the shenanigans.

"And what happened to Mason's lamp?" They walked through the Jack and Jill bathroom to Mason's room.

"Amanda, I cleaned up the pee." Her eyes opened wide. Bruce was laughing with his hand on his chest. "But Matthew dared Mason to pee off the top bunk." She pressed her lips together with her eyes closed; mostly to keep from laughing.

"He did it. Peed straight off the top," Bruce motioned with his hands in the air, "but it all landed on the lamp, smoke billowing everywhere… "

"Bruce!" Amanda put her hands on her hips, just then noticing that Mason's lamp was missing.

Bruce continued to laugh, then stopped abruptly when he saw his sister-in-law's face. "I couldn't save the lamp. Gotta new one out in the truck," he pointed downstairs.

"Unbelievable," Amanda shook her head and walked away from Bruce, now laughing. "I have laundry to do. I'll leave you to it."

"Thanks. I love you!" Bruce said as an apology and headed back downstairs. Amanda went to the master bedroom and, with a teasing response, said, "Love me less, Bruce."

They both laughed.

Bruce was in his truck when she gathered up all the dirty clothes from each hamper upstairs, went to the kitchen to grab dish towels, and proceeded to the laundry room. It was there as she sorted clothes that she found one of David's white shirts. The scent hit her.

It wasn't his smell, not an aftershave or deodorant. The smell wasn't familiar at all. It was Samantha; she knew it. It was sugar-sweet and artificial. Amanda felt her face get hot, and her eyes fill with tears. She felt angry inside. She quickly shut the door, remembering Bruce was now upstairs, hopefully too busy to hear her.

As Amanda sat down with her back against the washer, her knees up, and her hands out as if someone were sitting across from her to hold them, she let the tears flow. Silence fell upon her, then she started speaking.

"I'm just dumb. Do I even like myself? Who doesn't confront their husband about an affair and continues to have sex with their husband? At every turn, there is complete disrespect for me as his wife." Amanda thought about her conversation with Regina and what Vikki must think of her. Tears flowed.

Bruce trotted downstairs, headed to the garage in search of a new light bulb, when he heard Amanda in the laundry room. Was she crying? He listened. He wanted to call out to her, but he didn't want to embarrass her. Bruce just stopped moving and listened. She stopped crying to speak.

"It's not about what other people think, right? I mean, they thought you were crazy when you loved Zacchaeus? And you said that by a godly woman's behavior can change her husband. How am I doing? Is David changing? Thank you for protecting me from harm as he continues to sleep with her. Thank you for giving him the sense to wear a condom. I see you, God. I see you loving me."

Bruce was frozen but processing. *David is sleeping with other women?* At least Amanda thought he was. *Who was she talking to? Was she talking to Jesus?* Although Bruce didn't live by his Christian upbringing, he believed in Jesus. Someone was in that laundry room with Amanda, and all he could do was listen in awe.

"Heavenly Dad, I love my husband, and Samantha can't possibly love him the way I do. You said three strands are not easily broken; don't allow us to fall apart." She cried.

"You are powerful; you are the one in the heart changing-business. Please bring David home on Monday nights, and whatever it is that caused him to stray, and whatever keeps me thinking about Nathan, take away these desires and help us deal with them together with you. Keep me from deep despair and depression, and keep my eyes focused on you, no matter how afraid I am. I love you. I know you love me more. You said, you came so I could have life and have it to the full. Fill my life with your will and your goodness, your protection, your love, and your faith. I believe you will give me all I ask and more." Amanda took a deep breath and exhaled.

Bruce saw the goosebumps on his arms. He felt genuine love, yes, from a woman who loved her man, but also from a daughter who needed and loved her father. The fact that she prayed, what she prayed, how she prayed—he was more than touched, he was moved. He quickly went back upstairs. He spent the rest of his time putting together a baseball lamp and trying to process what he heard Amanda say. *David was sleeping with another woman. Really?* Bruce thought. Why hadn't David told him?!

This explains Amanda's behavior; she's been trying to keep him. Bruce was mad and broken-hearted at the same time. *Who the hell was Nathan?* "Damn," he said out loud. After making sure Matthew's fan was working, Bruce went back downstairs to find a new light bulb in the garage. Amanda was not in the laundry room, but the washer and dryer were running. He went back upstairs to install the light, and when he came back downstairs, he went looking for her.

There she was in the den, asleep on the sectional. He noticed a blanket on the chair and covered her with it. Bruce cleaned up his mess and locked the house upon leaving. As he drove away, he had that image of Amanda sleeping. He was broken. All these years, he was prideful, thinking the Lloyd's had done this wonderful thing of *accepting* Amanda into their family, when really, Amanda was doing this wonderful thing of loving them and making them a family. Bruce thought to himself that they weren't worthy.

CHAPTER 11

"Who was Zacchaeus in the Bible?" Bruce asked Marcus as they sat in his truck and watched it rain. Marcus Turner was Bruce's business partner. He helped him manage their construction team at Hyatt Construction. They were a small builder in the area. They built custom mid-level to high-end residential homes.

Marcus, an African American in his mid-40s, stroked his chin and continued to look out at the rain. "He was a tax collector who got rich by cheating people...overcharging people. Since he was short, he climbed a tree to see Jesus. Jesus saw him and called him out of the tree. The people of the day, of course, hated that; Zacchaeus was a sinner. But Jesus went to his house anyway. Zacchaeus repented and became a follower of Jesus."

"Ah." Bruce was trying to piece together Amanda's moment in the laundry room.

"What's up?" Marcus turned and asked Bruce.

"What? I can't ask a simple question about the Bible?" Bruce knew it was completely out of his character.

Marcus looked at him, doubting. "What's her name?"

"C'mon; it is not like that." Bruce sipped his coffee.

"Bruce, I've been knowing you for…" Marcus couldn't remember how long. "….Forever. You're honestly gonna tell me you're asking about the Bible has nothing to do with a woman?"

"Well…" Bruce couldn't lie. Marcus threw his hands up in the air because he was correct.

"Not a woman I like," Bruce said. "I overheard Amanda praying yesterday, and she mentioned Zacchaeus. It was an amazing prayer."

"I'm sure." Marcus said. "Amanda is a godly woman." Marcus had met Amanda and the boys numerous times.

"She is going through a hard time." Bruce thought about the situation. "I'm gonna hurt my brother. He and I need to have a conversation."

Bruce said nothing further, and Marcus knew not to ask. Marcus knew Bruce and David had a good relationship, but a sensitive one. David was the one who always seemed to have it together, and Bruce was the one who did not. But Bruce had it more together than his family gave him credit for. He had a reputation as a bachelor, but Marcus hadn't seen the women come and go like in the past. Lately, Bruce dated occasionally, but no one seriously since Chloe. Marcus never knew exactly what happened, but he knew his friend cared for Chloe deeply, and it just ended. Marcus knew Bruce lived modestly and didn't live paycheck to paycheck. Bruce had plans.

Amanda left the house before David got out of the shower. It was raining, so she knew he wasn't going to go for a run. It was Monday, and she just couldn't hear the lie about the late evening meeting. As she dressed in her jeans and Augusta Retail t-shirt, she thought about all the loose ends she needed to take care of at work. She left a note and fresh coffee at least.

When she got to work, she settled into her office and went through her messages and emails before heading to the warehouse. The essential oils and accessories were still in her office from Snowflake Ranch. Today, the scents were lovely to her. She got up to look at the contents of the box again.

The neck wrap was soft as she put it around her neck. With the rain outside, she was tempted to just lie back in her chair and get lost in the fragrance, but for the first time, she focused on the company logo. It looked familiar to her. It had a sky-blue background with one white snowflake and one gray snowflake. She couldn't place how she knew the company. Vanessa had looked up the company online weeks ago, and there wasn't anything coming up except that the company has representation at the Dallas Market Center. She was looking forward to going to the market center and visiting their showroom when she was in Dallas next week.

Then she thought about Nathan. The encounter would play over in her head, and she didn't know why; she loved David. But she couldn't help but wonder about Nathan's life. What was being divorced like? Leslie told her it was none of her business, but she couldn't help but wonder.

Amanda, for the first time, thought of herself as divorced. She felt confident that if David didn't treat her with love and respect, and didn't want her anymore, she could make it on her own. She couldn't have said that before the flowers came, before Nathan touched her, before she saw herself as beautiful, secure, and confident versus the foster kid that was abused and traumatized. She smiled. It was all going to work out regardless of what David did or didn't do. She had found peace within herself.

David had a full day. He kept Amanda's note in his pocket all day as encouragement:

Hey babe, summer hours, fresh coffee for you. I love you. See you soon.
-Amanda

Her handwriting was smooth and classic, like an English teacher's. He had a meeting with Gerald Acuff about the academy, which was stressful, but Gerald was supportive and wanted the program to work. He was encouraged to know about the downtown project early. Gerald had contacted the developers, and they were talking; he wanted David to make sure he told Amanda.

Then the meeting with Scott Acuff, equally stressful, about his new territory and his vision. Scott was all about the numbers and keeping up with the latest trends in grocery. Sometimes, those two things didn't always go together as far as David was concerned. Hence, there was friction between them.

While having a restaurant in the grocery store looked nice for certain areas, it made little sense. A *get it and go* approach was better over the lunch hour, especially. They would have a friendly conversation about it and decide the two stores in the territory needed two different approaches.

By the time he was to meet Sam, David was mentally exhausted. He used the hotel room shower to freshen up, and he put on a red polo shirt and khaki slacks that he always kept in the car. He was sitting in the living room area of the suite when she arrived. Sam was wearing a tailored V-neck blue dress, high heels, and her blonde hair in an updo. It was awkward for them to be in a hotel suite fully dressed, not in bed.

"You look beautiful." He rose, gave her a hug, and kissed her cheek. He sat back down and patted the sofa, inviting her to sit next to him.

"Thank you." She blushed and then took his hand. "He is taking me to dinner tonight. I'm actually nervous."

"Sam," David looked at their hands together, "you shouldn't be nervous about Terrance. Obviously, he cares enough about you to come here and help you with what is an extremely hard process." David was talking about Sam's old friend from Kansas. He had recently reached out to Sam, wondering why she had moved away so quickly. When she explained her mom's death and having to clear the family home,

Terrance, now done with his dissertation and oral exams, wanted to come and help.

"He wasn't a serious boyfriend, David. We were just getting to know each other back then, but lately... after several weeks on the phone, I want more with him." She rested her head on his shoulder. "Besides, you don't need me anymore." She looked up at him and smiled.

"Sam," David sighed, "I used you. I've been prideful and selfish." He now squared up with her face-to-face and held both of her hands. "Please forgive me for not being the man I know I should've been here."

"David, you and I were/are an emotional mess. At an intersection in our lives of *who gives a shit* and *I'm tired*, then the unspeakable happens. Your idea is now a full-blown program, helping 25 students who no one hardly ever thinks about. Who knows what this program will become? I'm honored to be involved."

"Yes, but this isn't/wasn't right. If I lose Amanda, it is no one's fault but my own. The best thing you can do is to move on with your life with a good man. No more married men, okay? You are better than a hotel room on Monday nights." David kissed her softly on the lips.

Sam had one tear fall from her left eye. She caught it quickly by releasing David's hand. "And you have got to tell her everything. Don't lie to her about how you got here emotionally."

He agreed. "Look at us, adulting."

"I am extremely excited about Saturday, but so sad for what I've done. I behaved badly, too. I knew you were married. I'm sorry. I wanted to feel good, so I ran here on Monday nights to get that feeling. I didn't care if it lasted for a few hours. But Terrance came along with one conversation and gave me that good feeling all week."

"I'm glad to hear that," David replied. "I don't know how to explain to Amanda that in the midst of me defending her honor, I ended up disrespecting her with an affair."

Sam sighed. "Somehow, someway, David, fight for your marriage."

David saw Amanda in his mind. He saw her sleeping next to him; he saw her across the table at Sunday dinner, and he saw her face looking at the boys and saying she loved them. He snapped out of the pause and said, "I will do that."

She took a deep breath and looked him in his brown eyes.

"David."

He looked into the depth of her blue eyes and saw the water in them.

"Sam."

"Thank you," she said.

"You're welcome," he said. "I care about you."

"I care about you, but this is how it ends," she whispered.

Now David felt a tear on his face. Sam wiped it with her thumb and let go of his hands. She stood up, quietly walked out of the hotel room, and shut the door behind her.

~

David got home, and Amanda was out on the deck with a glass of wine, looking out into their fenced-in backyard. She heard the sliding glass door open and was surprised to see David.

"Hey, babe. What are you doing here?" Amanda's tone was almost mean. She had decided she was going to drink wine until she got drunk or sleepy, and she was two glasses in.

David was too tired and emotional to challenge her response, but he took the wine bottle, noticed it was half empty, went inside with it, poured some wine into a glass from the cabinet, and joined her outside.

"No more Monday night meetings." David took a drink and stood next to her, staring out at the yard.

Amanda looked at him, but he was looking out into the yard. He looked tired and worn. At that moment, she was done drinking wine. With her eyes closed, she fought back tears. She remembered her prayer, *Please bring David home to me on Monday nights*. She rested her head on his arm as if to give him a hug, and then she went inside to the kitchen. David didn't follow right away; he continued to look out into the yard, remembering when they bought this home and how the boys were toddlers learning how to walk, playing in the sprinkler, and building snowmen.

When he returned to the kitchen, Amanda was eating a piece of bread and getting ready to prepare dinner.

"Amanda, stop," he said and put his wine glass down. "Don't make dinner for us."

She noticed he called her Amanda, not honey. He meant it. She knew he was serious, and she stopped moving.

David stood in front of her with his hands gently on her shoulders. "Please rest," he continued. "The boys are not here. Isn't it nice there are no LEGOs in the hallway and Nerf gun bullets flying across the television when you're trying to watch?" He laughed, and she smiled.

"You do so much here, at work, and beyond. You made such an impression on Gerald that he wanted me to tell you that knowing about the downtown project early allowed him to meet with the developers before solid decisions were made. Pop told me just how much you support the business, and I promised Mom I'd help out more and would stop thinking just about myself."

Amanda couldn't say anything except to give him a hug. She was tired of it all, especially him being so into Sam, work, and whatever else distractions she didn't know about.

"I'm having dinner delivered. Not *Lloyd's*, but something else you like."

David looked at her and knew she was out of sorts. "No more wine. I need to talk to you." He kissed her cheek.

Amanda was feeling guilty. Wine and crackers were going to be her dinner. She was expecting to pass out and be alone all week. She was tired of caring, giving, and wondering if anything was going to change.

And here it comes, she thought, the bend in the road, the curve she was waiting on, and she was about to miss it.

"I'll let you do that," she said. "I'm going to go upstairs and get myself together." Amanda disappeared upstairs.

David called The Front Porch, a small American restaurant less than a mile away that had Amanda's favorite Cobb salad, and David loved the grilled chicken sandwich. They would deliver, so David went to the laundry room, found a clean t-shirt and athletic shorts, put them on, started a load of laundry, and began to gather things for his trip tomorrow. He would drive west toward St. Louis, see a couple of stores, spend the night, and see one more store on the way back.

Amanda was upstairs in the shower, thanking God for the answered prayer. When she came downstairs, David had created a picnic on the living room floor. The lights were out, except for the glow of candles and the under-cabinet lighting in the kitchen.

David saw his wife in her white casual jumpsuit, looking comfortable. She wasn't trying to be sexy or sensual. With her curly hair damp, no makeup, and no lip gloss, she was gorgeous to him.

"David." She said. "This is sweet. The Front Porch. This is where I say... what's gotten into you?"

David answered honestly. "Perspective."

Amanda didn't say anything. She didn't want to talk; she wanted David to lead the conversation.

"I want to talk to you," he told her.

Amanda came closer to him, and their brown eyes met. He kissed her gently, not passionately, but caring enough that she knew he was present and wanted to say something important.

"I love your confidence." He was genuine, "I hope you are doing it for you. I love you, no matter what, and whether you initiate sex," he said, smiling. Amanda smiled.

"Making love to you lately… so good." They sat down on the floor—David with his back leaning against the bottom of the couch; Amanda with her back leaning against the bottom of the loveseat, their dinner before them on the floor.

"Initiate when you want, not to please me or because you feel obligated."

"Really?" Amanda was taken off guard. "You mean like sex is a thing I do to please only you? Or I can't say no if I'm tired or not in the mood? That I always have to say yes?" Amanda was trying to understand.

"Amanda, you hardly ever turn me down. Is there a reason why? Do you feel obligated? Then, I had it in my head that you, Regina, and Leslie had a contest or bet going on, the way you were acting, initiating…"

Amanda stopped him. "David, stop." She put her hand gently over her mouth, seeing his curiosity and insecurity.

She crawled and sat next to him. She turned his face towards her with her hand. "Oh, babe." She gazed into his eyes. "When I saw you for the first time, I quickly turned away because I just knew you could read my thoughts. Here we are twelve years later, and you still make me melt."

She kissed him on the lips. "You are handsome, sexy, and that wink/smile thing you do… Listen, I don't feel obligated at all."

Now David had his head down, blushing, and Amanda, with her newfound confidence, took his chin and lifted it so their eyes would meet again.

"There is no contest. Just me wanting you, desiring you—I wanted to draw you to me. I'm your wife," she told him, thinking about Samantha.

"I'm sorry I didn't initiate before now. I was shy about it, nervous, and I had to be ready to not be afraid the past would show up. I didn't know that not doing it would create doubt in you."

"Okay," David said with relief. He kissed her. He couldn't tell her completely where all of this was stemming from, but it was reassuring to know it was just her noticing his needs. It wasn't a stretch for him to accept that. She noticed everyone's needs.

"Amanda, I should have told you my needs." David was learning this from Dr. Nick. "There are so many things I need to learn about being a good husband to you."

Amanda tried not to act surprised. There he was, the humble man she married. Amanda thought about Nathan. If Nathan hadn't touched her, would she have figured out David's needs? Did it take David having an affair for her to figure it out? She didn't know.

They began to eat dinner when David heard his phone on the kitchen counter. He didn't move. Amanda, poised for whatever happened next, decided she would be indifferent.

"Have you heard from the boys or Bill?" David wanted to know, "because that's the only call I am taking tonight."

"Yes, they are fine. I'll send you the pictures. They are having a great time. Looking forward to your and Bruce's visit on Sunday," she replied.

David continued to eat his sandwich. Between bites, he said, "You are leaving for Dallas on Sunday. All next week, I'm going to miss you all. No one will be here. Well, Bruce will be here."

He rolled his eyes. "He wants Dad to add an outdoor sitting area at the restaurant, live music, etc."

"Great idea." Amanda continued eating. "I'll be home before you know it, and you need to rest, too."

David nodded. He stopped eating. "Amanda, this weekend. Vikki told me she had invited you to the Acuff Academy dinner. I swear, she is just like Mom. I told her I wanted to ask you and tell you about the Academy, but noooo."

"Vikki means well. She knows you and knew I needed time to find the right dress or whatever," Amanda interjected.

"Well, nothing elaborate." David requested. "This really needs to be professional but simple. I would love for you to join me early Saturday afternoon to have lunch with the trainees."

"Sure," Amanda said.

David explained to Amanda that the Acuff Academy was his idea; Gerald allowed him to pilot the program in his territory. The academy was a retail management and culinary arts training program designed to be a win-win for several community colleges in the area, especially Brookview Community College and Acuff. Acuff will have qualified, trained, entry-level management employees, and the graduating students will have jobs right out of college.

Amanda was pleased. "David, this is so great!"

"You think? The training sessions are about six weeks during the summer. Trainees will work in their designated store and sometimes come to the corporate office for training. After that, they continue to work in the store and hopefully advance within the company."

"Well, I think it is a fabulous idea. I am not sure why all the secrecy." Amanda figured Samantha probably helped him with the academy. Maybe they met while working together.

"Because the other vice presidents were definitely jealous of my longevity with the company, the fact I was put up for promotion under 40 years old, and the success of the two stores I have managed in the last ten years..."

David stopped speaking for a few seconds. He was going to say that the fact that he has an African American wife was just too much for some of the senior vice presidents. He didn't want her to know that he was still painfully angry about how that encounter happened.

"... I managed in the last ten years to keep quiet. The attention I was already getting was too much. This town is small."

"Well," Amanda saw her husband's face, red and stressed. "Babe, you have been carrying a lot in the past several months." She cleared their dinner trash and returned to sit on the couch with David between her legs so she could massage his shoulders.

"I'm sorry; when I say it out loud, I sound like a two-year-old," David said.

"You don't sound like a child; it's just a lot. David, you can tell me things. I'm not going to fall apart."

"I know. I'm sorry," he replied.

Then there was silence as she massaged his shoulders. Her touch felt incredible to him, but his guilt wanted her to stop. He touched her hand as if to tell her to stop, and he turned to her. "I love you." David leaned into her touch.

"I love you too." Amanda knew in her heart that David wasn't going to say anything more tonight. He looked tired and overwhelmed, and she could tell he wanted to sleep. She grabbed his hand, and he rose. Without saying a word, she blew out the candles and led him upstairs to bed.

CHAPTER 12

"I knew you would call me just as I'm getting ready to go to bed this morning," Jake answered Nathan's call.

"I'm sorry. I knew you were on stakeout, but I think I figured something out." Nathan poured his protein shake from the blender into a glass.

"What's our guy Ryan doing?"

"Acting like he is running a legitimate business, but we all know better."

Jake opened his refrigerator and grabbed a bottle of water. "What's going on? Amanda, okay?"

"Just fine. Nothing has happened since the box came. When I couldn't find this Snowflake Ranch, I decided to look up the business with the Secretary of State. Around the same time the box came here, paperwork went through there to change the name of Snowflake Ranch to SFR, and they are doing business as The Ranch."

"Let me guess, when you look up The Ranch, it's owned by our friend Ryan Barnes." Jake rolled his eyes. "That smooth operator says he owns a *boutique*. Now he owns a bath shop. You and I both know he is selling a little more than bras and body lotion."

"Yes, it's a front. His name on this paperwork is not Ryan Barnes, but Ryan Snowden."

Jake stopped moving. In the silence, Nathan knew Jake had already caught the connection.

"No way!" Jake was no longer tired.

"Yep. He killed his wife and thinks he got away with it because he took his dead wife's maiden name as his last name, then created a lingerie and bath store as a front to hide drugs, sex trafficking, and prostitution. Unbelievable."

Nathan states his theory. "Jake, this was an easy find. Can Ryan be this cocky or sloppy? Someone is leaving us some serious breadcrumbs because this new Ranch website is clean, basic, but not personal."

"I don't understand." Jake wanted to hear more.

"This box that Amanda got came with all this product and an invitation to come to the showroom at the Dallas Market. No catalog with prices, nothing. However, it was packed with care—the packaging and tissue paper; nothing like this on The Ranch website. Anyway, can we see the original Snowflake Ranch website? The catalog? I bet you it has answers. Can you pull some strings with the website developer? I wanna see it before I get to Dallas. I'm certain Ryan wants to get Amanda alone to see if she's gonna be a threat.

David woke up early. Amanda was still sleeping beside him. He watched her sleep for minutes. He thought about the first time he woke up next to her, and about how beautifully she was aging. No wrinkles, no laugh lines; her light brown skin just as smooth as the day he met her, but her face was mature. She had seen things, done things, and been places, and it showed on her face.

He kissed her lips; they were like velvet. She slowly opened her eyes with a little frown. She saw David. He was already dressed but lying next to her. She smiled sleepily.

"Don't move; it's early. I just wanted to let you know I'm leaving. Home tomorrow night late. Honey, take care of yourself. Lock up at night, okay?"

"I will. Drive safe. Text me." She closed her eyes, and he watched her drift back to sleep.

David was fifteen minutes into his drive with coffee and phone at his side when he heard the song on the radio that took him back to the first days when he met Amanda. He smiled big at the memory.

He remembered her ass as she was on her hands and knees chasing a lipstick when he first saw her. As she rose to greet him, she hit her head on the cosmetic shelving. He was left speechless with her beautiful light brown skin tone and golden brown hair with curls to her shoulders, but he managed to say two words.

"You alright?" He gave her his hand to help her up.

"I think so." She didn't take his hand but got up on her own and nervously laughed while rubbing her head.

"Need an ice pack or something for that head?" He was concerned about someone getting hurt in the store more than her well-being. After looking at her all-black outfit, he now knew who she was.

"Ana Cosmetics." He smirked. "I've been waiting for you all for weeks."

Amanda was now looking at him. David remembered that at that moment the atmosphere shifted. Her brown eyes were bright with golden flakes. Beautiful. *Where did the oxygen go?* He thought. David couldn't speak. He barely heard her say she was fine, no ice pack needed.

"Yeah, I'm sorry. The girl who was supposed to be here abandoned her job. We didn't even know, just decided not to come to work and didn't bother to tell anyone she quit." He could tell Amanda was frustrated.

"I see." David wasn't sympathizing, just a matter-of-fact. "I'm David, assistant store director." He held out his hand.

"Amanda." She took his hand and shook it confidently.

Her hands were amazingly soft. *God*, he remembered thinking, *am I going to make it through this without falling over?*

"Well, this is your fourteen feet of disaster." He turned and looked at the cosmetics wall. They both looked at the wall and then the entire area.

"Yes, abandoned. I take it you don't have a cosmetics manager?"

"What for?" David was sharp. "If we can't get her help from you all." He saw her roll her eyes.

David was not happy. The east wall of the store was a deserted mess. It wasn't organized the way he wanted. Truthfully, the cosmetics manager was fired, and he was trying to turn this part of the store, the non-food section, into something manageable.

Amanda followed David to the back-loading dock area. He walked briskly through the back of the store, showing her where they placed her pallet of fixtures, boxes of new products, and the supply closet of cleaning supplies. He introduced her to Seth Hawkeye, the back-of-the-store manager, and gave her a tour of the store. He then took her back to the cosmetics area to get started.

When David got back to his office next to the break room, he heard Corey, the front-end manager, talking to Ray in the produce section. "Did you see the hottie in cosmetics?"

"Hell yeah. She's got that Janet Jackson/Mariah Carey vibe with the natural curls. You talk to her?"

"Not yet," Corey replied confidently. "I know she's not married, but girls like her probably have an overprotective boyfriend."

David listened and shook his head. She was beautiful. David couldn't deny he was feeling a little light-headed from meeting her, and he wondered if she felt the connection too. By the time he made the rounds a couple of hours later to check on her, she had a grocery cart full of product, and she was on her cell phone.

"Well, it's a mess. I will be here all week…damages, discontinues, and shrinkage, yep. I'll turn in the paperwork. All the fixtures are here, new products, but will place an order for more…giving credit. Yes, I am." Amanda had her back to him.

"Calvin, you aren't here. This store director is pissed. He hates us, and the section is terrible. I'm calling Melanie with Insel and what's her name from Hindley? Yeah, Trisha. So who will maintain this store?" She began writing in her notebook, then stopped and looked up in the air. She turned around and saw David as she said, "That's the wrong answer, Calvin. Yep. Gotta go. I'm going rogue." Amanda ended the call and stared at David.

"Fun times," David said sarcastically, viewing her grocery cart of products and noticing she had made the cosmetic counter her office.

"Yeah." Amanda scratched her head and found the spot where she had hit her head and flinched.

"Are you sure you're okay?" David noticed her uncomfortable.

"Coffee?" Amanda looked at her watch. "Or something. I'm gonna be here all day." Amanda put her phone in her back pocket.

"My head is fine, really. Just tender. Probably knocked some sense into me." She chuckled, and then there was his smile. Not forced, just natural and pleasant, white, straight teeth, her eyes looking straight into him. Then she smiled. That's when David felt they both saw the connection.

"I'll take you over to the restaurant." David felt he needed to stop staring at her. His smile faded, and for the first time, she saw his name tag.

"David Lloyd," she said out loud as they walked across the store. "Are you related to Bruce Lloyd?"

Unbelievable, David thought. How did she know Bruce? Please, not one of the women he dated. Maybe that is why he felt a connection.

"Yes. My younger brother is Bruce. Just finished an apprenticeship with an HVAC company."

"Yep. I know him from college, Brookview Community College. I took a few classes there and then transferred to SIU."

"So you're a Saluki. I'm a Badger." David stopped at the customer service desk.

"Wisconsin," Amanda said. "Nice. How many Lloyd brothers are there?"

David looked at Ellen and asked her for a vendor card, and then answered Amanda. "Only the two of us, thank the Lord. My mom had her hands full."

Amanda laughed. "Yeah, I could see Bruce being a handful."

When they entered the restaurant and dining area, David explained that she could show her vendor card and her company could collect all her meal receipts to pay for them at the end of her stay.

"Thank you," Amanda said. David knew she saw him softening. Then there was a page over the store's intercom system, and he had to go. He saw Amanda grab her coffee and a cinnamon roll.

Amanda slept in. She called Vanessa and told her she would be an hour late. She enjoyed the quiet and stillness of the house. When she finally went downstairs, she noticed David had made coffee hours ago, but it was still hot. She turned off the coffeemaker, poured herself some coffee in her travel mug, and then saw the Acuff package. She closed her eyes and smiled. In the package was one cinnamon roll. Thoughtful that David remembered after all these years.

"Acuff's has grown up since I've lived here," Amanda remembered being on the phone with Regina that first day she was in the Galesboro store. "This cinnamon roll is amazing."

"How long are you gonna be here?" Regina asked. "Greg and I would love to see you, take you to dinner, and dancing?"

"Sounds fun. I'm here for a while. This girl who had this territory left the job, and Ana Cosmetics isn't going to replace her. I have an angry face," Amanda continued to sip her coffee and eat.

"I get it. Sounds like a headache. But, baby girl, you sound so good. Is the St. Louis area good to you?"

"Yes, good to start over, but I'm alone," Amanda said. "Don't worry, work keeps me busy." Amanda noticed a tall African American man with smooth brown skin, a short black fade hairstyle, and a flirtatious smile standing in front of her. It was Corey, the front-end manager. "Regina, I gotta go. Lunch tomorrow?"

They agreed, and Amanda put her phone away and greeted Corey. "Hi."

"Hi," he replied. "You okay? Is there something I can get you?"

"I think I'm okay. Can you point me in the direction of cardboard boxes? I gotta ship these discontinued items," Amanda explained.

"We will take care of it." Corey was excited to assist her. "I'll send someone over with those. Hey, a group of us sometimes go to this taproom bar after work; you're welcome to join us." Corey saw a pen on the cosmetic counter and wrote down his phone number in her notebook.

"Well, thanks for the invite." Amanda smiled. Corey winked and left. Amanda shook her head and thought of Corey as a college kid flirting.

She continued to take an inventory of the section. When David made his way back over, Amanda had her hair in a ponytail, the discontinued items were in boxes, and she needed David's signature on some paperwork.

"Wow," David said as he looked at the organized mess and continued to sign the paperwork she gave him.

"Sorry," she said. "It gets worse before it gets better."

Amanda explained her plan to get the discontinued items out, record the damages, and send them away. She would need to throw away all the old or broken fixtures, and then she could build the new section.

"Have you been selling a lot?" Amanda asked. "We haven't placed an order in a while, so I'll need to do that right away and put a rush on it."

"I fired our cosmetic manager for stealing." David was direct. Amanda didn't look up at him; she could tell he was pissed all over again.

"Okay. That explains some things. Tomorrow, I'll come in early. If someone can move the pegboard panels from the wall. The new fixtures require electricity."

"Lights, huh?" He looked at her, and she flipped to a page in her notebook and showed him a diagram of the section. "Okay. It's a start."

After an awkward silence, their eyes met. Amanda felt her insides quiver. This man was gorgeous; handsome with his dark hair, brown eyes, and tall build. He looked like Bruce, but nothing like him at the same time. He was professional, direct, and took charge of the store as an assistant, and she liked his mean-boy attitude but caring disposition. Amanda remembered looking away and quickly returning to the conversation. "I'll make sure we do right by Acuff."

Amanda's memory was interrupted by a chime on her phone. It was a text message from Vikki.

> The message I received from David this morning...

> Vikki, Samantha Coleman will no longer be our point of contact for the Acuff Academy and BCC. Morgan Davis is now the program assistant handling the logistics. Please correspond with Morgan going forward. If Samantha would like a meeting with me, please let's make sure either you or Morgan is in the meeting.

> Thanks for all you do. -D

Amanda felt tears on her face and closed her office door for privacy. She thanked God sincerely. She had asked God to fix it, and there he was in the fixing. David still had to explain, but she felt it would all come out this weekend. She called Leslie and Regina on a conference call.

"Oh, my goodness," Regina said, paying invoices. "I knew David wasn't in love with someone else, just confused as hell. No excuse, I'm still upset with him."

"Yes," Amanda agreed. "I'm done. I'm tired. Last night, do you know what he asked me? If I felt obligated to have sex with him?"

"Like you always have to give it up?!" Leslie asked. "No questions asked?"

"I guess. He literally asked me why I'm always willing."

"What did you say?" Regina asked.

"That I'm attracted to him and he turns me on. There is no obligation involved. When David smiles at me in the way he only can, I can't turn him down. It's the truth."

"Yes, I'm glad it is." Leslie had stopped grading papers to listen. "There is something going on with him. Just wait for him, Amanda. Too late to confront him now. He is turning around, trying to tell you something."

The women agreed with Leslie. Amanda told them about dinner and his thoughtfulness regarding the cinnamon roll.

"That meant he literally went to the store, got me one cinnamon roll, came back, and then got on the road," Amanda said.

"A man reflecting on what he has." Regina shared her thoughts. "I'm still upset, but with all that windshield time he has, it's making him do a lot of reflecting."

~

David remembered living in a two-bedroom duplex in Galesboro when he was single. He rented it from a University of Wisconsin alum in a neighborhood meant for families. It was quiet, and that is just what he wanted back then. Working retail could give him energy one day and wear him out the next. But he also remembered the lonely days he had forgotten. To think, he wanted to be single again because of other people's responses and actions. He found himself saying to himself, *Thank you, God, for helping me see my blessings before I really messed things up.*

He texted Amanda as promised and told her he would call her before he went to bed. Bruce had left a text that he needed to see him when he got home, but with all the rain, he didn't know when the Hyatt team would be behind. Amanda and Bruce—he saw their names on his phone and was proud of their relationship now, but he remembered when it made him nervous, and the night he called Bruce to ask him about her.

"Hey there. How was your day?" David asked as he stepped out of the shower. He sat on his couch with his phone on speaker.

"Yeah, it was alright. It's Monday. Too early for me to get in trouble," Bruce replied.

"I think I met one of your old girlfriends today." David went right into the conversation.

"Oh no. Who?" Bruce exclaimed. "Whatever she said, I probably did it, and I'll pay you later." Bruce was joking and laughed.

"Nothing like that. Amanda..." David was dumbfounded; he didn't get her last name. "She didn't give me her last name, but she's a beautiful, light-skinned Black girl. Says she met you at Brookview Community College. She's a cosmetics rep."

"Amanda Williams is in town?" Bruce asked with excitement. "Oh, she is sweet. She said I was her boyfriend?"

"No, I just assumed. You, a pretty woman. I was sure you and her..." David wanted Bruce to finish the sentence.

"Negative. Not at all. Not even interested. She is a good woman with a sad past. It's not even that. We met in English class, and I was into Maxine Lovefield. Now she was my trouble back then." Bruce went on about Maxine's body. Then he stopped and realized he was talking to David about a woman.

"David, you like her? You like Amanda?"

There was silence. Then David confessed, "It's been exactly twelve hours and fifteen minutes since I've laid eyes on her, and I can't stop thinking about her."

"Yeah?" Bruce wanted to know more. "Amanda is beautiful. I can only imagine what she looks like now. At twenty-two, twenty-three, she's a woman. Probably not the fragile young woman I knew."

David asked Bruce to tell him everything, and Bruce replied with a level of maturity he had forgotten his brother had.

"I can't tell you about her past. If she likes you, she'll tell you. I was sworn to secrecy in that classroom when we shared our papers, and I promised." Bruce was honest. "But Amanda came out of her shell, and she's fun. She helped me, Jeff Coffman, Marcus, and Tammi Stuart with a fraternity scavenger hunt."

Bruce told David that Amanda drove the car and was the photographer as they drove around town, taking pictures next to a list of people, places, and things. Amanda had to be the driver and photographer, only because the four of them had to be in all the pictures for it to count in the scavenger hunt. Polaroid pictures only.

"True story. On the list was taking a picture with a stripper. Amanda was the only one with the guts to go into the strip club with attitude and a lie. Before we knew it, we were taking our picture with Simone Sugar." Bruce laughed, and David remembered the picture and laughed.

"I need some advice. She is only here for the week." David came right out and laid his new fear on the table that night. "What if she is not into white guys?"

David could tell his younger brother was happy to see his older brother needing his help in the woman department again.

"David. Don't worry about race; it won't matter. Just kiss her before the end of the week." Bruce was forward.

"What?" David was shocked at his brother's response, and he grew more nervous. "That's a lot, Bruce. Amanda thinks I hate her. I came down on her pretty hard since her company left me hanging with dated products and fixtures. A kiss is just not gonna happen."

"There is a thin line between love and hate," Bruce said. "Yeah, I gave you shit about your love life in high school, but since college, you're not so uptight. I hear you are more than an average kisser and you can dance. Amanda will love you."

That she did. Bruce was right, David recalled.

Amanda could hear the tiredness in David's voice, and she encouraged him to go to bed. She, on the other hand, could not sleep. She enjoyed having the house to herself. She tried to remember the last time things had been this still. Amanda thought it had to have been when she was single, no boys, no David, no Bruce, or in-laws. She was glad that time was gone. Amanda loved family and remembered how she came to know David was more than the mean assistant store director in Galesboro.

Before David made it to the store, Amanda had Seth Hawkeye pull the cosmetic wall out from the wall and set it up to electricity. It was 7:00 am, and Amanda was all smiles because Seth had good news.

"Amanda, this whole wall has lights: we just never plugged this thing in." He was behind the cosmetic wall, pulling electrical cords.

"Seth, you've made my day!" She said.

"Amanda, my wife calls me Seth when I'm in the doghouse. Here, everyone calls me Hawkeye." Seth was in his late 30s, with blonde hair, brown eyes, a medium build, and old hands.

"Hawkeye. Thank you." Amanda was happy, then thought. "Is David gonna be mad? Expensive to keep these lights on all day?"

Hawkeye laughed. "He has that demeanor, doesn't he? But if you want my opinion, the lights are needed; these 35 feet needed some love and attention. I won't leave you hangin'. I will tell him I told you to do it."

With a few tries, Hawkeye had the wall lit. He had some night stock clerks just getting off their shift put the wall back in place, and the area looked 100 percent better in Amanda's opinion. She got an empty grocery cart and started discarding old, broken fixtures in the dumpster Hawkeye told her to use. When David came by, he had two cups of coffee in his hand.

"I like seeing progress over here." David handed her a cup of coffee.

"I'm sorry, I don't know how you take it, but it's fresh."

Amanda remembered taking the coffee with a surprised look on her face.

"Thank you. Black, two sugars," Amanda said.

David took two sugar packets out of his black pants' pocket along with two creamers. "I took a chance. After all, Bruce told me to be nice to you, Amanda Williams."

Amanda grinned. "You talked to him? Of course, you did." Her eyes rolled.

"Don't worry, he told me you were a good person. He told me I needed to come with a peace offering for my meanness yesterday, and if I ever needed to get into a strip club, to call you."

Amanda's mouth flew open. "Now, that's a funny story."

"He told me about Simone Sugar." David sipped his coffee.

Amanda laughed and caught David's smile. *Damn it*, she thought. *This man is so gorgeous*, and as the laughing died down, he looked into her eyes. She looked away before he could read her mind.

"What do you think about the lights? Hawkeye is a gem."

"Yes, Hawkeye is a good person. It brightens things up. Hope it leads people over here." David was back to talking business.

"It will. Hire a cosmetics manager, a good one, and watch and see." Amanda had her comeback.

David asked, "Do you want the job?"

"You can't afford me," Amanda sassed.

"That's probably true. Let's talk later; I've got a meeting." He winked and walked towards his office. Right there, Amanda melted inside, like a teenage girl crushing on a boy band.

By the time Regina made it over to Acuff's for lunch, Amanda had cleaned the mess she had made from the morning and had organized the cosmetic counter. The two women exchanged hugs and began walking to the Acuff restaurant, and that is when Amanda had the opportunity to introduce Regina to David.

"Hi," Regina said, shaking his hand and tucking her long black hair behind one ear, "I'm usually at one of the Acuff in Brookview, but I had to come see Amanda since she's in town for the week."

"Yeah, nice to meet you. You ladies should enjoy the patio. It is a nice fall day." David was brief and smiled at Amanda, then at Regina. He moved on to customer service to answer a call.

After Amanda and Regina ordered food and sat down at a table outside, Regina did say something and wondered if her friend noticed. "Amanda, are you awake?"

Amanda frowned at Regina as she put a straw in her water. "What do you mean?"

Regina took a deep breath and sighed. She looked at her friend, so naïve in a lot of ways, but thought she had grown in confidence. The woman she remembered as shy was no longer, but she was still innocent.

"David is so into you, he can't see straight."

"Seriously?" Amanda felt her face get hot. "You didn't see him yesterday. He was not happy. Today, he is better because his brother is Bruce Lloyd."

"Get out?! That's his brother? I can see the resemblance," Regina said.

"That doesn't matter; I saw the way he looked at you when you were looking and when you weren't."

"What does that mean?"

"Guys just have this way of looking at women they're interested in. He knows where you are at all times in this store, I bet you." Regina smiled.

Amanda kept quiet for a moment, then spoke. "Okay. I feel a certain way about him. I can't even describe it. My whole body does this quiver; what is that? When he smiles, I literally cannot see straight, and his take-charge attitude around here is attractive."

"What are you going to do about it?" Regina grinned, asking her.

"Nothing," Amanda said, "because I don't know what to do."

"That's not true. Against my better judgment, you had this six-month thing with Colin. That's over, right?" Regina was direct.

"Yes," Amanda was certain. "I should never have fallen for him."

"True. Be honest with me..." Regina looked at her friend now as her sister. "Are you okay emotionally? Mentally? Nightmare wise? They always seem to happen after major changes." She reached for Amanda's hand.

The server came by and gave them their salads. Amanda allowed him to leave, and then she answered.

"The breakup with Colin was mutual, so I don't feel any loss." Amanda was confident. "It's been two years since I've cut myself. I'm just lonely."

Amanda remembered that she and Regina enjoyed their lunch that day. They laughed as they told old stories. Amanda shared how Bruce told

David about the fraternity scavenger hunt and how she hadn't thought about Coffman in years. Both wondered what he was doing these days. Regina confessed she was slow to set a date to marry Greg, but she was happy they were engaged.

"All the more reason for me to move home," Amanda said.

"What?" Regina didn't see this conversation coming.

"I miss it here. You can't plan your wedding without me being close. I thought after Janice was gone, I'd need a change. I did. But I miss small towns. I hate that it takes a half hour to battle traffic, and I'm a single black woman in St. Louis. I'm careful of my surroundings. Don't worry, I live in a nice area, protected, but it's a city."

"I get it," Regina said. "So I say, allow David to pursue you. Accept every nice gesture. Do your job and only answer the questions he asks."

Amanda had the look of a teenage girl and was feeling like one. "Okay."

"Let him kiss you." Regina was sure.

"Oh, Regina. I'm here for three more days," Amanda doubted.

"Trust me, get prepared. Bruce didn't hang out with us a lot back then, but I know they're good people."

Regina gathered her purse and keys. "David seems more conservative, but loyal. Hard working, caring, and has a career. He can take care of you. Not that you can't take care of yourself, but a woman needs a man. A man needs a woman."

"Regina, I just met *this* man. I'm standing in day two." Amanda got nervous. "Is it okay that he is white?"

Regina and Amanda rose to leave, and Regina pressed her lips together to hold back her laughter.

"Amanda, you're half white. Did you forget your first mom was a white woman? Sure, your skin is tan, but embrace everything about yourself."

CHAPTER 13

$\mathcal{A}$s David walked the aisles of the Acuff stores he now managed, he couldn't help but remember how he learned of Amanda's past. Pausing in the cosmetics aisle and running his hands across the cosmetic fixtures, he was convinced that if he had remembered that day and the ones that followed, he never would have gone with Sam to her hotel. He would have gone home.

He remembered it as if it were yesterday. By Wednesday of that week, Acuff was remarkably busy. There was a weather report for snow Friday into Saturday, and that always caused an increase in customer traffic. David remembered Amanda making the cosmetic/health and beauty care area of the store clean and accessible as she continued the reset. She was kind enough to call the other cosmetic companies to update their sections in the weeks to come, and she organized the counter to the point where customers were asking questions and buying items.

After lunch, he went to check in on her. She was in a black t-shirt, hair up, and fighting to get a fixture to adhere to the cosmetic wall. Just when he was going to offer help, the fixture and the wall made their connection, and he noticed the bruises on her upper arms, as if someone had violently grabbed her arms and squeezed hard. They broke the blood vessels, causing these black and blue rings around her petite arms. His heart felt sad; his mind angry.

"Are you okay?" David asked before he knew it.

"Yeah," she replied regarding the fixture. "These boxes can be tricky, but after a couple of tries, they snap right in."

Suddenly, Amanda realized David was staring at her arms. She quickly put her cosmetic jacket back on and stated she was fine.

"Amanda, who did that to you?" David was concerned. "I can help you."

"David, I am fine." She was stern as she looked into his brown eyes so deeply that David had to blink. He saw her despair, and he was silent.

David quietly walked away and went straight to his office, shut the door, and sat down. He remembered what Bruce told him—*Good woman, sad past*. He didn't know what he was thinking, but he felt sadness, anger, and helplessness. *Stop*, he remembered telling himself. He didn't have to get involved; he just met Amanda. She doesn't live here. Not your problem. But he knew better.

He put his head down and pretended he was reading invoices just in case someone passed by his office window. David prayed for God to help her, guide her, and protect her. He prayed that if there was a way he was supposed to help, God would allow and bless it. David prayed for the connection he felt with her and asked that it would bring God honor. Whether he was supposed to be in Amanda's life for a season or a lifetime, he decided he would get involved.

First, he would give Amanda space. David spent the rest of the day helping on the front end of the store and informing the store director, Tom Cochran, of the happenings while he had been away on vacation. It was after 5:00 when he got the page to come to the pharmacy. With Tom back, he was ready to go home. But when he saw Amanda in the consultation room, with her arms wrapped around herself, squeezing the very places of her bruises, he realized he wasn't going home. Amanda's wounds were self-inflicted.

"What happened?!" David tried to be calm, but couldn't help but be stunned. There were at least three employees around besides Hawkeye and Emily Shepard, the store's human resource coordinator.

Hawkeye told David the story. Amanda was in the supply closet, and the door closed by itself, which made the light turn off, and she panicked. Hawkeye said he heard her crying for help. When he opened the door and turned the light on, he saw her sitting on the floor in a ball with her arms around herself. When she saw him, she got up, hugged him, and realized she was in the present.

"I walked her over to the pharmacy in the only private room I could think of," Hawkeye replied. "She said she was fine, but you know…"

David patted him on the shoulder. "Thank you. Go home." He looked around at the rest of the employees.

"If you are not Emily, go. We have a store full of customers, and I need you to do your jobs. Ms. Williams will be fine." With that authority in his voice, employees scattered, and Emily—a short, brown-haired, red-rimmed glasses-wearing, full-figured woman—was the only one standing in front of him.

"Em," which was her nickname given to her by him. "Now what?"

"Nothing," Emily stated. "Amanda is adamant that the store is not responsible for her panic attack. She says she was not hurt. I'm filing an incident report to note that it happened. She is not an employee of the store, but we will make sure the supply closet door doesn't lock behind a person, and the light needs to stay on." Emily left, and David was left looking at Amanda through the consultant room window.

"I'm going to go in and talk to her; take her blood pressure." David heard Karla's voice behind him.

"Thank the Lord you are here," David replied. Dr. Karla Peterson was a physician with the Southern County Urgent Care clinic, housed in Acuff, to provide medical care for non-life-threatening illnesses or injuries. David did not know Karla well but respected her presence in the store. He guessed she had to be in her 50s, with short blonde hair, light eyes, and medium height. She patted his shoulder, and from his peripheral vision, he recognized Regina heading his way. He took a deep breath.

"Is she okay?" Regina asked, now in front of him.

"Yes, she seems to be. I haven't talked to her yet," David said. "Can I get you something? Water…"

"No," Regina declined. "She called me, and she was calm but wanted me to come."

"Of course." David told Regina what happened, and she nodded her head in understanding.

"The door closing brought back painful memories," Regina explained to him.

"And the bruises?" David wanted to know. "She does that to herself?" They were now sitting alone in the pharmacy's waiting area.

Regina closed her eyes with a nod. "We talked about that yesterday, but she assured me they were three weeks old." Regina was remembered and then abruptly stopped talking.

David caught on. "Regina, I care about Amanda. For the life of me, I don't completely understand my feelings here, but I want to know so I can help her. That's all."

Regina sighed, reassured that she could keep talking. "Yesterday, Amanda said the medication she was on for depression was giving her violent nightmares of being scared, and she was hurting herself in her sleep. Since being off the meds for three weeks, she has been fine. I believe her; she wouldn't lie to me."

David saw Karla leave the consultation room. He stood up and introduced her to Regina.

"Amanda has post-traumatic stress disorder, known as PTSD. That supply closet door closing triggered it. She is okay now. Her blood pressure is high, and I'm not comfortable with her driving or moving from here for at least 30 minutes. She needs to be completely calm. She told me to leave her there to pray," Karla said. "I'll do whatever it takes to bring her pressure down. I am going to get her a blood pressure machine so she can take her pressure herself when she gets to the hotel. She says she is here on business."

"Yes," David confirmed. "Working here in the store on the cosmetic reset."

"I see," Karla said. "Well, no work at all tomorrow. She needs rest. I took her cell phone."

Karla handed the phone to Regina. "She may be here working on a cosmetic reset, but her mind is in three other places; it does not stop buzzing and chirping."

Regina stared at Amanda's cell phone. Of course, the latest phone with so many capabilities at her fingertips.

David and Regina talked about Amanda and her plans for the rest of the week, while she rested in the consultation room. As soon as Regina could, she visited with Amanda. David went back to his office for a moment and called Bruce.

"Hey there, checking in," David started.

"How's it going? Kissed her yet?" Bruce was carefree, and David wasn't.

"It's Wednesday." He didn't feel like unloading about his day onto his brother just yet. "I wanted to let someone know I won't be home this weekend. If the snow comes in like they are predicting, I need to be close to the store. I know Dad was looking forward to watching college game day football on Saturday, and Mom and Bill wanted a Sunday dinner since I had the weekend off, but there's a change of plans."

"Yeah, I get it," Bruce said, but heard anxiousness in his brother's voice. "You okay?"

David sighed. "Bruce, when I tell you it has been a day, it has been a day. This store has been an absolute zoo. I'll stay in touch." When he got off the phone, he paged Corey from the front end to call him. His office phone immediately rang.

"Yes, sir." David could tell Corey was at customer service.

"I need serious Corey right now. The one I hired that is reliable, discreet, and responsible." Corey laughed and then stopped. He now knew this was serious.

"David, you can count on me."

"Good. I need you to stop joking around so much. You're too smart for the bullshit."

Now Corey really knew he was serious. "David, man, what's up?"

David got Corey and another shift manager to drive his car to the hotel where Amanda was staying and then drive themselves back to the store. He then insisted Regina needed to go home.

"Please, it's getting late. Go home. I don't want your fiancé to worry about you being on the road at night." David was genuine.

"What is it about Amanda for you?" Regina asked. "You have altered your entire night. I can only guess what tomorrow looks like."

David had to think about her question, and he was honest. "I don't know her story, but somehow we clicked."

Regina smiled. "A connection. That's what Amanda said." David settled inside. Yes, he thought. She felt it too.

Regina held his hand. "I love her like my own sister. She has comforted me, protected me, and guided me. She is good, but has lost so much. If your care for her is self-motivated, then you go home. I've taken care of Amanda more than once; it has been my pleasure to do it."

"No, you go home. I want to help. My help is not self-motivated; it comes from a place of concern. I have feelings for her. They are not ones of sympathy; Bruce refused to tell me anything about that area of her life. I'm glad he didn't. That English class must have been quite something."

David and Regina exchanged phone numbers. She gave him Amanda's phone, and David walked Regina to her car. He then went back to Amanda at the pharmacy.

"How is she?" David asked Karla.

"Much better. Blood pressure is normal. I'm glad she got to talk to Regina. She needs to rest, not work, for a few days." Karla went back into the clinic area.

David looked at Amanda in the consultation room before opening the door. She was sitting up, looking at the wall, waiting, and then turned and saw David. He opened the door.

She put her head down.

"Don't do that." He whispered. "There is nothing to be embarrassed about."

"Okay," she said quietly. "I'm sorry, I was mean today. I was upset when you saw my arms."

"I understand. We don't have to talk about that now." David wanted to keep her calm. "I am ready to drive you to your hotel. Dr. Peterson says *No Work*. She wants that blood pressure to stay normal. Nothing needs to upset you."

Amanda nodded, and she rose from sitting, gathered her bag and purse, handed David her keys, and they left.

The car ride was quiet, except for a small conversation about the weather and how it was so nice out there now, but might turn into five inches of snow within 48 hours. He walked her into the hotel lobby and watched her pull out her key card. He was prepared to say goodnight.

"David," she said so tenderly. "I don't want you to go." She extended her hand.

David took her hand, and she led him through the outdoor courtyard and to her door. When she opened the door, it was like an apartment.

The living room resembled the hotel lobby with a full kitchen and a desk. The bedroom and the bathroom were two separate rooms.

She spoke. "I don't want you to feel uncomfortable, but I really want to talk to you."

David wanted to talk to her, too. For that matter, he just wanted to be in her presence.

"Okay," he said. "How about I make you some tea while you take a shower?" He now felt uncomfortable. "I meant while you get ready to go to bed."

She caught his awkwardness, and she blushed. "Yeah, I'll be back."

David began hunting in the kitchen for the kettle to boil hot water or something to put water in for the microwave. He called Regina to ensure she made it home safely and told her Amanda made it to the hotel. He certainly didn't tell her he was there, but assured her he would check on her tomorrow.

After twenty minutes, Amanda came out with damp curly hair, wearing a *Wake Up and Smell the Coffee* gray t-shirt and flannel pajama pants. David smiled inside; he thought she looked adorable and attractive.

He handed her a mug of hot water and a variety of teas to choose from. He made himself a glass of ice water.

"Thank you." She was still quiet and took a chamomile tea packet and invited him to sit down on the sectional in the living area. He allowed her to sit in the corner of the sectional, and she sat with her feet under her. He sat across from her.

There was silence for a minute. "I was a foster kid, in and out of the system since I was six years old. I started out in an orphanage, in and out of foster care homes, lugging everything I cared about in a single black trash bag," Amanda said, steeping her tea bag in the hot water.

David listened, though he was hurting inside.

"I was finally in a safe home when I was twelve. It took Janice Williams two years to adopt me. She was alone in the world, too, and we gave each other life. I am so grateful, David, to have known her and to call her mom. She taught me so much about life, human decency, love and loss, God and Jesus, womanhood, and caring for people. To me, she hung the moon."

Amanda was in tears now. David offered her the box of tissues from the coffee table.

"Thank you. Four years ago, when I was 18, she died of cancer." Amanda continued to cry.

David said softly, "I'm sorry, Amanda." He wanted to touch her, but something told him not to. He thought to himself, to be 22 in this world alone, with no relatives. Unimaginable.

"The good news is Janice was smart and saved money for me to go to college, and there were scholarships and grants available for me to attend college for free, thanks to people who knew my situation." Amanda continued. "But before Janice, life was dark."

"I was nine years old." Amanda sipped her tea and swallowed hard. "I was in my bed in the orphanage, asleep, sharing a room with my 13-year-old friend Stacy. A man in dark clothing came into our room, dragged me out of bed, and threw me in the closet. He shut the door."

Amanda had her eyes closed, trying to remember. David now understood.

"He then slapped Stacy. I heard it, and I opened the closet door to find him on top of her, so I screamed and tried to help her. The man punched me in the stomach, threw me back in the closet, and shut the door. I hit my head on an object in the closet. I don't know what it was, but it knocked me out. I never gained consciousness until I was in the hospital. When I woke up, my body told the rest of the story."

Amanda took a deep breath and yet remained calm. She was used to telling the story now.

David had his eyes closed for a moment to hold back anger, sadness, and tears.

Amanda continued. "He broke my jaw, gave me a black eye, and I was bruised. My body hurt everywhere."

Amanda did remember. "He raped Stacy first and beat her until she was unconscious. I was unconscious, and he raped me. I was nine. My innocence was gone. It took my body two years to heal."

David was literally speechless. He couldn't think of a single thing that could make what he just heard disappear from his mind.

"David, I don't remember the rape at all. I just know it happened because of my body. Stacy and I were separated. This was a human-trafficking situation. The plan was for him to take us and make us sex slaves, but this man was strung out on drugs and was not in a good frame of mind, obviously."

"They found Ms. Wilson, the orphanage director, dead at the bottom of the stairs, with a broken neck from her fall. It was a plan gone badly for the *organization*." Amanda put one hand in the air to symbolize quotes.

"As I got older and foster families wanted to understand my trauma, no one could find Stacy. I'm sure they told Stacy that no one could find me. Human trafficking is real, David. Police aren't always the good guys. When I was put in a foster family, I stopped asking questions. I went along to get along, and then Janice and I found each other."

Amanda repositioned herself. She put her tea on the coffee table and put her feet on the floor.

"I wanted to tell you why I panicked today. It triggered a memory I hadn't remembered in years. The supply closet door closing got to me. I pray I didn't scare Hawkeye too badly, and I'm terribly sorry I snapped at you." Amanda took his hand.

"My doctor in St. Louis wanted me to try some antidepressants for my loneliness and sadness. All it did was give me dreams where I was afraid and scared. I'd wake up with bruises on my arms and scratches on my thighs. I'm embarrassed by it."

"Don't be," David continued to hold her hand. "Amanda, I'm sorry for your loss. I'm sorry for every pain and suffering you remember and the pain you don't remember. I feel honored and blessed that you've trusted me with this precious, tender part of you."

David could tell he had said the right thing because Amanda let out a breath, and it was a true release for her. Because he held her hand, he felt tension leave her body. He rose, still holding her hand, and led her to the doorway of her bedroom.

"Go to bed." He let go of her hand. He took her cell phone out of his pocket and gave it to her. "I put my number in there, and I will call you tomorrow." David was pleasant.

"Thank you."

"Oh, I need to give you some directives." He was matter-of-fact but smiling. "Take not one phone call or message before 9:00 am. Calvin's text messages on your fancy phone would drive me to drink heavily. Send him one message that you aren't taking his messages. He won't die without you for a couple of days."

"After I call you, put that phone on silent. Nothing else will be important after that." He smiled, and Amanda smiled.

"Yes, sir," she said, laughing.

David walked to the door and closed it behind him.

CHAPTER 14

manda remembered waking up at that extended stay, feeling good. There were no nightmares, no fear, and today she wasn't missing Janice; she was remembering her. Amanda's sharing of childhood memories with David, combined with his listening and validation, put her at ease.

She heard her phone buzz next to her on the nightstand. She remembered the directions David had given her. It was only 8:30, but it was Regina.

"Hi!" Amanda remembered being happy.

"Good morning, baby girl. How are you feeling today?" Regina asked, still a bit concerned.

Amanda shared that she and David had talked, and she told him about the rape and how she appreciated his response. She even told Regina that David told her not to answer her phone before 9:00, but she figured she was an exception.

"Good." Regina was smiling now. "I told you, David cares about you. And..." Amanda waited. She knew Regina talked to David alone.

Regina stayed silent as long as she could. "He said he felt you two have a connection. He feels it."

Amanda was giddy, but tried not to be too obvious. "Thank you; I'm glad. Nothing worse than thinking someone is into you, and they are not."

"He is into you," Regina said confidently. "Do you know Bruce said nothing to his own brother about your past? I mean nothing. David said he was glad he didn't. That goes to show you who the Lloyds are."

"Yes," Amanda said. "So I get to enjoy the extended stay today. It will be hard not to respond to Calvin, but I promised David I would not. Honestly, I feel good..."

Regina interrupted her friend. "Amanda, I'm pregnant."

"Oh Regina! That's so wonderful! Are you excited?" Amanda sat up in bed.

"Well...yes, but I was hoping to be married to Greg. My mother has a frown that I'm sure you can see from two counties. I'm so vain, my wedding plans have accelerated to the ninth degree."

Amanda knew Regina's parents were strict and devout Christians. She understood Regina's feelings. "I get it. Here I am going on and on about my life. I'm sorry."

"No, it is alright. Greg and I will figure it out," Regina sighed.

"Regina?" Amanda said. She heard her friend respond, but she remained silent for a moment more. "Can I say what I think?"

"Of course," Regina waited.

"Get married now. Go to the courthouse, fill out the paperwork, get the marriage license, and get married on paper. Greg proposed six months ago in the park, orchestrating an evening picnic under the stars with no prompting from you. He is so in love with you and you with him that there is now a baby on the way. This is not an *oops*; you two love each other, and it is for life."

Amanda continued. "Find an apartment right away for your new family. Then, celebrate the love of Regina and Greg. Invite whoever you want, and ask for gifts that will support you, Greg, and the baby. Don't do what everybody else does; hide and pretend. Spend money on a reception where you can't drink, where your parents invite people you don't know, and you have ridiculous expenses."

There was silence. Then Regina spoke. "How do you do that?"

Amanda could tell her friend was crying.

"Amanda, how is it that you are so innocent and seemingly naïve one minute, and then in one moment, you can offer up this wisdom of someone well beyond your years? You are so right. I would hate for my baby to ask me in years to come if they were wanted or an accident. Even though I would say *you were wanted*, my actions of a shotgun wedding would make him or her feel otherwise.

"Regina, let me help you. It will give me something else to do besides focusing on lipstick, mascara, and being bossed around by Calvin."

Amanda laughed, looking at her phone and noticing three messages from him.

"Okay," Regina agreed.

"Now go talk to Greg and get his thoughts. Call me later?" Amanda got out of bed.

"Okay," Regina said, and changed the subject. "Just so you know, your whole weekend has been planned."

"Excuse me?"

"David is coming over tonight to cook dinner for you, and there will be a double date with Greg and me tomorrow night," Regina said proudly. "But act surprised, okay?"

Amanda was grinning. "I feel like those girls in those teen movies we used to watch."

"Good; you deserve it, baby girl."

Regina and Amanda said their goodbyes, and Amanda got in the shower, dressed, and sent Calvin a text saying she was sick. She then called Trisha Winters.

"Trisha, this is Amanda Williams with *Ana*. How are you?"

"Amanda! I am so sorry. I got your message about the Acuff store in Galesboro, but I was promoted at Hindley, and it has been one thing after another," Trisha said.

Trisha and Amanda had a basic professional relationship, working with one another by seeing each other in the field and at new store openings. Trisha shared that Hindley had decided not to fill her old field position.

"Yes, *Ana* will not be replacing Lisa."

"So there is a plan, isn't there?" Amanda replied.

"Yes. The powers that be don't want to say yet, but they are going to give these small-town accounts to a brokerage firm to handle. They can't afford the expense of a salary and travel versus how much places like Acuff sell in product." Trisha said. "They will treat cosmetics just like the health and beauty care sections."

"Simple enough," Amanda said. "Do you know which brokerage firm?"

"Augusta Retail," Trisha said. "Confidential."

Amanda finally said what she was thinking, now even more so with Regina being pregnant. "I'm looking to get out of *Ana*."

"I see, and I understand. Traveling alone, I'm sure, is challenging. Look up Norah Livingstone with Augusta Retail online. She is a good person; you won't regret it."

Amanda and Trisha continued to talk about options to stock the Galesboro store, promised to keep in touch, and then ended the call.

Amanda found herself emotionally exhausted. When she thought about the week, she had done a lot and felt a lot. Fully clothed, she got back into bed.

David was business as usual in the store, but his mind was on Amanda. With what she shared last night, he was taken aback by her maturity and strength. It just made her more attractive. Yes, he noticed the outer beauty first, but she had that good, sweet, caring inner beauty he loved to be in the presence of. While he was in his office, Emily was filing papers next to him.

"Em, I need advice." He thought he was being casual. "Amanda Williams."

Emily smiled. "Thank God you said her name before I was going to say something. The sparks that have been flying around here all week between the two of you!"

"What?" David gave that handsome smile.

"That smile right there makes all the female cashiers on the front end swoon and makes Amanda blush."

"This tells me that no one really does hard work here if everyone is watching me." David got a bit defensive.

"David, you have been out on the floor this week more than I can ever remember."

"I am always out on the floor. Tom has been on vacation, so of course I'm out here doing more," David explained.

"True. But this week it was different. You have been more personable, more solution-oriented, and I saw you bring her coffee and watch her work. Yesterday, when Corey drove your car to her hotel, and then Monty drove him back here, I knew you drove her home."

Emily had a face that showed she was lost in the romance of his actions.

"Em, are you done?" He was trying to keep from blushing, but it was too late.

"Look at you. You're asking me for advice. I haven't been on a real date in a couple of years," Emily admitted.

"We have to fix that," David said.

"So how can I help you?" She looked at him, all smiles. "I love this. Flowers?"

"Steaks," David said with a straight face.

"Oh." Emily was taken aback. "Help me understand."

"I need to get groceries for the extended stay because I am going to cook for her tonight. I thought of grilling steaks, but I do not know if the extended stay has a grill. It is a lot to think about if the grill is right outside her area."

"David." Emily shook her head in approval. "We are Acuff. We can make this happen. Make the list, and I will make sure the groceries get delivered. We have a catering truck. I think you have to come with flowers—not roses, that is too forward, but something that says, *I like you*."

"Okay," David agreed.

"We sell grills. At least we did this summer. If we still have one, I'll have Corey get someone to put it together. But I'll call the extended stay; you never know what they have."

Emily felt like she was on a mission.

"If you are going to call the extended stay, I need a room," David said with no emotion.

Emily's face turned red. David looked at her. "Listen, this has nothing to do with Amanda. If we have a snowstorm, you know I will never make it out of my cul-de-sac residential neighborhood. I need it on Friday and Saturday."

"I understand." Emily then turned serious. She finished filing the last of her paperwork in silence and then said, "David, I'm happy for you."

"Thanks, Em." David knew Emily cared, as she was a divorced, single mom, and saw him as her brother.

David waited until Emily was well on her way with his grocery list and grill mission, then he called Amanda.

"Hi," Amanda said, sounding sleepy.

"I am so glad you are resting, but I am sorry I woke you," he said.

"It is okay," she said, smiling. "I've done basically nothing all day."

"Perfect," he laughed.

"How is the store?" She asked.

Thoughtful, David thought. "Just fine. Insel Cosmetics came in today and updated its section. They said you called them. Thank you."

"It's the least I can do." He heard Amanda's sincerity.

"Well, I'm also calling to say I would like to cook dinner for us." David was asking without asking a question.

"Really?!" she sounded excited. "I'd love that. You cook?"

"I do." David was honest. "It was a requirement if I was going to eat with my family."

"Oh, okay. You'll have to tell me the story," she said.

"I will do that. So, in about an hour, the groceries will be delivered. One day, delivering groceries will be no big deal, but today the Acuff catering truck is coming," he chuckled.

Just as he was ending the conversation, Emily came in the doorway with a Fall bouquet. Orange daisies and lilies, with two white roses and red-orange fall berries. He gave her the thumbs up, and she handed him the card and a pen.

"So how does 4:30-5:00 pm sound? If I say that out loud, I will get help to get out of here on time." He looked at Emily.

"Perfect." Amanda hung up.

David wrote on the card, *See you soon.* D. "Simple, right?"

Emily nodded yes.

Amanda opened her door to the two people from the Acuff catering staff. She was impressed with what they were putting away in the kitchen—fruits, vegetables, seasonings, eggs, flour, and sugar. David was going to cook. By the way they were acting, they were doing exactly what David instructed them to do. Amanda was curious.

"Do you like David? The way he bosses you all around." She asked.

"Oh, Ms. Williams, it's not like that." One of the men said. "David cares about us. He tells us to *do it right the first time*, and he has helped me. We are family at the store. There was no one in my family to teach me how to drive. David did."

Amanda wasn't surprised. She let them continue with their task of unloading groceries. As the housecleaning staff came, she let them clean, and she sat in the courtyard across from her room.

"Are you serious?" Amanda said when she saw Corey with a brand-new grill, placing it next to her door.

"David is something else," Corey laughed. "I put it together myself." He touched his chest proudly.

"I don't even know what to say." Amanda smiled.

"David uses all his resources. I guess you like older men? My boss is easy on the eyes, but you could've let me down gently. I shouldn't have found out this way," Corey laughed.

Amanda laughed. "Corey, you are the nicest. Thanks for crushing on me. I'm flattered."

Then Corey handed her the flowers. "I wish I could say they are from me, but David is all class."

Amanda remembered thinking about what David loved: He loved Acuff, his employees, the customers, and what he was able to do for them. He was devoted to his work and his family.

"Well, tell him thank you. The grill?"

Corey laughed. "Oh no, that grill stays here. David bought it for the extended stay, courtesy of Acuff."

"Of course, he did." Amanda was getting to know David.

~

When he came to the door in jeans and a button-down navy-blue gingham shirt, she said hi, but she stood there for a few seconds staring at him. He stared right back as she had on jeans and an oversized chiffon yellow blouse.

"You're not in black." There was that smile that drove her crazy. "You look nice."

"Thank you," she said. "And you are not in black slacks and a white dress shirt."

He blushed as she allowed him in, and that's when she noticed the gift. It was a wine bag. He handed it to her. "Regina said you like red. I do too, but when I cook, I need a beer."

David went straight into the kitchen, opened the refrigerator, and grabbed a beer.

"What else did Regina say?" Amanda watched him in the kitchen as she sat on the barstool and watched him open the beer.

"Real food. Nothing processed. No ketchup, no box or microwavable macaroni and cheese. You are allergic to mangoes, but you love bacon. That fact that you love bacon makes me so happy." He took the bacon out of the refrigerator and put it on the counter.

"Ms. Amanda, what are you drinkin'?" He began unbuttoning his gingham shirt to reveal his basic white t-shirt. Amanda watched him put the shirt on the back of the desk chair.

"I have to drink with the chef. Beer."

David got her a beer, opened it, and gave it to her.

He grabbed his beer and put it in the air to offer a toast. "To us getting to know each other."

She smiled, and their beer bottles touched.

"Okay, so can I be the sous chef?" Amanda asked.

"Of course." David shared how he puts the salad plates in the refrigerator to chill. He pre-heated the oven and pulled out stuffed mushrooms and sweet peppers for appetizers. He went outside the door to start the grill. When he came back in, Amanda was opening the bacon and placing it on a foil-covered cookie sheet, per his instructions.

"That's fabulous." He said to her as he put the mushrooms and sweet peppers in the oven. "When I was ten years old, my parents divorced. My dad had a mistress for years and decided to leave us with our mom. One day, he was home; the next day, he wasn't. That was how I saw it as a boy, but I'm sure looking back, there was a progression only known to my parents." He leaned against the kitchen counter, finishing his beer.

"My dad and his girlfriend, Sheila, had their place; Mom had our place. Divorced, you go back and forth. After a year, Sheila leaves. By the time my dad figured his life out, Mom and Bill, my stepfather, were a thing. They married, and to this day they live on his farm, which has been in his family for generations."

Amanda took all that in and thought, *Everyone has a story. The sweet parts, the sour ones.* She could tell David made everything sound so clinical, but she felt emotions yet to be uncovered.

David continued. "My dad's broken heart was healed by cooking. Bruce and I learned right along with him. There was no money to eat out, so if we wanted to eat, we had to cook."

"That is good. You learned how to cook." Amanda finished the bacon. David pulled the mushrooms and peppers out of the oven and put the cookie sheet with bacon in. Amanda could not help it; he bent over to open the oven, *his ass in those jeans. Damn it,* she thought.

"Yes, and these stuffed mushrooms with bacon are an Acuff favorite of mine. These sweet peppers are wrapped in bacon. Bacon in the oven for our salads... see, I love bacon." He was happy, Amanda noticed.

He cut a little piece of the stuffed mushroom, moved close to her, and put it up to her mouth to feed it to her. Amanda felt warm in the face as she opened her mouth and took the mushroom. She closed her eyes to savor the taste and the moment.

"Is that cream cheese?" Amanda exclaimed. "Wow! That is good. Really good."

"I know, right?" David said. Amanda could feel his nervousness; his innocence in giving her food to try was on his face, and she knew he wasn't trying to seduce her, but there they were. She changed the subject.

"I completely took your advice." She finished her beer. "I sent Calvin one text message today versus his seven. I simply told him I was sick."

"Good for you. He sounds intense. I know I can be a hard ass, but really? How much talk can there be around mascara? Ew, was that sexiest?" David asked.

Amanda laughed and was reminded of Colin. "You sound like my old boyfriend, who was an avid hunter. Apparently, you can buy dirt wafers. You put them in a bag with your hunting clothes so the deer won't pick up your scent. I told him, if he can buy dirt wafers, I can talk about mascara and lip gloss as long as I want." David agreed.

They laughed, cooked together, and shared fun stories about themselves. As David would reach over her or brush against her, she could smell hints of his aftershave and masculinity. He was a man. She could tell he loved being in charge, being an authority figure, strong, smart, and confident. Yet, she saw his softness and caring nature.

He showed Amanda how to make lettuce wedge salad with fresh bacon, Hasselback potatoes, and the key to a good steak was a hot grill. Since the extended stay did not have a table but a bar with stools, they ate there. They positioned themselves so they could see each other and enjoy dinner and each other's company.

"David, this was wonderful. Thank you." Amanda poured more wine. "I don't think anyone has cooked dinner for me like this."

"Great, I'm glad you liked it. You deserve it. I hope you are feeling better." He held her hand. He noticed they were finished eating and helped her down off the bar stool. "Can I?" He didn't let go of her hand.

Amanda's eyes said yes. David pulled her into him and put his arms around her. Amanda placed her head on his chest, her hands on his muscular, strong back. His hands were on her lower back.

"Ever since last night," he whispered, "I've wanted to hug you; comfort you."

"Thank you." Amanda meant that and allowed the hug to last as long as he wanted it to. His arms felt good. She closed her eyes and took him in —his smell, his hands on her.

He released her and looked in her eyes. Then he got embarrassed, looked away for a moment, and then back in her eyes. "Ah, Amanda. You leave me with no words to say except, You are beautiful."

Amanda blushed, looked away from their eye contact, but he took her chin and lifted it. "I hope today and every day I get to spend with you, that you would feel appreciated and honored. You deserve it, not only because of your past hurt, but because you are a good woman."

David placed his lips on hers without a single sound.

Amanda opened her eyes and sighed with quiet pleasure. The tension in the room lifted. She gave him his wine; she took hers and invited him to sit on the sectional.

"Dishes later, okay?"

"Yes. After Regina explained your dessert preferences, I was completely confused, but I have an idea that we can discuss later." David purposely sat in the corner of the sectional this time with his left arm resting on the back of the arm of the couch so she could curl into him, and that is exactly what she did.

"Regina tells me we have a double date tomorrow?" Amanda loved this position.

"And so much for me asking you to dinner tomorrow with friends," he said, taking a sip of wine, smiling and shaking his head. "You women have got to let a man lead." He leaned forward for a moment, just to put the wineglass down.

"We do," she whined. "Regina told me before I could state my plans. I'm a planner. I wanna know stuff way in advance."

"I'll remember that." David now had his left arm on her left shoulder, confirming he liked her there. "I don't want you to think I'm stalking you, but after Friday's dinner, I'll be staying here. I mean, at the extended stay."

"Okay?" Amanda questioned. David explained about the potential snowstorm, where he lived, and his ability to get to the store. "I understand, but I thought you had the weekend off?"

David smirked. "It says that on paper, but we are salaried and in retail management, well..."

"I already know..." Amanda piped in. "I worked a stint managing a dress shop. No thank you."

"I decided when I came in here yesterday and saw this was like an apartment, and it is close to the store," he said.

"You love your job." Amanda was confirming. "The employees love you."

David didn't deny it. "They are my family."

"I see that. Corey played like he was disappointed that he and I didn't *get together*, but he was joking. The pride he had when he showed up with the grill; priceless."

David smiled. "He is a good person. Reminds me so much of Bruce. Amanda, I remember the day I decided to work for Acuff. It was with indignation."

"Really?" She wanted to know more.

"Yes. I was 14 when I started working there with my friend, Brad Frahm. When my mom married Bill, I was pissed and confused. My dad was finally humble, but it was too late for him to get back with my mom. She was with a good guy, but secretly, I wanted my parents back together."

"I get that," Amanda said.

"So when Bill put us to work on his farm, I did the chores, but I didn't like it. I got a job that would get me out of cleaning up after chickens and building stuff."

"At first, all I did at Acuff was sack groceries and clean the bathrooms. Here I am, 11 years later, an assistant store director."

"David, that's amazing," Amanda remembered being immensely proud of him. "I was ready for you to tell me you were 30."

David played with her hair. "Just had to grow up fast. When my dad left, at my mom's, I was the man of the house. I took that to heart. Maybe a little too much."

They sat in silence for a bit. Amanda remembered enjoying every bit of David's embrace.

Amanda finally got up and turned the television on after David said something about the weather. Even though she had nothing waiting for her in St. Louis, she had to think about getting home, and David wanted to know if the store was prepared.

"It's just Thursday night, but tomorrow the store will be insane. You can say two inches of snow around here, and it is like the end of the world." He began gathering the dishes in the kitchen.

"Oh, I know," Amanda said. "It looks like it is going to hit this area pretty hard, though. I will need to extend my stay." Amanda went over to the desk and pulled the car rental contract out, exposing her resume.

"Darn," David teased her. Of course, he wanted her to stay. He hugged her from behind, planted a kiss on her cheek, and noticed the resume. "You're tired, aren't you? Of what you are doing now?"

Amanda saw him look at her resume. She confessed that St. Louis was good for a time, but she was sad, depressed, and still mourning the death of her adopted mom. "Something I need to pray about," Amanda said, and saw David smile differently.

CHAPTER 15

David arrived at Acuff early. He wanted to catch the night stock manager, Dan, before he left for the day to make sure his crew had stocked the shelves fully. The storm was on track to leave Galesboro with five to six inches of snow, and David wanted to be prepared.

Corey had already put a full palette of ice melt up front; storm rugs were already laid to prevent slips and falls in the front entrance. Shovels, hats, gloves, and ice scrapers were all on the front end.

He gave David a high-five. "The front end is winterized."

"Looks good." David was glad to see him proactive.

"How's Ms. Amanda?" Corey elbowed him.

"Just fine. We had a nice dinner. I need to say it again; thank you. You went above and beyond; you didn't have to," David told him.

"But I did, though. You've been there for me like now because I need twenty dollars for my dry cleaning," Corey teased, and David laughed.

David walked through the store doing a quick assessment, but his mind was on Amanda. Last night was perfect, he thought. Not too much, too soon. The kiss was soft, the hug and cuddling sincere. He loved how teachable she was; she let him show her things, and she listened. Most of all, Amanda was humble. She didn't have to be in charge to display her confidence. He even respected that she didn't kiss him back. His heart smiled to know she was praying, and she wanted to move back to the area.

It was 9:00 am when he saw Amanda with two coffees in her hand. She stood before him in her black outfit, sunglasses, gloss on her lips, and her bag across her body. Completely sexy, David thought, and how comfortable he would feel kissing her.

"Good morning," she said pleasantly. "Me, medium roast black coffee and two sugars. You, dark roast, two French vanilla creamers."

"Thank you," he smiled. "How'd you know?"

"Emily is amazing. She needs a raise." Amanda paused and then kept walking. "I'll see you in a few? I want to finish the reset and get your thoughts."

David winked at her and then felt Tom's hand on his shoulder. "Oh, she is a cutie." Tom Cochran had fading blonde hair. He was thick-built, stocky, and a few inches taller than David.

"Yes. I didn't see this coming." David watched Amanda disappear.

"Yeah, Gail and I, 12 years in June," Tom said. "Amanda gave the cosmetic section life, and she gave me some advice on health and beauty care. She is bright, has vision, and knows this business."

"Tom, I like her." David gave his boss an honest smile. Tom was like a father to him.

"Then don't let her go," he chuckled. "Or let her know where you stand; something. Don't leave her guessing."

"I won't; we've got plans tonight," David mentioned.

"Listen, the store looks good. The kids and I got this. You've been holding this place down for two weeks. Gail's got jet lag bad from our being in Europe. You don't have to be here this weekend." Tom and he began walking to the frozen food section.

"I hear you," David said. "But…"

"And that is why you will manage this place when I'm gone," Tom interrupted David, got a page, and headed to customer service.

When David made it to the cosmetic section, he was shocked. To think on Monday, the section was dark, and now it was bright. The cosmetic counter was clean with cotton balls, makeup sponges in glass jars, a stool, and mirror for makeup application. David shook his head in disbelief.

"When did you have time to do all of this?" David asked. "I was in this store earlier than you. You did this in three hours?"

"I promised you I'd make this right," Amanda said, with one hand on her hip and her cell phone in the other. "This little phone you hate came in handy when I sent Emily pictures last night of everything I needed."

"Emily is amazing. I've gotta find her a date." David walked around the counter and noticed the $2 off coupons. He picked up one.

"So I created those. I'll give a dollar for each one you redeem. Calvin said fifty cents, I told him…" Amanda stopped herself with her hand in the air.

"Asking God's forgiveness for the response I had."

"Remind me not to make you angry." David had his hands in his pockets, looking around. "You, of course, did what you wanted."

Amanda gave him a closed smile of justification. David loved that she was determined to do the right thing.

"Amanda." He took her hand; their eyes met. "Will you go to dinner with me tonight? At Charlie's? I've asked Regina and Greg to join us. If you are up to it, then let's go dancing."

She looked at their hands connected and, biting her bottom lip, said,

"Mr. Lloyd, thank you for being a complete gentleman. Noted. I won't run past your intentions again."

"So...?"

"Yes, it would be my pleasure to go to dinner with you. I can't wait for you to meet my friends." Amanda smiled as he kissed her hand.

"Okay, I'll pick you up at 5:30 pm." They went their separate ways.

David went to his office and finally had a moment to call Bruce. He caught him up on the happenings from the week—Amanda's panic attack, her sharing about her past, and dinner last night.

"Bruce, she's so beautiful...and I mean that in so many ways." David was serious. "She's business savvy, respects me as a man..."

"Did you kiss her?" Bruce asked, waiting for the answer.

"Yes. One sweet, tender one. Just a nice evening; I want to go slow."

"I understand," Bruce said. "Tonight is her last night here?"

"Not with a snowstorm looming," David told him. "I won't let her go, even if she said she can make it."

"David, you really like her. She likes you, too; she shared a lot about herself," Bruce noted. "So what's the plan tonight?"

"Could you meet us at the dance club on 49th and Collins? I'd love for her to see you." David was shutting down his computer and grabbing his keys. He gave him the details.

When David and Amanda arrived at Charlie's, Greg and Regina were seated at a corner table meant for four. Greg saw Amanda and beamed. If she didn't know him, she would believe he played basketball. The height and physique gave it away. His dark chocolate skin was still without one blemish. He wore a goatee and dressed in jeans and a sports jacket. Amanda noticed his expensive shoes as he rose from the table and greeted her.

"Look at you!" He hugged her and kissed her cheek. "You look great." She did, David thought. Her jeans just accentuated her curves; a men's style white dress shirt was long to her mid-thigh. She left a few buttons undone to show the white lace tank top, a hint of cleavage, but the silver teardrop necklace resting on her chest was meant to be the focus. A long, salt and pepper colored sweater covered her arms.

"Thank you." Amanda was always polite. She turned. "Greg, I would like you to meet David Lloyd, assistant store director at Acuff, and my friend." The two men made eye contact and shook hands.

Regina then rose to greet David with a side hug. "Thank you for taking such great care of Amanda this week. She looks so much better than the last time I saw her." With everyone seated, Amanda said, "Okay, this will not be a *babying Amanda* session. I'm fine. Blood pressure is normal, and I'm rested."

David remembered he took a moment inside himself and noticed he was the only white man at the table. He was happy on the inside because he felt at ease. Madison, Wisconsin, had changed his views on race.

When he would go to the gym at night with his black classmates, he was never questioned about his comings and goings or what was in his pockets, but they were. Being detained by the police at the nearby convenience store was a regular thing for his classmates, and he realized that when he finally asked the police what the problem was, they quit harassing them. His privilege and their treatment angered him.

"So, ladies, what are you drinking?" Greg asked. "David and I can go up to the bar."

Regina and Amanda gave their orders and watched the two men head to the bar.

"You look great!" Amanda turned to Regina and said brightly. Regina had the ends of her hair full of curls, a red-colored shoulder top against her skin. Amanda saw her glowing. "Are you feeling okay?"

"Perfect." Regina genuinely smiled. "Greg was grateful, as was I, for your wedding suggestion. We talked to our parents, not to get their permission, but to tell them that this is our responsibility. We told them that while this pregnancy was not planned, we are engaged and want children."

"And…" Amanda waited.

"We are going to get married in three weeks, if you can get back here." Regina was excited. "A courthouse wedding will be beautiful. I have it all planned in my head. Our families are planning a big barbecue afterwards. Greg is looking for a house to rent."

"This is so good," Amanda said. "I will be here. But you have to promise me something."

Regina waited for Amanda to say it. "Allow Greg to be in charge of some things. Don't take over finding the house, and don't allow your mom to dictate the things you and Greg are responsible for. I know Momma Janae; she means well, but…"

Regina knew her friend was right. Greg was gracious with all the women in her family, but they could be controlling.

"Don't do this again." Amanda took her friend's hand. "You made Greg wait with no end in sight."

Amanda explained to her friend that Greg had wanted to marry her six months ago, and they should've sent a date then to marry. With Greg not being sure how long it would be before Regina would set a date, her mom and sisters, with all their opinions, he wanted her sexually the moment the ring was on.

"I'm gonna find out very soon how strong my self-control is, so I'm not judging, and your sex life is none of my business. But don't make him wait when self-control is hard enough."

"Yes, wise soul," Regina commented and looked at her friend lovingly. "We started acting married," she winked, "weeks into the engagement, so desire heated up for sure."

"I'm done," Amanda said. "Sorry."

"Don't ever be sorry for helping me keep my relationship with God in order," Regina said. "Your turn. How was dinner last night?"

Amanda told Regina about the groceries being delivered, the flowers, and that even though the dinner was simple, David knew the kitchen and she loved being in there with him. She told her about the soft kiss, being in his arms, and holding his hand.

"David sounds like a good man," Regina said. "He is like you in a way, thinking about others, loving...you two do have a connection."

David followed Greg's lead at the bar, except to say, "Hey, allow me to take care of the drinks."

"Okay, man," Greg said. "But Regina and I are treating you and Amanda to dinner." David nodded.

Greg ordered a rum and Coke, David a beer, and they sat and enjoyed their drinks. Greg had a good basketball career in college, played overseas for a year, but came back to Brookview to open a personal training business and gym. David, listening, was now familiar with his name, Greg Phillips, leading his conference in rebounds and assists. Greg, knowing about Bruce Lloyd, but gaining respect for his older brother. "You just met Amanda."

David smiled, then laughed. "Monday. She left me speechless with her beauty, her attitude, and her graciousness."

Greg smiled back. "Well, Regina tells me you are making her happy."

"Good," David said.

"If there is one thing Amanda deserves, it's happiness." Greg acknowledged. "She told you about parts of her childhood quickly. That means she trusts you, wants to get to know you, and she feels you are safe."

"Yes," David agreed. "I think it helped her to know my brother Bruce."

"Bruce and I have played basketball a few times at Brookview gym. He and Marcus Turner are close friends." Greg sipped his drink.

"Yeah, Bruce could've told me about Amanda; he knew her from Brookview Community College before she transferred to SIU." David took a drink. "Out of respect for her, he didn't. I'm glad he didn't. Her panic attack kind of accelerated things, but I feel honored she trusts me with knowing the intimate parts of her."

"Yes." Greg liked David's answer. "Listen, Amanda doesn't have a dad or any men in her life to question the intentions of the guys who come circling around. That is where Stan and I come in. You keep hanging around, you'll meet him and his wife Leslie."

David understood Greg. If he were in his situation, he would protect Amanda too.

"You Lloyd's are good people. Your dad was the only food truck not afraid to park in my 'ole neighborhood and tell the kids they didn't have to steal from him, but to just ask. Bruce walked Regina home many times from class to the dorm. Now Regina's pregnant, but you saw after Amanda, so she didn't have to drive to Galesboro again."

Greg looked at David. "I'm happy for you and Amanda," he said, raising his glass to toast.

David held up his beer. "Congratulations on the baby!"

"Yeah." Greg smiled purely. "I know it's supposed to be marriage, then baby, but here we are. Amanda and Regina are talking right now about the wedding."

"Fantastic." David waved the bartender over.

"I know Amanda lives in St. Louis, but I don't give that long. The wedding is in three weeks, all Amanda's idea. When the baby gets closer to being here, Amanda won't be able to stay away," Greg said it with certainty.

"Yes," David sighed. "I want to spend as much time with her before she has to go."

"Yes," Greg said. "Real conversation… God made Amanda to be this gentle, humble, and powerful soul. In the quietest of ways, she's an influencer. Right now, she is telling my fiancé to consider me in our future plans. Regina has been around strong women her whole life. She means well, but she has had to take charge. Men in her family ain't shit."

Greg ordered Regina a non-alcoholic sparkling wine; David got Amanda a glass of Merlot.

"Amanda is soft-hearted, teachable, and you'll say to yourself, *How sweet*. Then, out of nowhere, wisdom, maturity, servanthood, and loyalty flow. She sets us all straight. I tell you this in confidence because she says she feels connected to you. That's a big statement coming from her."

David put his money on the counter, and God reminded him what he had prayed, that if Amanda were to be in his life for a season or a lifetime, he would be all in.

"Greg, just between us, I see all the things you are saying you see in Amanda. It is hard for me not to fall in love with her. I'm taking it slow, but now that I've held her, touched her hands, looked in her eyes, and she's seen straight through me and knows my intentions, she is downright captivating inside and outside." David took Amanda's wine, and Greg took Regina's non-alcoholic sparkling wine, and they headed back to the table.

"You see her, David? Hold on to her; you've been given a gift."

The men joined the women at the table. As they enjoyed their dinner, they laughed and told stories. Greg had to share that the first time he met Regina was in college, and how he purposely invited himself to her study group in kinesiology so he could get her number. David told them about his time at the University of Wisconsin and how Acuff had held a job for him when he would come home in the summers. The Wisconsin winters were terrible, and he loved living close to his family.

"So that is the one thing that is new, Amanda. *Lloyd's*, David's dad, has a new deli-style restaurant," Regina said. "He makes these chocolate brownies; goodness, they are so good!" She closed her eyes in memory.

"Yeah," David had to agree. "They are good. But it's my dad's apricot-braised pork loin when I want comfort," he sighed.

Greg saw the connection David was talking about as they continued to talk. The way Amanda looked at David with interest and the way David allowed her to share a thought completely, he wanted to understand her.

As they finished dinner, Greg made it clear. "Hey, this dinner is on us, Amanda. It was more than nice to put eyes on you."

"Greg, thank you." She pouted as a sister would to her brother. "I'll be here for the wedding. I'm more than excited."

The couple continued to talk and exchange hugs and handshakes as they left the restaurant. Regina and Greg would've loved to have gone dancing, but with Regina's pregnancy she was tired, and Greg insisted she rest. They went on their way.

David got a limousine service for himself and Amanda. The extended stay had suggested it as parking ordinances were going into effect early due to the storm. As they waited for the black four-door Lexus to come around, he held her hand and pulled her into him. "I enjoyed meeting your family friends," he whispered in her ear. The night was getting cooler, so he hugged her, and their eyes met.

When their lips met, their eyes closed; it was a purposeful and sweet kiss. He opened his mouth slightly to give her upper lip his time and attention. He pulled away just a little, as a quiet way of saying *kiss me back*, and Amanda did. Her lips took hold of his bottom lip gently. A warmth was felt between them as they stared at each other.

"Mr. Lloyd." The limo service had driven up; the chauffeur was out of the car with the backseat door open for David and Amanda to move inside. They did.

David allowed the chauffeur, Jack, to get settled back in the car, told him their destination, and the car merged into traffic. David sat close to Amanda, stared at her, and kissed her again softly. "I'm not going to get tired of kissing you," he whispered in her ear.

Amanda, this time more confident, kissed him back just as softly. "Good." She put her head on his shoulder.

Amanda remembered feeling secure, and David remembered he was right where he was supposed to be in that moment. When they got to the club, Amanda waited for David to give Jack some directions and some cash. They walked hand in hand into the club, the pop music playing, and David looked around the crowded dance floor. He headed to the bar when he saw Bruce coming towards them. Amanda's face lit up as Bruce came up to her, hugged her, and picked her up off the ground for a second. Bruce led them both over to their table, away from the music.

"Bruce!" Amanda was happy to see him, looking well and gorgeous, with that dimple on his left cheek. She could see the resemblance between David and Bruce, but it was the way David looked at her, his smile that could move her insides. "I'm so glad to see you." She saw everyone else and tried to catch the introductions over the music. The brown-haired girl and the blonde hair guy, Tammi and Paul, were married. Kenny, with dark hair, and Marcus, a black guy, were Bruce's best friends. Amanda and David nodded over the music.

David asked Amanda if she wanted a drink. She asked for water, and David left her at the table, went to the bar, and came back with bottled water for Amanda and a beer for himself.

Bruce smiled at his brother and whispered in his ear, "She likes you."

David drank his beer. "I like her too. She's beautiful." He watched her talk to Tammi.

"I'm happy for you. Amanda needs someone like you, and you need someone like her." Bruce was sincere. "Enjoy the time."

David and Amanda's eyes met for a moment. She indicated that she was good and having fun. During their time in the club, David made sure everyone knew she was with him. She liked that. She heard one of her favorite songs and pulled David out onto the dance floor.

Amanda thought she would get resistance, but David was eager to dance with her. With her hands up above her head, her hips swaying, and David behind her with his hands on her hips on beat, feeling the rhythm, she turns to face him in awe.

"You can dance?" Amanda shouted, admiring his moves. He was smooth, sexy, and they could see Bruce and his friends cheering.

"Yep. This white guy can dance," he shouted back over the music. He winked and continued to dance with her until the song was over. The next song was slower, and that's when he took her hand and put his other hand on the small of her back. "Dance close with me." He had her ear.

Amanda stayed in the embrace and danced with him. She was done. David checked off all of her buttons. He was more than handsome, more than kind, generous, and a good cook. He had the approval of her friends; his brother was like a brother to her already, and his kisses reminded her of a good song while driving fast in a convertible with the top down, the sun in her face.

His embrace was quickly becoming a security blanket. He reassured her, validated her, and made her feel special. As the song ended, he led her back to their table, and the group enjoyed each other's company. David watched Amanda just request water again, and he reminded himself to ask her about it when they were alone.

Amanda seemed to be okay, but he had to admit he was curious about her as she made conversation with the table. She loved college football;

she was a cook herself, and yet did not take over once last night. She was helpful, telling Tammi beauty secrets and not to worry about her upcoming job interview. He found out that if she wanted to know how to do something, she read how to do it. How to paint, use a lawnmower, or write a check. Of course, there would've been no one around to help her completely understand those things; he found her to be resourceful.

When the table was empty, and with Tammi and Paul on the dance floor, Bruce found a brunette at the bar. Kenny and Marcus headed out before the snow. David held her hand and said, "Are you ready? There's one more place I have to show you."

David saw her face of approval and touched her cheek. They waved goodbye to Tammi and Paul and hugged Bruce one last time. When they stepped into the night air, it was cooler, but it felt good after being in the club.

David held Amanda in his arms. "Let's go." He led her down the block, and just as they turned onto a new street, there were steel stairs on the side of an old brick building. There was a black door at the bottom of the stairs. It read, BLUE NIGHT OWL. David took the first three steps, turned around, and offered Amanda his hand. "Trust me, but watch your step."

When they reached the door, and David opened it, she heard band instruments tuning up and people rustling about. It wasn't loud like the club, and David let out a sigh of relief.

"This is me." He led her down the hallway that had pictures of musicians on the wall. As a white-haired, white-bearded, heavy-set black man passed by, he said, "Lloyd, it's been a while, man. Good to see you."

"Yeah, you too, Sebastian." David kept walking, holding Amanda's hand. At the next door there was another man—bald, white, tall, and big in stature. Amanda got it. Security. He looked tough and mean until he smiled at David and Amanda. "Hey, Lloyd, where have you been?"

The men nodded at each other. "Working. Finally able to get out and enjoy some music."

"Alex, this is Amanda," David said, introducing them.

"Amanda, the pleasure is mine." Alex nodded again. He smiled, but he wasn't the handshaking type.

When Amanda entered the club, it was like a modern vintage Cotton Club. The floors were dark oak, the walls in white with wainscoting, and the light sconces were dimmed. The bar was huge and took up an entire wall—solid oak, mirrors behind it, with glasses and liquor resting on glass shelving. There were at least three bartenders preparing for the night. The stage was intimate, with a place for a band and an orchestra off to the right, and a grand piano just off center.

Center stage was a microphone on a floor stand. In front of the stage was a dance floor surrounded by small square tables with white tablecloths and tea light candles glowing in small jars. Behind the tables were semicircular booths with white leather high backs and round tables in front of them.

"David, this place is incredible." Amanda continued to look around. No other customers were in the club except them. David's eyes were bright.

"Yeah, the doors open in half an hour."

Amanda followed him up to the stage, and from the left-hand side came a voluptuous woman with alabaster skin in a tailored black V-neck dress. She had loud ginger hair, red lips, and red nails.

"David." She said in this husky velvet voice.

"Mel." David looked her in the face, ignoring her curves, cleavage, and lips. Amanda noticed. He grabbed both her hands and gave her a polite peck on her cheek.

"Mel, this is Amanda." He turned to Amanda as if to formally introduce her.

She looked at Amanda out of the corner of her eye and smiled. "Amanda, nice to meet you."

"Good lookin,' where have you been?" She teased David by running her fingers through his light brown hair. He blushed and flashed his smile. Amanda laughed.

"Mel, stop flirting." David rolled his eyes. "Amanda, this is Melanie Leaf."

Melanie relaxed and gave an honest, pleasant response, "You're a pretty girl. Are you the reason we haven't seen him around?"

"I wish." David winked at Amanda, "Work. The boss went to Europe and left me in charge."

"Well, since you're here, help me warm up." Melanie walked up to the piano and leaned against it.

David sighed happily; he was glad she asked. Amanda was excited. David took off his blazer, handed it to Amanda, and rolled up his sleeves.

Amanda stepped off the stage and sat at the closest table as David sat at the piano with a microphone. Melanie took the microphone from the stand on the center stage.

When David played, Amanda closed her eyes to enjoy the sound. But when he started to sing, well, she opened her eyes and looked at him, breathless. His voice was clear and precise. Melanie's voice touched Amanda deeply. It was soft, sure, and creamy. She made each word come alive; it was her gift. She had a vibrato that was smooth and controlled.

Their voices complemented each other and were conversational. It was a nice rendition of *Breaking Up Is Hard to Do*. Just when she thought there were no more surprises for the night, there it was. David was a crooner, and a decent one at that.

Amanda stood and clapped. "You never cease to amaze me." She went to him as he sat at the piano, put her hands on his shoulder, and kissed him on the cheek.

Melanie caught David's response. He put his hand on top of her hand that was on his shoulder and kissed her back. Melanie smiled as if she knew something they didn't.

"David, you're fun. You're welcome here any night." Melanie said. "Adam still plays for me, but you know he'll step aside for you to play a couple."

"Oh no, not tonight, Mel." David rose from the piano, rolled down his sleeves, and took his blazer from Amanda. "It's all about Amanda tonight."

Amanda looked humbly at him.

"Are you and Adam still a thing?" David raised an eyebrow.

"Aren't we always? Today we are, tomorrow he'll piss me off, but that's how our chemistry works." Melanie answered, then asked, "You and Amanda, are you a thing?" She mocked him.

David didn't even give Amanda time to answer. "Yeah." He stared into her eyes. "We're a thing."

Melanie nodded in approval before she left the stage. "Hey, David." She turned back to look at him. "Is she your Saturday sweet or Sunday honey?"

David chuckled at Melanie, her code way of asking if Amanda was the real thing. It was charming, he thought. He took Amanda's hand and helped her off the stage.

"She's my Sunday honey." David replied, and Amanda wasn't sure what it all meant at the time, but she loved the sentiment.

"Well," she said, "the first slow song is for you and your Sunday honey." Melanie disappeared backstage.

David and Amanda sat in a booth as other customers began to file in. "This is the best seat in the house," David said.

"When did you become a crooner? I mean, we live in the environment of country and pop music down here."

"In high school. When everyone else was playing sports and crushing on girls, I was playing the piano and in the swing choir. I was a baseball player, but that was a summer sport; school was out. No popularity contest there. Now, after high school, being in musicals and choir is popular," he laughed.

He talked about his dad loving old country and the blues growing up. David admitted he knew his parents were fans of Diana Ross; he watched *Lady Sings the Blues* and *Mahogany,* and reminisced about how they fell in love in the 70s.

"I should've known then I'd fall for a sweet, brown, beautiful woman," he whispered in her ear.

"David," she whispered back and then kissed him. "You win. If you were aiming for this week to be memorable,, you could've stopped at your kind words on Wednesday," she said.

She looked at him and touched his cheek. "I like you."

"I like you." He winked at her, knowing that when he did that, it made her blush.

"Stop that!" She laughed, nudging his shoulder.

"Okay, so are done drinking for the night? One glass of Merlot with dinner?" David was trying to find out why she was just drinking bottled water at the club. "Are you okay?"

"Perfect," Amanda eased his mind. "I just don't drink at a club like that or where the bar is open on all sides. Anything can happen, especially to women."

After hearing her give the explanation, he was proud of how she kept herself protected, but sad men had made it that way.

"I had a foster dad when I was ten. He was a bartender. Sometimes I would have to do my homework at the end of the bar if the babysitter didn't show up. We finally found a good one, so it didn't happen too often." Amanda remembered.

"That is why I don't eat processed food, mac and cheese in the box, and ketchup. I was left for 12 hours when I was seven, with just that to eat."

"Amanda," David touched her hand. "I'm sorry."

"Yes, all of that. Over," Amanda said, and then continued. "But Clay, my foster dad, taught me some survival skills, like how to cook. So when a bar is floating, I don't drink, especially if there is only one bartender. She can't see what's happening once the drink is made. And when a woman comes to the bar and asks for an angel shot, that means *call the police*."

"Really?" David was curious.

"Yes. Depending on the bar, there are safe drink codes. So if a woman feels uncomfortable with her date, she can order the *safe drink*, telling the bartender she is in trouble."

"Wow," David thought out loud. "I'm so glad I'm not a woman. I could not do it." He shook his head. "I'm glad you protect yourself."

When the waiter came to the table, David insisted she try dessert.

"This place has the best tiramisu, cheesecake, flourless chocolate cake, and apple crumble." David looked at the menu.

"You have a sweet tooth, because that is just about every dessert on here," Amanda said, laughing.

He ordered the apple crumble. She ordered the flourless chocolate cake along with coffee. David did the same, but with creamer.

"No sugar?" David tilted his head.

"No. There is sugar in the cake," Amanda said. "Balance."

David then remembered what Regina had said. Amanda had a way she ate desserts, just watch and learn, Regina said when he asked. He laughed inside.

She was curled in his arms for the rest of the performance. It was an intimate place. The semicircular booth made their conversations and kisses private. She asked him about his favorite childhood memory. She wanted to hear how a real family *operated*. Her wording was awkward to him; he knew she didn't know any other way to put it.

He could tell she craved a mom and a dad who loved each other, ate dinner together, and played football in the backyard. To his shame, he had some of those things, and he took them for granted. He thought about his mom. He hadn't thought much of those Sunday dinners, but now he had a new appreciation.

"Good lookin'." Those words were spoken from the stage. David's attention was now on Melanie. Her red lips close to the mic, she said softly, "This is for you and your Sunday honey." She found David in the audience with her eyes. He stared back at her as an indication that he was listening. She closed her eyes and started singing.

Her voice touched the inner parts of David and Amanda; their eyes closed just as they heard her. They felt every word. There was a touch of silk and desire in that first chord. She sang about a Sunday kind of love, one to last past Saturday night. Amanda knew then that this was for her. God was telling her to get prepared for her love of a lifetime with all its twists and turns, but David was hers. He would be hers to take and hers to let go of.

David looked at Amanda's hand in his as he heard the band supporting Melanie's voice. Her voice was soft and sounded sad when she sang about not being able to find someone to love or care for, being on a lonely road. He could relate. He went to work and came home. As handsome as everyone said he was, he couldn't handle the women who couldn't see past it or didn't want him to lead in the relationship as a gentleman. Then, Amanda changed it in five whole days.

He felt it when he looked in her eyes, when he saw her bruises, heard her story, in his prayer, and in their kiss. This was his wife. They both enjoyed Sebastian's saxophone solo at the bridge of the song. Melanie went up an octave as she sang about arms needing to keep her warm. The audience whistled.

Melanie's soulful voice captivated everyone as she gave her voice full power as she listed off all the days of the week, but she wanted a *Sunday Kind of Love*. David thought even Etta James herself would be proud. That night, that song was one of the greatest gifts life had given him.

CHAPTER 16

Amanda got out of the shower, dried off, and while her hair was still wet, she styled it. Today, it would be a bun, not too high on her head. She played with her hair a bit to find the right placement, and making a ponytail first. Then, she used her comb to pull out several strands to give herself soft, long, natural bangs. She then twisted her hair around the bottom of the ponytail and pinned the end. She saw herself in the mirror and was pleased. Then suddenly, she heard shouting. She quickly grabbed her robe, put it on, and stepped out of the master bathroom.

David had left the bed hours ago, and he was downstairs, but Amanda wondered who else was there? She swiftly went to her walk-in closet, put on a bra and panties, and then put her robe back on. She heard the shouting again; it was David's voice. It was coming from the backyard.

She left the master bedroom and went to Matthew's room and peeked out of the blinds. Amanda closed her eyes and felt her stomach drop. David was in the backyard with Bruce.

Bruce pushed his brother's shoulder with one of his hands because David's cell phone was in the other. "You're shit. You're sleeping with another woman?!"

Bruce was indignant. "Who is this, Sam? And why didn't you tell me? What is wrong with you?!" Bruce gave David back his phone by slamming it in the middle of his chest. Bruce turned his back to David in disgust.

David put his phone in his jean back pocket. "Bruce! Stop! My relationship with Sam is over."

"Well, it shouldn't have started in the first goddamn place." Bruce had his hands behind his head, then turned around and faced David again.

"You promised. You know that?! You promised her and the entire family you would love her, honor her... she's like the sister I never had, but didn't know I needed, David."

Amanda covered her mouth and felt tears forming.

David couldn't speak because Bruce kept talking with an elevated voice. "Mom is gonna kill you! I won't have to..."

"God, Bruce, do not tell Mom. Amanda and I will work this out." David wanted to tell Bruce so many things, but now, all he wanted was Bruce to just stop ranting and listen. "This is my life; I will fix it. I love my wife."

With that statement, Bruce faced his brother. Their brown eyes locked, and Bruce caught David by surprise and punched him in the stomach. David bent over.

Amanda gasped. She quit looking out of the blinds but kept listening. "You know, I wish I had one of those. A wife." Bruce's voice was normal now.

"Don't tell me you love Amanda. You love you, and your new job and the power it gives you, right?"

Then Bruce really got to his feelings. "Why didn't you tell me? I'm your brother; we share so much. Don't you remember what Dad did? What about Matthew and Mason? Did you think about them as you were sneaking around?"

David was now standing upright. Amanda heard the garage door open. *Who's that?* She thought.

"Good luck on fixing it," Bruce continued. "Because of the neglect you created, Amanda is thinking about someone else. Who's Nathan?"

Amanda closed her eyes and let out a sigh.

David's mind was in shock, and his face must have exposed it. "What?"

Bruce was smug. "I bet all this wonderful sex you've been having has been an effort to keep you home and to keep her mind from thinking about him, but she thinks about this Nathan."

How did Bruce know this? Amanda was curious, but she would not intervene.

Bruce continued. "You guys tease me about the women in my life. Yeah, I'm not proud of the revolving door I've created, but I know women. I haven't slept with all the women you think I have, but I know them and how they think. Amanda is hurting, something you were not supposed to cause."

Bruce got up close to David again. "I love you, but I'm hurt and I'm angry." Bruce punched his brother in the stomach again. That's when Michael came out in the yard.

"Hey, hey, boys; you're not 18."

Shit! Amanda couldn't listen anymore; she had to get moving. *What is happening?!* She asked herself. *How did Bruce know about Sam? And Nathan? Did Regina or Leslie call him?* She didn't have time to find out. She and David were supposed to be at Acuff Corporate today to greet trainees and say a few words.

Amanda picked up her phone and called Vikki. "Vikki, it's Amanda."

"Amanda, please tell me you and David will be here in an hour."

"Vikki, can you talk? Anyone around that shouldn't be?"

Vikki paused and moved herself outside of the room she was in. "Amanda, is everything okay?"

"Yes." Amanda was now in her walk-in closet, looking at her blouses.

"Drama. Bruce found out about Sam. There is an intervention going on in my backyard, and I need to get out of here to make it to Acuff on time. I can't guarantee David will get out of this. His dad and brother are asking him about his love life right now. I can't get involved."

"Oh no! You don't want to get involved." Vikki closed her eyes. "I need at least one of you here."

Vikki started walking down the hall of the conference center and saw Willis standing in the entrance.

"Amanda, darlin', I'm going to have Willis come to get you in an Acuff company car. He is an intern here in marketing. Nice kid with brown hair, a tall stature, and freckles. Be ready in 30 minutes." Vikki ended the call.

Amanda remembered this was a casual gathering. The trainees would be touring the corporate office and meeting in the conference center for lunch. She went with her white jeans and turquoise long blouse. Amanda found jewelry to match her white wedge heels, and she did light makeup with lip gloss. She made it downstairs and out the front door without being seen. She waited for Willis.

"What the hell?!" Michael looked at his sons as he stood between them.

"Please tell Bruce to stop punching me," David said, breathing hard.

"He obviously feels that he has reason to punch you." Michael looked at his son. "David, please tell me you are not having an affair?"

David couldn't meet his dad's eyes. He closed his eyes. "Had an affair. It's over. We ended it."

Michael hung his head. "I could ask, *What the hell were you thinking?* I could ask *Why?* But all of it would sound self-righteous and hypocritical, wouldn't it?" He sat down on the steps of the deck, his sons still in the yard catching their breath. "Is she pregnant?"

"No." David was ashamed that it was even a fair question to ask.

"STD?" Michael asked.

"No."

"Do you love her?"

There was silence. Michael had struck a chord from David's childhood, and he knew it. At that moment, David looked at his dad with contempt.

"No, I'm in love with my wife, Amanda." David was clear with his words as he looked at his dad and then his brother.

"This is how you show it?!" Bruce interjected.

Michael silenced Bruce with his hand in the air. "Listen, I know I am not a good example in this situation, but you are my sons. Yeah, you may think this is none of my business, your love lives. I agree to a point. But I didn't stand up for you at your wedding in front of God, family, and friends for you to quit like I did."

Michael rose. "You didn't get married by yourself, and you're not staying married by yourself. We are a family."

David was angry now. Michael could see it. "Bruce, go home now. You've made your point."

Bruce couldn't even say anything. He just left the yard through the fence to the driveway. Michael watched him disappear and heard his truck back out of the driveway. Bruce didn't notice Amanda sitting on the front porch.

Father and son were quiet in the yard for a moment.

"David, I was selfish back then. I lied to your mom, to you, and to myself. I have never stopped loving your mom." Michael approached David.

David couldn't look at his dad. "That was a long time ago, Dad. That's over."

"Is it?" Michael asked him. "Because in our relationship, we get right to this moment, and then you shut me out."

David didn't speak.

"All this time, I have been apologizing for what I did to your mom, and how I lied and told her I didn't love her anymore. I've apologized for not being at your piano recitals, swing choir shows, and baseball games. I was too busy with Sheila." Michael was saddened now by his behavior back then.

"I've apologized for leaving you to help Bruce more than an older brother should. But I haven't said, I'm sorry, David, for leaving you. I left you with all of it, didn't I?"

David finally looked at his dad.

"So much to carry for my boy; my ten-year-old son." Michael touched his son's shoulder, and David rejected the touch.

"Yeah, you left me with the heavy. I didn't know Mom cried herself to sleep every night. I didn't know how to deal with that. I didn't know what to do to get Bruce to stop sitting in your chair, thinking that night Dad is coming home. How do I tell Mom we didn't want another night of spaghetti, only to realize that is all she could afford? And still tell her she was pretty, and I was grateful for her. You left me with a lot of things, but I felt like nothing."

David was surprised when the tears developed, and then he exploded.

"I want to be mad at you! I don't want to love you! You caused me so much pain! Why did you move out?! Your clothes were not in the closet anymore. Not a word about where you went until two months later with Shelia. I want to hate you!" David had his face in the air, crying aloud.

Michael touched David again. It was as if David were ten. He hugged his dad. "I don't hate you, Dad; it just hurt." Michael embraced his son with tears on his face and relief in his heart. Maybe now, he thought, he could have a real relationship with his son. Michael and David held each other in the yard that day for minutes. With just

Michael saying a few times, "I love you, David. I'm sorry, David. Forgive me, son."

David broke the embrace. "Now, look at me. I'm just like you. I was going to tell Amanda about Sam today, but Bruce came in… I'm gonna hurt her. It was a mistake; I wasn't thinking clearly. I was thinking about myself."

"Well, you're not like me," Michael said, looking firmly into his son's eyes. "I know something happened at work where Amanda is concerned, didn't it? Gerald came to the restaurant to apologize; he assumed I knew what had happened. Does this Samantha have something to do with it? Can you and Amanda figure it out?"

Then David remembered. "Oh Dad, yes, but…I have to go. I'm late. The Acuff Academy is today." He grabbed his phone and saw a text from Amanda:

> Babe, don't worry. I'm here. Vikki had a company car come and get me. Get here when you can.

When Amanda made it to Acuff, Vikki was waiting for her outside the convention center. She gave her the instructions, and Amanda was in awe. David had done all this work; it was beautiful to hear it all from Vikki, and she was about to see it. When she walked into the center, there were some of David's colleagues. It was intimate. Amanda noticed this wasn't a crowd of people.

The first person she saw was Corey. He looked more mature and handsome, Amanda thought. She remembered attending his wedding just five years ago, and now he was the second assistant store director at a store in Galesboro. The city had grown and developed; now there were two Acuff stores.

She saw Tom Cochran, David's old store director, back when they first met. He was bald now, but still carried a warm smile. Brad Frahm was there. Amanda always imagined this blonde-haired, blue-eyed kid with

David's brown hair and brown eyes saying they were brothers, sleeping over at each other's houses, making forts in their backyards, and daring each other to eat gross things. They had a million and one stories. All of them were happy to see Amanda, and she graciously apologized for David not being with her. She assured them he wasn't far behind.

When she made it through the entryway, she went into the conference area and saw the trainees. Amanda was overwhelmed. There were only 25 trainees in the small conference area. So much of the room had been closed off to make it look like a large room in a home.

The environment was perfect, and she knew David had a hand in the layout. Six large tables were in the room, which looked like dining room tables you would find in a home. Cherry rectangular wood tables with placemats, cloth napkins, and candles were at each table. But what surprised her the most was the trainees.

They hadn't noticed her yet; they were busy talking to each other, laughing, and enjoying each other's company. All the trainees were multicultural: Black, Latino, Asian, or biracial. Vikki stood next to her. "Are you ready? I want you to meet the trainees."

"Yes."

Vikki came from the side of the room, went to the center of the room, and got the trainees' attention. "Hey there." Vikki's southern drawl just added to the hospitality. "Take a seat. Just sit anywhere for a minute."

The trainees found seats. They looked like sets of families sitting at a family dinner table.

Vikki had all eyes on her. "I want to introduce you to someone." Just as Vikki said that, in the back of the room, everyone from the entryway filed in. Brad, Tom, Corey, two white men she didn't know, a white woman, and in the flesh herself, Samantha Coleman. Amanda remembered her picture on the website. Blonde, tall; today in blue jeans and a Brookview Community College t-shirt.

"She has been in retail for at least 16 years, in retail management for 13 of those years. She works for a retail brokerage firm, Augusta Retail, here in the city. And yes, she is David's wife. I introduce none other than Amanda Lloyd."

The trainees smiled sincerely and offered warm applause. But one student, a young black, light-skinned man dressed in jeans and a red polo shirt, made Amanda completely relax.

"Jacob, you owe me twenty bucks. I told you Mr. David had a black wife. Pay up."

Amanda went to the center of the room and thanked Vikki, stating she didn't have to be so formal. "And Jacob, you should pay… what's your name?" Amanda wanted to interact with the trainees.

The young man said, "Malcolm."

"Well, you should pay Malcolm because I am black. At least, that is part of my culture." The room laughed and whistled. "I am married to David Lloyd."

They looked at her majestically. She wasn't sure what David had told them, but they were ready to listen.

"So, Jacob, where are you? You have twenty dollars less than you had a few seconds ago." Amanda spanned the room. The students loved her sense of humor.

Another young black man stood up from a table towards the back. He was darker-skinned, had a warm smile, took off his baseball cap, revealing that he had barely any hair. "Yes, ma'am."

"Please call me Ms. Amanda; that works." Vikki handed her a bottle of water. She thanked her.

"What are you doing here? Why are you here? I just want to get to know some of you." Her tone was soft, but assertive and caring.

"Ms. Amanda, I wanna be a chef." Jacob said. "I wanted to be a chef ever since my grandma taught me how to make macaroni and cheese from scratch. Before my dad left for prison, he was a master on the grill; nothing like his char-broiled steak." The trainees were feeling his story. "I just want to cook; it relaxes me. I hope it takes me somewhere, everywhere, and keeps me out of trouble."

Amanda felt Jacob. So honest, filled with hope, and ready to put the past in the past.

"What about you, Malcolm, who is twenty dollars richer?" They all laughed.

"I have got to own something." Malcolm rose from his chair. "I'm an entrepreneur at heart," he said. Then, a Latino woman with sandy-colored hair with big curls added, "And crazy as hell." The room broke out in laughter again.

"Where I'm from," Malcolm put his hand on his chest, "it's called risk-taking."

"Whatever," the Latino woman bantered back.

"And what about you?" Amanda touched the shoulder of the young black woman next to her. She was quiet, with her hair in long braids in a ponytail.

"I'm Chelsea." She didn't rise from her seat. "I love to create and make things. I make my own soap, tub teas, bath salts, and bath bombs."

"That's wonderful. It's nice to meet all of you." Amanda asked them by a show of hands how many of them met with David one-on-one. All of them raised their hands. She asked how many of them felt that David and the Acuff family genuinely cared about them. All of them raised their hands. She finally asked if they felt this was their opportunity of a lifetime to turn their lives around. All of them raised their hands.

"Thank you for sharing. I'm sure that over time we will see each other. So, a bit about me." Amanda sighed pleasantly. She noticed David was now in the room next to Brad. He was in his jeans and a white button-down shirt. He smiled and gave that look of *don't tell them I'm here.*

"I was born Amanda Flakke. My mom, Cathy Swanson Flakke, was white and married my dad, Dwayne Flakke, a black man, a realtor; well, he wanted to be. He was ready to take the test when tragedy struck."

The students were listening carefully. The joyful laughter in the room changed.

"When I was six, my mom was going to school to get her Master's in Higher Education. She wanted to help low-income students stay in school. She took me to school, and then she went. My mom worked at the local diner at night to help make ends meet for our small family. My dad worked at the real estate office and picked me up from school every day. I was never alone."

"The neighborhood we lived in was not safe for a six-year-old girl, but it was all we could afford. One night, a drug addict left the stove on in their apartment, and the whole building caught on fire. My dad scooped me up out of bed, and my mom was right behind us as we made our way down the stairs and outside. But when my dad sat me down across the street—in my light blue nightgown with my bunny house shoes, and my stuffed animal in my hand—my mom was not behind us. He ran back to find her, and neither of them ever came back out."

Silence filled the room.

David hated the story. He was mad at himself that he was going to hurt her. Bruce was right; he failed her. He was proud of her for sharing, but she stopped abruptly. He knew she wasn't going to share the rape, but he could tell she had a thought, and she dismissed it. She sipped her water. She told them about foster care and the long journey until she was adopted at fourteen.

"So, I'm not short of hard times. In a lot of ways, I understand you, and you understand me. When I entered this world of retail, I was naïve, but I worked hard and I'm proof that if you do that, it will pay off."

"Ms. Amanda," Jacob called to her. "I gotta get my twenty dollars back."

Amanda laughed. "Okay."

"Is it true you met Mr. David in retail with your butt in the air?"

The room erupted in laughter and gasps. Amanda looked at David. He smiled, arms folded, and head to the ground. Brad elbowed him.

"Yes," Amanda said, now exposing that David was in the room. "Babe, you're wrong for telling them the story like that." Amanda smiled at him. The room looked at David.

"Is it not my fault; that's how they remembered it," he said with his shoulders by his ears. The room laughed.

"This is how the story should go: David saw the back of me first. I was chasing a lipstick that had rolled onto the floor. I saw his shoes first, an expensive pair of Johnson & Murphy black leather shoes. I also remember him being angry, and rightfully so. The cosmetic company I worked for at the time abandoned his store. Retail management rule number one—do the right thing and make the customer happy."

David chimed in. "And she has been doing that for ten years." The women trainees found the sentiment sweet. Jacob and Malcolm realized neither of them was twenty dollars richer.

Amanda saw Samantha's face. It was pleasant the entire time, but there was something in her eyes that looked familiar. The trainees enjoyed Amanda. She thanked them and encouraged them.

Vikki told the trainees that lunch would be in ten minutes. The meal would be served family style, and then they would take a tour of the test kitchen before they would go back to the hotel. Vikki escorted Amanda to the side door as trainees surrounded David.

As Vikki and Amanda were in the entryway alone together, Samantha came up to them.

"Hi, Amanda," Samantha said, looking into Amanda's eyes. "I'm Samantha Coleman. My friends call me Sam. I just wanted to thank you for what you did today. I would never have been able to share the way you did. I appreciate your support." The women shook hands.

Amanda smiled at her and now saw what was familiar—the sadness in her eyes. "Thank you, Samantha." Amanda was not going to call her Sam. "I will always support my husband," Amanda said, "and that is why it is best that you don't take things that don't belong to you."

Vikki immediately pressed her lips together and put her head down, scratching her head casually.

"Yes," Samantha said. Amanda saw the sadness and humility again. "You are absolutely right. Have a good day," she said, smiling with realization, and walked away.

Amanda was angry at first, but she had to hand it to Samantha; she would not shy away from what she did. She felt Samantha did that for David.

"Amanda, you can handle yourself, can't you?" Vikki whispered. "I underestimated you. Let's get you home. You and David have a lot to talk about, don't you?"

Amanda sighed. "We do."

Vikki found Willis. He had an interoffice envelope in his hand and handed it to Vikki. He then left and brought the company car around. Amanda texted David and told him she would meet him at home. To Amanda's surprise, Vikki got in the backseat with her.

"Vikki, I can take no more surprises today." Amanda was tired.

"I know, but I have to give you this envelope in the event David doesn't give you the full story," Vikki said. "It's about him and the Acuff Academy." She handed her the interoffice envelope.

"I'm sorry." Vikki said, "... that I didn't come right out and tell you about David and Sam."

"It was not your story to tell. In a way, David told on himself."

Vikki took a deep breath. "I gathered you knew when I first met you and how you came to the office after that."

Amanda gave a little smile.

"You are a beautiful, godly woman, the way you fight."

Amanda frowned. "Fight?"

"Sweet girl, what you did by not telling David you knew and loving him anyway, hundreds of demons had to flee. You covered over a multitude of sins with your *visits* to the office. You took on all this pain for your covenant marriage." Vikki made everything Amanda was feeling have value.

"I am just thanking God you are his executive assistant. I couldn't imagine the scandal and outrage." Amanda looked at Vikki now.

Vikki told Amanda that she had a casual conversation with Samantha about appointments and stressed that David didn't have appointments after five. David understood what that meant, so wherever they went, it wasn't there.

"Thank you," Amanda said. She respected Vikki even more.

"Amanda, I love the Lloyds. You have no idea how I begged God and Gerald to be with David." Vikki spoke with such confidence and certainty.

"Vikki, I'm so grateful for you. Thank you for protecting David and keeping this quiet. Yes, this all hurts, but this is by God's design for a reason we may never know. It will all come full circle."

Vikki looked at Amanda and took her hand.

"When I was a freshman in high school, I thought I knew what I was doing hanging out with Bobby Baldwin under the bleachers at the varsity football game. I wanted to be rebellious and tell the freshman girls I kissed a senior boy." Vikki shook her head. "I was stupid."

Amanda listened carefully.

"Bobby came onto me fast. With his hands everywhere, he was stronger than me. His kisses were no longer soft but forceful, and he was hurting me."

"Vikki!" Amanda said and covered her mouth.

"I shouted no," Vikki recalled with her eyes closed. "And there he was."

Vikki opened her eyes and looked at Amanda.

"It was dark, so I couldn't see who it was at first, but he pulled him off me. Punched him and told him to go and never bother me again."

Vikki continued. "Bobby Baldwin ran. He asked me if I was okay or hurt, and I said I was fine. Back then, no one cared about assaults like that. If it weren't for Michael Lloyd under the bleachers trying to sneak a cigarette, who knows what would've happened to me. Bobby Baldwin is in the Illinois state prison right now serving two sentences for rape and assault."

Amanda gave Vikki a closed-mouth smile and hugged her. Vikki folded into that hug, and they held each other for a few minutes. Amanda didn't want to let go.

"Vikki, I thank God it was Michael. I thank God David has you. I thank God that I have you."

Amanda let go of Vikki and kissed her on the lips, like she used to kiss her mom. Vikki was touched deeply. She appreciated the sentiment.

"Amanda, please." Vikki touched her face. "Please know how much David loves you. Don't doubt it for a second. Samantha was a stupid fling, not to be taken lightly, but compared to what you are to him? There's no comparison."

Willis drove the car up onto the driveway.

"I love you, Vikki," Amanda said sincerely. "I truly do."

"I love you too." Vikki hugged her again and let her leave.

CHAPTER 17

*A*manda opened the door to her home, and it was quiet. She locked herself in. *Thank you, Lord*, she thought. She went upstairs to her walk-in closet, shut the door, and put the interoffice envelope in a vacant bottom drawer. She took off her clothes and drew a bath. As she waited for the tub to fill up, she sat by the side of the tub and screamed, then she cried. Not because she was sad. She was just filled with so much emotion.

David had created huge opportunities for 25 underrepresented multicultural trainees well beyond what they could even imagine. Samantha Coleman actually came up to her. *Did that even happen?* She asked herself. Then she thought about Vikki and her story. If Michael only knew how important his life was and what he did back there covered his son up here.

Then there was the mystery of Bruce. How did he know about Samantha and Nathan? A mystery. In this moment, Amanda thought about a million things and released them all with tears.

She had been in the bath for fifteen minutes when she heard the garage door. She didn't care; she was relaxed now and ready to listen to David. Amanda let the water out of the tub and stepped out, taking the towel from the towel bar. David opened the door to the master bedroom. "Honey?"

"Yes, I'm just getting out of the bath. I needed to soak for a minute." Amanda elevated her voice. "Can I meet you downstairs?"

David was unbuttoning his shirt and untucked his t-shirt underneath. "Sure. Coffee?" He asked.

Amanda looked at her watch. It was lunchtime, but she wanted the security of her coffee mug and caffeine. "Yes."

She heard him leave the room, and she came out of the bathroom, moisturized her skin, and put on a multicolored sundress. When she reached the kitchen, David was making coffee.

"I figured I would make single cups. That way, I won't get it wrong." He kind of chuckled.

Amanda smiled and went to the cabinet to get two coffee mugs. She met him at the counter and handed him one. He selected his dark roast from the box and her favorite medium roast. David started Amanda's first and handed her the sugar. They stood in silence for minutes, watching their coffee brew.

David touched her hand, and Amanda welcomed it. She opened herself and extended her arms for a hug. He fell in. She was hugging him, not the other way around. He smelled her fragrance as she had just gotten out of the bath; he loved it. She could feel the weight of all he was carrying emotionally and mentally.

She said in his ear, "I couldn't be prouder of you."

"Please don't say that," David replied.

"No, David, the Acuff Academy will be life-changing for these 25... do I dare say kids? We are getting older. We've got about 12 years on them."

Amanda let go of him and looked into his eyes.

"Yeah," David said. "They are good kids. I want them to go on and have a good life. They are deserving and talented, but just needed the resources."

David handed Amanda her coffee. She dressed it with sugar from the dispenser and opened the drawer for a spoon.

"I thought about the first time I bought you coffee." David was nervously talking. "I thought a lot about us this week."

Amanda stared at her coffee and said she did too.

David now had his coffee and was in the refrigerator looking for the creamer.

"The trainees got a kick out of our meeting. They didn't believe me when I told them about you. Not just that you were black, but how you worked hard, created a place for yourself in this business, and loved me."

David poured the creamer in and stirred. "Thank you so much for today. You made it all richer, meaningful, and fun."

"I loved it," she said.

There was quiet. David and Amanda held their coffees in one hand and took each other's hands as David led them to the den. When they were both inside, he shut the French doors and allowed her to sit wherever she wanted. Amanda sat in the corner of the sectional, so David sat next to her.

They sipped their coffee, and finally David spoke.

"I have been a mess all week. Trying to find words that don't sound so flippant, nonchalant, or selfish. But that is exactly what I did, so it is going to sound like that. I wasn't thinking about anyone else but me and what I wanted."

Amanda sat there and looked at David with his head down, looking into his coffee.

Then, no more hesitation, he looked her in the face and said, "Amanda, I have been having an affair with another woman. It was a mistake that could cost me all that I care about. I ended the relationship on Monday because we both figured out that our behavior was ridiculous, reckless, and selfish."

Amanda sat without words. She was glad he owned it, and she felt a tear fall from one eye. The tear surprised her. Perhaps it fell because the truth was finally out in the atmosphere. She put her coffee cup on the table, got up, went to her desk behind the sectional, and found the floral card she had moved from her purse, now in her Bible. She handed it to him and sat back down. This time, she got comfortable in the corner of the sectional with her back resting on the pillows, her feet tucked underneath her, and she faced David.

He looked at the card and asked, "How did you get this?"

"Well, in a way, you sent it to me," Amanda said, and then explained how the floral shop made an error. "I thought it was a mistake, but that is your handwriting and your signature at the bottom." David faced her and sighed in shame.

Amanda continued to be calm. "To realize your husband is not only sending flowers to another woman, but that they had an amazing time. I worked it out with the floral shop to resend Samantha her flowers with your sentiment. She's not me. She didn't know, nor did she care about the handwriting on the card."

"You know her name?" David said.

"I'm a woman, David. I know Sam is Samantha Coleman, program sales director at Waters Square Hotel," Amanda said. "I saw her today. She approached me. I told her it is not good to take things that don't belong to her."

David wasn't surprised; he knew Amanda could be fierce when she wanted.

The couple sat in silence. Amanda took the blanket off the back of the sectional and used it to wipe her tears, which were now flowing frequently. David rose and got her the box of tissues from his desk, and sat back down.

"Why didn't you tell *me* you knew?" David asked her.

Amanda found herself upset at the question. "I don't know, the same reason you didn't tell *me* you were with another woman, and you came home to *me*, showered and slid next to *me* into our bed."

That statement deeply convicted David. What Amanda said was fair.

"True."

"David, I was afraid of the answer, or worse, a lie." Amanda paused and then asked, "What *time was amazing?*"

"Amanda, don't ..." He didn't want to hurt her more than he already was. But he did promise himself that he would answer every one of her questions honestly.

"I want to know. Was it the sex?"

"Yes." Again, David looked at her.

"Did she give you blowjobs?"

"Yes."

"Did you taste her?"

"Never," David said, looking at his wife. "Amanda, in my mind, I wanted to please myself. I thought I wanted to be single again."

David explained how he met Samantha at the young professional event and how one thing led to another. He told her his mind was on escaping the stress of applying for the promotion. David confessed he should've told her about the pressure, but she was in the middle of a busy season of resets and remodels; she had just gotten promoted. He didn't want to burden her, but he should have.

"Amanda, in no way am I excusing my behavior. I want you to know what I was thinking. Sam and I were a release for each other. Like stupid teenage kids, running to a hotel room to think a physical sexual release was going to rid us of the emotional situations around us."

She quietly sat with what he said, taking in all his words. She closed her eyes, and God reminded her of Nathan. David's first night with Samantha was no different from her night with Nathan. God continued to calm her, and she knew it would be wrong of her to be self-righteous.

After several minutes, she spoke. "I found your condoms in the car."

David had guilt on his face. "I'm sorry, Amanda, that I have done this."

"Do you know if Samantha is pregnant?"

"She is not," David answered.

"Any STDs?"

"No." He recalled his dad asking him the same question.

"I know," she said. "I went to the clinic to address my weight loss. I had them check me."

"Amanda, I'm sorry." David said, but it felt empty to him to say just two words. But Dr. Nick said it would be, but the words were necessary.

"What was it?" Amanda finally asked with tears in her eyes. "What did I do to make Samantha the escape?"

David took her hand and looked at her wedding ring. "Amanda, I love you. I love providing for you and the boys. I am proud to be your husband. But I pride myself on taking care of you and protecting you, especially because of all the pain from your childhood and the postpartum depression after Mason."

"I felt that going to work and bringing home a paycheck was good enough. If we were going to secure our future, I needed to do this. Matthew and Mason would have to understand that Dad is working. And I told myself I was doing this for you."

Then he felt tears on his face, and Amanda leaned into him, making the hand holding more meaningful. He said with a voice cracking, "Because I couldn't do it for my mom when dad left. But I wasn't going to be like him. I was going to provide for my family." The tears continued.

"Now, here I am like him." David shared with Amanda what had happened in the yard that morning, and for the first time, he felt his dad understood him. Amanda and David cried together. Wiping tears and blowing their noses, releasing emotions. Amanda couldn't deny that what happened between David and his father was years in the making. Michael had tried to get David to be honest about his feelings towards him, but David would shut down or avoid the confrontation. To Amanda, it appeared everything was out in the open, and now healing could begin for father and son.

"Bruce asked to see my cell phone this morning and saw my text messages to and from Sam," David said. "He is so upset with me right now. He has every right to be. Bruce loves you. He sees you as his sister, and did even before we married."

Amanda didn't want to share that she overheard that.

"I want to ask you about Nathan. Bruce told me that you think about him. You have a relationship with him." David was afraid to ask. "Are we talking about Nathan Montgomery from Augusta?"

"We are," Amanda said, letting go of his hand. She re-adjusted herself.

"Before I explain, I have to share how you have neglected me and the boys."

"Yes, I have." David was quiet.

"I am hurt by it, and I'm angry," she said. "The boys hate your phone. Matthew told me that when you are with them, it's like you're not. You're on your phone most of the time. So you are present but not engaging."

She tried to dry her eyes, but the tears were rolling faster now.

"Mason is so scared of you."

David, now with more tears and a look of surprise. "Scared?"

"Yes, he's afraid that you don't like him, think he is slow, and that he takes too much of your time," Amanda sobbed. She couldn't say anymore, and David was trying to take it all in.

"Amanda, I'm sorry. I want to fix this. I love our sons." David was truthful.

"I've hurt them too; I now see that. I love Mason so much. I need to take time with him, and I am prepared to do that."

Amanda slowly stopped crying. "I guess you will have to prove that to him."

"Yes. I will see them tomorrow. I need to apologize to Matthew, too," David said.

Amanda sighed. It was not a sigh that David was going to apologize, and all would be better. No, it was good to get all of this off her mind and her heart and release all that she had been holding in. She told David that he was taking his family for granted, and his parents were not going to live forever. Amanda talked about the plans her parents had one day, and their lives were gone in a flash because of the house fire. David understood.

"For a while there, I felt used," Amanda told him. "I'm the driver of the kids to school. Sure, you pick them up, but because you're not engaged, it's an empty service. I still am the one with dinner and homework, class projects, laundry, and keeping their calendars, and I work too. You get to go out with the guys, come home buzzed and horny. I say nothing and give you what you want."

David was now hurting. He was seeing his landscape of selfishness through the lens of his wife, and it was painful.

"Please don't misunderstand. When I say I need rest, you do help. But if I don't, I'm just invisible to the entire house, like no one sees, recognizes, or appreciates me." Hearing her words, David reminisced about the image she drew in her journal.

"I admit it; I desire you, and I love our sex life. I say yes most of the time because I want it. But when you came home from Prairie Heights, it was about you, not me, until I started initiating sex. You were the one feeling good. Sure, you would touch me in my pleasure places, but it was for you, not to connect with me."

"I'm sorry, Amanda." David knew he had done that, and now he deeply regretted it.

"When I found out about Samantha, I cried all week that week. I figured I did something, or created an environment at home not worthy of the love and lovemaking I desired. I was not myself at work. I would often close my office door to cry, take frequent trips to the bathroom, and space out in meetings. By Friday, I was in the conference room, and I honestly couldn't tell you how many times Nathan had called my name before I answered him. I tried to play it off, but I was crying."

David finished his coffee and held the mug with both hands, rubbing his thumbs around the rim.

"I had no idea Nathan felt the way he did about me until that moment when he was consoling me. He kissed my hair and said I was beautiful."

Amanda told David about the encounter, and she gave Nathan permission to touch her because she felt neglected. David bit his lip hard and slammed his coffee mug hard on the table in anger. Amanda jumped.

"David, the way he touched me... it was lust. I was the one who went for his belt buckle before he stopped me. Nathan told me to come home to you."

David balled his hand into a fist and put his forehead on it.

"Nathan turned me on. He didn't know about my childhood trauma or my depression, and he didn't handle me with kid gloves. He made me look at myself and notice the sexy, the fire, and the beauty."

Amanda addressed David's anger with indignation. "What?"

She looked at him with his lips pressed together, and he was now rubbing his forehead. "You don't have a monopoly on being angry. I spent months sharing my husband with another woman, and you're gonna get angry that your neglected wife desired another man? I didn't have sex with Nathan in a hotel room for months. You did that with Samantha."

The room grew quiet again. The pain of her last sentence lingered in the air. Amanda took more tissues and formed the used ones into a pile next to her.

"Amanda," David closed his eyes and was now calm. "All of this is my fault. I caused this, and it hurts."

"Welcome to the party," she said sarcastically.

"So all this initiating sex was an effort to keep me home?" David asked. The question angered Amanda, and she got up. She was enraged and tired. David remained seated.

"After I left Nathan, I called Regina. It was not a girls' night; it was more of a night of conviction and confessing to Leslie, Regina & Greg. I told them sex for us was so *married-couple-like*; wrong. I just let sex happen; I wasn't the initiator. Maybe that was the problem."

"Greg agreed with me and what Nathan said—not having sex with you would mean more neglect for me and give you a reason to keep Samantha around." Amanda shared how her friends did her hair and encouraged her to keep her husband interested in being with her.

All David could do was shake his head. "Look at my mess," he said under his breath. Amanda heard him and promised God that where there was humility, she couldn't continue in hurtful anger.

"When I initiated, I came alive, and I wasn't expecting that. I saw your response—that you were slowly engaging and paying attention. Finally, I felt more confident. I knew work was stressful, so I tried things to relieve your stress, and it worked. When I came to the office and told you to touch me, I was glowing for days after. I prayed for you to end the affair, and you did."

David got up and hugged her from behind. Amanda felt numb. His right cheek touched her left cheek. There were no words.

Then, he softly said, "You have every right to be angry at me. Thank you for telling me about Nathan, and for not giving up on me and praying for me."

Amanda softened.

"Please go rest," he said. "Thank you for listening and sharing your feelings."

He let go of her and left the den.

Amanda wrapped herself in the blanket and continued to cry silently until she fell asleep on the sectional in the den with tissues all around her.

David went downstairs into the guest bedroom and shut the door. He grabbed a pillow from the bed and sat in the corner, between the dresser and the wall. With his back against the wall, pillow in his lap, he put his knees up and buried his face in the pillow, and cried. Of course, Amanda's scent on the pillow made him sob even harder.

He cried because he had hurt her. He cried because there was Nathan, and he was pissed about him touching his wife, but if he hadn't neglected her and taken her for granted, that probably wouldn't have happened. David cried that there was another Lloyd who cheated on their wife. He cried about his relationship with his dad; he knew he couldn't keep the anger in after all this time.

David cried when he thought about his relationship with Bruce. Such a sensitive little brother was hurt that he hadn't told him about Sam or how he was feeling. He laughed because when he cried, he felt the pain in his stomach from the punches Bruce gave him. Then he realized he couldn't laugh or cry anymore. The pain made it uncomfortable to do either. He sat in silence, then he prayed.

"I know, it has been a while. I'm sorry," David had tears.

"It's me, trying to do life without you, and, of course, it's not working out very well. I don't even know what to say except, Help me. Help me not just out of this mess, but help me. Help David, the ten-year-old boy who is still angry at his dad. Help me, the brother who has been so selfish and prideful with his younger brother, more often than listening to him. Help me be a better father."

David cried now, not caring that it hurt. "God, help me to be a better husband. Amanda deserves someone better, but I love her, so make me better. You're the only one who can do it. My sons need me to be better. Help me! Help me!" he sobbed.

"Help me, God, be a better son to you. Please forgive me for the adultery, the foolishness, the pride, the selfishness, and placing more value in all your blessings: Amanda, the boys, the job, the car, the house, and the success. I deserve to lose it all, but please, teach me how to walk with you again."

"I can't do life without you; it hurts."

David buried his head in the pillow, exhausted. He quieted himself. He rested in his breathing. He got up and lay across the bed.

CHAPTER 18

David and Amanda arrived at the Acuff corporate offices to welcome Acuff employees, trainees, their families, and community college partners. While many events at Acuff were sit-down dinners with placement cards and five-course meals, David knew that such an atmosphere would highlight trainees' lack of resources instead of the program's benefits: a new beginning and career path.

Many of the trainees did not have families. David made the event an outdoor gathering in the courtyard of the Acuff restaurant; an informal buffet style, so everyone felt comfortable and would interact with one another. When it came time to welcome Samantha Coleman and her boyfriend, Terrance Winters, Amanda thought there would be an awkward moment, but it wasn't for her.

Terrance was an average-height white man with glasses, light brown hair, and a nice smile. Amanda learned he had just obtained his Ph.D. in engineering from the University of Kansas, and he was in Brookview to help Samantha with the family home, as her mom had passed a year ago.

There it was, Amanda thought. She had seen the familiar sadness in Samantha's eyes earlier. "I'm sorry to hear about your mom," Amanda found herself saying, and Samantha's response was a simple nod, but the look in her eyes was one of humility and appreciation again.

David looked at Samantha with sincere kindness. They exchanged a look, Amanda noticed. It was a clear *we-have-history exchange*, but Samantha held Terrance close and leaned her head on his arm to communicate she was happy. She did look happy, and Amanda could tell David was happy about that.

After all the guests were welcomed, Vikki handed David a large interoffice envelope. David took Amanda's hand and led her out of the courtyard and into the abandoned Acuff building. Nothing was going on early Saturday evening in the corporate offices, and it was clear to Amanda that David wanted a quiet space to open the envelope. They sat in a small conference room, just the two of them.

David spoke first, opening the envelope, and Amanda took a seat in a rolling chair next to him.

"I have so much to say, Amanda," he said. "I feel like our conversation today took the pressure off, but I still got a knot in this mess of a life I created. Please bear with me."

"Okay." Amanda was hesitant.

"When I got promoted, I got the bonus, and we celebrated. I expected a salary increase, but nothing like what I got. There was a reason for that, and I want to tell you after the event, okay?" David looked at the papers that were in the envelope and put them out in front of them.

"I created a separate account for the extra because, quite frankly, I wasn't sure if I wanted it. But Acuff did the right thing. So what you are looking at is how much extra Acuff has given me. Well..." He looked at her and saw those brown eyes. He smiled and remembered the first time he had seen them. "... how much extra Acuff gave us."

Amanda looked at the amount in surprise. "In the past three months, this is how much money is in the savings account?"

"Was in the savings account," David said with a chuckle. "Today, we are giving it away."

David explained that there were eight trainees with no parent representation at all. He said Acuff, the corporation, paid for the trainees' moving expenses, just as they would pay for any Acuff employee relocating to accept a position at a store. The savings would cover the first month's rent for the eight. David explained it would help them use their first paycheck to buy things they need for their new apartment or clothes for work.

Amanda had a closed smile on her face as she saw the receipts from the rental properties with each trainee's name on it.

"As you can see, it leaves money in the account. It's for Chelsea and her mom. You met her earlier. Amanda, Chelsea rests in my soul like hot chocolate after sledding with the boys. She is soft, warm in spirit, quiet, but a bit giggly because she is a young girl." David and Amanda both smiled at his description.

"She's only twenty and advanced to have earned her bachelor's degree at her age. But her dad was removed from their home for opioid addiction and for the physical abuse he caused her and her mom. They needed a car, so I got them one of our fleet vehicles. It has a few miles on it, but it's nice; brand new, really," David said.

He told Amanda, Chelsea and her mom will move to Galesboro. Chelsea would train and work in Corey's store. He wanted her with someone he truly trusted to look after what he called this "sweet family." The rest of the money would be used for whatever they needed.

Amanda was overwhelmed with joy. This was the man she married. The take-charge but caring guy who saw the bruises on her arms and wanted to know how he could help. The one who drove to St. Louis more times than she could remember for just a night curled up next to her with kisses and chocolate chip ice cream. She turned her chair towards him and rolled it so they were face-to-face. She closed her eyes and placed her lips tenderly on his.

Amanda remembered that day she went through David's desk and saw the congratulations letter for the bonus and salary. She remembered her anger and confusion when she called the bank and discovered the savings account without her name. She was grateful that she had waited to say something. Amanda realized from this day on that she would just ask him.

David took her kiss in and how happy it made him. "Oh Amanda. I don't deserve that."

"God's mercy and grace." Their eyes met.

David was clear he didn't want to make a scene out of Amanda's and his gift-giving. Vikki had arranged for Chelsea's car to be at the hotel tomorrow morning so she could drive it to Galesboro.

All the trainees received envelopes at the end of the evening and were told not to open them until they got back to the hotel. They were asked to have enough integrity and respect not to compare the gifts but to be grateful that a gift was given.

David and Amanda didn't arrive home before David's phone was buzzing with *Thank Yous* and *Love Yous* from the trainees and their guardians. David told Amanda the sentiment he and the trainees and have—*It's like that*. It means *you're welcome*, as in *you and I have it like that*. Amanda liked that sentiment and began texting it back to the trainees as David drove the SUV into the garage.

As they sat in the car in the garage, David sighed. "Amanda."

"Yes." She could tell he had more on his heart. "Vikki gave you an envelope."

"She did," Amanda said quietly. "She told me to read it because you might not tell me, but she felt I needed to know."

David put his head on the steering wheel. "I love Vikki," he said in an attempt to convince himself that his new executive assistant was good for him.

"Vikki loves us," Amanda remembered her conversation with Vikki that morning.

"Yes, she does," David said as they got out of the car.

As they got into the house, Amanda put her shoes and purse in the mudroom. David was behind her and put the keys on the kitchen counter.

"You don't have to get the envelope, but we do need to keep it in a safe place, okay?"

"Okay," Amanda said. She took his hand. "What is it about? Please, from here on, don't keep things from me."

"I agree," David said. He confirmed he could not eat or drink anything else. Amanda agreed. David lay on the couch in the living room, looking up at the ceiling. Amanda lay on the sofa in the same position.

"When I get to Dallas, I am going to sleep like a baby," she said. "You leave tomorrow?!" David remembered and immediately didn't want her to go.

"Yes." Amanda didn't want to talk about it the way he wanted to. "Please tell me about this envelope."

There was silence because David had many emotions about his wife going to Dallas with a man who had feelings for her.

"My stress with this whole promotion was crazy. It got out of control." David was ready to explain, not moving from his position.

"I got a letter from Gerald and the senior vice presidents stating I had been nominated for a promotion. They looked at my longevity with the company and the success of the stores I managed. Letters of recommendation were required, and I had to write a letter and a paper/proposal about what I would do if I were a vice president."

"Wow," Amanda said. "I'm stressed for you. Why didn't you tell me?" She didn't move from her position either.

"My pride. And this was your first season overseeing the resets and remodels for Augusta in this area. You had your own things going on," David said.

"I thought if I didn't have all these responsibilities, life would be easier.

It hurts to even say what I was thinking. 'I'm working here, is anybody noticing?' I would say to myself."

"The boys were misbehaving. Matthew was not turning in his homework. Mason was crying all the time about the boys at school not liking him, but he just had two boys over for a playdate, and they had a blast. I just did not understand, and I was frustrated. I'd go out with the guys, come home, have sex with my wife—who I now know hated that sex—and get up in the morning to write the paper."

"I didn't hate the sex, David," Amanda added. "I just knew it wasn't …," Amanda thought hate was too strong a word. "… right, but go on."

"So I turned everything in. I went to the young professional event, and that's when I met Sam. We knew we had made a mistake. We both agreed at the time it would be a one-time thing, no one would ever know."

Amanda sat up. All this time, she thought Samantha and David had met with no break in their relationship; this was not the case. She was listening more intensely.

"After a week, I got a call from Emily Shepherd." David was still lying down, but noticed Amanda was now sitting up. "Emily is now at Acuff's corporate human resources. I'm so proud of her."

"Me too, but why did she call you?"

"She said she was coming by as a friend off the clock. She had to tell me something. It was serious." David now sat up.

Amanda was waiting for David to continue.

"Emily gets to the store, and we are in the restaurant talking. She wanted it to look like we were catching up like old friends. We were until she told me she saw my application for vice president. Very impressive from my end. Everything was in order. The senior vice presidents voted, she said."

David told Amanda that Acuff has seven senior vice presidents. One in each state and three that remain in the corporate office to oversee human resources, finance, and logistics. He told her that three of the senior vice presidents did not want him to be a vice president.

Amanda, now leaning in, asked, "Why not? What did she say?"

David sighed hard. "Emily said they cited my moral character. Immediately, I thought of my night with Sam. Who found out? But that wasn't it."

David was silent.

"David?" Amanda said.

"It was you." David looked at her so softly. "Emily said three of the senior vice presidents considered my interracial marriage as a reason why I didn't get all the points for good moral character."

"Unbelievable!" Amanda threw her hands up. "So let me get this straight: You can sleep with another woman—a white woman—but if you have a black wife, THAT is cited as bad moral character? What the hell, David?!"

David didn't think about it that way, but she was right. "Yes, but no one knew about Sam. They still don't. Please don't get mad at me. Emily and I were having a conversation in the restaurant. She was telling me what she knew."

Amanda covered her mouth with her hand and looked at him to continue. "I'm floored."

David was recalling the day. "And so was Emily. She told me that *not in good moral character* usually includes things like stealing from the store, embezzlement, misusing funds, a police record for driving under the influence...things that could affect the image of the company and your work ethic. But this was a serious problem for the company. She told me the senior vice president in HR held my application and gave it to Gerald."

"Emily went on to tell me that Acuff was an equal opportunity employer. They agree not to discriminate against any employee or job applicant because of race, color, religion, or marital status. This was a mess." David was getting anxious.

Amanda was connecting the dots. "So there is actual documentation that three members of senior-level management did not want an employee to be promoted because they considered him having an African American wife was not in good moral standing for the company?"

"Correct," David said.

"My Lord. Well, you are standing here as a vice president. What happened?" Amanda was angry that she was just now finding this out.

"Emily said that, as her brother-friend, she had to tell me. But the three vice presidents would re-vote, and they could not cite that reason."

"When they re-voted, what did they cite?"

"They miraculously gave me all the points I needed," David sighed. "But I'm angry, Amanda, and hurt. I've been with Acuff for 23 years, and because the love of my life is a different color, they were not going to promote me? How wrong and illegal? And how do I tell you and have you not feel upset, disappointed, and hurt?"

"But you didn't tell me!" Amanda said heatedly.

"I'm telling you now," David said, raising his voice. "It was not over! I felt like my bonus was justified from the Lindale store. We met our sales goal as a store, and I was happy to bring that money home to our family."

Amanda could tell there was more to come, and David was on his feet, pacing. He was irate.

"When the increase in salary came, I created a savings account. I didn't want that money. Was it hush money? Sympathy money? I was trying to decide if I wanted to be with a company that didn't accept me and my family. It was a complete slap in the face. Brad and Tom both told me that just because three people felt that way doesn't mean the whole company felt that way."

Amanda listened, and she understood where David was coming from. He had devoted so much of his life to this grocery store chain. It was his refuge when his parents' divorce; most of his friends were from the stores he managed. He met her there, along with Tom and Gail Cochran, Alice and Gerald Acuff—both couples were like second parents to him.

"Emily told me she did not get rid of the first vote, and she kept the papers. She also said she kept the second vote. She knew Gerald talked to those men, and their vote changed." David was still pacing.

"So we celebrated the vote." David was still fuming; Amanda was anxious, trying to grasp it all.

"It's an all-day store leadership meeting. After 5:00 pm, the vice presidents and senior vice presidents meet in the executive conference room to celebrate my becoming the newest vice president. Of course, Tom and Brad were there. Gerald stopped by, congratulated me, and left; he had a flight to catch. The senior vice president of HR is the only senior vice president not there. It's a guy thing; you celebrate with a cigar and Scotch."

Amanda frowned, but understood.

"After the laughter and the congratulations, there were toasts from Tom and Brad. One vice president, Galvin, says. 'You'll go home and celebrate with your wife.'"

"Oh no," Amanda imagined the next comment.

David put one finger in the air. "Honestly, Galvin's comment was innocent. We've played golf together. He had no clue the can of worms he opened. When the next comment came, Galvin was a bit uncomfortable, but he laughed."

"The next comment was..." Amanda said.

"David likes his coffee like he likes his women—hot and black." David rolled his eyes. "We all laughed."

Amanda chuckled but wasn't amused.

"It was okay until another senior vice president went way left with his comment." David's heart was racing, and he stopped pacing.

"He says, 'How does it work at home, David? Is she the house slave and you the master?'"

David put his hand out to Amanda, gesturing for her not to say a word. "I swear to you, Amanda, I rose from the table that was between us, and he continued saying, *I bet she is beautiful and delicious; you can bring her here for us all.*"

"After that goddamn comment, Brad and Galvin held me back, telling me he wasn't worth it, so I spat in his face. I told him he was never to put my name or my family's name in his mouth again." David was shaking; his face was red and hot with tears.

Amanda sat there in complete silence with tears in her eyes. She had no words. She gave David a moment to calm down, but he took a pillow from the couch and threw it across the room in disgust.

It was quiet. Amanda recalled her chance meeting at the grocery store. "That explains the senior vice presidents at the Brookview store and you meeting me for lunch that day."

David closed his eyes and gave her a look of yes.

"Those are awful words, David." She was deeply offended by them. "Words, I am sure you probably had a hard time repeating to me."

She went to him and made him sit down.

"Yes," David was calming down. "I'm sorry, Amanda. I'm sorry for all of it."

She rubbed his back.

"The audio was recorded," David finally said.

"What?" Amanda was stunned.

"In that executive conference room, there was a meeting forty-five minutes prior, and they didn't shut off the audio equipment."

Amanda shook her head. "Let me guess, all that documentation is in the envelope?"

"Yeah," David said. "When all of this came out, Julie, the administrative assistant, found the recording. Emily had the original vote documentation and the series of memos to encourage the second vote. The senior vice president of HR had no choice but to sit down with me. He clearly had to admit this was discrimination because there was no other basis for me not to be promoted. Since I was promoted, could we forget all of this?"

David hung his head. "I sat with this for a while."

"I'm sure you did," Amanda said.

"What benefit would it bring? I got the promotion. What case could I bring but bad misconduct? It was easy when Gerald came to me completely humbled and broken-hearted. He begged me not to publicize this and hurt his 85-year-old family business," David said.

"Gerald told the senior vice president he had grounds to fire him, so it was his choice to retire and take what Gerald was offering or be let go. He chose retirement at the end of the year. Then Gerald came to me asking what we should do."

Amanda figured it out. "The Acuff Academy."

"Yes," David said. "I heard department stores do it all the time, so I read about them and contacted community colleges and remembered Sam. We thought we could keep our relationship professional, but we couldn't."

"David," Amanda sighed.

"Amanda, I'm sorry. I told Gerald today that I didn't want this job if I couldn't be a godly man. He gave me a bonus for the Acuff Academy. It was reasonable; not hush money for what happened. We just gave Chelsea and her mom a car with it. I didn't want it."

Amanda took it all in. David had been carrying all this stuff for months. It started with frustration right here at home. Amanda felt more tears coming, and her frustration with David increasing. Like a light switch, a surge of emotion came over her. "We aren't going to make it."

"What do you mean?" David was settled now. He was relieved he got everything out.

Amanda got up and disappeared into the mudroom. David heard her rummaging around and heard the garage door open, close, and then open again. Amanda came back into his view with her tennis shoes on, in her t-shirt dress, which she had on from the evening, and a big cardboard box. She began opening the cabinets in the kitchen, taking the plates, glasses, and mugs from the shelves, and just putting them in the box with indignation. She opened the sliding glass door to the deck and turned on the outside lights.

"Amanda, what are you doing? Honey, it's getting late." David was concerned and got up from the living room and went towards her.

But Amanda was already outside with the box of dishes in the yard at the edge of the basketball court, which was a concrete slab in their backyard with a basketball hoop at one end. He saw her take one plate from the box and throw it on the concrete, breaking it into pieces.

"Why does everyone think I'm this fragile thing? Not able to handle life."

He quickly put on his shoes and ran out in his t-shirt and jeans. "Amanda, what are you doing?!"

"I'm in my right mind." She broke another plate. "I'm angry at you for treating me like your child and not your wife!"

She threw another plate down. "We are not gonna make it, David. We will be divorced in a year."

"Please don't say that." He stood on the deck and decided she needed to get her frustrations out. "I'm so sorry."

"Don't be sorry. Stop holding things in and keeping things from me like I'm going to break." Amanda broke another plate.

"I'm stronger than you think. I am tired of you and all my friends thinking I'm like this fragile piece of glass." She took a drinking glass and dropped it on the concrete. She took another plate and broke it.

"David, Samantha is just a by-product of what is really going on. You'll be stressed out again. Where, who, and what will you run to?" Amanda stopped for a moment and then broke another dish.

"Amanda, I won't do this again…"

She didn't let him finish. "That is what you say now. But you are not engaging with anyone, especially me. Do you know I am here to help you?" She threw another plate.

David noticed the word. He was now standing in the grass, still several feet from her.

"When God made Eve, she was a suitable helper for Adam." Amanda looked at her husband. "She didn't have kids to take to school or dry cleaning to pick up. I wonder if she cooked dinner or made sure he was sexually satisfied? Or whatever subordinate role men think wives just do." Amanda broke another plate and then a glass.

"No, as your wife, I have aspects of God's character. I can be your strength and your rescuer. Through prayer alone, David, I've protected you." She stopped.

"Be honest right now. What did I do? What kind of environment did I create in this home that made you give in to Samantha? You didn't answer me today. I'm a big girl, David. I can handle the answer."

David came closer to her and fell on his knees. He had asked God to help him today, and God's answer was right in front of him. Amanda.

"You weren't happy anymore." David finally said. "My fault, I'm sure. Both of us are going through the motions. *I am* treating you like a child; taking care of you like I took care of my mom, I guess."

"David, you can tell me what you want. I'm not going to break. Yes, as a child I was abused and raped. The best thing you can do for me now is love me for real." She broke another plate, then a mug, and then a glass.

"I hate that this has happened," she sobbed. "I hate that you ran to her, and you didn't come to me!" Amanda broke more plates.

She stopped and wiped her hands on her dress, breathing hard, and saw the blood. She fell to her knees. David crawled to her and held her. He took her hand and saw the cut, but she took her hand back and hit him in the chest.

"I'm so broken. This hurts; you hurt me so bad!" She saw that she had put blood on his white shirt, which caused her to pause and put her head down.

"Aren't I teachable? I pray for you, us, the kids, Mom, Dad, Bill...we are the family I wanted. Why am I seen as this fragile black woman when I am so much more than that?"

"Honey, to God and me, you are beautiful inside and out." He stroked her hair. "I'm sorry I didn't come to you. I should've. I'm so sorry I hurt you," he told her, with tears in his eyes.

Amanda continued to cry, but she was listening.

"Jesus is our standard; the world is not. It doesn't matter what kind of environment you created here at home; I should not have had an affair with Sam, period." David was clear. He gently took her head and lifted it so he could see her eyes.

She saw his clear indignation, but she also saw kindness.

"No matter how much neglect you felt, you should have never allowed Nathan to touch you," David said.

Amanda was convicted. She just realized she hurt him too. She put her head down and spoke.

"You are right. I'm sorry."

They both held each other in the yard, crying with broken plates around them.

"Amanda, don't go to Dallas." David dried his tears and was direct.

Amanda looked at her hands covered in her blood and David's shirt. He got up first and helped her up. "Leave this," he said, looking at the broken plates and glasses.

David led Amanda up to the deck. They took their shoes off, turned out the outside lights, and locked the sliding glass doors. David turned on the cold water from the kitchen sink and placed Amanda's hands in the stream of water.

"David, I am going to Dallas for work. Nathan will be there, but he will not be my focus." Amanda wanted to be honest, so she took over washing her hands.

David caught her every word. "Well, what will he be?"

Amanda sighed. "A colleague; it's a company-wide conference."

"You told me Nathan stopped by here. What happened that night?"

David didn't like Nathan being at his home.

"I told you. Because I was absent-minded, I left my office keys in the door. Nathan came by to check on me, gave me my keys back, and told me to take the week off. He never came into the house. We talked outside," Amanda said.

She shared what Nathan told her about his life; he was divorced with a son who was graduating high school, and how he gave his life to Christ. "He knows..." Amanda felt the sting of the cut on her hand. She sucked air in.

"He knows what?" David wanted her to finish, but directed her to sit on one of the barstools in the kitchen.

"He knows I want to save my marriage."

David's emotions settled. He examined her hands and found the cut on her left index finger. Without a word, he went for the first-aid kit in the drawer, found the anti-bacterial cream and a Band-Aid.

"And now there is this company that reminds me of my childhood. I need to go see it at the Dallas Market Center."

"How does it remind you of your childhood?" David asked as he treated her finger.

Amanda told him about the bath products and accessories from Snowflake Ranch.

"Today, as I was sharing about my childhood to the trainees, I hesitated for a moment because my mind went somewhere in the past. And that Snowflake Ranch logo was there, but I don't remember." Amanda was frustrated she couldn't recall.

David remembered that moment today where she paused, but his mind was still on Nathan.

"Okay. I get you will be working, Amanda, but it's a week with a man who is attracted to you. Are you traveling with him?"

"No. I have no clue about his flight itinerary. Vanessa booked me on the last flight tomorrow at 4:00 pm. Leslie is coming to get me and take me to the airport."

David sighed. Amanda could tell he was not satisfied with any of her answers. But he took her finger and kissed it. She slid off the bar stool and gave him a hug.

"Thank you," she said quietly.

He didn't speak; he began unbuttoning her dress, exposing her champagne-colored bra and panties. He took the dress off her shoulders, and it fell to the ground. David pulled her close with one hand on the back of her neck at her hairline, the other hand on her creamed caramel skin-toned waist. Amanda was breathing hard as their lips barely touched.

He kissed her with such intensity, she couldn't help but accept his wanting. She couldn't remember the last time David had taken her where she didn't feel an air of selfishness. The hand that was once on her waist had now moved to her butt and upper left thigh. He had her in a position of admiration, close to him. He finally whispered in her ear, "Remember, I am your husband. I love you. I know every inch of you. I am yours, and you are mine."

Then he softly let her go. David picked up her dress off the floor, took off his shirt, and headed to the laundry room. He spoke in his normal tone, just as if that moment hadn't happened.

"Amanda, go to bed. It's been a long day." She smiled and got the point he was trying to make. She belonged to someone who loved her, and she had better not forget it.

CHAPTER 19

*A*manda woke up at 4:00 am. David's side of the bed was abandoned. She sighed and remembered yesterday. All of yesterday.

Amanda thought it was a sigh of relief that all was out in the open—Samantha Coleman, Nathan Montgomery, the Acuff Academy, and the discrimination around David's promotion. She thought about David and the way he touched her last night before bed. She smiled and thanked God David was home.

Then she thought, did she want to get out of bed this early? Tea and the sunrise on the front porch suggested yes. She got out of bed, put on her oversized sweatshirt and leggings, and headed downstairs.

The house was still. She went to the kitchen and opened the cabinet, but there were no mugs. She closed her eyes and remembered. After Dallas, she would have to buy new dishes. She went to the pantry and found plastic cups and plates. She started the hot water, leaned against the counter, and saw it.

On the dining room table was the Bible; David's Bible. It was black leather, worn. She went to it and opened the front of it. There was the dedication she remembered and loved:

To my grandson, David. Allow this book to forever be your compass.
—Grandma Em.

If there ever was a great loss for David, Amanda thought, it was Grandma Emma, Meri's mom. David described her as one of a kind, and would not have cared if Amanda was yellow. The first thing she would've asked was, *Does she know Jesus?* Amanda smiled at the thought and wished she could've met her.

The sound of the tea kettle's whistle pulled her back to the kitchen. Her heart was more than glad when David pulled out his Bible, but she thought about how many times she had run to her Bible when she was in trouble, only to put it back down again. She caught her doubt. Faith was needed here.

She grabbed the heaviest blanket she could find and carried it outside with her to the front porch with her tea. As she watched the sunrise, she prayed and asked God to give her deep conviction about Nathan. If there was self-righteousness in her about her and Nathan and her comparing it to David and Samantha, she prayed that God would show her the sin.

David was right. She shouldn't have given Nathan permission to touch her, and she felt David's disappointment. Now she needed to feel her Heavenly Father's sadness and to help her see. She thought and meditated on the scripture that there is no one righteous; all fall short of the glory of God.

~

David woke at 5:00 am to his phone. It was a simple text from his dad: *I'm praying for you and Amanda now.*

A comfort, David thought, and so needed. He felt the weight of all he was carrying gone, but now the consequences. He would see Bruce today, the boys, and what about his mom and Bill? He had to apologize to everyone and tell the truth.

He turned over on his back, his eyes on the ceiling. *How do I tell my mom? She warned me.* He remembered her telling him to stay home and spend more time with the boys. The hurt in her eyes would be just as bad as Amanda's last night.

He played yesterday like a movie in his head. He rolled over, hugged the pillow, and cried. He thought, *Forget being strong; admit that you are weak and in need of a Savior.* He was so grateful for his Grandma Em, who told him all about Jesus growing up. When he left for college, he fell into drinking, partying, and that relationship with Holly. But when he found the campus ministry, The Way, it all changed.

The Way was a fun group of people who didn't make loving Jesus weird. They played cards, drank beer, went on group dates, studied the Bible, and lived life responsibly. He remembered being baptized in a horse trough after a revival on a farm in Wisconsin. Then he thought about yesterday and what the group of guys used to say when they fell into sin: "Jesus, you're still saving me." David took comfort in the memories. He drifted back to sleep, thanking God for his mercy.

It was about 7:30 am when Bruce showed up at David and Amanda's to get ready for the parent program at Sugar Creek Farms to see Matthew and Mason. David was still sleeping, and Amanda had drifted to sleep, lying down in the den, when Bruce came to the door.

"Bruce," Amanda said softly, leading him to the kitchen. "I haven't seen David, yet. I'm sure he set his alarm for 8:00. I can make you a cup of coffee if you'd like?" She leaned against the kitchen counter and offered him a sit across from her on one of the barstools.

"Sure. I actually came early to talk to you. How are you?" Bruce looked at her sincerely. For once, he wasn't wearing his construction t-shirt. He was dressed in khaki cargo shorts and a solid navy t-shirt.

"I am well." She had now made a pot of coffee and poured him a cup. "Plastic cup this morning," she said, scratching her head with embarrassment.

"Okay." Bruce took the cup, asking for sugar and cream. "Since you haven't seen David, I assume he is in the guest bedroom. You guys talked about Sam, Samantha... whatever her name is?"

She gave him the sugar and cream. "Yes, we did. We had a very full day yesterday. You and David will have a good drive time today. He will fill you in."

"I'm sure," Bruce was quiet. He wanted to make her smile with a joke, a smart remark, or banter, but he had nothing.

"Bruce..." He already knew what she was going to ask.

"I know. You want to know how I knew about Sam. I'm sure David told you I knew you were thinking about some guy named Nathan." Bruce said exactly what Amanda was thinking.

"Yes." She frowned, wanting to know.

"I'm sorry, Amanda." He held his head down. "That day, I was here fixing Matthew's ceiling fan. I came down for a light bulb, and I heard you in the laundry room crying."

Amanda closed her eyes. They were both quiet for a moment. Bruce tried to read her reaction, and Amanda remembered the day. With her head down, she looked at her hands on the kitchen counter. Bruce covered her hands with his.

"I didn't want to interrupt. I didn't know what to do, but I heard you," Bruce said, almost tearfully.

"Sis, my heart went out to you."

"Yeah, I felt pretty stupid that day." Amanda looked at their hands together. "To know your husband was having an affair and not say anything, like I was tongue-tied or waiting for him to say something?"

"Amanda, I know. I'm sorry. I took David's phone yesterday and saw all his messages to this Sam woman, and I unleashed," Bruce said. "But what you said that day in the laundry room changed me."

Amanda finally looked at him. She saw a glow in his eyes.

"You prayed, I mean you really prayed, and He heard you!" Bruce let go of her hands and used his hands to express his excitement, but tried to stay quiet so he wouldn't wake David.

"Who heard me?" Amanda was not understanding, and she was trying to grasp what he was trying to say.

"Jesus," Bruce said quietly. "I know," Bruce said with certainty. "I know HE heard you."

"Of course, HE did," Amanda said, remembering her prayer. "David came home that Monday night and had ended his relationship with Samantha."

"That is so great! I knew something good was going to happen." Bruce smiled.

Amanda looked at him now in amazement and surprise.

"Amanda. That day, I was listening to your prayer, and at first, I was overwhelmed at how much you love David. I mean, you really love him. If he only knew! I'll really try to tell him." Bruce was talking fast and now standing.

Amanda was in Bruce's eyes, and he was like a child for a minute.

"Then, I was just speechless—what do they say, undone—as you prayed to God. Amanda, you did not feel what I felt. You did not see what I saw in my mind. Jesus heard your cry; I felt Him. I felt you—a daughter talking to her Father in heaven and Him listening so concerned." He had tears on his face, and Amanda did too, smiling.

"Bruce, what a beautiful thing you are telling me," she said.

"Amanda, our family isn't worthy of this love you bring to us."

Amanda went around the counter and hugged Bruce for a moment. "Bruce, it isn't me. It is Him inside me."

"Yeah, I get that," Bruce said in their embrace. "You showed me that day."

"Bruce." She released him and then really looked into his eyes. "If through all of this, you become a believer of Christ, I'm the one undone."

He smiled with that dimple. "It's happening."

"Yes!" Amanda hugged him again but stayed quiet.

"Let me tell David, okay?" Bruce said. "I have to tell him…"

Amanda dried her happy tears.

"Chloe," Amanda said her name.

"Yes, I'm ready," Bruce said.

"I'm glad," Amanda said. "No more secrets."

"Speaking of that, who is Nathan?" Bruce sat back down and finally sipped his coffee.

Amanda explained.

"I'm guessing all of that didn't sit well with David?" Bruce asked. Amanda mouthed the word *No*.

"And he will be in Dallas this week with you?!" Bruce's eyes got big. "Amanda, c'mon, this is not going to end well."

"End well? It never really started. Nathan knows I love David," Amanda said.

Bruce let out a breath. "Amanda, it's not that simple for a man."

"Okay, so what is he going to do? I'm in love with my husband. You think he is going to try to convince me not to be?" Amanda whined.

"If I were him, I'd point out all of David's faults."

"Nice try. Nathan is no better. He cheated on his wife. No thanks, I'll take the cheater I already have." Amanda was sharp.

"Wow. This is all a lot of drama with lots of episodes." Bruce shook his head. "Be careful. I want you and David together, as it should be."

Bruce and Amanda heard the basement door open. David came from the lower level. He faced his brother.

"My stomach still hurts."

Just as if his mom were right there telling him what to say after an argument with his brother, Bruce said in a monotone voice, "I'm sorry. Please forgive me. I was angry."

"Whatever," David said, giving his brother a hug. That was how they apologized to one another.

David looked at his wife. Amanda looked at him. Bruce was the one who spoke.

"Listen, I'm going to the lower level. David, you need a new filter for the furnace; the weather has changed." Bruce disappeared downstairs.

David went to Amanda and moved in close. "I missed you. I'm trying to give you space."

"I know." She took his hand. "Thank you. I'm sorry about Nathan. I love you, and I love us."

David was happy with that statement. "It makes me feel good to hear you say that."

They held each other for several minutes. David wanted to remember her smell and her touch. Amanda missed him, this David, the one who was sincere and cared. She was grateful for his touch.

"Please send me pictures of the boys and call me. I promise to be in the hotel room by 7:00 pm," Amanda said.

"Okay," David smiled. "Can we video chat with each other?"

"Sure." She kissed him on the lips tenderly. David closed his eyes and sighed happily. He let go of her hand and went upstairs to get dressed.

David and Bruce drove David's sedan about an hour and a half north to Sugar Creek Farms. On the way, David shared with his brother how he confessed to Amanda about Sam, the success of the Acuff Academy, and the incident and pressure surrounding his promotion. David apologized to Bruce for not sharing it all as it was happening. He told him their mom would be disappointed. David planned to tell her when she returned from her conference in Nashville.

As they entered Sugar Creek Farms, the trees were perfectly manicured down the road to the main entrance. A wooden cross was in the center of the circular drive, but David followed the signs for parent parking and parked in the grass designated for them. When they entered the front entrance, all parents were greeted by college students wearing hunter green Sugar Creek t-shirts with a yellow paper listing the program for the day. They found Bill at the resource table, directing people to various areas.

"You guys clean up nice." Bill saw David and Bruce in their khaki shorts and t-shirts; their personalities shining through in their wardrobe. David looked as if he were ready to play golf. Bruce looked like he was ready to entertain his friends on his back deck with barbecue ribs and beer.

They exchanged hugs with their stepdad and told him there was much to say, but today was not the time. Bill communicated Meri was having fun at her nurses' conference, and he wasn't sure how much she was learning, as much as she was enjoying the country music and food. He showed David and Bill the direction to see the boys and their activities from the past week, but to make it to the auditorium in twenty minutes.

David and Bruce walked into one classroom and saw the theme was *Fisher of Men*. The children were pictured with the fish they caught, and what it meant to go make disciples. David was all smiles when he saw Matthew pictured with a good-sized bass. Matthew's caption stated he wanted to go *make disciples at Disney World, teaching the other kids there that it is a small world after all*. David and Bruce shared tears of laughter, with David expressing that Matthew got Bruce's sense of humor.

When they got to Mason's picture, there were tears of endearment. Mason was pictured with two small fish, one in each hand. He was grinning in the photo. Mason's caption said he wanted to go *make disciples wherever God places me, teaching everyone that God will use the small and multiply it*.

David saw so much of Amanda in his son. His eyes watered, and Bruce tapped him on the shoulder, expressing Mason gets what life is all about. David took pictures with his phone and would send them to Amanda.

The next classroom was themed *Light of Mine*. There were pictures of the children catching lightning bugs, learning how to make a fire, eating hot dogs, and roasting marshmallows. David loved seeing Mason with a group of boys in a tent. His face was glowing and laughing. Matthew had his mouth stuffed with marshmallows. Bruce saw the picture and laughed, saying to David, "I bet you this was a chubby bunny moment." David agreed.

But the touching part of the room was the laminated papers the Sugar Creek teacher gave David as he and Bruce left and headed to the auditorium. One was from Matthew; the other was from Mason. Matthew and Mason both said the person they admired the most was their mom. Matthew said it was because she is always there for him. Mason said it was the time she takes with him. Their favorite person to spend time with for Matthew was Bruce. That hit David hard. He was grateful it was Bruce, but it was a consequence of his sin of abandonment.

Mason loved to spend time with Bill. That made David realize that Bill loved his family. It was time he accepted his stepdad fully. The rest of the paper told David that his boys loved him. He was seen by them as a hard worker and made the best hamburgers. The boys loved going to the movies as a family and wished for later bedtimes and more video games.

When they arrived at the auditorium, the children were on the stage getting ready to sing their favorite camp songs. Matthew spotted David and Bruce right away and waved. Mason was on the front row at the end. He smiled with his dimple and tried to wink at them, but both of his eyes closed. David and Bruce loved his try. All the parents enjoyed their performance, with David videotaping periodically. No one but Bill was prepared for the last performance.

As Mason stepped forward, David was surprised and was recording the performance. Mason's small, sweet voice singing, "God is beautiful to me." The other children joined him with, "He made the birds, land, and sea."

Bruce was in tears right away by the sure image of Mason in his yellow camp shirt and jean shorts, his smooth face sincere, and he saw a spirit like Amanda's in him, but he had David's voice.

Mason continued. "His love is beyond what the eyes can see."

David held the video steady, but he was in tears, saying, "My sweet boy can sing. How beautiful."

The children sang with him in a round as they ended with, "... Please worship the Lord with me."

The audience gave the children a standing ovation, and David mouthed to Mason, "I'm so proud of you."

As the auditorium cleared out, Bill said he would send Matthew and Mason to their assigned table so David and Bruce could have lunch with them. Bill said he would love to join, but he had a leadership meeting to attend.

David hugged his boys so close when they ran to him. He held them until Matthew said, "Dad, we missed you too, but you're squeezing me."

David let go, and it was Bruce's turn to exchange hugs. "Daddy, how are you?" Mason asked.

"Oh, Mason, I am so happy because I'm seeing you and Matthew," David said sincerely.

"Where's Mom?" Mason asked.

"She so wished she could be here," David said as the boys sat at the picnic table, sitting across from him and Bruce. "She is on her way to Dallas for work. She will be home when you are, at the end of the week."

"Yeah," Bruce piped in, "she will be so proud of you both today. Your dad took a video, so he will share it with her."

Both boys smiled.

"Boys," David looked at them both before lunch came. "I need to tell you how sorry I am."

Matthew was the first to respond. "Sorry?"

"Yes, I've been working a lot and on my phone when I should have been paying attention to you two." He looked at them.

"And Mom," Mason said.

"Yes," David agreed, "but now I will not do that anymore. You both are too important to me. I promise when I am with you, I will be with you. No more, see?" David pointed to the phone in his pocket.

"That makes me happy, Daddy," Mason said.

"Okay, Dad." Matthew was less convinced, and David saw that and got up from his side of the picnic table and sat next to his son.

"Matthew, it's okay that you don't believe me. If we can spend time together this summer, I'd like to show you." David looked in his son's eyes.

Matthew looked at David and smiled. "Okay, Dad, I'd like that very much."

Matthew fell into his dad's arms and told him how much he missed him. David's heart melted. Right then, David thanked God for this time with his sons. Bruce was listening pleasantly, happy to see the reunion.

"And you, Mr. Mason." He looked at his youngest son and put him on his lap. "You were amazing today!"

"Yeah," Mason smiled. "Did you like the song?" His brown eyes showed excitement.

"We loved it!" Bruce chimed in. "You know you sound just like your dad."

Bruce told the boys that their dad used to sing and play the piano. David rolled his eyes, but the boys were excited.

"Your dad used to sing to your mom," Bruce said, remembering their engagement party.

"Bruce!" David said, annoyed. He didn't want his sons to feel pressured to do the things he used to do. He wanted his boys to do things they enjoyed, to be their own persons.

"Did Mom like his singing?" Mason asked.

"Yes," Bruce replied.

"Well, maybe you can sing to her, Dad. Mom hasn't been happy," Mason told his dad.

David looked at Mason on his lap.

"Mason, you weren't supposed to say anything," Matthew snapped.

David put Mason on the picnic seat next to Matthew. As their box lunches and bottled waters were delivered to the table, Bruce thanked the counselors and resumed their conversation.

"Boys..." David wanted to know what they knew.

"Matthew, I know we said we weren't going to say anything, but it's Mom, and she was crying," Mason told a bit more of the story.

"But it's my room," Matthew whined back to his brother.

David cleared his throat, and the boys knew what that meant.

Matthew started. "Mom cries at night in the lower-level bathroom. I hear her sometimes through the vent in my room."

David closed his eyes for a moment as Bruce said, "Poor Amanda. Is there any place in her house she can go for privacy?"

David looked at him and frowned, but addressed the boys. "Mom was crying?"

"Yes," Matthew said, "she was crying about you, Dad. She was sad about what you did."

David sighed. Bruce looked at him sternly.

"Yes. It is my fault that Mom is sad," David told his sons.

"Yeah, you cheated on Mom with condoms," Mason said.

Bruce quickly pressed his lips together to keep from laughing and covered his mouth with his hand.

"Mason, that is not how that goes. She was sad Dad was using condoms," Matthew corrected his brother. "Blake Canterbury's brother, Scott, who is in the sixth grade, said boys use condoms so girls don't have babies."

Bruce, now looking at David as if to say, *you-are-on-your own*, continued to hide his mouth, now twisting his lips with his hand.

"Okay, boys, I need to be honest with you," David began to explain. "I hurt Mom because I had a girlfriend. It is sinful to have a girlfriend and a wife."

David told his boys that he made a mistake, and Blake Canterbury's brother, Scott, had it almost right. Men do use condoms so women don't have babies. He told them contraceptives are an adult thing, nothing boys their age should be talking about. He told them he would explain it all to them soon enough.

"So, did you tell Mom you were sorry?" Mason asked.

"Yes, I did," David said, kissing Mason's forehead.

"Are you going away with your girlfriend? Blake Canterbury's brother says that is what happens when the dad cheats. He leaves, there is a divorce, and the mom always gets the kids," Matthew told David and Bruce.

David had tears in his eyes. Bruce saw his brother struggling, but he nodded as if to encourage him.

"Boys, I love your mom. I'm in love with your mom. I'm not leaving. Your mom and I are not getting a divorce. I have to show you both and your mom how sorry I am for thinking just about myself."

David put his head down and told his sons to eat their lunch. They ate in silence for a few minutes. Mason whispered to his brother, and Matthew whispered back. David and Bruce looked at them and waited for the boys to share, but they didn't.

David didn't feel like he was breathing through the entire conversation with Matthew and Mason. It was clear his sons needed his love and guidance as well as his paycheck. He thought about all the young people he had managed over the years and how their fathers were missing or had just left them. Amanda was right; his neglect was real, and he saw it. It affected him, and he felt convicted and sad.

"Dad," Matthew finally broke the silence. "I'm so glad you are here." He glanced up at David. "We have been learning a lot about Jesus."

"I bet you have. He is the greatest," David replied.

"Yes, and he is the only one who is perfect," Mason pointed out.

"True," Bruce said, and David was surprised Bruce even commented.

"We're glad you are our dad. We know you're not perfect," Matthew said.

"Daddy, Mom knows you're sorry. If you told her you love her, I know she will love you back," Mason said with confidence.

David looked at his boys with tenderness.

"Dad, we forgive you. That is what Jesus would do," Matthew said, and he and Mason put their fists together.

Bruce had tears in his eyes.

"Thank you," David said to them. "I love you both so much."

"So, did you and Mom make up? Blake Canterbury's brother says you'll kiss and make up in bed," Matthew said.

Bruce couldn't hold it in; he laughed. David laughed too.

"Listen, I don't want you hanging around Blake Canterbury or his brother. Talk to me, okay? I'll tell you both the truth about girls, Jesus and life, alright?"

"Okay, Dad. But next year, it's fourth grade, and I'll be in the big kid building with the fifth and sixth graders. We will study science and girl parts and boy parts," Matthew stated.

"Yeah, I know," David said. "You come home to me and ask questions. Those Canterburys—they don't know what I know."

"Daddy. I'm sad," Mason said. The atmosphere shifted from humor to serious again.

"Why Mason? Your mom and I will be fine."

"But you're not together; you are alone." David realized only Mason would put those pieces together.

Matthew was matter-of-fact, "Dad, just go to Dallas and be with Mom."

"Matthew, buddy, it's not that simple. Mom has to work and so do I," David answered.

"But you have a corporate jet, right?" Matthew asked, and David smiled, thinking that out of all the conversations he had with his sons about his new promotion, the only thing they remembered was the company's corporate jet .

He chuckled at his son. "It isn't that simple."

"Why not?" Bruce answered and raised his eyebrows.

"That way you can kiss her and make up," Mason said. "But Dad, does it have to be in bed? That's just weird," Mason said.

Matthew started to speak, and David and Bruce both interrupted him. David spoke first.

"Okay, no more Canterbury brother explanations. The conversation we had today is for the boys and men in this family only. Promise?"

The boys and Bruce promised with their fists out and a wink. Mason was still practicing his wink, and David loved his cute innocence.

After the boys showed their dad and uncle their cabin, they said their goodbyes. Mason took longer to let go than Matthew. When David got in the car with Bruce, he put his head down on the steering wheel and sat there in silence. David didn't care that his brother was right there witnessing his tears of sorrow, gratitude, and laughter.

"I'm so sorry, God, for all my selfishness and pride," he said out loud. "Thank you so much for your mercy and grace! This could've been so much worse. You are saving me. Thank you, thank you."

"My boys, please help me, help them. And these Canterbury brothers? Put that on pause..."

Bruce couldn't help but laugh and say Amen.

Again, David frowned at his brother's response, and Bruce noticed.

"David, just start the car and drive. I have a lot to say."

CHAPTER 20

*D*avid drove out of the parent traffic area. It was a beautiful drive. The trees were full and green, complementing the blue sky.

Bruce noticed a private drive on the Sugar Creek property. "Can you turn here?"

David granted the request without any question. He realized his brother was serious. He parked the car at the curve that would lead them back to the main road. There was a bench in front of the view of countless trees and endless green grass. David was ready to listen as the brothers sat down at the bench.

Bruce began to explain how he became aware of his brother's affair and how Amanda's prayer changed him. David hugged his brother with so much emotion. He couldn't stop crying and smiling.

"Oh Bruce, you won't regret the decision. Just don't forget this moment or this feeling. I did, and look at me."

"David, I always look at you. You made a wise decision when you married Amanda. She loves you more than you know. One day, you will really feel it. I felt it that day, I swear to you, it was mind-blowing."

David smiled.

"You just wait. I know she is your wife, and you love her, too. Neither of you realizes what you have."

David understood what Bruce was saying. They sat in silence for a moment, taking in the view.

"I was hoping to build that with Chloe," Bruce said.

"Yeah, Bruce, what happened there?" David was grateful for the opportunity to finally ask.

"Her husband," Bruce replied. "I mean, really, can the Lloyd men escape infidelity?"

"And you punched me in the stomach?" David looked at his brother, almost laughing.

"My story is nothing like yours; it really isn't." Bruce had a serious tone.

"Chloe told me she was single. She didn't wear a wedding ring and had her own apartment, but she was living a double life."

David's face went flat.

"I loved her, David. I know you and Dad think I sleep around a lot. I flirt, and there might be some fooling around, but I reserve some things for *that woman*. I thought Chloe was *that woman*. After six months with her, you can imagine my devastation when I realized I had made love to another man's wife." Bruce touched his chest.

David couldn't imagine. "How did you find out?"

"I was with the boys at Wayne's—you know, the video arcade with the go-karts? Just as we were leaving, I saw her with her family!"

"No way." David's eyes widened.

"A boy and a girl," Bruce said. "She didn't see me, but I saw her, the wedding ring, the children calling her mom, and the husband kissing her lips."

David apologized for what he had said before. Bruce's situation was entirely different. David felt Bruce's devastation was about lies and deception, which crushes trust in relationships.

"So, I take it you confronted her?" David asked.

"Yep. She didn't deny it. Her reasoning was, *it all kind of happened quickly, and they were separated at one time.* It was clear she didn't know what she wanted. I ended it abruptly."

"Good for you. You're my hero. I wish I had walked away from Sam," David admitted.

"Not that I am making excuses for you, but your head was in a million places. You have a job with a million parts to it, a wife and kids, a brother who is in your face 24/7, a dad who you have issues with, a mom, and a stepdad, and now an executive assistant, who is like a second mom. My head hurts just thinking about your life."

"I wanted to tell you about Chloe. My heart still hurts, David." He put his head on his brother's shoulder.

"Why didn't I see the signs? Like her cell phone being locked, or her apartment with hardly any pictures of friends? What was I really to her... just her *you know what* on the side?" Bruce was trying to clean up his language.

David could tell this was still a fresh wound for his brother. "I'm sorry. Lies are hard and damaging. Even though I didn't lie to Amanda directly, I did. I came home and slept with her, slept next to her, while I also slept with Sam. The way Amanda told me she knew about Sam, and she was still having sex with me, and good sex with me... I haven't begun to fully unpack that."

"Yeah, that's a lot to take in. Chloe said she loved me. Can you love two people like that?" The men had a conversation and decided they couldn't.

"Do you think Amanda cares for Nathan?" Bruce asked.

"Yes," David sighed sadly. "To hear your wife say another man *turned her on*, I'm crushed, and it's partly my fault."

"Wow," Bruce sighed. "I tried to talk to her about that this morning. She got angry and said she wants her marriage to work. Nathan cheated on his wife, so she isn't going to go from one cheater to the next."

"Fantastic," David said sarcastically. "She's right; I'm a cheater. Nathan is too. What is wrong with us men? God help us?!"

"Well, I didn't know I was lied to," Bruce said, highlighting his innocence. "Amanda saw my face the day I found out. I was white as a sheet. She came to pick up the boys and asked me one question about Chloe. I don't even remember what it was. The moment she asked, I ran to the bathroom, shut the door, and was sick all night."

"David, Amanda didn't say anything to you because I asked her not to. I'm sorry. I bet she felt obligated to do that because I kept her secret about her past while you were dating."

David said he understood, and he did. As they rose to get back in the car, David shared more of his feelings with his brother.

"I ended things with Sam. It is over. There is no need to have contact. Her ex-boyfriend is back in the picture. But Amanda...she works with this guy, Nathan. He hid his feelings, found a vulnerable moment, and now she is there with him for a week. I know there are other people around, but I'm dying."

"This is emotional. Women desire intimacy over sex. If he even buys her lunch, opens the door for her, helps her in any kind of distress, it just makes matters worse. Go there, David. Take the flipping week off and go to Dallas to be with your wife."

After taking a moment to send Amanda the kids' videos and pictures, David and Bruce began the drive home. The car ride back was lighter in spirit but didn't lack depth and perspective.

"David, you got balls; can I say that now?" Bruce asked, thinking about his Christianity. "You spat in a man's face?"

"I wanted to hurt him badly, but I didn't want to go to jail. What he said was racist, derogatory, and poisonous. He got in my head and made me think distorted things about my relationship with my wife."

Bruce didn't understand, "Help me out…"

David hated bringing the incident up. "When Allen said I was the master, and she was the house slave, so many things played in my head. Just knowing the untold history of that gross part of America—the house slave felt obligated to give the master whatever he wanted because he would threaten to trade, beat, or kill her husband or children who were still living in slave quarters. Even her marriage to the man she loved was not recognized by all. The slave woman was property, not a person. She was shared sexually if the master wanted her to be."

David kept driving, and Bruce had a disturbed look on his face.

"Here I was with Amanda, this beautiful black woman, having an affair with a white woman. Amanda manages our household, hardly denying my needs, because that is her role as a godly woman. Because I am not in my posture as a godly man, it all seems painfully like slavery."

"Well, damn, David," Bruce said it before he knew it. "That explains the whole initiating and if Amanda felt obligated to have sex with you conversation."

David took his eyes off the road for a second. Bruce saw the glance of guilt and shame.

"So, I've been talking to Dr. Nick Harris, a friend and marriage counselor in Lindale. He is helping me see my selfishness, my pride, and, as a black man, he is helping find the right perspective."

"Okay," Bruce replied. "How do you think Amanda feels about all of this?"

"Bruce, you should've seen her face. There was a silence that felt like years."

David told Bruce that when he and Amanda married, she told him to get prepared for the prejudice, the discrimination, and the racism. But he felt he had taken all God had given him for granted, and now he was sobered.

"Amanda was gracious. She knew it was hard for me to tell her what Allen said, and she knew I was angry. Her face was full of hurt and disgust. Dr. Nick says this is what I signed up for when I married Amanda, and I have two black sons to raise."

"Well, he's a straight shooter." Bruce was picking up on Dr. Nick's personality.

"You know it, which is why I need him." David was clear.

"Bruce, I had forgotten what I told God when I met Amanda. I told Him I would be all in. Dr. Nick told me I need to gain a better understanding of African American culture and be prepared for microaggressions. What am I going to do when my sons come home with a grade based on their skin color and not on merit? Am I going to spit in someone's face?"

Bruce approved of Dr. Nick's advice. David felt he could share so much more with Bruce now that they had talked about Sam and Chloe, and with Bruce on his journey to become a Christian. God was making things right, and David was feeling grateful.

Amanda and Leslie talked on the way to the airport. Amanda viewed the pictures and videos of the boys David sent, and she laughed and cried, reading and having Leslie listen in the car with her.

"Sounds like you and David are trying to stay married." Leslie was ready to have a serious conversation with her sister-friend.

"Yes. I want my marriage, and he does too. It's just that there is this distance now, hurt between us. I never thought about how my situation with Nathan hurt, angered, and disappointed him. On the outside, I was glowing in my newfound confidence as a sexy woman. I thought he would be happy I was initiating sex, which he was, but I think it cost me his trust."

"Yeah, I get that. So, a week in Dallas with Nathan?" Leslie asked, continuing to drive.

"No, a week in Dallas with Augusta Retail and at the Dallas Market Center," Amanda corrected.

"Did you shave your legs?" Leslie abruptly asked, kind of laughing but serious.

"What?" Amanda frowned, laughed back, and sat up straight in the car.

"No. If I did, what does that mean?"

"Did you bring sexy underwear and clothes? Think something is going to happen between you and Nathan? You can be honest with me."

"Leslie, I would not lie to you. Ever since Nathan and I shared that moment in the conference room, I've thought about having sex with him. Before David ended things with Sam, and I felt like an idiot for not confronting him, Nathan consumed my thoughts. But I prayed to God about David ending his affair, and he did. I prayed to God about my thoughts about Nathan, and God is removing those. With David coming home, Leslie, the way he touches me now is so different. We haven't had sex for some time, but David's love and consideration during this time overtakes me."

Leslie smiled. "I know you love David."

"So, no. I don't want to sleep with Nathan," Amanda told the truth.

"But what if the opportunity presented itself this week?" Leslie pressed.

"Dear God, I pray I would think about all I have with David, the boys, and my family, and run in the opposite direction." Amanda sat with the thought. "Leslie, I will be careful."

"Please," Leslie said. "I know I joke around and make you and Regina laugh, but all that you are going through right now... it's a lot."

Amanda agreed.

Amanda told Leslie about the snowflake logo and how she was determined to figure out why this company was so pressing on her mind. As her friend dropped her off, she was happy she had someone like Leslie in her life.

"Leslie, I gave you the wrong answer. If the opportunity presented itself this week, I hope I would think about my relationship with my Heavenly Dad and how that sinful moment would separate me from Him."

Leslie held her friend close and whispered to her, "Now that is why you are the gracious warrior. I can now stop worrying about you."

Amanda promised to call Leslie and Regina once she got to Dallas, and she headed into the departure terminal.

When David and Bruce got home, it was after 5:00 pm, and David knew Amanda was gone. His sadness overwhelmed him. Bruce saw it on his face, called their dad, and invited him over.

David had never invited his dad over to his home. They met at the restaurant most of the time, and David would bring the boys to the restaurant, and Michael lived up above in a spacious, open loft apartment. David kept his dad at a distance.

"Pop." David always greeted his dad with that name, usually calling him dad. He hugged him.

"Son, how are you?" He had bags in his hand and a case of beer.

"He is terrible," Bruce interjected. "We saw the boys, and he left them for another week at camp. Amanda is in Dallas for a week with another man, and David is here alone."

"Thank you for the recap." David was tired. "It's all my fault, and I need a moment to figure out what to do about it all." He sat on the couch in the living room.

Michael went into the kitchen with the bags and put the beer in the refrigerator. "I brought dinner for later. You said you had a mess? The house looks clean, David."

David closed his eyes. "It's outside on the basketball court. I told Amanda to leave it, and I'd take care of it."

Michael and Bruce opened the curtains in front of the sliding glass doors. David heard them step out of the deck, and Bruce's comment was clear. "Holy shit, what happened out here?"

David couldn't help but snicker. He thought to himself that God would have his hands full with Bruce for a while. David rose and met his dad and Bruce outside.

"David, what happened?" Michael exclaimed.

"Yeah, this isn't a mess, David. This is a damn crime scene." Bruce started picking up large pieces of plates and putting them in the cardboard box left in the yard.

"And whose blood is this on this plate? Are you sure Amanda is in Dallas?"

Michael laughed at his son. "Bruce, stop." Michael knew his son was teasing, but asked David, "What went on here?"

David looked at the yard. He was surprised—it was a bigger mess than he remembered. It was a good reflection of the damage he caused his family. One decision affected their family dynamic. Shattered glass, pieces of plates on the basketball court and in the grass were the equivalent of feelings hurt, trust broken, and tears shed.

"Amanda told me exactly how she felt about me keeping things from her by breaking every dish, plate, cup, saucer, and mug we had."

"Wow," Bruce said.

"It was good for us. She let out her feelings. All of us need to stop treating Amanda like she is still that nine-year-old girl who was raped while unconscious. The fact that Nathan knows nothing about her past and treats her like a woman was obviously attractive."

Bruce and Michael were silent. They helped pick up the plates. The only sound in the yard was the broken pieces hitting each other in the box, and David's sniffing from his tears.

"David," Michael spoke.

"Dad, it's okay." David wanted to reassure his dad that he was fine.

"No, it's your phone. It's Amanda." Michael handed his son the phone. David took his phone and went into the house in the den.

"Honey, how are you?" David tried to dry his tears quickly.

"I'm good," she said. "The flight was delayed for forty-five minutes, and I wanted to call you."

David closed his eyes, grateful. "Did you get the pictures and videos of the boys?"

"Yes," Amanda's voice was happy. "They were priceless. I miss them. It was so good to see them having a good time."

David loved that too. "Yeah, I spoke to them, Amanda. They know more than I thought, so I told them how sorry I am."

Amanda felt a settling in her heart and mind. "I am so glad."

David went on to tell her about the boys and their forgiveness; Bruce telling him about Chloe, and how much he now wanted a relationship with God. He told her he imagined it was easier for him to share after his older brother screwed up everything.

"David." Amanda was tender and broke the topic of discussion with a whisper. "I miss you."

David didn't speak and took that in as notes to a song he loved.

"Your humility is pleasing to God," she said. "It is time to turn and forgive yourself. Please don't spend the week being sorry. I know you are; we know you are. Start moving forward in the life you want now. Forgive yourself."

Beautiful words, David thought. Words he needed to hear. "Thank you, honey."

"Amanda?"

There was a long pause followed by silence.

"Hey, babe. Sorry, but I have to go. We are boarding."

"Please forgive me," David begged her.

Amanda stopped moving about and gave her phone her full attention. She spoke clearly and with such a sincere tone.

"The moment I knew those flowers weren't for me, I forgave you," Amanda said and ended the call.

It was in that sentence that everything came together for David. He was broken.

She had loved him the entire time?! Not once did she call him outside his name, come up to his office angry, or turn the kids against him, as so many women who have been cheated on do. In fact, she did the opposite. David wouldn't have been angry with her for any of those responses, but God called her to a greater response, a sweeter response.

Tears flowed as he remembered her still making him coffee, taking care of the dry cleaning, dinner, the family, initiating sex, and giving massages, while dying to herself and knowing about Sam the entire time. He thought about her trips to his office to make love to him. How she made the everyday chores of dishes, homework, and laundry in the house feel alive as she danced to music with the boys. That amazing day she came to the office in that tangerine-colored dress, the love they made that day... and she knew about Sam! Who does that? Who loves so crazy, so unconditionally, and without even a thought about themselves? David thought of Christ, but God answered, *Your helpmate*.

David felt it, that feeling Bruce told him about. The feeling was deep and intimate, and the Holy Spirit surrounded him. God was speaking to David in thought, and the scripture that says a woman who fears the Lord is worthy of praise. She submits to her husband because her hope is in the Lord. God told him that he was pleased with Amanda and no harm would come to her.

David imagined the image of three strands interlocking and holding on. He said to himself, *I get it, not easily broken.*

CHAPTER 21

*A*manda relaxed on the plane, taking a deep breath in before settling in her seat. After the flight attendants did their routine safety instructions and final cabin check, Amanda closed her eyes and imagined the hotel room in Dallas. She looked forward to a nice warm bath, a glass of wine, and a comfortable bed. When she closed her eyes, David and his smile came to mind. She remembered their first months together and how he told her he loved her.

David said goodbye to his dad and Bruce after their feasts of brats on the grill, *Lloyd's* potato salad, and a few beers. It had been a long time since David had been in the house alone. He walked around and entered every room. He felt the need to sit in each one for a minute in a spirit of gratitude.

When he reached the master bedroom, David opened the armor in the corner and found the glass trinket box with an *A* etched on the top. He opened it, took out the five stones, and smiled. He took out a photo album, sat on the bed, and began turning the pages, seeing their younger faces. So many happy memories.

David took out one picture where he and Amanda were looking at each other and were so in love. He decided right then, and there, he didn't want their love to die. He remembered their first weekend.

David recalled that when they discussed their first weekend together, Amanda remembered how he tucked her in. She said she woke up smiling as she replayed the night before, which she described as perfect. The evening started with a delicious dinner with Regina and Greg, followed by dancing at the club on Collins Street. Amanda said she was pleasantly surprised to look up and see Bruce again after so many years. She thought that was such a sweet gesture by David. The Blue Night Owl was magical to her. To hear David play the piano and sing. She fell in love right there.

Amanda fell asleep on his shoulder during the car ride home. He was just across the courtyard at the extended stay, but with the snowy cold weather, he took her to her door, let her get dressed for bed, he kissed her, and tucked her in. *He's so sweet*, she thought, putting himself last. David laughed as she recalled telling him that she didn't know whether to be scared or thankful.

He hasn't crossed the line or appeared to be interested in sex. Most guys she knew would never go to such extremes unless they knew they were getting some by the end of the night. For a moment, she felt insecure. Then she thought, *Good grief, it has just been six days. What if he were a normal guy who just wanted to get to know her?* She decided she would enjoy the moment and not speed ahead. Today, as he recalled their conversations throughout the years regarding their fond memories of that weekend, he realized she was wise beyond her years, even back then.

~

A Flashback

Amanda turned on the television and saw all the weather alerts stating bad icy road conditions, highway and road closures, store closings, and canceled activities. She went to the window and saw the snow as it was slowly falling. It looked innocent, blanketing the cars, tops of buildings, and trees, but it was causing chaos, confusion, and havoc.

Cars were in the ditch on highways, in accidents on side streets, and accompanied by power outages west of town. She immediately wondered about David. Did he have to go to work? Amanda looked at her phone; it was after 8:30 am. She was sure he had gone to check on the store and smiled at the thought of his dedication. After Amanda showered and found the warmest thing in her suitcase, David called.

"Morning," he said. Amanda loved hearing his voice. She couldn't deny it; she was smitten with a man named David Lloyd.

"Good morning. Did you go to the store?" She asked.

"No, the store is fine. They will have to close at noon, though No one will be able to get to the store after the morning. The snow is beautiful, but the wind is not," David said.

"How are you? Did you sleep well?"

"Perfect. Thank you for tucking me in," she said, blushing.

David couldn't see it, but he knew the look she had on her face. "Coffee? I'm making breakfast over here."

"Oh, that sounds so good." Amanda was hungry, but more excited to see him.

"Amanda..." David said, with nervousness in his voice. "Spend the weekend with me?"

Amanda paused. What did that mean?

"At least, can we talk about it over breakfast?" David asked.

"Okay," Amanda said.

"So...open your door," David said and ended the call.

Amanda walked to her hotel room door and opened it. There, David stood in his winter coat with fur on the hood, in sweatpants, and snow boots. He had battled at least 35 feet of three inches of snow to make it to Amanda's hotel door.

"Morning," he said, with a coat in his hand. "I figured when you left St. Louis, at a nice fifty degrees on Monday, that you didn't think you would need a heavy winter coat by Saturday morning. You can borrow one of mine."

She let him in the door and shut it. "Good grief! It is cold!"

"Yeah," David said, standing there. "So, coffee and breakfast are about 30 feet that way," David pointed back to his hotel room. "They say we can expect at least four more inches of blowing snow. In our little courtyard here, we will not make it going back and forth. So, I suggest you grab a few things and spend the weekend with me."

He handed her the coat with a smile that drove her crazy.

"Okay." Amanda disappeared from David for a few minutes. She found a medium laundry bag in the closet and put a few clothes in with her overnight makeup bag. He waited for her to put on her tennis shoes. As she put on his coat, she chuckled. It was long in length and in the sleeves, but it would work to make it across the courtyard.

He held her hand and her bag and made big footprints in the snow so she could put her feet in his footprints. Amanda was cold when they made it to his hotel room. The wind went straight through her jeans, and she wished she had socks. The falling snow found its way onto her ankles, and her feet were wet. David helped her out of his coat and got her a towel and socks.

"Wow," Amanda said, sitting on the barstool, drying her feet and putting on David's oversized socks. "Winter came overnight."

"Yes," David said, standing beside her. "You look cute." David laughed as he looked at his socks on her feet. They reminded him of clown socks since they were so big on her small feet.

Amanda sled off the barstool with her hands on her hips. "My feet are warm, though. Thank you."

David faced her, gently pulled her close, and kissed her softly.

Amanda looked up at him. "Thank you for last night. I had a great time."

'I'm glad." He gave her coffee and two sugars. "You are beautiful company."

"I don't think anyone has ever said that to me." Amanda was touched.

"It's true," David said. "Breakfast? Your wish is my command." He went into the kitchen. "French toast, pancakes, hash browns, bacon, sausage, eggs? Omelets?"

"Chef David." She joined him in the kitchen. "How 'bout French toast, scrambled eggs, and bacon. Let me help you."

David got the eggs out of the refrigerator, and Amanda remembered how David liked to cook bacon on the cookie sheet, so she preheated the oven. They were both very relaxed in the kitchen together this time. David kissed her on the cheek as she scrambled the eggs, and Amanda put her hands on his waist to move past him. They were laughing about their date last night when Amanda assumed he couldn't dance. As they sat and had breakfast, David loved his time with her, and he wanted her to feel more at ease, knowing more about him.

"I didn't mean to put you on the spot this morning about spending the weekend with me," David finally got the nerve to say. "It is just that the snow isn't going to allow us to go back and forth to our rooms and, honestly, I want to be in your presence." Now he was blushing.

Amanda took all of that in her mind and felt honored.

"Dating is so complicated," David blurted out.

"True." Amanda thought about Colin for a moment.

"I'm a Christian, so it makes things awkward for some people." David put it out there, and he felt good just saying it. He figured Amanda was also; he remembered her praying in the pharmacy and saying she would pray about her job situation, and he remembered what Greg told him about her.

"I'm a Christian, too. However, I have been behaving badly in the men's department. My last boyfriend was not a Christian and, well, let's just say we ended it. He moved to Minneapolis to work for a marketing firm."

"Okay." David didn't want to pry. "I understand; my college days were not my best moments in the women's department either."

David looked at her and took a breath. "Listen, I have dated a few women only to find out they don't share my same values. They say they are Christian, and then they act all weird."

"Like how?"

"Well, some feel it is completely wrong to touch at all. Okay? That is simply weird to me if we are dating. Can I hold your hand? Do we hug? For how long before someone *struggles*?" David sounded exhausted. "I don't struggle with things like that, so it all sounds like legalism to me."

Amanda understood.

"I have dated women that want to talk about Jesus and the Bible all night long. I can't do that either. They will ask me about my favorite book of the Bible. I like the whole book. When is a good time to tell them I drink beer?" David was now sharing his frustration, and Amanda laughed.

"I wanted to kiss you." He looked into her eyes. "Because I couldn't let you believe I wanted to just be friends."

Amanda touched his cheek. "You're sweet."

"So, I wanted to clear the air." David took a deep breath. "I just know from experience when you lead with the physical, everything bottoms out."

Amanda thought about what David said and had to agree. Her past relationship with Colin was all physical. She was lonely and vulnerable. He didn't offer her more of himself than a warm body and dinner.

David took a breath and went there. "I like sex, but I don't need sex right now."

"Okay." Amanda could handle what he was saying.

"Please, the moment you feel uncomfortable with a touch of mine, promise me you'll tell me?"

David was sincere.

"Yes, I will do that." She leaned in and kissed his cheek. "Will you tell me if I do something?" Amanda was timid to say.

"Of course." David smiled.

"So…" Amanda got off the barstool and started clearing dishes. "I'm so embarrassed to ask this question." She covered her face with the dish towel.

"What?" David laughed.

From behind the dish towel, she spoke. "I cannot even believe this question came into my mind. Forget it."

David got up and sweetly removed the towel. "Amanda, just ask the question."

She buried her head in his chest. "For you, is it easy to be self-controlled here?"

He caressed her back. "You are the sweetest thing." David took a breath and recognized Amanda's insecurity and her question. He raised her head gently, took her hand, and looked at it.

"When I first saw you, I couldn't breathe." David had to be honest. "I only heard half of what you were saying because you are physically beautiful. Don't think I'm not attracted to you physically." He continued to look at her hands. David's own shyness wouldn't allow him to look at her.

David told Amanda he cared for her, all of her. Especially her integrity and her respect. Right then, he set the boundaries for the weekend. If a conversation, kiss, or moment got too physical, they were to give it a number. If it was a six or greater, it was time to change the conversation or go home.

"Amanda, when I was a teenager, this whole self-control thing was hard. I didn't care. I was 15, and in one ear, I had a Sex Ed teacher telling me it was perfectly natural to have these feelings. In the other ear, my youth minister was telling me about self-control. What? I wanted what felt good. Period."

Amanda listened as they sat on the sectional.

"That was until Aunt Melba." David made a sound of disgust and shivered.

"Bad?" Amanda looked at him.

"It was a Saturday morning. The Friday before, my buddies had given me a Playboy magazine to *use* for the weekend. During that time in my life, it was mostly just my mom, Bruce, and me in the house. Saturday morning, the hall bathroom was mine." David started his story, and Amanda wasn't sure if she wanted to know this story, but she let him continue.

"But this Saturday, my Grandma Emma was in town with her sister, Melba. Aunt Melba was pale, full-figured and blunt. Nothing like my Grandma Em, who was soft, quiet, petite, and loved God. Of course, I went to use the bathroom that morning, with the magazine in my small duffle bag. Looking forward to my time, you know. I get to the bathroom, and I am mortified."

Amanda closed her eyes, not knowing what David would say next.

"Aunt Melba wasn't in the bathroom, but the bathroom reeked of the old lady perfume she wore. She had put her big lady underwear on the towel bar, and her dentures were in a glass by my toothbrush dispenser." David recalled the morning with distaste.

Amanda covered her mouth, then laughed out loud uncontrollably.

"Amanda, to see her teeth floating in the glass!" David closed his eyes and shook his head. "No."

Amanda was trying to find air. She imagined the image of a young David and found his story funny.

"As I left the bathroom, I heard her footsteps down the hall behind me. Why did I turn around?! She called to me in her old lady voice with no teeth, *David, do you need to get in the bathroom?*" David mocked the old woman's voice.

Amanda was laughing now with no sound.

"I turned around, and there she was with no teeth in her mouth, in her light pink housecoat, where I could clearly see her breasts hanging down to her waist," David said.

"I told her *no*, with my head quickly looking at the floor and my duffle bag in my hand. *It's okay, Aunt Melba, I'm good*," David remembered saying.

Amanda was now in tears from her laughter. David was laughing too.

"The erection I wanted or thought I was going to relieve was gone completely. To this day, if I ever need to bring about sexual self-control, I think about Aunt Melba, God rest her soul."

David and Amanda enjoyed each other's company the entire weekend. There was college football to watch, stories to tell from their childhood, and brownies and cookies to make. David was still trying to figure out Amanda's sweet tooth. He loved how she could adapt to anything and yet be clear when she didn't care for something. She loved action movies, romantic comedies, and some psycho thrillers, but no horror films. She was comfortable curled up next to him, giving him kisses on the cheek, but she only kissed him on the lips after he kissed her. *Sweet*, he thought. He suspected those were her boundaries.

Amanda was careful not to assume things were moving ahead. During their weekend, she only left once to grab her laptop for work and hot chocolate to warm up again. She worked on her resume and left an email for Norah Livingstone at Augusta Retail. Amanda loved David's leadership and care; he wasn't afraid to ask questions about the cosmetic and beauty industry. He wanted to know what it was like growing up half African-American and half Caucasian. He took great interest in the things she cared about, like injustice, human trafficking, and children being homeless. Amanda could tell that her caring for others pleased him. David slept on the sectional and gave Amanda the bed. As much as he wanted to, he couldn't sleep next to her. He knew himself to be a morning lover; the temptation was too great. He was falling in love, and he wanted to do it right.

The winter storm passed, and by Monday morning, it was cloudy and forty-five degrees. Amanda was heading back to St. Louis for the night, and then she would drive to Columbia for a cosmetic reset. David didn't want her to go, but he knew they had Regina and Greg's wedding to look forward to. Amanda would be in town for that, and he saw her this weekend on her laptop, looking for job opportunities to return to the area.

"Who knew a week ago today I'd feel this full." David looked at her as she stopped by the store before she left.

"I know, right?" Amanda was a bit sad and disappointed. Nothing awaited her in St. Louis but an empty apartment and eating alone. She was not looking forward to it or the drive to Columbia with Calvin in her ear either. David held her hands as they sat at a table on the Acuff restaurant's outdoor patio across from each other.

"David, thank you for making this week so lovely."

She was being kind. David felt her withdrawing. He hated it.

"I will be back in two weeks," she smiled. Amanda was scared. She thought without her emotions for the first time in a few days. David was a kind, privileged white guy. Would a relationship with him really work, especially in this town? He was handsome, caring, with a brilliant smile, and a huge future at his job. What did she bring to the table? David read the look of doubt on her face.

"Amanda, don't." He got up from the table and sat next to her. He turned the chair so that he was facing her. She did the same. With their knees touching, he took her hands and covered them with his. Her hands were cold, so he rubbed them to give them warmth.

"Don't act like this week wasn't something special. That you and I didn't feel this connection or attraction." He was direct and frank.

"I see you, Amanda. You don't go around telling everyone your story, and I don't take just anyone to the Blue Night Owl. I shared the innermost parts of myself. You did too."

Amanda looked at their hands together. "I'm just afraid. Afraid of this. Things I've always wanted for myself never seem to work out the way I want them to. Perhaps I'm meant to be alone."

"Well, I don't believe that. I told you that you deserve so much more than life has offered you right now. You are worthy of so much happiness."

Amanda looked at him and smiled.

David let go of her hand only to brush her cheek and make eye contact. "You are beautiful."

She put her head down, and he raised it with one finger, her brown eyes looking into his. As he stared, he saw how the golden flakes caught the morning sunlight.

"Amanda Williams, be my girlfriend." He was confident and sure. "I think we are too young to remember when people went steady. We are too old to give each other pins or for you to wear my school letterman's jacket, and flowers just die. But I promise to call you every night to hear about your day and wake up every morning thinking about you and your amazing smile."

Amanda laughed sincerely and searched his eyes. They sat in silence for a moment. She could tell he was quietly begging her.

She nodded yes. There was that smile, the one that melted her and made her stomach quiver. He leaned in and kissed her softly, whispering, "Thank you." They exchanged several kisses in a row, and they put their arms around each other.

David sighed in pleasure. "I promise to make sure you never feel alone. I'm here."

They broke their embrace and put their foreheads together.

"So, now that you are my boyfriend," Amanda said, smiling. "Will you be my plus one at Regina and Greg's wedding?"

"I was waiting for you to ask me," David replied, grinning.

They rose from the table and kissed again. David noticed Corey and Emily in the restaurant, pretending like they had work to do, but he knew they were being nosy.

"You need to get on the road. I want my girlfriend home before dark." He held her hand and walked her to her rental car. "My management staff is wondering which David they are going to have to deal with until you return: the happy one or the crabby one?"

Amanda pulled her keys out and said. "Well, I am glad there will be a smile on your face."

They prayed together. David prayed for her safekeeping on the ride home. Amanda prayed for David's day and their relationship, and that God would continue to bless it. She got in her car, and he watched her disappear.

David remembered re-entering the store through the restaurant patio door to find Emily still standing there. Emily smiled when he said to her that he was done dating, and the women in the store needed to stop flirting with him. David told her in confidence that Amanda was the one for him.

CHAPTER 22

Amanda remembered making it home to St. Louis in the early evening and David having roses waiting for at her door. In the coming weeks, David was true to his word. He called her every night, and she was on his mind all the time. Without being overbearing, he made sure that she felt safe traveling for her job and wanted others to know Amanda belonged to someone.

Regina and Greg's wedding was beautiful and intimate. David thought Amanda did a great job helping Regina plan the day. The courthouse in Brookview was majestic in its architecture. The arches and staircases made the wedding photos vintage and historic.

Regina wore a beautiful, white, tailored suit with a chiffon floor-length sleeveless duster. Greg was in a charcoal gray suit with a burgundy tie, which matched the simple, deep red roses Regina carried in her tight wedding bouquet. On the steps of the courthouse, Regina and Greg said their vows with their parents, Greg's brother, Regina's two sisters, Leslie and Stan, and David and Amanda by their side.

The barbecue, on the other hand, had at least fifty to a hundred friends and family. Amanda was worried whether David would be comfortable being the only white person at a black gathering. When she shared her feelings with him, David asked her if she was comfortable being the only black person almost everywhere she went in Brookview. He simply told her that if she could do it for 365 days, he could certainly do it for one.

David wasn't uncomfortable. He helped grill the meat and sat with Greg and his brother drinking beer, talking basketball and sports medicine, played cards with Regina's sister and friends, and chased the kids around the yard. Amanda rested easy from that day on about David and the issue of race. He told her he believed in only one race: the human race. David shared with Amanda that the African American culture wasn't too far from his own culture growing up. He lived by the mantra *Just love God and treat each other well.*

Within three months, Amanda landed a field representative position with Augusta Retail, and David was officially named the director of the Galesboro store. Tom Cochran was promoted to Senior Vice President of Logistics.

Since Bruce was in residential construction, he had helped Greg and Regina successfully find a home to rent for their growing family before winter settled in. David had secretly asked Bruce to find him a home for Amanda and him to share one day. For now, on a cold winter Saturday, David and Amanda were packing up her apartment in St. Louis to head to her new apartment in Lindale.

"Amanda, honey, is this the last box?" David pointed at a large cardboard box in the corner of the living room. "Please say yes."

Amanda could tell David was done for the day. Although she was moving fifteen minutes from him as opposed to two hours, he was frustrated by all the books and magazines she had.

"No," Amanda gave him the wrong answer. She approached him in her winter coat, hat, and gloves and hugged him.

"Just one more in the bedroom. It can fit in the back of the car, and then we can leave."

David loaded the car with the last two boxes. He told Bruce and his friends to leave for Amanda's new apartment, and they would follow after Amanda turned in her keys. A large, rotund white man wearing a black coat, brown hat, and gloves was behind David as he headed back up the stairs to help Amanda close up. When he continued to follow him to Amanda's door, he frowned with concern and said, "Can I help you?"

"I hope so." He was a little winded from the stairs. "I'm looking for Amanda Flakke."

David didn't know that last name, but Amanda heard the foreign voice, her old last name, and stood at the door. "Who's asking?"

Amanda was defensive and gave David a look not to speak.

"Ms. Flakke?" The man looked at her. She was all grown up and prettier than he could've imagined; long hair full of curls, the brown eyes were the same, but the sadness was gone. He humbly took his hat off, showing his gray hair.

"I mean, Ms. Williams. I'm sorry. Do you remember me?"

Amanda came closer to him with David standing between them. She looked at his rosy cheeks, blue eyes, and a simple gold wedding band on his left hand.

"I'm sorry, I don't." She went to him and invited him into the kitchen.

"It's okay. I'm Martin Walker. I was there the night your parents didn't come out of the fire." He rested on the kitchen counter.

"I'm glad I caught you. You're moving?"

"Yes," Amanda replied, offering no more information on purpose. "Mr. Walker?"

"I know, I don't wanna cause any trouble." He didn't want her to ask him any questions.

David stood next to Amanda on the other side of the kitchen counter. The high-top counter was now between Martin and the couple.

He opened his coat and pulled out a brown, expandable file. He explained he was in his thirties when her parents died, and that this was one of his first cases as a transition specialist for the foster care unit.

"My heart broke for you," Martin remembered, "so I followed you in the system. I couldn't do much to help you once they moved me around; my position changed over the years. The orphanage..." He stopped, but his head was down in silence. Amanda could tell he felt sadness.

"Mr. Walker, it's okay. I don't recall any of it. The trauma was too great..."

He interrupted her; he didn't want to relive it.

"This folder is now yours." He handed it to her. "Your file. With the database in the department getting updated, and since I'm retiring from this work, I officially aged you out of the system."

Amanda was puzzled. She explained to Martin that since she was adopted at fourteen by Janice Williams, she didn't understand how she could *age out*. Martin told her Janice died when she was exactly seventeen and four months old. The case worker at the time quickly put her back in the system. Then, she aged Amanda out at exactly eighteen to enroll her into the state's aftercare program until she reached the age of twenty-two.

"Here is your signature. You don't remember?"

Amanda remembered signing a lot of papers around that time. She looked at David, stating that all of this did happen, and there were a lot of things going on with Janice's will and her funeral. Janice had a lot of friends at the time willing to help with her college applications, financial aid, and various programs to keep her in school once she got there.

"I've been trying to find you. The letters we sent to you asking for your input were returned. So, one of the case workers found me; they knew I followed your case. I used my resources to get your file and update the new database to reflect that you aged out," Martin said. "And that you are not alone." He looked at David.

Amanda looked in the folder. There were forms, progress reports, school transcripts, and two envelopes labeled *pictures* and *cash*.

"Mr. Walker, the cash? What is this for?" Amanda was surprised. "I'm just not understanding any of this."

"Listen, Ms. Williams. I don't trust anyone in the department these days. Especially the files that are pending on young girls who appear vulnerable and alone. If I had left your file with return to sender letters, checks never collected, and your file exposed for anyone to see, the not-so-innocent case workers who might work both sides of law enforcement, could take advantage of the situation and..."

"I get it," Amanda said.

"Now, your file is closed. You aged out, and you are done. Your file looks like everyone else's from the 90s," Martin said.

"Thank you." She looked him in the eye. She tried to place him, but she couldn't.

Then she asked, "Mr. Walker, what really happened to Stacy Snowden?" Amanda wanted to know what happened to her best friend at the orphanage after the rape.

Mr. Walker put his head down and then looked at her. "She went missing. At age sixteen, she didn't come home from school one day. Her foster parents didn't care, except when the money stopped coming. She was difficult and a burden to them; not a good situation," Mr. Walker told her. That was when he saw the sad face he remembered.

"Listen, Amanda," Mr. Walker said. "I'm sure this young man will agree with me. Don't look back. Don't go diggin' up bones that have already been buried. Start your life wherever you're going. This is the last address I have for you. Of course, none of us are hard to find anymore with our jobs and these cell phones nowadays, but don't go lookin' for trouble."

"Yes, Amanda. Can you let go?" David touched her hand.

"Yeah, I wanted to ask." Amanda took a deep breath.

"What about the guy from the orphanage who attacked them? I know it was ages ago, but since we are asking." David was curious.

"Sure. A copy of the police report is in the folder." Mr. Walker pointed to the file.

"They shot and killed him weeks later while he was committing another crime. I'm afraid the gang he was affiliated with is still out there."

Martin reached inside his coat pocket and took out a piece of candy. Amanda followed Martin's hand, unwrapping the clear plastic wrapper, and he put the red-colored ball in his mouth. She noticed his hand again with his gold wedding band.

Amanda saw it in her mind. She went around the high-top counter, faced Martin, and reached out for his hand. The movement was awkward to David and Martin until Martin gave Amanda his left hand.

"Mr. Walker, I do remember you. You held my hand and led me to your office."

Martin smiled. "I did."

"These candies in a crystal candy jar that sat on your desk. You gave me one. You have a wife named Mona. I went home with you and slept in a bed with pink hearts on the sheets that first night."

Martin smiled with water in his eyes. "Yes."

She hugged him for minutes and cried on his shoulder.

David felt tears forming for him. He imagined Amanda at six years old, trying to grasp the tragedy. He thought about this man, younger, and his wife, trying not to get attached to the numerous children who would stay with them for a moment until placed. David felt grateful for his parents, even though he was still angry at his dad for the affair; he had a loving family. He was ready to share it all with Amanda.

"Thank you for caring for me." Amanda released Martin. "Thank you for finding me and bringing it all to a close today."

"My pleasure, Amanda," Martin said. "You have turned out to be a good woman. Finished college, good job, and a nice man who I see cares about you."

Amanda looked at David and winked. "Yes. Currently, he is not exactly happy with how many boxes we've carried to the car, but he is sweet to me."

Martin smiled and shook David's hand.

"You kids look out for one another." Martin put his hat back on his head, gave Amanda another hug, and said, "Oh, Happy Birthday; well, two weeks early."

Amanda smiled and watched Martin disappear. When she turned to face David, he had a surprised look on his face.

"Birthday?!" David couldn't believe they had been dating for three months and not once had they mentioned birthdays.

"I'm the worst boyfriend ever. I do not know your birthday! Were you even going to tell me?" He tickled her side and got that giggle he loved.

He grabbed her hand, pulled her close, and kissed her.

"Amanda Flakke Williams? Honey. Seriously, talk to me. I thought you trusted me?"

"I do trust you." Amanda saw the concern in his eyes.

"It is Amanda Nicole Williams, okay? Flakke is sacred. It is to be said only by my future family and me. It is not meant for common everyday use, like my driver's license or on my checks. It is special."

David understood. Amanda kissed him. "When is your birthday?"

"February 11th."

Amanda smiled. "I was born on January 23rd, and I remember my sixth birthday and my sixteenth birthday the most. I was with people I cared about, and they cared about me. The other times, no one remembered; uneventful or in the hospital with my mom, Janice."

"Well, now that you live closer, we are celebrating your birthday, okay?"

David learned to stop saying he was sorry for her past; he would quickly bring up the future. He saw the brown file on the kitchen counter and moved into the kitchen to grab it.

"C'mon, Amanda, let's go. Bruce and your friends have probably made it to your new place by now. Lock up. And this..." He looked at the folder and looked at her.

"Can we do this together?"

Amanda loved this part about him—the leadership. The encouragement he gave so softly while making sure he wasn't stepping on her independence.

"Yes," she said to him, checking all the empty rooms.

"David, I feel free, sad, and emotional, so if I cry all the way to Lindale, it is just a release."

As they locked the door to the empty apartment, David kissed her forehead and said, "I get that." David did understand.

Amanda was overwhelmed by the love David showed her on her birthday. They had not said the word *love* to each other, but Amanda had to admit to herself, Regina, and Leslie that she felt David's love for her.

She enjoyed a full morning at a spa and lunch with Janice's friend, Kate. Now that Amanda was back in the area, David encouraged her to reach out to the people who had helped her when Janice died. Kate was excited and pleased to see Amanda doing well.

It was then dinner with Greg, Regina, Stan, and Leslie at Amanda's new apartment, but she did nothing to prepare. Between David and Emily from the Galesboro store, the decorations were simple. David cooked dinner, and the chocolate cake with chocolate frosting was from the Acuff bakery, although it looked homemade.

As her dearest friends celebrated her, David got to know Amanda better. Her friends bought her books to read about living well and helping others. He gathered she loved to journal, cook, feel pretty, plan, and attend events. Regina and Leslie showered her with notebooks, recipes, makeup, bath products, and a list of all the wineries, music festivals, and concerts to attend in the spring. Amanda waited for everyone to leave to open David's gift in front of him alone.

She sat at the end of the dining room table in her apartment, and he sat adjacent to her, both enjoying coffee. He gave her the brown cardboard box. It wasn't wrapped. David was nervous.

"I need to learn how to wrap presents. Emily was disappointed in me."

Amanda chuckled. "She is really your sister from another mother."

Amanda began to open the box. "I like that it isn't wrapped. It's who you are."

"I'll remember you said that." David was thinking about their future as he sipped his coffee.

When Amanda saw the glass trinket box with an *A* etched on the lid, she gasped. To her, it was so perfect. The glass was tinted pink, and the trim and latch around the glass were oil-rubbed bronze.

"Oh, David, I love it." She looked at him.

"Open it," he told her.

She did, and she found a black velvet pouch inside. She opened the pouch and found five smooth stones with *I love you* engraved on one side of each stone and on the other side, five reasons why:

because you are so much fun
because I just do
because you are an inspiration
because of your great smile, and
for always being so giving

David and Amanda's eyes met. He said, "I love you. The way you respect me, the way you allow me to do for you, and the way you do for me since you have moved here. Thank you for calling me and asking me about my day, and on late shifts, you sit and have dinner with me."

Amanda leaned in and said, "I love you too." For the first time, she kissed him first. It was a long kiss where she took his upper lip and didn't let go for seconds. When she did, David kissed her back with intensity and passion; their tongues meeting for the first time.

"Whoa," David said, opening his eyes. He smiled and took a breath.

"David, I'm sorry. That was clearly a six."

"Honey, an eleven," he winked.

"Don't wink." She hid her face. "That is a total turn-on, and you know it." She got up from the table and went to the kitchen.

"I better go," he said, following her. He couldn't resist taking her hand and pulling her in close.

"David..." she said with their noses touching.

"I know, I'm sorry, but for the first time I told my girlfriend I love her."

"I know, and for the first time I told my boyfriend I love him, and I kissed him; really kissed him."

"I know," David said excitedly. "And he kissed you back, really kissed you."

They searched each other's eyes. David kissed her again, this time softly and briefly. He whispered in her ear, "Happy Birthday, honey."

Amanda felt her desire for him rise. She closed her eyes.

"Thank you for the wonderful evening. I love you," Amanda said. She broke their embrace and went to the front door.

"Thank you for being the strong one tonight," he said, grabbing his coat. "I love you too."

David left, and Amanda leaned her head against the door and smiled.

CHAPTER 23

David woke up with pictures all around him on the bed and on the morning news. He had fallen asleep looking at old pictures and was in yesterday's clothes. He looked at his phone, and the battery was dead; he forgot to charge it. "Damn," he muttered, and lay back down on the bed.

This was his reality this week—a mess. It all came rushing back.

He had the affair, abandoned his wife and children, and was feeling the consequences. Although he thanked God that the boys forgave him, he was eager to plan the rest of the summer by their side. Amanda had forgiven him, but it was awkward between them. Then he thought about Nathan.

While David had to share in that blame, Nathan would be in the same hotel as Amanda all week. He hated that. He trusted Amanda, but she was vulnerable. David recognized that he had hurt her, and between her vulnerability and hurt, it was the best recipe for temptation to win.

He plugged in his phone and began to put the pictures away. The television told him it was 8:30 am; there was no way he was going to make it to the office in a reasonable amount of time. David was sure Vikki had tried to reach him on his phone.

He showered, skipped shaving, and found a dark blue pair of jeans, a pale blue t-shirt, and a dark gray sports coat, which was all he wanted to do this Monday morning. He remembered there would be a contract on his desk today from Gerald. He had no clue what his role would be at Acuff now. The Acuff Academy launch was over, and with all the drama around his promotion, he wanted a position that didn't pull him away from Amanda and the boys.

There was now enough charge on his phone to see that there were 14 text messages. He continued to charge his phone on the kitchen island as he made himself coffee for his travel mug.

Amanda had texted saying she needed a favor, but when she didn't hear from him in thirty minutes, she texted back

> Never mind; Leslie is helping.

He was disappointed. Vikki had a text saying to call her. The rest of the text messages were from some of the Acuff Academy trainees, starting their first day as Acuff employees. They shared pictures of their red and black shirts, Acuff name tags, and aprons. David was proud. Just as he was ready to grab keys and go, he heard the doorbell. To his surprise, it was Leslie.

"Hey," he said, greeting her with a hug.

"Hey, you look..." Leslie lowered her sunglasses to make eye contact with David.

"I didn't shave..." He opened the front door wider to welcome her in.

"I see that. You actually look really handsome." Leslie was honest, and then she hit him in the arm as hard as she could.

"Ouch!" David pouted, rubbing his arm.

"What were you thinking? Messing around with another woman? Now Amanda is acting all crazy because she's hurt..."

Leslie moved herself inside and followed David to the kitchen.

"Leslie, I know," he replied. "I deserve way more than a punch in the arm. I promised you, Stan, Regina, and Greg that I would take care of Amanda."

"You did." Leslie sat on one of the barstools. "But, it sounds like you and Amanda want the marriage to work, so you have work to do."

David remembered that Leslie drove Amanda to the airport yesterday. He was curious about the conversation.

"What did she say yesterday?"

"That she still loves you." Leslie smiled. "So please don't take this chance for granted."

David told Leslie he realized God's mercy and grace in the situation and would do whatever it took to regain Amanda's trust.

"What brings you here? I was just leaving. My phone died. When I didn't answer Amanda right away this morning, she said she contacted you?"

"She did," Leslie said. "I'm not teaching this summer session. I'm teaching in a few weeks. I told Amanda I would stop by. She told me where the hidden key was, but I thought I would ring the bell first."

"Did she forget something?" David frowned and then looked at his phone, deciding to plug it back into the charger on the kitchen counter.

"More like remembering something," Leslie said.

"Okay." David was now multitasking quickly, telling Vikki that he was on his way.

"She wanted me to see if there was an envelope of childhood pictures in the back of her desk drawer. If not, I need to ask you about a skeleton key that goes to a safe deposit box at the bank."

Leslie was looking at her phone, reading Amanda's message.

David froze, eyes wide. "What?"

David explained that the pictures Amanda was looking for are from the orphanage, long ago.

"Yes, I remember, Amanda told me." Leslie rose to go to the den.

"Why does she need them? Yesterday, she said she had a flash of a memory. Something about a snowflake logo?" David asked.

"Yeah. She is forcing herself to remember why this snowflake logo from this company in Dallas is familiar to her. This morning, she said she now remembers this logo was in a picture from the orphanage."

"Really?" David moved past Leslie and went to Amanda's desk and sat down.

"Wait a minute. If this snowflake logo is from the orphanage, who sent her the logo? They must have known Amanda as a child. Who could that be?"

"David, I don't know. But Amanda told me this company sent her a large box of essential oils, bath products, and accessories with this snowflake logo on the tags. She now remembers this logo from the orphanage."

David searched Amanda's desk. He knew the envelope well, but didn't see it.

"Leslie, I don't like the sound of this at all. If Amanda's memory is right, which I believe it is, someone knows her from the orphanage."

He took the skeleton key from a glass cup that sat on her desk. He knew he would have to go to the bank and get the brown expandable file.

He remembered that cold January night when Amanda went through the file Martin Walker left the afternoon she moved from St. Louis to Lindale. Amanda was a smart and intelligent little girl. He remembered the photograph of an innocent four-year-old with her mom and dad. Amanda looked like her mom, David thought. Amanda's face was the same shape as her mom's, but she had her dad's eyes. It was the only family picture Amanda had, and a copy of that photo blessed the fireplace mantle in their home.

After the fire, Amanda did well in grade school, but kept to herself. He remembered her eyes in the pictures before the rape, then after. Amanda cried that night, looking through all the pictures of her and her friend Stacy. It was clear they were happy together for the short time they were together. Then David saw it in his mind—the snowflakes. Of course, there were pictures of the girls showing off their drawings of the snowflakes. Stacy Snowden. Amanda Flakke.

David explained his memory to Leslie as they left the den, and he went to the phone he had left charging in the kitchen.

"Vikki," David said her name quickly when she answered the phone.

"David? I thought you were on your way. Nothing is going on anyway, but Gerald already came by here once, wondering if you saw the contract on your desk."

David sighed to calm himself. "Vikki, I need you to ask Gerald to call me. It is important. Tell him I am coming to the office today, but I wondered if the plane is available. I need to go to Dallas."

"Dallas, Texas?"

"Yes." David imagined the face Vikki was giving him. He finished the call and put the skeleton key in his front jean pocket.

"You have access to a plane?" Leslie said, smiling. "This is so romantic?!" Her eyes kind of glowed.

"Seriously, Leslie?" David rolled his eyes. "Listen, Amanda is being completely naïve about this snowflake logo. Someone knows Amanda from her past, in a location where she was raped. She wants to go see this company, I get it, but she cannot and will not do that alone."

Leslie understood. "But she is not alone. She said Norah and Nathan were going with her to the Dallas Market Center."

"Nathan." David closed his eyes and sighed in frustration. He thought about what Bruce said about women loving men who come to their rescue.

"I can't have Nathan do that. I don't care if that's part of his job."

Leslie understood. "I'll call her and tell her…"

"No," David interrupted. "Well, yes, call her and tell her not to go until tomorrow."

David was anxious and confused. He started pacing.

"David," Leslie made him sit on the other kitchen barstool next to her. She closed her eyes for a second.

"I get it. If you call her and tell her you're coming, she will think you don't trust her."

David knew Leslie did understand it all.

"I will call Amanda. I will tell her that the pictures were not in the desk. I will tell her I found the key, and I will go to the bank if she can go to the Dallas Market tomorrow."

Leslie was calm, and then she thought, "Could this be Stacy?!"

David put his head down. "No."

David explained to Leslie that it was one of those secret things Amanda and he shared. Amanda didn't want her friends to worry about her, but she wanted Stacy at their wedding if they could find her. Martin Walker investigated with the police and found Stacy was a Jane Doe. They had found a dead woman in an abandoned crack house on the south side of Chicago with no identification. After DNA testing and dental records from the Department of Human Services, *Jane Doe* was identified as Stacy.

"I'm concerned about who knows Amanda and Stacy, and why now, after all these years, they've contacted my wife," David said.

Leslie texted Amanda just as Regina knocked on the door.

"Regina?" David answered the door. "What are you doing here?!"

"Could you please call or text your wife? She asked me to stop by when she couldn't reach you. I'm supposed to check on you without saying she is worried about you."

Regina was in her white spa smock as she came into the house and saw Leslie.

"What's going on?" Regina was confused.

Leslie filled Regina in about the picture and the snowflake logo. "Amanda says okay." Leslie looked at her phone.

"That's all; okay?" David was anxious.

Leslie looked at her phone. "… umm, she is in meetings all day." Leslie looked at her phone, then at David.

"And?" David could tell there was more to the message. Then David heard his phone. He went to the kitchen and saw it was the office, most likely Gerald.

"Regina, I gotta take this." He took his phone and headed towards the den.

"Please text Amanda and tell her I'm fine; my phone died."

Regina and Leslie sat in the kitchen on the barstools, looking at Amanda's text.

"She is having dinner tonight with Nathan," Leslie said, looking at her phone. "Norah got called to attend a special dinner session with other senior directors."

"Ugh," Regina said. "The devil is just sitting this up to be very tempting. Please tell Amanda to be careful and stay alert."

Leslie texted exactly that. They both noticed Amanda's kitchen missing dishes, and they laughed.

"That Amanda. I didn't believe it when she told us last night, but she did it. She finally got angry." Regina smirked and texted Amanda that David was fine.

"You know she is going to be okay," Leslie said, sharing with Regina her car ride conversation with Amanda yesterday to the airport.

"I know. She's smart," Regina said. "Quick on her feet."

They sat there and discussed all that Amanda had shared with them when she arrived in Dallas last night. She shared how David had confessed to the affair, the racist incidents surrounding his promotion, and the touching Acuff Academy.

"I was exhausted hearing the damn story," Leslie commented. "I pray she got some sleep."

"It's clear David didn't get much," Regina commented, and brought up his five o'clock shadow. "David and Amanda really love each other. They will find their way back to each other, right?"

"Yes," David heard Regina as he came out of the den and into the kitchen. "Yes we will."

David apologized to Leslie and Regina.

"Leslie, I know I hurt Amanda. I promised to be faithful. I didn't do that."

"True," Leslie had to agree.

"David, I'm so upset with you." Regina finally said it. "You love Amanda. I know you do."

"Regina," David said with watery eyes. "I'm so sorry I hurt you and Greg by hurting Amanda. I was selfish; I believed a lie instead of going to Amanda. I'm doing whatever I can to get her to trust me again."

"Yeah..." Regina got off the barstool and stood in front of him. "Did you really spit in that white man's face defending your wife's honor? And did you create a program for underrepresented college graduates so you could change the face of your company for generations, so discrimination wouldn't happen to another family like yours? Did you just tell the CEO of your company that you didn't want your job if you couldn't be a godly man?"

Regina was in tears. "Did you do that?"

David looked Regina in the eye and responded with one tear on his face, "I did that."

"That's repentance." She hugged him. "I can't be upset at that."

David hugged her. "Thank you." He took Leslie's hand for a moment.

"I need to go pack. I have to go to the bank, go to my office to grab this contract, and then I have a plane to catch." David headed towards the stairs.

"You got the plane?!" Leslie smiled.

"Yes, Gerald and Alice are headed to Los Angeles today. They can take me to Dallas," David said.

"You have access to a corporate jet?" Regina was surprised. "You're going to Amanda?!"

"I am. Something is not right with this snowflake logo; I don't feel right about it, and I love her." David looked at the women.

"This is so sweet," Regina said. "So like Whitney Houston and Kevin Costner in that Bodyguard movie." Leslie nodded.

David rolled his eyes. "It is so not. Whitney Houston owned the plane in the movie; she was the movie star. You sound like my mom when I had just married Amanda. She made me and Amanda watch the movie. She and Amanda both cried when the characters kissed at the end."

"It is like the movie," Leslie argued. "You are the bodyguard going to defend your woman. It's romantic."

David sighed. "I know better than to argue with the two of you."

"I have to go back to the spa," Regina said. "But I like this look on you; don't shave. Amanda will love it." Regina headed towards the door.

Leslie told David to go pack, and then she needed to pack a bag for Amanda.

"Leslie, really? She already has clothes." David was getting frustrated.

"Trust me, David. Amanda needs another bag. When you see her, you tell her, with you in town, she can now shave her legs."

CHAPTER 24

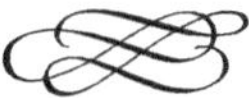

David went to the bank first, then to the office. Immediately, when he saw Vikki, she said, "You look like you haven't slept all weekend? How is Amanda?"

David sat at his desk, knowing he could be honest with her.

"Well, I told her everything. She has been angry, breaking every dish in the kitchen. She cried, and the boys felt neglected. Now she is in Dallas with a colleague whom she kissed because of my absence, and now someone knows about her past. Her plan is to go check it out with the guy she kissed and her boss. I'm so uncomfortable with that. I'm headed to Dallas."

"Wow. So, what are you going to say when you get there?"

"Vikki, I don't know…tell her that I love her? We need to take care of this together?"

He saw the contract. "Plus, I cannot make this decision without her."

"Where are you staying once you get to Dallas?" Vikki said with no emotion.

"Ugh…I have no clue." David put his head down and got humble. "Could you find me a house to rent for the week?"

"Sure. Why not just stay in the hotel with Amanda?" Vikki asked.

He looked at Vikki, ashamed, and turned away.

"After Sam, I can't be in a hotel with Amanda right now. I need a comfortable place for us."

Vikki agreed. She went around the desk and touched his shoulder.

"Amanda loves you. This is just a bump in the road for you kids," she said.

"Thank you." David felt Vikki's compassion. "Don't worry," David added, looking at the contract.

"Worry?" Vikki wasn't sure what David meant.

"Wherever I go, you're going with me," David said. "Please tell me you're okay with this?"

Vikki smiled as his office phone rang. "More than okay."

She picked up the office phone from his desk and answered, "David Lloyd's office."

Vikki went silent. She listened and then hung up the phone.

"Who was that?" David asked, curious.

"Your mom. She's on her way up," Vikki said, leaving his office.

"Great," David said sarcastically. He rose from his desk and followed Vikki, except he continued down the hall and met Meri at the top of the stairs. She was dressed in plain clothes: a pair of khaki-colored capris, an oversized black blouse, and sunglasses on her head, adorning her blonde hair that was pulled back with a black and white polka-dotted headband. He figured she wasn't working today.

"Mom." He gave her a long hug.

"David." She hugged him, but she said his name quickly, staccato and firm.

By the look in her eyes, David knew she knew everything his dad knew.

They walked down the hallway quietly. He offered her coffee. Vikki poured Meri a cup.

David closed the door to his office, and Meri sat at the conference table. He joined her, sitting at the end of the conference table next to her.

There was silence.

"Mom, I'm sorry," David said quietly.

"I know," Meri said. "Your dad told me ALL about it. Bruce too."

"Okay."

"David, this is a lot to take in. Not just the fact you were unfaithful to your wife, but I pray you and Amanda consider what divorce will do to your children and this family."

"Mom, we are not divorcing. We haven't mentioned the word. We are trying to work this out." David explained himself the best he could. Meri noticed her son's humility. How he didn't make excuses for himself; he confessed to being selfish, reckless, and disrespectful to the family.

Meri put her head down, looking at her coffee. While she was proud of the man her son had become, she had words for him.

"David." She looked at him intensely. She saw those brown eyes. For a moment, she saw that ten-year-old boy who was so sad his dad had left them.

"You are blessed beyond measure to have the love of a woman like Amanda and the life you both share."

"I know, Mom." David was still quiet. He respected his mom's thoughts and her wisdom.

"No, I don't think you really understand. You're a white man in corporate America who has cheated on his black wife with a white woman. In this community, there should be a scandal, an outrage, a *see, I told you* so."

Meri mocked. "All the different angles and spins that would come along with that. Our world is unkind, prejudiced not just on the issue of race, but on gender, economics, and social status. All disgusting to our God."

David sat and listened with his stomach aching.

"Because you have owned your sin, this will not happen; watch and see. Because Amanda has prayed for you, been selfless and cleaved to her relationship with God through Jesus, you will be hidden from your own unrighteousness."

David took a breath and took in the empathy. His mom was right. God had hidden him. No one knew about Sam, really? He didn't lose his job over it; his business was not in the streets. Why?

Amanda and all of her family friends said not a word. Vikki protected him. Sam was not vengeful, even though he used her to help him with the academy. All God's doing. He saw the blessing but felt awful.

"You are right, Mom," David said convicted. "I don't deserve this life. I'm ashamed of what I have done, but I don't care what anybody else thinks. I care about Amanda and my sons. I love her, I love you, and my family. I cry tears of joy that through this Bruce has made a decision to follow Christ and dad... well, the animosity is gone."

"I know." Meri gave a closed smile. "I'm not happy at all about what you have done, David, but I am so proud of your response. It will continue to produce great fruit."

"I give credit to the Holy Spirit within me," David confessed. "He continues to make me feel uncomfortable when my pride shows up."

Meri sat quietly for a moment. "Amanda's face at Sunday dinner and the night she invited me over for dinner crushed me. I knew something was very wrong. I had that face for years; empty. I will pray for the restoration of your marriage."

"Thank you, Mom," David said. "I appreciate you coming to talk to me. I love you and owe you so much."

Meri rose from the conference table and hugged her son. She felt her eyes start to tear, but she tilted her head back and then spoke.

"So, Bruce says Amanda is in Dallas with Nathan?"

David told her yes and that he decided to take the week off and go to her.

"Good." Meri was glad to hear her son wasn't waiting for Amanda to return. "You make Amanda make her decision clear. I love Amanda, too, but you deserve a wife who is all in. I love you, but Amanda deserves a husband who is all in."

Meri went to the door and opened it.

"Yes," David agreed and gave his mom a look of appreciation.

In front of Vikki, Meri said, "I can see myself out." She smiled at Vikki.

"Thank you for being the best gatekeeper and administrator for my son."

Vikki smiled and said *Thank you.*

Meri turned to David and faced him. "David, if you love her and she loves you, don't come back home without her. Thank you for the Acuff Academy; your dad told me about it. I'm grateful you are using your privilege in this way. Now, you allow this company to promote and give to you what you deserve. They can't possibly give you what you're worth."

"Okay, Mom."

"Remember, I raised you to leave this world better than you found it." She hugged him again, kissed his cheek, straightened his blazer, and told him to have a safe flight.

David watched her disappear down the hallway.

~

While David was meeting with Meri, Vikki found a house in Dallas to rent for the week. David looked over Vikki's shoulder as she showed him the house that was just minutes from the Dallas Market Center.

It was more house than they needed. Secluded by trees, an outdoor swimming pool, and a large great room with a real fireplace, David loved it. He told her to book it and to send the information on his phone. He went back into his office, shut the door, and read the contract Gerald had left for him.

Nathan sat in the back of the auditorium on his phone, looking at the old Snowflake Ranch website and seeing the picture of Amanda and Stacy in their youth holding up the snowflakes they drew. He now understood it all. These snowflakes inspired the logo of this company.

This online company housed beautiful bath products and accessories until a drug lord hijacked it. When he shared this with Jake and the team, there was no more mystery. Ryan didn't send the box to Amanda; he only found out about it. Now, Nathan knew Ryan had to meet with Amanda to see how much she knew and remembered.

As Amanda sat in the meeting with seventy other Augusta Retail sales representatives in the auditorium, she felt good, rested, and focused. She was glad to talk with Regina and Leslie last night, telling them all about her weekend. She was glad to receive their text that David was fine, and Leslie was trying to find the picture she needed. She remembered it all now.

She and Stacy were drawing snowflakes, and Ms. Donna had stopped to take Polaroid pictures of them. Amanda now understood that those pictures were to capture the smiles that were few and far between. Amanda felt a sadness come over her; she prayed silently for it to pass by her. It did. Her thoughts were interrupted by her cell phone.

It was a text from Vanessa. She was confirming a reset in Lindale upon her return. She approved the date with a yes. Then Amanda heard one of the sales representatives whisper to another sales representative,

"What happens on the road stays on the road, right?" He showed a picture on his cell phone to the other sales representatives. One elbowed the other, silently laughing.

Amanda could only imagine what that picture showed, as she noticed both men wore wedding bands. Amanda felt another wave of sadness coming on, so she opened her phone to Sugar Creek Farms' photos of Matthew and Mason, and one Bruce sent with David and the boys. She smiled.

Amanda returned her attention to the presentation. Augusta Retail was expanding and creating new offices. In this meeting, they made it official that more retail stores needed their help with the increase in online sales.

David went through a quick security check, handed over his luggage, met the pilot, and sat on the plane alone waiting for Gerald and Alice. At that time, he texted his friend and counselor, Dr. Nick. He told him the weekend went well, and what he was doing by going to Dallas. Dr. Nick told David to take it all slow and, no matter what the outcome of Amanda's relationship with Nathan, he needed to listen and care. David understood. He called his dad and brother and told them about Meri's visit and asked them to check on the house while he and Amanda were away.

David got up from his seat as Gerald and Alice boarded the plane.

"David." Gerald shook his hand, and David placed a kiss on Alice's cheek.

"Gerald, Alice, thank you so much for your generosity." David was humble.

"No, no, the pleasure is all mine."

Gerald made sure Alice took her seat first, and then he sat next to her, across from David. The corporate jet allowed them to sit across from each other face-to-face, and when in flight, a table could be pulled out for them to use.

"David, how romantic it is that you are going to Dallas to be with Amanda," Alice said. David smiled and told her just about every woman he talked to told him that.

"I pray Amanda thinks so," he replied.

"When we return from Los Angeles, you and Amanda need to come to the house. I would love to build a better relationship with Amanda." Alice was sincere.

David gave a pleasant smile. "Gerald and Alice, Amanda and I are as simple as they come. Can we just be honest here?"

"See?" Gerald looked at his wife. "Another reason why I like David."

"Gerald, Alice, we have known each other a long time. I've worked here for 23 years. I was a young boy who thought scrubbing toilets, sacking groceries, and getting paid for it was a way better deal than hanging out with my stepfather and his farm chores at the time." David chuckled and then was serious.

"I know it wasn't your fault regarding the issues around my promotion. I'm in trouble with my wife, not only for the infidelity but for not confiding in her. I am certain she is feeling some insecurity and that she and I need to revisit our conversation on racism."

"David, your incident has caused us to look at the whole process," Alice interjected before her husband could. "I'm sorry. What happened was wrong, period. I'm grateful for your understanding and graciousness."

David just nodded.

"I'm not offering you what I'm offering you because of what happened." Gerald wanted to be clear. "You and Amanda talk it over."

"We will, Gerald." David was honest. "If you are not offering me this because of what happened, why are you offering this promotion to me?"

Gerald looked at him earnestly. "There are so many reasons, David. Every store you have managed, the people flat-out respect you. There is nothing on your record of treating anyone with disrespect to get ahead or any amount of selfishness."

"Gerald needs someone with him he can truly trust," Alice said frankly.

"Scott is my son and I love him, but he is too thirsty to make a name for himself," Gerald said. "I know he respects you, but I know the two of you have had heated discussions; he needs someone to challenge him."

"Gerald, I'm not going to come between you and your son."

"David, I'm not asking you to. Scott will take over Acuff when I want him to and no time sooner. But I cannot overlook this Acuff Academy. These trainees are amazing. We are one day into trainees being at their store. Three store directors have already called me personally with rave reviews, saying what a difference it makes when new employees know how to operate the register before being on the front end. When they know the procedures at customer service and know what is on the menu in the restaurant before dealing with their first customer."

"That is great." David was proud of the trainees.

"The way Amanda came into the office, like she was one of us, and you both shared about the Brookview Downtown project. We need to be involved in these decisions, not to overtake them, but I want Acuff to be a corporation with good citizenship, a responsible community leader, caring about what happens in all areas where we have a store." Gerald was passionate and serious.

"Amanda is amazing in that way. One minute she is sweet and caring, and the next minute there is this fight that comes out of her, and you wonder what hit you." He laughed, thinking about the dishes in the yard, and Vikki shared how she responded to Sam.

"Yes. All the more reason Amanda and I need to be better friends." Alice smiled.

David smiled back.

"Listen, those other senior vice presidents are embarrassed by their behavior and know what I did to Allen can happen to them. I'm not scared," Gerald told David.

David appreciated Gerald's generosity with the contract of promotion and his commitment to inclusion and equity for all the Acuff employees. David was excited and anxious to share with Amanda all he was thinking regarding his career with Acuff. He shared with Gerald and Alice pictures of the boys and his plan to spend more time with them.

When they landed, David said his goodbyes and wished them a productive and safe trip to Los Angeles. A car service took him directly to the house rental. As the car service waited, he walked to the house and dropped off the luggage before heading to Amanda's hotel.

CHAPTER 25

$\mathcal{A}$manda entered the hotel after a full day of meetings in the Augusta Retail corporate office two blocks away. She was tired and went up to the front desk to ask for more bottled water for her room. She heard the woman behind the hostess desk say, "Ms. Snowden, here is your room key card. Enjoy your stay."

Amanda turned to the woman—blonde hair and no rings on her finger, but her hands were beautifully manicured. It was the pale blue nail polish with tiny rhinestones and a snowflake on the left pinky that caught her attention. As she left the reception desk with her rolling suitcase, Amanda noticed her designer jeans and black slingback high heels as she headed to the elevator with a bellman.

Amanda got her bag of bottled water and followed them into the elevator. Amanda said her floor number and noticed the bellman pushed eight for Ms. Snowden. No one spoke. Amanda had to get off on the sixth floor, but she noticed the bellman's name and thought she would befriend him later.

When David made it to Amanda's hotel in Dallas, he sat in the lobby. The lobby was large enough that no one really noticed him. He sat on a soft, blue suede sofa by large windows with a view of the hotel's well-manicured front entrance lawn. He knew Amanda had dinner plans with Nathan. Leslie tried to hide that from him, but David overheard her conversation with Regina. He prayed for Amanda. As he read a local Dallas magazine and checked his email, he welcomed Brad's phone call.

"Hey, how are you?" David answered his phone.

"The bigger question is, how are you?" Brad said.

David had confessed everything to his friend after his first session with Dr. Nick. Brad knew his friend had a full weekend and really wanted to check in.

David filled him in on the success of the academy after one day. The trainees texted that they were having a good experience. Store directors sent Gerald good ideas and wanted to know if this academy was going company-wide.

"That all sounds promising." Brad was excited for his best friend. "How's Amanda?"

David explained that he was in Dallas and why.

"David, you and Amanda are IN love. I'm jealous. Renee and I are getting a divorce."

"No!" David sat up straight in his chair. He quickly looked around the lobby and brought his voice down. "Why are you just now telling me? I know I have had a lot going on, but you could've said something?!"

Brad went silent long enough for David to notice this wasn't an easy subject.

"David, c'mon; this isn't a complete shock. Renee and I have had our issues over the years. I should've known when she told me she didn't agree with your marriage to Amanda. Let's not start that conversation."

"Yeah, Renee is a bit judgmental," David sighed.

"I love Renee, but she abandoned Abby and me the moment she went back to school. New friends, a new outlook on life altogether. She loves the money I provide, but I am not sure she was interested in being a mom or a wife anymore in small-town America. She prefers Nashville."

Brad sounded bitter to David in one way, but he had known his friend since grade school. He was hurt.

"I'm sorry," David said and paused. Another moment in his life to be grateful to God for his life.

"Brad?"

"Yeah?"

"I love you, man. What can I do?" David meant that, and Brad knew he did.

Brad explained his situation: The divorce would be final next week, and Renee gave him full custody, only wanting Abby a few holidays and weeks in the summer. No lawyers, she argued over nothing. Brad agreed to pay for his wife's schooling and a down payment on her new home in Nashville, and he would establish Abby's college fund with both contributing monthly.

"Sounds so sterile. No emotion; done," David said.

"Yep," Brad agreed. "I'm alone with a 12-year-old girl who is going through puberty, feels completely unloved by her mom, and I have 200 employees to manage. I'm tired."

David heard Brad. "Well, you are not alone. Can you hang in there just one more week until I get home?"

"Of course. I have my mom and dad. But the *I told you so* works my nerves." Brad gave a half-laugh, and David did too, but reassured his best friend that he would support him and love him during this difficult time.

≈

Amanda and Nathan made their dinner a working one. With memos, documents, and their phones on the table, they confirmed resets and strategized how their office could help their clients with online sales. When dinner arrived, they cleared their papers and enjoyed their food, glasses of wine, and conversation.

"Wow," Nathan said after hearing about Amanda's weekend. "How do you feel? That's a lot to take in. I'm glad he told you everything."

"Yes," Amanda said, moving a strand of hair out of her face. "Now that things are out in the open, I pray for healing. I feel the man I married coming back to me." She gave a little smile.

Nathan was happy to see her smile. It was beautiful. After seeing her childhood picture, he noticed that she had grown into those brown eyes, and the golden highlights only grew more profound as she aged.

"I'm glad," Nathan finally commented after a few seconds of silence. He hesitated for another moment and then said, "I took your advice."

"You did?" Amanda frowned. "What advice was that? I don't remember; I've been preoccupied for weeks."

They laughed.

"I apologized to my ex-wife," Nathan told her and took a deep breath.

"To say she needed to hear it would be an understatement. She thanked me, and we talked for a while. So thank you for prompting me to do it."

Amanda gave a smile of contentment. "That's wonderful. Now she can have closure and not bring baggage into her second marriage."

"Well..." Nathan said, sipping his wine. "Jill told me she broke off the engagement. She said Jeff became very possessive after the engagement, and she ended everything."

Amanda's eyes grew large and started dancing. "What?!"

Nathan told Amanda what little Jill had said on the phone that night and that their son supported her decision.

"Why haven't you made it to Briton to have that coffee?" Amanda asked.

"Are you blind?! She wants to talk to you; perhaps the two of you can build a brand-new relationship."

Nathan could hear the excitement in Amanda's voice, but he was doubtful.

"Amanda, you are kind, but I'm not so sure she can open her heart to me like that again. I was bad."

"The keyword is WAS. You are now a new person. You are the handsome, thoughtful gentleman in the office who thinks about everyone else. You care about each of our representatives and want what is best for them, not only professionally but personally."

Amanda meant it innocently, but the way Nathan looked at her now, she stepped into a tender territory of his emotions.

"Amanda..."

"Nathan, I'm sorry..."

He touched her hand briefly. "I have so much to tell you, but I can't or shouldn't." Nathan wanted to tell her about the investigation and how much he knew and cared for her.

Amanda felt it. It was time to go. It was a nice dinner; the wine and the conversation were good. She felt the atmosphere changing. "We should go."

"I'm sorry... I didn't want this to get uncomfortable." Nathan was clear.

"I know you love David. And the truth is, I do love Jill."

Amanda settled.

"I want you to know I care for you," Nathan said. "No matter what happens, we shared a moment, and I regret it. Then I don't."

Nathan and Amanda stared at each other for a moment and held hands.

Jake, disguised as a room service attendant, knocked on the door of Room 825. She opened the door and allowed Jake to take the cart that was stacked with dirty dishes. He saw the brown, full-size envelope under the plates. She nodded and made a comment that her salad had tomatoes, and she specifically told the kitchen she didn't want them. Jake apologized, realizing that it was a code that she was not alone or was being recorded.

He left the room, got on the elevator, and made it to the kitchen, where the hotel kitchen staff cleared the cart. Jake took the envelope and headed to the hotel security room. Law enforcement had been invited three months ago to share the space with hotel security. One side of the wall had screens displaying what was going on everywhere cameras were in the hotel. Two federal agents were on their laptops, and two Dallas detectives were examining the whiteboard of timelines and the happenings of Ryan Barnes.

Jake sat in the vacant chair and pulled out his laptop, which he had left at one of the desks. He opened the envelope and saw the SFR catalog and copies of pages of a ledger. He snapped his fingers, and that got the attention of the two detectives. They made their way to Jake.

"This right here connects our friend, Ryan, to all of this." Jake handed the papers to Stu.

Then Jake noticed a real employee from the hotel kitchen appeared in front of him. She handed him a USB drive and said, "I found this in the pile of tomatoes."

David noticed a woman walking across the lobby to the front desk with a room key card and an envelope in her hand. No mistaking the walk—it was Amanda. A golden yellow blouse with a matching shawl, skinny blue jeans, those wedged heels, and a clutch purse on the other hand. She wasn't even trying; she was a pretty woman.

David saw her give the room key and envelope to the woman behind the reception desk. She turned back towards the lobby; she was looking for someone. She didn't see David, but she saw the bellman who assisted *Ms. Snowden*.

"Hi." She smiled at him.

"Mrs. Lloyd, right?" The young man said. He was wearing his uniform that fit his thick frame perfectly. He had innocent brown eyes and a conservative brown haircut as if he were running for political office. His skin was fair. He was friendly.

"Yes," Amanda answered. "Can I ask you a question about the woman in the elevator earlier this evening?"

David saw Amanda give the bellman money. He took it and looked at Amanda as to size her up and figure out her purpose.

"Mrs. Lloyd." The bellman said.

"Derrick." Amanda looked at his nametag.

"Listen, you are a nice woman. Here on business from the Midwest, Augusta Retail. I make it a point to know guests who are here for more than one day. Please, don't get involved in local affairs," Derrick told her.

"But what if those local affairs sent you a box interrupting your business in the Midwest? I don't want to confront anyone I don't know, nor the response I'm going to get," Amanda said strongly.

"I get it," he said to her, pulling out a map from the tourist wall. He pretended Amanda had asked a question about a tourist attraction.

"Mrs. Lloyd, my father runs security here. My job is to keep my eyes and ears open all the time." He pointed to a part of the map. "The rooftop bar here has gotten out of hand," he said, glancing at her ever so often, but he told her about the sex and the drugs.

"Ms. Snowden?" Amanda wanted to know.

"Nicci," Derrick said her first name. "She's caught in the middle of a dangerous world. Mrs. Lloyd, don't get involved, no matter what these people sent you. Between you and me, please don't say a word. Police are undercover all over this hotel."

Amanda heard her phone buzz in her purse. She thanked Derrick and sat in one of the lobby chairs, opening her purse to reach her phone. David saw her closed-lip smile as she saw the text message.

How was your day?

Better now that I have heard from you. I miss you.

I miss you too. You are beautiful.

Thank you.

Amanda was now blushing.

I love making you blush.

You know me so well.

You know, I've always loved yellow on you.

Amanda looked up from her phone, then texted:

Where are you?!

Look straight ahead.

When Amanda rose from the chair in the lobby, there was her husband. His brown eyes stared at her as he displayed that smile that made her smile back at him. She liked that he hadn't shaved; he looked sexy to her, standing there looking at her with his hands in his pockets.

She took four steps, and she was face-to-face with the love of her life.

"So Mason realized that I would be all alone this week. Matthew reminded me I have a corporate jet, and Gerald and Alice were happy to give me a lift." David smiled.

"Oh babe." She touched his face and kissed his lips. She closed her eyes and hugged him.

"All the women said this would be romantic. I'm guessing, yes?" David said, rubbing her back.

"Yes," Amanda said, breaking their embrace only to look at him again.

"I like this new look," she said as she looked him in the eyes. "So handsome, are you coming up to my room?" Amanda smiled, and then she saw David's guilt.

"Amanda," David said, looking down at the hotel lobby floor. He didn't have to say anything more. Amanda's eyes, which were once sparkling and happy, now fell flat. She thought of his affair, too.

"I rented a house. It's beautiful. If you gather your things, can we stay there together? It's just four miles away," David said.

Amanda took her husband's hand. "Sure." She was silent for a moment and wondered how she would trust him again. The love was there, but how would he regain it? She smiled at him lovingly, wanting to move on. After all, he was in Dallas with her and for her.

"I'll call the car service while you go and get your luggage." David kissed her hand and let her go.

Amanda headed towards the elevator, thinking of her conversation with Derrick, the bellman. Perhaps it was good for her to leave the hotel. It sounded like a raid was going to happen sooner or later.

Amanda walked around the house in awe. The entryway was circular, with a staircase that led to a loft with a view of the neighborhood and downtown Dallas. Coming back down from the loft to her right was an office with a twin bed; to her left was a high-top table and wine bar. Behind her was a long hallway revealing the rest of the home, featuring a beautiful kitchen with a full kitchen island, a prep sink, a gas stove, black granite countertops, and white cabinets with oil-rubbed bronze hardware. Amanda spotted the stainless steel wall oven and French door refrigerator.

The kitchen opened into a large dining room and great room, with a big sectional couch that circled a wood-burning fireplace. The great room windows were floor-to-ceiling, showing off the backyard that was secluded by trees. The mauve, orange sunset captivated Amanda for minutes.

Out from the dining room was a beautiful cedar deck for gazing at the sunrise in the morning. Past the dining room was another hallway leading to two master bedrooms with a master suite in between them. One master bedroom led to a private outdoor shower. A tall fence was located near the outdoor pool, which was just a few steps away.

"David, really?!" Amanda came back to him in the great room. "This is wonderful."

"Thank Vikki. I told her I wanted us to be comfortable." David opened the refrigerator.

"And Vikki had groceries brought in. Unbelievable; she thinks of everything."

"Wow," Amanda said, leaning against the kitchen island.

"So, how was dinner?" David asked nervously. "Are you still hungry? I was going to make coffee, but I didn't sleep well at all."

"No," Amanda said, looking at her husband sweetly, "I'm fine, but if there is tea..."

He found the tea and started the hot water.

"David, I was supposed to have dinner with Nathan *and* Norah tonight. But as it turned out, it was just Nathan and me."

"I know. I overheard Leslie's conversation with Regina—that in and of itself is a story—but Nathan is not the only reason I came here. I love you, and I want us." He went up to her and kissed her forehead.

"I love you too."

David gave her the hot water and a selection of tea bags. He decided he wanted cheese and crackers, so he began to prepare a plate for himself. After tea was made along with his plate of cheese and crackers, David and Amanda sat on the big U-shaped sectional couch. As always, David allowed Amanda to sit in the corner of her choice, and he sat next to her.

Amanda shared that she and Nathan worked over dinner and mentioned there was a chance he could reconcile with his wife.

"Interesting," David said. In his mind, he knew he would be miserable if he and Amanda divorced.

"David, I'm sorry. I didn't realize how much my encounter with Nathan and the temptation all around me hurt you."

"I trust you, Amanda." David made the statement, and then he saw the eye contact she gave him.

"I kissed him tonight. He invited me to another hotel across the street, where he has another room. He gave me the keycard. I left the table, wrote him a note of '*no thanks*' and left it at the front desk." Amanda got it all out quickly, then corrected herself with her eyes closed.

"No, he invited me with the keycard. We exchanged glances, I said *no*, and we kissed. I left." Amanda felt her face was hot.

David continued to sit quietly. Immediately, he felt anger. But the more he sat, the more the Holy Spirit dealt with him. He was reminded of Sam, and his anger disappeared.

He knew Amanda was telling the truth. He saw her give a keycard and an envelope to the woman behind the front desk at the hotel. It was honorable; more than he could say for himself.

David played his first night with Sam in his head for the millionth time. He wished he had thought of someone besides himself. He also thought about what Dr. Nick had told him: stay calm, listen, gather facts, and then emotions.

David took her hand and held it.

"Please forgive me, David," she said quietly.

"How can I not with the way you come to me, soft and broken? I started this mess."

Curiosity got the best of him. He softly asked, "This kiss; did you like it?"

Amanda closed her eyes, and a tear fell. What an awkward question for her husband to ask, she thought.

"It was foreign because my lips already have a home."

David smirked a little and looked at their hands together.

"It wasn't a *hello, see you later* kiss," Amanda said. "It was a *goodbye* kiss. I stopped Nathan from speaking. I was calm, but clear, and I told him I wouldn't do it."

David kissed her hand that was inside his. Amanda moved closer to her husband so that they were inches away from each other. David placed a tender kiss on her lips. Amanda gave one back.

David gave her another tender kiss and gently spoke. "I love you. I'm sorry I had an affair with Sam, kept it a secret, and still came to you like it was all normal. Forgive me, Amanda," he said, looking into her eyes and kissing her lips.

"Babe, I told you, it's forgiven. I'm sorry too. I shouldn't have kissed Nathan. Can we fix us?"

"I want that." David hugged her.

David released her, slid Amanda's heels off, and then took his shoes off. They readjusted themselves on the sectional so he was in the corner and could put his arms around her. They exchanged a series of kisses, and they held each other with no words for a moment.

"Honey, when Leslie came to the house asking for old pictures of you from the orphanage, then asking for the skeleton key to the safe deposit box at the bank, did you think I was just going to say okay?"

David stroked her hair gently. "I brought the file with me. Please tell me what is happening here."

Amanda was almost asleep, her head resting on his chest. The smell of his cologne and masculinity had almost hypnotized her. She couldn't remember the last time they slept in the same bed. When they did, their backs were to one another, or one of them was already asleep before the other got to bed.

"Babe," she said with her eyes closed. "Thank you. I love you. It all doesn't matter right now. You're here with me. My man is here to help me, support me and love me."

"I am." David felt his soul flip with joy and security. He could feel her body relax even more. Amanda was tired.

He rose and kissed her cheek. "C'mon."

He took her hand and led her to the master bedroom with the outdoor shower. "I put your luggage here. Go to bed; get some rest."

She saw her suitcase from the hotel and then another one.

"Babe, you didn't have to bring me more clothes!"

David kissed her hand before he closed her door and said, "Let's talk about Leslie tomorrow. She insisted you needed more clothes and said something about you can now shave your legs."

Amanda smiled and then laughed.

"Good night."

CHAPTER 26

*A*manda was awake at 2:30 am; too much tea before bedtime, she figured, but she was wide awake. As she climbed back into the bed alone, she thought about how much she missed sleeping next to David.

She knew he was giving her space, but she wanted to be near him. Amanda felt God sharing His satisfaction with David's humility and brokenness. His trip to Dallas was orchestrated by God. He wanted her to reconcile with her husband.

Amanda decided to go to her husband. She brushed her teeth, washed her face, put on her red mid-length satin robe that Leslie had put in the second luggage, and peeked into David's room. The bed was empty. She heard a noise.

As she made her way down the hallway to the kitchen, there was David at the kitchen sink, in nothing but his athletic shorts. He still hadn't shaved. As she looked at his muscular arms and chest, and how refreshing that glass of water looked as he put the glass to his lips, she wanted him.

"Amanda, I'm sorry, did I wake you?"

"No," she continued, leaning against the wall.

"I couldn't sleep." David didn't want to confess that he was missing her. His guilt and shame convinced him that he did not have the right to miss her. After all, he was sleeping with two women at the same time.

"Me neither," Amanda said, as she untied her robe and let it open naturally to expose her naked body.

David saw his wife standing there. He didn't know if he was more stunned by her invitation or captivated by her beauty.

Amanda smiled and motioned him to come near her. "I'm here for you," she said demurely.

He went to her, putting his hands inside her robe, on her bare waist. He gave her a hug with his right cheek touching her right cheek. David took in her smell, and Amanda loved the feeling of his unshaven face. To her surprise, it was soft and warm.

"My Sunday honey," he whispered in her ear.

With her back now against the wall in the kitchen, Amanda whispered in his ear, "My morning lover."

He kissed her passionately. Amanda grabbed his face, taking in the passion, her tongue in his mouth, wetness on their lips from the heated kiss exchange. David pressed her against the wall, kissing her neck, his tongue enjoying her pleasure spot under her ear. Amanda's hands were on his bare back.

He loved her moan as his right hand was still at her waist, but his left hand was on her breast, enjoying the feeling of her erect nipple. His left hand continued down her body until he reached between her legs. She was open for him, and he pleasured her there, looking into her eyes before she closed them in delight. He loved her breathless voice saying his name. She loved his gentle touch and his tongue on her neck at the same time; she couldn't control herself anymore. Her release was so intense; no words, just hot breath and kisses on his shoulder.

She then pushed him against the wall behind him. Her hands massaged his bare chest until they reached his waist. She pulled down his shorts as she got on her knees. She opened her mouth and took him in, to the back of her throat. Amanda heard David's approval as she gently pulled away for a moment to catch her breath. With her mouth and her lips doing all the work, David liked her warmth and her rhythm. It didn't take long for him to stroke her hair as a signal. Amanda swallowed all he released, and she rose slowly, kissing him on the neck, her tongue in his ear as she whispered, "I love you."

David held her close. He was still quivering and felt so undeserving of what had just happened. There was silence until David spoke.

"God's grace overwhelms me." He was quiet.

"Amanda, with God's help, I promise to love you and the boys better. I desire to cover you and protect you. Tell me what you need, and I will do whatever I can to make it happen."

David meant those words sincerely. He pulled his shorts back up.

"God woke me up and told me to come to you. Here it is early in the morning, and you couldn't sleep."

"No, I couldn't."

"You wanted me?" Amanda asked.

"Badly. I wanted to give you space and time, but not having you next to me..." He blushed.

"I missed you, too. I couldn't remember the last time we..."

David took Amanda's hand and led her to his master bedroom. He faced her and said, "Come to bed with me. If it's too soon, tell me, but..."

Amanda didn't allow him to finish the sentence before she took off her robe and uttered, "Make love to me."

He did; several times. David took nothing for granted in those hours. He thanked God for every touch and the fact that he could watch her drift to sleep in his arms. He noticed her hand resting on the pillow and saw her wedding ring. He remembered the day he bought it.

She was on a weekend trip with Regina and Leslie, a weekend without him, so he went ring and house shopping. The moment he saw it, he bought it. White gold, one and a half karats, and a princess cut with three small diamonds down each side. The wedding band had seven more small diamonds. It reminded him of her—soft, beautiful, and noticeable, but not flashy.

For three months, he kept it close, just waiting for the right moment. After Sunday dinner at the farm, they went on a private walk around the lake. Amanda had just laughed about the popcorn he burned in the microwave the night before and how she loved his socks over hers. The sun went behind the clouds, and the rain came down quickly. Her hair was instantly wet with its beautiful, tight curls, raindrops on her face, and the golden flakes in her brown eyes. The scene hit him with such love and beauty that day.

He proposed and got down on one knee, ring in his front pocket. Her face glowed and her yes was satisfying. As he remembered, he leaned in and kissed her cheek as he continued to watch her sleep.

Amanda woke up, got out of bed, and texted Norah that David had come to Dallas to surprise her. She told Norah that she would go to the Dallas Market today with him and would touch base with her soon. Then, Amanda climbed back into the bed with David, resting her head on his chest, feeling loved.

She thought about the hours before. She felt David's tenderness in every way he touched her, and thanked God for giving her the husband she married, wanted, and needed. She could tell that David was different in all the right ways.

He stroked her hair and warmed her body since she had left the bed for a few minutes. David laughed at his thought, *I guess we kissed and made up in bed.*

Amanda laughed as she remembered David telling her about his conversation with the boys at camp, *Yeah. I will tell Matthew this is none of his business.*

David was right about one thing: she did need to find a private place to pray in the house. The boys only knew about the affair and her resulting pain because they overheard her pleas to God through the floor vents. Still, she saw the good that came out of it. If Bruce decided to get saved and follow Jesus from hearing her prayers, it was worth it!

They were both excited about Bruce and how his life seemed to be turning around. They both acknowledged that, out of all the things going on, his decision was a blessing. They didn't know what else could make the highlight of their year.

"Honey, I have a few more confessions." David sat up a bit. He rearranged the pillows and invited her to take her place back on his chest.

"What?" Amanda frowned.

"Since we are being honest, I invaded your privacy too," David said.

"You did? How?"

"I opened your art journal," he said. "Amanda, it was so beautiful. Why don't you share this part of you with me?"

Amanda kept her position on his chest. "It's therapy. You weren't listening then."

David took her hand and kissed it. "I'm listening now."

"Yes," Amanda confirmed. "When I feel...well, when I'm not sure what I feel, I draw."

"Well, it's beautiful. When I saw that you saw yourself as invisible, I couldn't bear it." David told her that the picture motivated him to call Dr. Nick.

"I am happy you are talking to someone." Amanda was calm and felt gratitude.

"Are you disappointed that I opened your journal? I would never do it again, but I couldn't figure out the change in you. Now, I get it," David said.

"Babe, just ask me." She looked up at him. "I'm not hiding; I just want you to notice me."

David felt a wave in his stomach. He recalled those nights when the boys didn't want to go to bed, and Amanda would clean the kitchen, get the laundry done, and she just wasn't in the mood, but she pleased him anyway. He knew he didn't notice her feelings then.

"Honey, you have been so gracious and patient. Look at me."

She sat up.

"Please come to Dr. Nick with me. Who do you share your feelings with?" David asked, touching her face.

Amanda smiled. "Sure. I have Regina and Leslie, but I promise not to keep things from you."

"Okay." David looked at her seriously. "Going forward, what should our intimate and sexual relationship look like? Dr. Nick says not to make it like it was; we have to create something new."

Amanda looked at David, pleased.

"I don't want answers now. Think about it. It is easy to have mind-blowing sex here with no kids, household responsibilities, dinner to make, activities to get to, schoolwork to help out with, a job, or our family. Don't get me wrong, family is a blessing, but we are always doing something with family."

"Yes," Amanda said. She was happy David was saying all the right things, and she was enjoying it, but she also knew the hard part was awaiting them at home. The familiar day-to-day, running into Samantha and Nathan. *Lord, make us strong*, she thought. She shared her thoughts with David.

"One day at a time," he told her. "You are promising you won't keep things from me?"

"Yes," Amanda said, smiling.

He suddenly started tickling her. "You are in trouble." Amanda fell into the bed laughing and giggling. He loved to hear her and see her smile.

David now hovered over her. "Have you lost your mind? Asking Leslie to get the brown expandable file from the safe deposit box at the bank."

"Yeah... about that?" Amanda covered her face with her hand.

"Yeah, honey, about that?" David mocked her. "That... more than anything, made me ask for the plane ride from Gerald."

"When I couldn't get a hold of you, I just went to Leslie. I remembered where I saw that logo, and I went for it," Amanda said.

David shook his head but told her he understood. He told her he remembered the picture too.

Amanda lay in the bed and told David about Nicci and what Derrick, the bellman, said.

"Amanda, who do you think we are?" David got out of bed. "Snowflake Ranch, sex, in the area of human-trafficking, prostitution, and drugs? We aren't going anywhere but to the police."

CHAPTER 27

avid and Amanda got dressed, had breakfast, and coffee. Amanda listened to her husband and called Vanessa, asking her to take a photo of the packing slip from the Snowflake Ranch and send her a picture of the logo. They sat at the kitchen table and discussed what happened and their next steps.

"I got the box the same day you came home from Prairie Heights," Amanda remembered. "I didn't pay it any attention. The website for the ranch just sent me to the showroom at the Dallas Market Center. No note, just an invitation to the showroom."

David looked at the picture from the orphanage and the logo. His wife was correct; it was remarkably similar.

"Yes, whoever this is knows you and Stacy. So let's think about it."

"Babe, I already know." Amanda looked at the logo and the picture. "If we have a brown expandable file with this picture in it, Stacy did too."

Amanda used her phone to call the police. After several minutes on hold and talking to a detective, the detective insisted that he come to the house.

"Honey, I don't want you to be afraid," David said, embracing her from behind as she now looked out the large window overlooking the backyard.

"That's easier said than done." Amanda loved his arms around her. "Can I tell you something?"

"Of course."

"I don't want to work anymore. I'm mentally exhausted, and there are too many things to keep track of at work. As the boys get older and discover who their friends are, your travel schedule, and Augusta Retail's upcoming changes, what if I travel too? Seeing my colleagues' adultery and being in the office with Nathan, that is not the life I want."

"I understand." He kissed her cheek. "Well, I'm pleased to tell you that you don't have to work if you don't want to."

"David, I completely forgot. What did Gerald say to you?"

"That's another reason I'm here. We have a contract to look over. I've read it; now you need to read it. If I accept it, you don't have to work. Alice would like to talk to you, but the salary... I'm humbled."

David closed his eyes. "This is it. What Gerald is offering... I don't want to advance any further in this company. You know how they talk about wickedness in high places. This is high enough."

Amanda looked at David. "Well, let's just ask God to put you where He wants you and leave it at that."

They both heard a knock at the door, followed by the doorbell's ring. David went to answer it, and Amanda went to the kitchen to make coffee.

When David opened the door, there stood two men in plain clothes. They extended their hands. Sergeant Stu Rollins had black hair, olive skin, and brown eyes. He wore jeans, a Dallas Cowboys' t-shirt, and a leather jacket. Officer Jake Harmon had army short strawberry blonde hair, pale skin, and blue eyes. He wore jeans and a white t-shirt with a small logo of a local restaurant on the upper right side. If David had to guess, Sergeant Rollins was closer to his age, and Officer Harmon was younger.

"Please, come in." David opened the door wider.

Sergeant Rollins and Officer Harmon stepped out of the way, and there was Nathan, who was standing behind them, now in full view.

"David, you have every right to punch me in the face, but I've asked Stu and Jake to give me a moment with you and Amanda." Nathan stood before David, with his head down and his hands by his side.

"Okay." David frowned but allowed Nathan in as the police stood outside.

When Amanda saw it was Nathan and not the police in front of David, she was puzzled.

"Nathan, why are you here?"

"Please, can we sit?" Nathan felt awkward, but knew it was time to tell the truth.

David and Amanda led Nathan to the great room. They offered him coffee, but he refused. David and Amanda sat together holding hands on the chaise of the sectional, and Nathan sat next to them on the couch section.

"When you called Norah this morning and told her David was here with you, I was so relieved," Nathan started quietly. "And when you called the police, I am grateful that you are now aware."

"Okay, I'm missing something. I don't understand what's going on here," Amanda said.

Nathan took a breath. "I started with Augusta Retail just like you, in a field position. But before that, I was a police detective in Cunningham County. I got shot in the line of duty, and that is when the drug addiction started. I felt that the loss of my job due to injury was a loss of my life's purpose. So I began using and destroyed my marriage, my relationship with my son, and couldn't keep a job for a time."

"I went into a bar to get a fix and ended up in a fight with broken ribs, and along with my back injury, I was found next to a dumpster, left to die. Another officer on the police force recognized me and took me to the hospital instead of jail. That's when God got a hold of me and started changing my life. I began physical therapy, started a drug-free recovery program, and Augusta Retail took a chance on me."

Amanda digested the information and now understood Nathan. David sat surprised, but he was ready to know what all of this had to do with his wife.

"At the retail level, I was noticing petty theft, and I helped the police with a few store robberies. It was when I got promoted to this position that I started working with the FBI."

"The FBI?" Amanda was shocked. "Nathan, you're an informant?"

Nathan nodded yes. "Do you know Lucas McCormick?"

Amanda rolled her eyes. "Brown hair, blue eyes, handsome, but he knows it? Mr. Arrogant? I wish I did not. He has your job in Michigan."

"Well, kind of. He is a senior account representative, so he goes to the same meetings I do. We were here in Dallas at a meeting right after you got promoted. Lucas and some other male Augusta colleagues went out for drinks one night. Lucas pulls out this catalog that was like a lady's lingerie catalog. I'm shaking my head, not getting why these guys are pointing and telling him what they like out of this catalog."

"Oh boy," David scratched his head. "I've only heard about these things, but I can't believe this is true."

"Yes," Nathan said. "So Lucas tells me not to worry about it; he will treat me this time."

Nathan told David and Amanda he was completely naïve to the entire incident until a woman showed up in his hotel room in the lingerie, which he guessed Lucas picked out for him.

"Her name was Eva, and she told me she was hired to have sex with me or whatever I wanted. I was numb and gave her money to tell the guys I slept with her, but I didn't. Instead, I asked her how the operation worked. How did she get involved, and how deep was Augusta Retail into this?"

"And...?" David asked.

"It's bad. I shared what I knew with a friend on the police force. He told me not to tell anyone else what I knew and said someone from Internal Affairs would call me. Long story short, I began working with the FBI."

"Nathan, what does all of this have to do with me?" Amanda asked.

"I'll let the officers outside explain. When I found out these people knew you and you didn't know them, the FBI wanted me to keep an eye on you. I already had a secret crush on you." Nathan couldn't look at the couple anymore; he stared at his hands. "To now have to look out for you, that just deepened the infatuation."

David let go of Amanda's hand and shifted his posture.

"The Snowflake Ranch box came from Dallas, and I knew this company wanted to meet with you. I attempted to find out as much as I could about the company without making anyone in the office suspicious. But Vanessa and I knew something was wrong with how much merchandise they sent you, and to no one else, company-wide. I told her to tell me if anything else came for you from this Snowflake Ranch and reassured her not to worry. You didn't do me any favors leaving your keys in the door and racing off to a doctor's appointment without telling anyone."

Amanda sighed, and then Nathan sighed. He then looked at David.

"What I didn't see coming was David's affair." Nathan's eyes met Amanda's. "I thought it strange the flowers ended up in the breakroom, you with your office door closed all the time, absent-minded, in the bathroom, and that Friday night. I was there because you were there. I was worried you hadn't gone home, and you were in the conference room in a daze."

No one spoke. Then Nathan continued.

"David, I'm sorry. I lost control of my emotions. Before it went too far, I thought about my life and what my ex-wife endured. My job was to help and protect Amanda, not cause more problems."

David let out a sigh of relief at Nathan's confession, but was trying to capture the story.

"This is hard to grasp. Let me see if I'm getting this. You innocently found out about a sex trafficking/prostitution operation. The FBI asked you to be an informant. You realize that these sex traffickers know about my wife, and the FBI asked you to keep an eye on her because...?" David was lost after that.

"Because they know who Amanda is, but she doesn't know them. The officers will explain."

Nathan repeated himself, then continued.

"I just wanted to clear the air. Last night I wanted to tell you this. I gave you a keycard to my hotel room across the street because the FBI did not want you alone after the confrontation and the raid."

"Amanda, I'd like to think we would've kept our emotions in check, but the enemy could've worn us down. I'm grateful God sent your husband to do what I probably would've messed up. After work today, I must be at the hotel across the street. These people are smart; they can't know I'm the informant."

Amanda took it all in. She wasn't sure what to feel. She knew the officers outside would explain what Nathan would not, and she saw Nathan in a different light. Nathan pulled an envelope out of his back pocket. Amanda recognized it.

"David, before the police come in, I wanted to share this with you. Amanda, thank you for this." Nathan took the letter out of the envelope, and he began to read:

Dearest Nathan,

Thank you for dinner tonight. It was good to hear about your conversation with your ex-wife. Nothing would please me more than you having a second chance with the woman you love.

Please take this keycard. I couldn't be alone with you in a hotel room. It is easy to think one night, and no one would know. But we would know. Shame would follow us and separate us from our God.

I honestly believe the encounter we shared, the enemy wanted it to destroy my marriage and destroy your second chance. But what the enemy intended for evil, God used it for good.

Thank you for telling me to go home to my husband and love him. I did. He came home to me, and I am looking forward to building a new life with him.

Nathan, I have eyes for no other man. David covers me, and I live and breathe inside of him; my heart and soul belong to him. I love him. What God has put together, let no man separate.

Blessings upon you,

Amanda

David looked at his wife with adoration. "Nathan, thank you for sharing that."

"Sure," Nathan said as he got up from the couch.

David got up and shook Nathan's hand. Amanda gave Nathan a long hug.

"Thank you. I'm not sure I understand all you have done here, but I do know you have supported me."

Nathan gave her that closed smile Amanda was used to seeing when she paid him a compliment at work. He left the room. The Lloyds heard the door open and several footsteps enter the house.

Nathan officially introduced the Lloyds to Stu and Jake. Amanda put a pot of coffee on the dining room table as everyone took a seat.

"Thank you for coming to us," Amanda said.

"We appreciate the call," Stu replied. He poured coffee into a mug. "Mrs. Lloyd, we saw you leave the hotel with your husband, but you didn't check out of the hotel."

David and Amanda both had surprised looks on their faces, and Jake swiftly said, "Yeah, we know all that is going on at the hotel; sorry. The moment you called and said who you were, what brought you to Dallas and Snowflake Ranch, we got it."

Amanda sat next to David. "So, what is going on?"

Stu was ready to answer. "Well, a couple of things, but why don't you tell us again why you called?"

Amanda explained how she received the box of Snowflake Ranch bath products and accessories at her office in Brookview. She showed them her phone that displayed the packing slip and the snowflake logo. She told them she recognized the logo several weeks later. She explained her childhood trauma affects her memory, but by the look on their faces, they already knew.

"Norah, Nathan, and I had agreed to go to the Dallas Market Center today, but when I landed here in Dallas, I remembered that I drew that logo as a child with Stacy Snowden. She was my best friend at an orphanage we were in." She showed them the Polaroid picture.

Everyone at the table recognized the picture.

"Then, when I saw a woman at the hotel using my dead friend's name with a snowflake painted on her pinky, I asked Derrick, the bellman, to tell me what was going on. He said the rooftop bar has turned into a place for sex and drugs?”

Stu and Jake both looked at each other and realized Amanda knew more than they thought.

“Mrs. Lloyd, we are incredibly grateful your husband is here with you, and you are safe.”

David and Amanda were waiting for Stu to say more.

“There is a drug lord, Ryan Barnes, who hijacked a business called Snowflake Ranch to camouflage his sex trafficking and drug business. The original owner of this business was manipulated and bullied into giving it to him. But what he didn’t know is that this owner built her business on a legacy that involves you, Mrs. Lloyd, and Stacy Snowden.”

Jake tried to professionally present the story without too much sentiment.

David touched Amanda’s hand to reassure her.

Stu cleared his throat. “Let me start with 12 years ago. It’s funny how criminals think they can get away with a crime, and then something so simple happens, and it becomes their Achilles heel.”

“Stacy Snowden was a cold case in Chicago. As you know, she was labeled a Jane Doe at first. Who cares about a 26-year-old woman found dead in a crack house on the south side of Chicago? But you cared, didn’t you?” Stu looked at Amanda fondly.

“Yes,” David remembered. “We wanted Stacy to come to our wedding. We asked our friend, Martin Walker, from the foster care unit in Illinois, to find her. It was then we found out she died two years prior.”

“Correct,” Stu said. “But no one would have known Jane Doe was really Stacy Snowden if you and Mrs. Lloyd hadn’t asked Mr. Walker about her.” Stu took a sip of his coffee.

“Because Stacy was in the system as a foster youth, the state of Illinois had her records, and now someone cared. Police began to investigate this

Jane Doe, now Stacy Snowden. What they found was a missing person's report."

"Stacy was a receptionist at a car dealership, nowhere near the south side of Chicago. She worked in a small town named Oakley near Springfield. She wasn't a drug addict either. Her job filed a missing person's report because she didn't come into work for several days. They tried calling her on her cell phone, but there was no answer."

"Her roommate, a 30-year-old woman with her 10-year-old daughter, said they hadn't seen her. There was nothing out of the ordinary when they visited the apartment complex, but the police noted that the roommate's daughter was upset beyond normal."

"Then we found out that the dealership got a phone call three weeks later, after the missing person report was filed. The new receptionist says the woman on the phone said she was Stacy. She apologized for the scare but stated she was fine. She claimed that she moved to be with her boyfriend."

"For small-town America, believable. The missing person report was dropped. But after further investigation from the Feds, years later mind you, that phone call was made after the police had already found Stacey's body and tagged it a Jane Doe. Something was wrong there."

Amanda was trying to follow the story. "So then what happened?"

"It's complicated, Mrs. Lloyd." Stu continued. "Now we know Jane Doe is Stacy, who was not a drug addict but found in a crack house, miles from her home. It was a body dump for sure. But we also know that someone pretended to be her, so the missing person's report gets dropped. With this paper trail, we can open the case and rule it a homicide."

"Why didn't anyone tell us?" Amanda was immediately sad. She remembered desperately wanting to know what happened to Stacy.

"Mrs. Lloyd, when it comes to these human-trafficking cases, drugs, and gangs, I'm sure the police at the time felt all you needed to know was that your friend was gone. They freed you to grieve and go on with your life."

"They didn't want you involved for your safety," Jake added.

Amanda understood and let Stu continue.

"So, we watch this roommate with the 10-year-old daughter, who is now older. That's all we really had. For what that roommate said she did for a living, she and her daughter had brand new cars and nice wardrobes. Suspicious people visiting their apartment duplex, like organized crime drug dealers. We couldn't do anything but watch because we are investigating a murder."

"We saw no drug dealings; we just saw known drug dealers supporting our suspect. When this 10-year-old girl turned 18, we noticed her college tuition was paid for in full every year. Now we can see it's her drug lord father who is doing that, Ryan Barnes."

Jake spoke. "We start thinking this roommate had a more meaningful relationship with Mr. Barnes. Turns out not. The huge discovery was that this young girl is Stacy's daughter. We found the marriage certificate from a courthouse in Tennessee. Ryan married Stacy as soon as she turned 18 and had the baby two years prior."

Silent tears begin to fall from Amanda's eyes.

Stu could see Amanda piecing the story in her head and goes on. "Stacy's daughter creates this sweet business to honor her mom and her mom's best friend. After a year of success, her father, the drug lord, takes it over to hide his sex trafficking and drug business because we, the police, were getting close to figuring out his operation, thanks to Nathan."

"But it's awfully hard to catch the drug lord at the top, so we began to think what else can we charge this guy with," Jake said.

"Murder," David said.

"Correct. We believe Ryan killed Stacy, and he dumped her body," Stu said.

Amanda tried to keep her composure.

"We got a little help." Nathan shares. "Amanda, Stacy's daughter is smart. She told her father that he would need to change the name of the business. He agreed to the initials for Snowflake Ranch, SFR. She did the paperwork through the Secretary of State, and I found it. Ryan Barnes, no longer going by that name, but Ryan Snowden."

"The fact he comes out of *hiding* using his dead wife's maiden name leads us to believe Ryan has no idea what has happened in this case after the missing person report was dropped or that we are still trying to solve what happened to Stacy." Jake raised an eyebrow. "So we just watch him."

"Ryan is a monster. He made his daughter a prostitute and 13 other women, using a Dallas hotel," Stu said in disgust.

David closed his eyes in unbelief and then opened them. "How is this man getting away with this?"

Jake explained that Ryan uses a popular cash app on smartphones for people to use. It looks like they are purchasing lingerie, bath products, and accessories, but they are buying drugs and having a good time, right in local hotels. No money exchanges hands; it is all in regular accounts and small bills, consistently.

"Mrs. Lloyd," Stu says softly. "Nicci Snowden is Stacy's daughter. She's 22 years old, and she sent you the box."

Amanda's tears were now flowing faster.

"She took a chance and sent you the box with an invitation to the Dallas Market Center. It was her hope to meet you there and tell you who she was. She has been leaving us clues regarding her father's business, but he found out Nicci sent the box to you. This is now dangerous," Stu said.

"Ryan has now connected some dots. He now sees his daughter's business meant something far greater than he thought. He has seen this picture and the logo." Jake placed an identical picture of Amanda and Stacy next to Amanda's picture that was already on the table.

There was quiet. David knew this was now serious.

"Ryan knows you are the other girl in the picture with the snowflake logo. He is thinking you got this box, wondering who this company is, and you have a Polaroid, just like he does. He made Nicci take down the website, destroy catalogs to buy him time, but he can't destroy a picture you've had your whole life. He now wants to talk to you."

"A murderer wants to talk to my wife." David got up from the table. "This is insane."

"Mr. Lloyd, this is a lot," Stu said, standing up.

"If you only knew what my wife and I are going through here," David said to Stu directly. Amanda got up and faced her husband, looking into his eyes. David saw it in her face; she was ready to do whatever the officers wanted her to do.

"Amanda...," David said.

"David, I'm not afraid anymore. I am certain." Amanda's eyes locked with his. "I want Nicci out of this mess."

David's eyes softened toward his wife. Amanda turned towards Stu.

"Sergeant Rollins, what aren't you telling us?"

The three men looked at her and knew they could say it out loud.

"Ever since Ryan took over Snowflake Ranch, he has been watching you and your family," Nathan said. "When I got back from my trip from Dallas, I met with the FBI and found out you, the woman Augusta Retail just promoted to work alongside me, was connected to this investigation."

"It didn't take long for me to realize you had no idea about this operation or Snowflake Ranch. It was clear, Amanda; you have moved on from your childhood, and I'm sorry it has come up in this way."

Jake interjected quickly. "Please know, Nathan and I made sure your family was protected. Ryan pretty much knew what we found out; you are a regular working mom trying to take care of your family."

Amanda felt peace and put one arm around David's waist, facing the other men. "Now what? The way I see it, if Ryan wants to talk to me, let's get it over with."

David knew Amanda was going to be direct. It was what he loved about his wife. She could be soft one minute and then, in another minute, focused and determined.

He understood that she didn't want to always be looking over her shoulder for the rest of her life, but he also knew she cared deeply for Nicci Snowden because of Stacy.

"Mrs. Lloyd, are you sure?" Stu said.

"Well, please call me Amanda." She went to the kitchen. "More coffee? What's the plan here?"

David sighed, confirming he agreed with his wife's decision.

"Let's figure this out. Know this: I'm here to protect my wife. If you think I'm just going to sit here in this house alone waiting for this to be over, you're wrong," David declared.

CHAPTER 28

David and Amanda went back to the hotel to Amanda's room on the sixth floor. One by one, Stu, Jake, and Jenna Watkins came into the room.

Stu was the only one in his same clothes. Jake dressed in a hotel uniform. Jenna was the receptionist at the front desk, and like Derrick, the bellman said she had been undercover for months.

David held Amanda as they stood in the hotel room with Stu on his phone. Jake was at the desk with his laptop open, with Jenna over his shoulder.

"I love you." David gazed into her eyes. "You look beautiful. I can't believe we are doing this."

Amanda wore a black high-collar, but sleeveless, chiffon dress hemmed at her knees. She was in full makeup with her hair pinned up in the back with a twist design.

"You look handsome." She smiled and then laughed.

"Amanda, I'm glad you are joking." David shook his head. He looked at himself in black pants and a white button-down dress shirt. "The only thing different from my regular work attire is these cufflinks."

"I love my grocery man." Amanda encouraged him, continued to laugh, and gave him a kiss.

"You guys look great." Jenna Watkins smiled. "I'm crushing on you both. The moment I saw your reunion in the hotel lobby, I loved you both." She stared at them like a child begging for candy.

"Jenna, it's hard to believe you carry a weapon," Jake snapped back at her teasing. "Officer Watkins is a hopeless romantic."

"And Officer Harmon is a heartless nerd," Jenna snapped back.

David and Amanda recognized the banter, noticing that neither Jake nor Jenna was married, and wondered if their relationship was strictly professional.

"Amanda, Jenna needs to set up your two-way listening device." Jake handed Amanda a small device that looked like a hearing aid. "I will be in your ear, listening and helping."

"We need to go to the bathroom and put this small black box somewhere in this dress," Jenna said.

Amanda understood and disappeared with Jenna into the hotel bathroom. When Jenna closed the door, she started. "Oh, please tell me how you met that handsome man who clearly loves you."

Amanda laughed and turned her back to Jenna so she could unzip the dress. "Only if you tell me why you and Officer Harmon aren't together."

Jenna sighed. "You don't miss a beat, do you?"

"I'm a wife and a mom; it comes along with the job. Oh, my insides are going crazy right now. I'm so nervous," Amanda said.

"Don't be. You go to the rooftop and do your parade: make your selection, table 21 is Erika's table. She's a federal agent, a beautiful black woman posing as a prostitute. Choose her as I showed you. Dance with your cutie pie husband, escort him to meet Erika, then you both leave," Jenna said.

"Ryan watches all of this?" Amanda questioned.

"Yes, he watches the rooftop bar from his suite. We need him to see you're not on our side, and you are new swingers. It is already believable. He saw you having dinner with Nathan, knows about David's affair with the blonde-haired lady; she's not as gorgeous as you, just saying."

Jenna placed the small black box in Amanda's bra with Velcro strips, stating they were new best friends as she touched one of Amanda's breasts. Both women started giggling.

She remembered Jenna's last comment and felt shame.

"I don't have feelings for Nathan like that. I feel stupid being the woman David cheated on, and all of you know." Amanda closed her eyes.

"Don't worry," Jenna stated. "We have seen it all. You are not stupid, and we don't know everything. Don't think we bugged your house or had 24-hour surveillance on you. We know your comings and goings and what's in your bank account."

"Well, we are clearly not laundering money."

"Exactly." Jenna zipped Amanda back up in her dress. "When you gave that keycard to me with the envelope, I admired you."

"Thank you."

"You know, your husband saw the whole thing happen," Jenna told her.

"What?" Amanda was surprised David didn't say anything.

"Yep," Jenna said, fixing the dress and examining if she could see the box. "Grocery man, admiring his wife's integrity."

"Jenna, the moment his brown eyes met mine, there was an instant connection." Amanda smiled, remembering.

Jenna smiled back. "Good. Well, you guys look very much in love."

"What about you? Jake?" Amanda raised an eyebrow.

"Oh, Jake is my partner. We've been through hell and back, but we don't go there, do we, Jake?" Jenna was aware Jake could be listening.

Now, as a voice in Amanda's ear, Jake said, *I remember the hell. I think we are still there.*

Amanda's eyes widened. She repeated what he said and snickered.

"No privacy," Amanda said.

"None," Jenna said. "Don't worry, nobody else can hear what you said. Jake is on a cell phone. Unless, of course, the cell phone is on speaker."

"No," Amanda repeated. "Jake says no one else can hear."

Jenna and Amanda finally opened the bathroom door.

Jenna announced. "The princess is ready."

Jake checked Amanda's device for volume and looked at David. "Grocery man, you good?"

David laughed. "Yeah, I'm good. Honey, this is just like home. You get to be the princess. I'm just the grocery man."

Amanda laughed as she headed to the hotel room door. "I'll see you soon."

David saw the door close behind his wife, and he prayed to himself for her bravery. He heard Jenna on her cell phone, "The princess is on her way to the elevator."

Amanda walked out into the hotel hallway to the elevator and heard Jake in her ear asking if Derrick, the bellman, was in the elevator and if anything was out of the ordinary. Amanda confirmed everything was as it should be.

～

The elevator opened to a hallway. To the left were glass double doors leading to a restaurant with a large patio open to the outside. When

Amanda walked into the restaurant, she felt the mix of air conditioning and hot air as the patio doors opened, as hotel guests went in and out. The bar was long and wide against the left back wall, with three staff members making drinks. There were high-top tables on the perimeter of the restaurant with a few square tables hugging the spacious dance floor. It was busy but not overly crowded. Jake told Amanda he could see her, and she needed to go to the bar and order a drink.

"Jake, I'm a wine drinker."

"Tonight, you're not. Wine is the wrong image. Ask Ricky, blonde hair, for a New York Sour. Trust me; it's got red wine and bourbon in it. You'll thank me later," Jake said in her ear. "Just sip."

Amanda obeyed. David was watching his wife on Jake's computer. She was confident as she ordered the drink and turned her back to the bar, scanning the room. She got her drink and sipped it.

"This is completely sinful," Amanda said. "This drink is incredibly smooth."

Jake laughed. Amanda noticed Erika in the corner of the room to her left, but went right first and carried a pleasant look on her face as she said hello to people as they passed by her. When she finally reached Erika, she whispered in her ear, "princess and grocery man," and gave her a kiss on the cheek.

Amanda placed her drink on the high-top table. Jenna told her the move was an indication she had chosen Erika for the night, and Ryan would be watching to see if Amanda knew how the game was played. Erika smiled at Amanda and encouraged her with a kiss back and a whisper back in her ear, "You are a natural. Smooth girlfriend. Now go mingle until the grocery man gets here."

Amanda didn't make it to the next table when Lucas McCormick stopped her. "Amanda Lloyd?"

Amanda closed her eyes for a moment. Lucas was standing in his well-fitted jeans with a charcoal gray button-down shirt. She responded.

"Lucas, what a surprise. How were the sessions today?"

Jake was in Amanda's ear. "Lucas…" Jake remembered the name from Nathan. "David is on his way up."

"The usual. I didn't see you today," Lucas answered.

"Well, I was checking out new products at the Dallas Market Center," she told Lucas.

"You look amazing." Lucas's blue eyes looked Amanda over suggestively.

"Thank you," Amanda blushed. "You are looking well."

"I have to say, I am quite surprised to see you up here. I mean, you know, as a Texas native, I know what happens up here."

"Yes," Amanda said. "David and I are trying something new."

"I get it," Lucas winked. "Way to keep the home fires burning."

"Amanda, honey, you promised me a dance." David came up behind her and planted a kiss on her cheek.

Jake whispered in her ear, "Thank God. But you all are actually making this story more believable."

"Lucas, it was good to see you," Amanda said graciously. She introduced David to Lucas. The men shook hands, and Amanda gave Lucas a hug to say goodbye. Lucas rubbed her back and took full advantage of the opportunity; he lowered his hand and passed her back to stroke her butt. David took Amanda's hand as the embrace ended. Lucas went on in the opposite direction.

"Amanda," David kept his face composed. Amanda could tell by his tone that he was less than pleased with Lucas McCormick and his inappropriate touch.

He led her out onto the dance floor, then drew her into him with one hand around her waist and his other hand in hers. "I'm a very jealous man."

Amanda stared back at him. "I'm a very jealous woman," she said, thinking of Samantha.

"We couldn't have this lifestyle for real. I'm already pissed off," David said.

"See? When it happens to you, it's not so fun, is it?" Amanda was sharp with her words. As soon as she said it, she regretted it.

"I deserved that."

Amanda saw the guilt and shame in his eyes. They both were thinking of the affair. Jake was too and had compassion for his new friends.

She whispered in his ear, "David, it's forgiven. I'm sorry. I'm trying to leave it at the foot of the cross."

He kissed her. She kissed him back. They smiled at each other. There was silence among them as they enjoyed the dance. Jake was silent in her ear until the dance was over. "Whenever you're ready, introduce David to Erika and come back down."

Amanda and David did exactly what Jake ordered them to do, and it was just the two of them in the elevator holding hands as they reentered Amanda's room on the sixth floor. Jake was standing in the room between the queen beds.

"Nice job," he smiled. "I believe Ryan is completely convinced, especially how you sent SFR money through your cell phone like the rest of the customers. Nicci says he wants to meet you at the rooftop restaurant at 8:00 pm. He believes you and David have an *open* marriage."

David sighed, "Great."

There was a knock on the door, and Amanda opened it. It was Erika. She smiles at Amanda, then David, took off her shoes and sat in the desk chair. "I hate high heels." David and Amanda sat together on one of the queen beds.

"I'm leaving to make a few rounds," Jake said, straightening his gold-plated name tag. "Jenna's at the front desk, but watching Ryan on surveillance cameras. Stu is preparing SWAT for tomorrow. Erika, there is a maid in the bathroom; introduce her to the Lloyds," Jake said as he closed the door.

Suddenly, the bathroom door opened, and out came a woman with short blonde hair. One side was noticeably short; the other side had long bangs that almost covered one eye. She wore heavy makeup and false eyelashes, but was dressed as a maid. She quietly came up to sit across from David and Amanda on the other queen bed with her head down.

"Amanda, David, this is Nicci Snowden," Erika stated and kept silent.

Amanda saw Nicci's hand and noticed her manicure. On her pinky were the snowflake and the rhinestone. Amanda got up and moved to share the bed with Nicci. Immediately, Amanda opened her arms, and Nicci enfolded her. "I've been waiting so long to meet you, I don't know what to say now that you are in front of me," Nicci said as she held on to Amanda.

Amanda released her to look her in the face. She lifted her chin and then moved her long blonde bangs behind her ear. She stared into her blue eyes, and that is when Amanda's tears flowed. She noticed Nicci had Stacy's eyes.

"Look at you!" Amanda smiled through her tears. "If only I had known of you, I would have come for you, looked for you."

Nicci sighed with gratitude. "This man, your husband?" She looked at David and tried to smile.

"Yes," David answered, handing both women tissues from the box on the nightstand between the beds.

"My mom would be so happy that you're married. He is good to you, obviously, for him to be here and help."

"Yes, he is," Amanda said. "We have two boys, Matthew and Mason, nine and seven years old."

Nicci smiled. "Wonderful."

"I'll show you pictures when all of this is over." Amanda held her hand.

"Please tell me, why has your father been watching me, and why does he want to talk to me?"

Nicci felt her heart racing as Erika handed her a bottle of water from the mini refrigerator. "Father thinks you could cause trouble for him and his business. By sending you the Snowflake Ranch box, I woke up a sleeping giant—you."

"I didn't know. I wanted to share with you what I created. He took the catalog out of the box, then told me my business was now his. I shipped the box anyway. When he found out about it, he...hurt me." Nicci couldn't look at Amanda anymore.

"I changed the name of the business in the hopes someone would notice that and his name changed. Father asked me about the picture in the catalog. I told him where I got it: Mom's foster care file. After some calls, he found out you had the same picture in your file. He sent *someone* to watch you for a week. Father quickly realized you were *clean*, and he could wait for you to get here to Dallas."

Amanda encouraged her to take a breath and drink some water. Nicci opened the water, drank half the bottle, and took a deep breath.

"I'm not understanding. You sent Amanda the box. Why did your dad think that was a problem?" David asked.

"Father... Father never told me that you..." Nicci looked at Amanda and began crying. "... that you made the police look for my mom. Yeah, it was too late, but I now know what happened to her."

"I know Father did it. I can't prove it, but he killed her. So, when I sent the box to you, he knew you were the one who made the police look for Mom; she was no longer a Jane Doe thanks to you. But Father was angry that I brought you back into his life because, after all, he has gotten away with murder."

Amanda and David now understood. Ryan was paranoid; the FBI was right. Ryan couldn't get rid of the picture Amanda had of herself and Stacy. He couldn't erase the use of the snowflake logo that was in the picture and was being used on all the products he was supposedly selling to cover up what he was really selling: young women and drugs. Amanda was connected to Stacy, Snowflake Ranch, and Augusta Retail.

Amanda took one of Nicci's hands; it was cool and pale compared to her own. She couldn't help but think of her childhood friend. They sat in silence for a minute. Amanda admired the snowflake painted on her pinky and the rhinestone.

Nicci told Amanda that Stacy ran away from her foster home because she was pregnant with her. Stacy's boyfriend at the time was 20-year-old Ryan Barnes. He bought an apartment, gave her all she needed and wanted. Ryan cared for Stacy during the pregnancy and beyond. Nicci said Stacy felt it was a dream come true. They were in love and got married as soon as they could.

Stacy didn't know Ryan was a drug dealer; he never bought that life around her. But Nicci told Amanda and David that when she left the house for kindergarten, things changed.

"Only two young girls would live with us at a time. I didn't know it then, but he manipulated my mom into helping him with his sex trafficking business. He told her that he had taken care of her all this time, and she owed him; married or not, she had to start contributing."

Amanda continued to hold Nicci's hand as she continued to share about her life with her parents. Stacy gave Ryan whatever he wanted of her mentally, emotionally, and sexually. She protected Nicci from seeing the men come and go, as the *meetings* would happen during the day, while Nicci was at school. But Nicci saw the cash, and Stacy managed it all, while Ryan still dealt with the drugs outside the home. Stacy was very smart and kept a secret account for herself.

"She wasn't greedy; Father couldn't even tell," Nicci said. "On an ordinary day, my mom and I went to the grocery store and didn't return home with the groceries. My mom threw her cell phone in the garbage at the grocery store. We went to a motel on the outskirts of town long enough for Mom to change her appearance, and a man came to give us a new car."

"Did he find you?" Amanda asked quietly.

Nicci said Stacy only went three hours away from home. Amanda's heart hurt. The conversation they had earlier with the police and Nathan confirmed through Nicci; all this time, she and Stacy lived in the same state, but they were living two separate lives. Nicci said Stacy really loved Ryan and didn't really see him for the dangerous man he was.

"She worked at the car dealership in Oakley. We never drew attention to ourselves, but Father found the secret account years later. He knew he couldn't come at mom threatening her or acting violently, so he came soft, apologetic and said, 'Let's talk'."

"She went with him on a *date*, and she never came back. When the police came to the door asking questions, I knew."

Amanda hugged Nicci and apologized for all her hurt and pain. "But you asked about her," Nicci smiled. "Though gone, they found her because of you."

Nicci continued her story. "When the police left that day, when they looked around the apartment, they didn't know what I knew. They didn't see the foster care file or Father's bookkeeping notebook. Neither saved her life, but they saved mine. I kept those things secret for years, waiting for the opportunity to use them."

"Nicci, thank you for your bravery." Erika had been listening and took the opportunity to add her gratitude. "By your coming to the authorities and bringing us that notebook and the files, we have months of your father's dealings and understand his money laundering pattern."

Looking at Erika, David asked, "What is next for Nicci? After this, what does she do?"

"She gets complete witness immunity," Erika stated. "Nicci can start over."

"Nicci, you can do whatever you want. Amanda and I can help you do whatever it is you want to do, okay?" David moved and sat next to Amanda. He held his wife's hand.

Nicci made eye contact with Amanda, then David. "I want my name back. I was named after you, Amanda, and my mom." Nicci explained her name was Nicole Marie—Amanda's and Stacy's middle names combined.

Amanda kissed her cheek. "Easy enough, Nicole."

"Listen, sweet girl, you have to go," David told her. "You have *rooms* to clean. Amanda, Erika and I...well, our good time is about over," he rolled his eyes.

Erika looked at her watch. "Yes, we need to get ready for the next move."

"I love you," Amanda said, hugging Nicci. Nicci let go abruptly.

"But you don't know me, and what Father has done to me; what I've done."

"I'm sorry, Nicci. I'd give anything to remove all the awful that has happened to you," Amanda cried. "But I don't care where you have been nor what you have done," Amanda told her. "You are my niece now, and I love you."

Nicci hugged Amanda again for a quick moment and went back into the bathroom, put on her black wig, grabbed the towels, and left the room.

Amanda fell on the bed, turned on her side, and sobbed. David took off Amanda's slingback high heels, kicked off his shoes, and snuggled up behind Amanda and held her.

Erika witnessed David's love for Amanda. He was still in his crisp white shirt, his arms around the bare shoulders of his wife. She was still in her black cocktail dress, looking like an adult but curled up like a child.

Amanda knew Ryan had assaulted and prostituted his own daughter; she felt it. She saw it in Nicci's eyes. It grieved her. If she allowed it, it was going to make her sick.

David was in her ear. He was holding her, comforting her, and reassuring her. He spoke no words, just began to hum. Amanda wasn't listening, but she began to hear David humming *You Are My Sunshine*. It was the song she heard when she opened her childhood jewelry box.

For years, her childhood jewelry box managed to travel with her to each foster home she went to, until it was accidentally thrown away. Whenever Amanda felt sad or troubled, she would hum the tune, and it calmed her. Now, David would hum it to her for a moment and hold her. The room was still, even though Erika and now Jake were present. Amanda stopped crying, and David was gentle but firm.

"Amanda, honey, I need you to open your eyes." David wanted Amanda to be present. He understood the longer Amanda closed her eyes, the more she could evoke past trauma. Amanda knew it to be true, and she opened her eyes and listened to David.

He kissed her on the cheek. "Honey, I love you. Please don't worry; God has you in His care. I know this is a lot to take in. I'm so sorry; I haven't made this any easier, but if you've changed your mind and you don't want to meet with Ryan, it's okay. I'll take care of it."

Amanda put David's hand inside hers and brought their hands together to her chest. She could smell him, and it reminded her of the devotion she had for her husband. Her wedding day flashed before her—David waiting for her as she walked down the aisle. The certainty on his face that day made her feel secure in this moment.

"No," Amanda cleared her throat. "My heart aches for Nicole. I just wanted to release that right now."

"Yeah," David felt that within her. "Honey, I also know that triggered a lot of past hurts for you."

"Yeah," Amanda repeated the rhythm of his voice. "But I'm better now. I have a thousand amazing memories with you that seem to erase some of those." She brought their hands together to her lips.

After that comment, Erika found a tear on her face and quickly wiped it away. She was skeptical of interracial relationships, but she found her mind changing and believing love doesn't care about race.

David loved her comment too. "Ahh, honey, I am yours."

She turned around, faced him, and gave him a soft kiss.

"Ready?" He wiped her tears from her cheeks and smiled.

CHAPTER 29

After a shower, Amanda went back up to the rooftop bar in her skinny jeans, wedged heels, and black scooped neck blouse. Her hair was wet, in tight curls, and her makeup was soft. Ryan saw her sitting at one of the high-top tables in the corner with her drink. As he approached her, he immediately had to say what he was thinking, "You are beautiful, Mrs. Lloyd."

Ryan was in a black button-down shirt with two buttons undone, barely showing his white undershirt. The shirt was tucked into his crisp, pressed tan dress pants with a black skinny leather belt matching his black leather laced shoes. He looked relaxed, yet prominent; his white pearl cufflinks obviously communicated that money was not an issue. His pale skin had warm tones, and he had a full head of blonde hair that stood up. Amanda had to admit he was model-like, and his smile complimented his looks.

"Mr. Barnes, you're easy on the eyes."

Jake was still in Amanda's ear. *"Take it slow."*

"I see you are straight and to the point," Ryan said, hearing his last name and not Snowden.

"I am," Amanda said. "You know who I am, and I know who you are. Let's not tease one another."

A bartender came over right away, and Ryan refused the gin and tonic. "This is your first time in Dallas, at the rooftop. Are you enjoying yourself? Did you and David had a good time tonight?" He asked, raising an eyebrow. "I notice everything."

"I see," Amanda acted surprised. "We are still having a good time..." Amanda found herself blushing, and Ryan noticed.

"Aren't you the cutie?" Ryan was genuine. "I can see why David keeps you on a leash. I get it, he doesn't mind sharing, but he's the only man in the room."

"Absolutely. My husband is a jealous man," Amanda replied, and took the toothpick of blackberries from her drink and suggestively took one and put it in her mouth. Ryan intently watched her.

Ryan shook his head, completely taken by Amanda's sex appeal. "You are amazing. Beautiful, cute, and sexy. Do you wanna move to Texas?"

"I most certainly do not," Amanda said frankly. "You called this meeting. I met Nicci in the elevator. She called me; we talked. She told me you wanted to meet me. I'm here."

"Right." Ryan got distracted by Amanda. He needed to focus.

Jake in Amanda's ear, *"You are doing great."*

Ryan looked around and reached for Amanda's hand. "Let's go."

Amanda got off the barstool and took his hand. He was gentle in his leaning into her ear. "I'm not asking, so think carefully about your response. Let's go up to my suite."

Amanda immediately got nervous. Ryan didn't see the listening device as his mouth moved away from her ear and looked at her face for a response.

Jake quickly responded in her ear, *"Amanda, this is completely up to you. We have your back either way."*

"Okay," Amanda replied. She acted shy. "I will need to call my husband when we get there. When I change locations, I must call him."

Jake heard Amanda and snapped his fingers at Erika, who got on the hotel phone to Jenna at the front desk. Erika let her know Amanda was going up to the suite. David saw Jake make two swift clicks on his laptop, and the screen immediately had six squares, all different angles of what David assumed was Ryan's suite.

Jake continued to talk to Amanda through his cell phone, *"Okay, you are one brave princess. Right before you enter the suite, you must tap your ear device twice; that will turn off the device. Ryan's suite is bugged. If you keep this device on, the interference will give you away. We can see you and hear you, but I cannot help you. Once you get into the bathroom of the suite, you can turn it back on, and we can talk."*

"Fair enough," Ryan said, looking at their hands together. "We can relax, and you can tell me about your quiet little life in small-town America, right?"

"Mr. Barnes," Amanda said, looking over at him sheepishly. "I know you know all about me."

He kissed her hand he was holding. "True."

They walked out of the rooftop bar with Ryan leading Amanda out the door and into the hotel hallway. Amanda hadn't noticed it, but there was another elevator, but this one when it opened required a keycard. As they got on the elevator, Ryan put his card in and pressed 20. He softly brushed Amanda's right cheek and insisted she call him Ryan.

David stared at the laptop screen as Amanda and Ryan got off the elevator. He put his head down briefly and prayed. He and Amanda were not prepared for this moment. As if he knew this moment was even going to be a thing. He said to himself, *How'd we get here?* He blamed himself, asked God to intervene, and to give Amanda courage.

Just like she was told, Amanda tapped her ear twice without Ryan noticing, and when he opened the door, three men in suits stood up. All of them were middle-aged, well built, attractive, and relaxed when they saw Ryan with Amanda. They sat back down one by one as Ryan introduced them by their nicknames. "This is Dirt, Shade, and Puck. My guys keep me informed."

Amanda nodded at them as they sat on the caramel-colored tweed couch and sofa in a spacious living room area, on their phones, watching sports highlights on the flat screen television. The suite was modern and large. Black and white photos of farmland, cattle, and ranchers laced the room.

Amanda noticed the desk in the corner with two monitors. The desk chair was empty. The kitchen was clean but abandoned.

Ryan led her up three steps, and when he opened the solid white double doors, there was the master bedroom. Right away, there was a well-made king-size bed with a thick, smooth gray duvet cover and several pillows in a variety of textures and sizes displayed in a pattern. Two dark wood nightstands complemented each side of the bed with light sconces on the wall above them. The charcoal gray and black curtains hid the ceiling-to-floor glass windows. Amanda noticed the stocked bar in the corner.

Ryan sat on one of the matching chocolate-brown velvet sofas in the sitting area in front of the bed. Amanda sat across from him on the other side of the rectangular glass coffee table between them. She tilted her head and looked at Ryan, then opened her clutch purse to retrieve her cell phone. Ryan leaned back, opened his arms, and rested them on the back of the sofa. He watched Amanda. Amanda saw scrutiny and desire in his hazel eyes. She pushed the button on her phone, then returned to staring at Ryan.

"Hey, babe." Amanda was soft.

David, with the phone up to his ear, Jake and Erika listening but also watching on the laptop. "Honey, how are we doing?"

"I'm fine." Amanda let out a unique sigh. David knew it meant she was uneasy. "Listen, this meeting is gonna take a while."

Ryan winked at her. She smirked at him and slid off her shoes slowly, and put her feet on the shag rug that was underneath the coffee table.

"You okay? I promise to make it up to you," Amanda seductively pouted.

"Do you have a plan here?" David asked her. "I hate the way this man is looking at you. Stay focused."

"I will," Amanda said, being truthful. "Okay, yes. I love you too." Ryan saw her put her phone away.

Amanda grabbed her purse and stood up. "How about room service? Fruit, chocolate? May I go to the restroom and freshen up a little?"

His eyes examined her silhouette as he stood. "Sure. The bathroom is there." He pointed to the door almost behind her and next to the bed. He walked closer to her, brushed her right cheek again, and then put his lips close to hers and said, "If you were my wife, I wouldn't be able to share. I'm sorry, he is either too generous or a fool. You'd be more than enough for me."

"Look at you with your soft brown skin, head full of curls, that innocent, sexy, but humble look you give." He kissed her lips. "I'd come home every night ready to satisfy you anyway I could. That Monday night bullshit wouldn't have existed."

Amanda didn't respond. His words landed deep within her. Ryan knew he had touched a tender part of her as one of her fingers touched his lips. She gently said, "I'll be back."

Amanda went into the bathroom, locked the door, and turned the faucet on. She sat on the floor in front of the cabinetry. David watched her disappear off the screen. Jake told him there were no cameras in the bathroom. After a few seconds, they heard her.

"Jake, I need some help."

David sighed in relief. The room felt his posture shift.

"Name it, princess." Jake was quiet in her ear. *"Dirt is an undercover cop. Say the word, and he will escort you out."*

David leaned into Jake's phone and spoke. "Amanda, honey. I'm sorry."

Amanda didn't want to cry now, but her emotions were everywhere. Ryan was smooth. She could see how Stacy fell for his charm, care, and concern. How did a drug dealer, a pimp, a murderer know what she felt her husband didn't appreciate?

"Amanda, Ryan is right. Samantha and Monday nights with her were bullshit. I was a fool. This is not our life; I am yours and you are mine." David didn't care who heard. Jake looked at David to continue.

"The enemy does tell the truth. Honey, Ryan spoke the truth, but he knows nothing about righteousness. He told you the truth for his own benefit; he doesn't care about you or us. Ask him about Stacy and get out of there."

Amanda took in what her husband said. He was right. The fight going on was not between her and David or her and Ryan. It was spiritual. She washed her face and then asked Jake about the device. He told her how to remove it and to hide it in the bathroom trash can under the toilet paper.

Amanda felt the pull in her stomach; she could feel Ryan. "Angel shot," she said.

David's eyes widened. He remembered that was code for distress at a bar.

"Jake, Ryan has slipped something into my drink. I need Dirt to help me with room service."

Jake looked at Ryan in the room behind the bar. He admired Amanda for her sharpness. She was clear and swiftly discussed her plan.

Jake agreed. Amanda told David she loved him, and she disconnected the device and put it in the trash.

Amanda came out of the bathroom to find Ryan on his cell phone, giving orders. He was back on the sofa, and this time Amanda sat next to him. He put his free arm around her and smelled her hair.

"Listen, I need to go. You know what to do. Call me when it's done," Ryan said and ended the call. He told Amanda she was lovely and felt like he already knew her.

"My Stacy talked of you often and wanted to reach out to you, but when she saw you got adopted, she just didn't want this life for you."

Ryan started in. "I regret the day I invited this part of the business into our lives. I'm sad we lived in the same state and never connected."

Amanda was honest. "Nicci took my breath away. She looks so much like Stacy. She told me she had sent me the box. She wanted me to see her accomplishment."

"Yes. I told her not to send that damn box." Ryan showed a glimpse of his temper. "She did anyway, and now this is a mess."

"Well, I was minding my own business when this box of bath products and accessories showed up with a snowflake logo I drew as a little girl. I researched Snowflake Ranch; nothing but an invitation to Dallas. It's not completely unusual for Midwest companies to find and buy products from the Dallas Market Center, but come to find out, there are no bath products and accessories anymore, are there?"

Ryan adjusted his position and looked her in the eyes. "Amanda, Nicci shouldn't have sent you the box." Amanda felt he wanted to end the conversation.

"You and your husband already have this open marriage; it can be arranged if you want a share of this business. Do you want compensation for the logo? There are bath products if you want them, and there is pleasure if you want that too." He kissed her softly.

Amanda lowered her head, looking embarrassed and shy.

Ryan handed Amanda a drink from the table. He grabbed his. Before Ryan could speak, a knock came to the door.

David finally took a breath. As he watched Amanda, he thought to himself, he couldn't do this every day. The watching of surveillance video, being undercover, and the danger. He was looking forward to home; spreadsheets, delayed shipments, hires and fires, and store closures didn't seem bad after all.

"Hey, room service," Dirt said as he opened the door. "I also need your signature, man. That shipment in Oklahoma is ahead of schedule."

Ryan put his drink down. "Let me take care of business. You eat, baby." He rose, and Amanda followed him to the door.

Dirt looked her in the eyes and saw she was fine. Amanda wheeled the room service cart in and shut the door. She acted fast and dumped both drinks in the bar sink and put the empty glasses underneath the room service cart.

Amanda made new gin and tonics and noticed the date drug was exactly where Jake told her. By the time Ryan made it back, Amanda was on the sofa eating grapes with her scooped blouse now off her shoulder.

"Okay, baby, where were we?" He sat next to her. She fed him a grape, and he sucked her finger.

David rolled his eyes. *"I'm ready for this guy to drink this drink and go to bed."*

Jake nodded. *"I owe you both. Praying Ryan gets comfortable and says something."*

"A toast," Amanda said. She gave him his drink, and she took hers.

"To Stacy," Ryan said, and he took a healthy sip. Amanda imitated him and frowned.

"Yes," she shook her head. "You make a stiff drink." He put the drink on the table, leaned in, and kissed her neck. Amanda tried to concentrate.

"Now, I asked you a question. You want into this business, money for this logo? What can I do for you?" Ryan began to kiss her bare shoulder.

"Ahh, you are making it hard to stay focused here. I get it. Bath products and accessories have a nice front. I'm not interested. I'm not here to rat out my best friend's husband," Amanda lied.

"I want to know what happened to Stacy?"

Ryan looked at Amanda. This time, she kissed him and searched his eyes. That's when she noticed it.

"Stacy was like you. Beautiful and smart." Ryan broke eye contact. "She got too caught up in this business, the drugs, the sex...she knew too much about it, and she abused it. They found her OD in a crack house in Chicago. Devastated all of us." Ryan told his story, clean, matter-of-fact, and abrupt.

"Thank you for inquiring the way you did. Stacy was brought home to us, no longer just missing. No longer a Jane Doe. It brought closure to Nicci."

Jake was excited. *"Yes. This man has no clue this case is open."*

"Sure," Amanda closed her eyes for a moment. "They just told me she was gone." She interlocked her hand with his and put it to her cheek.

There on the inside of his wrist, she saw the heart tattoo with *R&S* inside it. Now, Amanda knew she was going to have to start showing signs she was drugged, so she took a deep breath and began unbuttoning his shirt.

"Are you hot? I'm hot."

"Yes, you are." He kissed her on the lips, and he began taking off his cuff links to help her take off his shirt more easily.

Amanda helped him out of this button-down shirt, and he pulled the white t-shirt over his head. His bare chest was tight, firm, and smooth as she caressed it. She noticed he waxed. No hair, just muscle and soft skin. Amanda was aroused.

She stood up in front of him, holding one of his hands. "Do you think Stacy would be okay with us…"

Ryan stood up to face her and pulled her close to him. "She'd be glad we met." He stumbled a bit and laughed. He finished his drink. Amanda took another sip of hers. He led her to the bed. She forced him to sit down, opened his legs wide and got on her knees.

David's heart was racing as he watched. He was angry, remorseful, and wondered if she was pretending. He was nervous Ryan would turn violent.

Amanda was in control. She took off his shoes and socks, allowed him to fall back onto the bed, and removed his belt. She straddled him.

"Come here," he demanded. Amanda leaned into his face, and they kissed. Ryan's tongue in her mouth took her breath away. As she was dazed from the passion, he rose and took her blouse off. Her black lace bra was exposed. Ryan sighed at the beauty in front of him.

David was breathing hard, biting his lip, and covering his lips with his hand. He found it hard to sit still.

Jake said what was on his mind. *"I can't believe you stepped out on that. Princess is beautiful."*

"Yeah, and she's pissed about your affair." Erika watched Amanda take Ryan's hand and place it on her chest. *"She knows you're watching. Payback is a bitch, isn't it?"*

David didn't want to think Amanda would do that, but he couldn't say anything. He had no reply. He shouldn't have had the affair. Now, he was noticing Amanda was triggered by it all.

When Amanda saw the tattoo on wrist up close, she kissed it. Ryan looked at his tattoo and then at Amanda.

"I loved Stacy. I really did. If I hadn't done it, they would've killed all of us."

"I'll be damned." Jake was shocked. *"Did he just confess?"*

"That's it." Erika gave Jake a high five. *"It's enough for us to ask him later what he meant."*

Ryan stopped talking and closed his eyes. Amanda got off him and took the rest of his clothes off. Ryan was lethargic and got into the bed under the covers on his own. Amanda was in the bed too, still in her bra and jeans.

She began to twist and turn and mess up the sheets. She started moaning and breathing hard, saying Ryan's name and telling him how good he was. Ryan had a smile on his face until he truly passed out.

David closed his eyes as he heard his wife fake an orgasm. He was relieved; she sounded nothing like that earlier that morning. No doubt in his mind, Amanda was present in those hours, loving him, and he loving her. But he was saddened because he did recognize it. He could now compare.

On those days when she was so tired and yet wanted to please him, the rhythm of her voice was the same as when she was there with Ryan, and he wasn't even touching her. Her word choices, her facial expressions. David realized Amanda and he had so much more to discuss regarding their marriage.

Amanda went to the bathroom to retrieve the two-way listening device. She put it and her blouse back on. She looked at herself in the mirror and wasn't sure if she was proud of herself. Ryan was clueless about his daughter's betrayal. Amanda thought Nicci was the real hero.

What was really on her mind was her husband. How much of this would further hurt their marriage, and would they be able to go back to Brookview and live a normal life? She tapped her ear twice.

"Jake…" She was quiet.

"Oh princess!" Jake was happy, and Amanda could hear it. *"We owe you and David so much. Thank you."*

Amanda found a smile. "Yeah, I think you got some answers. Thank you. There's no telling what Ryan would've done to me if I had come to Dallas on my own."

Amanda left the bathroom and saw Ryan passed out in the bed. She put her wedge heels back on and grabbed her purse. As she opened the master bedroom door to leave, Dirt was right at the door.

"Where's Ryan?" Dirt asked for the other men in the room.

"He's sleeping. I gotta go. Tell him I had a good time," Amanda thought she was speaking softly.

"Yeah, we heard," Puck snickered.

"C'mon; I'll escort you out." Dirt took Amanda by the arm assertively.

As they got out in the hotel hallway and the elevator door opened, Dirt flashed her a smile. "You did us a favor."

"You saved my life." Amanda was sure of that. "Could you do one last thing for me?"

"I'll try." Dirt held the elevator open for her, and she stepped in.

"Let Ryan believe whatever he remembers about tonight. Tell him he accidentally drugged us both; I don't know. I just don't want this following me home. I have a job, kids to raise, and I hope I still have a husband."

Dirt nodded in agreement and approval. Amanda took the elevator ride to adjust her clothing better, and as she got off the elevator, she tapped her ear twice. "I'm on my way. I'm on the rooftop. Can you see me?"

Jake looked at his computer screen and told her yes. As she was in the hotel hallway waiting for the next elevator, Jake heard her say she was relieved.

Then, from behind, Amanda felt a grab at her waist. As she turned around to see who it was, he slapped her in the face.

"Lucas?!" she screamed.

"Princess, what the hell?" Jake said, as the scream in his ear made him jump. *"What is going on?"*

"Shut up!" Lucas told Amanda as he pulled her arm, opened the steel door, and pushed her into the stairwell. He pushed her against the wall, his body close to hers, and he covered her mouth with one of his hands. "I told you not another word. Shut up."

David's eyes widened, and he stood to his feet. "What just happened?"

"I don't know?" Jake said. "I can't see her…"

Jake said he saw a guy come up behind her and then nothing. "She said *Lucas*," Jake recalled.

"Lucas McCormick," David said. "Ugh."

Erika and Jake looked at each other quickly. Erika got on her phone and computer. The hotel room phone started ringing.

Jake ran to answer it, but still had his cell phone to his ear. *"Princess, if you are still listening, stay calm. We're coming."*

Jake answered the hotel room phone. "Jenna, what happened?"

He listened and then spoke. "Okay, this Lucas has her in the stairwell."

David didn't wait; he left the room and headed towards the stairwell.

"Damn it, grocery man," Jake said, holding two phones. "Jenna, get two men in the stairwell right now!" Jake gave the hotel phone to Erika.

"Does Lucas McCormick work for Augusta Retail in Michigan? He was caught with possession of narcotics a year ago," Erika stated, reading from the database displayed on her computer.

"Here we go. He is from Garland, Texas." Jenna told Erika and Jake what room Lucas was staying in and that he was a regular at the hotel.

"Now listen, I'm going to uncover your mouth. Do not scream, and I will not hurt you." Lucas stared at her.

Amanda calmed down and closed her eyes. Lucas slowly released his hand, and when he did, Amanda took his hand and bit it as hard as she could. She kneaded him in the groin and ran down the stairwell.

"Damn it, Amanda," Lucas said, doubled over in pain, running after her. Amanda came out of her shoes and continued to head down the stairwell until Lucas caught up with her by grabbing her hair. Amanda fell backwards and hit her head on a concrete step.

Lucas slapped her face again. Amanda was now on her back, Lucas over her with one hand on a stair and the other on the wall. He leaned in and whispered in her ear, "You're a fighter. I like that."

He put his lips on hers, and Amanda felt pain from the back of her head. She finally spoke, "Fifteen." She whispered, then said louder, "Lucas, what do you want?"

"Why is it you can be with Nathan, and you can be with Ryan, but you wanna fight me?" Lucas asked as he pulled Amanda to her feet and put her in one of corners of the stairwell landing, pinning both of her arms above her head with one hand. Amanda was a bit weaker and dazed.

"Lucas, you're high." Amanda was breathing hard and saw his eyes. "What did you take?"

Lucas lifted her blouse to feel her breast, and he felt the box of the two-way listening device.

"Shit, Amanda! Who in the hell are you working for?"

David came up the stairwell, and he saw Lucas had Amanda cornered. Immediately, David pulled the back of Lucas's collared shirt to get him to release Amanda. Amanda's arms quickly fell beside her, and her body slid down the concrete wall.

David recognized her frail state. He stood in front of her, and the two men began to push each other. David punched Lucas in the stomach and then across the face. He stumbled and backed into the opposite wall.

"Lucas," David declared, catching his breath. "Stop." He stood between them. Lucas looked up and charged at David. David punched him again.

This time, Lucas fell down a flight of stairs and didn't move. David turned to Amanda. She was in the corner of the stairwell's landing, half-conscious.

"Honey, are you okay?" David examined Amanda's face. "Can you hear me?"

"Yes," Amanda said with her eyes closed. "I can hear you."

"Grocery man!" Jake shouted in the stairwell. "You got eyes on the princess?"

"Yeah, Jake. I got eyes on the princess," David said, as he took his white shirt off and covered Amanda's shoulders.

Jake saw Lucas at the bottom of a flight of stairs, unconscious, and checked Lucas for a pulse. David now heard several footsteps coming from the stairs above and below.

Jake put his hand on David's shoulder. "You didn't kill him, thank God. Stu is gonna chew my ass if we don't get this cleaned up before tomorrow morning."

CHAPTER 30

avid, Jenna, and Jake sat in the hospital waiting for Amanda to return from her MRI.

"David…" Jake was ready to apologize, and David, with an ice pack on his knuckles, would not let him.

"Officer Harmon, don't go all soft on me now. Amanda wanted to help, I supported her, and here we are. Lucas was not a part of the plan." David looked at him. "You and Officer Watkins are good at what you do."

"Thank you," Jake said. "But you're crazy to leave the damn room without me. You had no weapon."

David didn't look at Jake. He just stared at his hands and the ice pack. He remembered God told him that no harm would come to Amanda. This looked like harm to him, but he knew God was a God of His word.

"God was with me. He's the greatest weapon there is."

"Ain't that the truth?" Stu stood before him.

David got up and shook Stu's hand with his uninjured hand.

"You love your wife. I'd go inside a volcano for mine." Stu patted him on the shoulder.

Jake and Jenna stood up out of respect for Stu as a sergeant.

"Oh for goodness's sake, as you were," Stu said.

Jake and Jenna relaxed but stood next to David.

"Make sure the princess is okay." Stu gave a pleasant look. "The plan is still a go. I got Officers Memphis and Jesse moving the Lloyds' things back to the house rental. They have completely checked out of the hotel. The front desk is to give no further information to anyone who asks."

"Thank you," David said.

"It is the least we can do," Jenna said, which was what the other officers were thinking.

"Where is Lucas McCormick now?" Stu asked Jake and Jenna.

"On the third floor here, sir," Jenna said. "Police are outside his door. He will be okay and in custody before the morning."

"Good." Stu liked things to be in order.

Jake shifted as he saw Dr. Jeffrey Goodwin heading in their direction. Dr. Goodwin was an average-height, black man in his fifties with a small afro.

"Officers, David." He nodded.

"Dr. Goodwin, please tell me my wife is okay." David wanted confirmation.

"Yes, she is fine." Dr. Goodwin smiled. "She got a nice goose egg on the back of her head. The MRI shows a mild concussion, but I expect a full recovery. Follow up with her doctor when she gets home."

As Dr. Goodwin led David to Amanda in the observation room, he told him that Amanda had experienced dizziness, nausea, and needed a light meal. He knocked on the door and opened it a little to hear Amanda give permission.

"You've got a visitor." Dr. Goodwin came in with David behind him.

When David saw Amanda lying on the hospital bed with an ice pack on her cheek, his heart fell. "Honey." He went to her and held her hand, then kissed it.

"I would smile, but it hurts." Amanda took the ice pack off her face. David saw the bruise on her left cheek.

David with tears in his eyes, said, "I wish I had gotten there sooner."

Amanda closed her eyes because the light was uncomfortable. She rubbed his hand. "You were on time."

Dr. Goodwin noticed Amanda's sensitivity to the light, and he turned the lights as dim as they would go. He tested her eyesight one more time, told her to rest, and to call him if her symptoms got worse. He left the room to give Amanda and David a moment. David found a chair, moved it next to the bed, and sat down.

"Babe, I love you," Amanda said, with her eyes closed and tears flowing. "I'm sorry; I took things with Nathan way too far. I did it again with Ryan. The truth is, I am secretly angry, wanting to hurt you, I guess. David, I'm hurting, I'm broken."

David sat quietly with the word *broken* in his mind. He heard her crying and held her hand. He loved Amanda. He loved how she didn't hide her emotions; they were always front and center. She was honest. If she lied, she said she did. If she took it, she said she did, and had a solution to give it back. Here she was, admitting the truth: she was hurt, angry, and broken by his betrayal.

He needed to be serious. He cleared his throat as tears were forming in his eyes.

"Amanda, I'm broken too. To know, hear, or see other men look at you, desire you...In one moment, I'm proud because you are mine. But to know and see they've touched you the way I'm supposed to, I'm enraged."

David clenched his other hand into a fist and felt tears fall past his face onto his neck.

"The truth is, I'm angry at myself. I'm not loving you enough. I was sad tonight more than anything, that all I did was watch. What a coward."

"What?" Amanda wasn't understanding. "You have always given me room to be independent while encouraging me. Did you not just punch a man in the face? Lucas was out of control. You came to Dallas to rescue me from my naivety, using your company's corporate jet, putting your promotion on hold, mind you."

"Let's not talk about you spitting in a man's face for me. David, you're not a coward," Amanda said. "You're my husband, if you still want to be."

David let go of her hand, wiped his tears with his sleeve, and joined their hands together again. "You're my wife, if you still want to be."

There were no words between them for a moment. David got up to assist Amanda to sit up. She realized quickly she was tired and in pain, but she wasn't dizzy anymore.

David stood in front of her. "I love you. I'm so proud of you. You were brave and showed courage tonight." He kissed her forehead.

"Thank you," Amanda said. "You're my hero. You've shown up for me from the day we first met to now. I love you."

Amanda got on her feet, requesting fresh air. She held onto David's arm as they left the room.

Dr. Goodwin greeted them in the hallway with pain medication. Amanda refused it, saying she could recover with over-the-counter pain relievers. Dr. Goodwin led the couple to the outdoor sitting area and said he would send the officers out to them.

Amanda instantly felt less nauseated when the night breeze hit her face. When Jake and Jenna saw her, they were relieved and thanked her for her courage. David sat next to Amanda on the outdoor patio couch, Jake and Jenna sitting in the chairs across from them.

"I'm fine," Amanda said. "I will be fine."

Amanda shared what happened between her and Lucas. David was happy and surprised that Amanda wasn't crying or showing signs of trauma. She was clear-headed and was proud that she fought back the way she did. Holding her hand, he felt honored to be her husband.

"Amanda, Lucas is going to be fine. He is a drug dealer with Snowflake Ranch and, unfortunately, a drug addict also," Jake told them.

"He and Ryan befriended each other in Dallas years ago. The main reason Augusta Retail is involved with this operation is that Lucas networked it all together and tried to get Nathan involved. Of course, Nathan, with his law enforcement background, notified us. Here we are."

"Tonight, Lucas saw you leave with Ryan from the rooftop. He had a few lines of coke, went back up to the rooftop, and had several drinks. He saw you and turned aggressive and violent." Jake wanted to make sure she knew the full story.

"I'm grateful to God; this could've ended a lot worse," Amanda had to admit. "Where is Lucas now?"

"Here," Jenna stated. "David's punches and a trip down a flight of concrete stairs led to him getting checked out."

All four of them were quiet for a moment. Dr. Goodwin's nurse came out to give Amanda an over-the-counter pain reliever, a bottle to take with her, and several ice packs for the freezer at their house. Amanda took the pills with the bottled water the nurse supplied. Amanda leaned against David's shoulder.

"Princess." Jake looked at Amanda now, like a sister. "You put yourself out there tonight. The video of you and Ryan is valuable; it tells us Ryan doesn't have a clue about Stacy's case or what Nicci has done against him. The glass you put under the room service cart did show that Ryan spiked your drink. Great forward-thinking on your part. You can go undercover for us anytime," Jake said.

"It was the Holy Spirit, and, no thank you." Amanda chuckled. "I'm looking forward to going home."

Jake saw her glance at David and asked, "Is there anything you want us to know? Anything you remember about your time with Ryan?"

Amanda enjoyed the outside breeze and took a moment to gather her thoughts. She began:

"Ryan didn't expect me. My temperament reminded him of his wife," Amanda said. "This is going to sound crazy, but I believe he loved her."

"Amanda, how do you love someone and then kill them?" Jake wanted to know.

Jenna pulled out her cell phone. "Can I record you?"

Amanda agreed and answered Jake. "I believe when Ryan met Stacy, they both could relate to each other. Every adult they knew was using them for money. Foster care people take you to get paid. For Stacy, probably a small percentage of foster parents wanted to deal with her trauma. Ryan was making someone a lot of money. By being a runner, if someone on the streets asks you to deliver a package for hundreds of dollars as a teenager, and you can get the things you need and want, why not? It is not a far reach for me to see them fall in love, especially if he got her pregnant at sixteen."

"That's statutory rape," Jake said.

"In some states. It's more of a reason for Stacy to leave the foster care home where they didn't care about her, and go with the boyfriend who had money and promised to take care of her and did it."

Amanda showed compassion. "Jake, I'm not saying it is right. Life is complicated."

"Nicci shared that Ryan never brought drugs to the place where she grew up. I believe Ryan was a good businessman, and the person he answered to was pleased with him, until they wanted more money out of him and wanted to get into prostitution. Having women on the street is too dangerous. Knowing his wife was from the foster care system, young girls age out of the system with no place to go—easy money."

"I'm sure Stacy didn't want to do it, but better than young girls being on the street or worse, dead. She takes them in, and for a while, I believe she felt she was doing something good."

Amanda then took a breath and took David's hand, interlocking it with hers.

"It becomes a routine. Take Nicci to school, come home, and the girls are having sex two times a day, a thousand dollars each. I'm guessing the business was good and the men weren't abusive. You tell yourself, *it's just two people having sex*, and they don't mind paying for it. But then, more darkness begets more darkness. I'm sure Ryan had sex with the girls in his house and had sex with his wife. Awful. And who is to say Stacy didn't do the same?"

David felt his stomach turn and stared at their hands together. Jake and Jenna knew Amanda and David were thinking about their infidelity. Jake felt sadness. Jenna saw the love between David and Amanda as they sat there together.

"I'm sure Stacy blamed herself, felt stupid, and couldn't stop what she helped start. So, she came up with a plan, created the secret account, and left." Amanda could relate to her deceased friend.

Jenna felt Amanda's account was completely believable, and she leaned into it and asked, "So, why not really leave? She moved three hours away, and the secret account was not closed, just buried."

"Jenna, you love who you love," Amanda said, looking at her. "Stacy loved her husband, hoping he would find her and leave his life and change. Who knows? She was out. I don't believe Ryan didn't know about the *secret* account; he knew. I think his boss didn't know, found out, and told him to *take care of your wife*. Tonight, Ryan said she knew too much. That part of his story is truthful."

Amanda told them about Ryan's tattoo.

"He loved her. I am willing to bet there was a tattoo on Stacy's body somewhere. He didn't want to kill her; he kinda said that and insinuated that he and Nicci would be killed if he didn't do it."

"Amanda, what if he didn't kill her? Perhaps someone else did, but did he know?" Jake asked.

"No." Amanda looked at David, then back at Jake. "When I asked him what happened to Stacy, I saw that look."

Jake and Jenna waited for the answer. "Regret," Amanda said quietly.

David felt his eyes water, and he tilted his head back for a moment.

"Based on him having a date drug readily available, I believe he secretly drugged her. I'd like to think she just fell asleep."

Jenna turned off the recorder on her phone and said, "Thank you, Amanda, for making this all human."

"Well, it is still criminal. Ryan is controlled by dark, evil people. To take your daughter's company, assault her, and make her prostitute for you, unthinkable." Amanda felt her tears hit her face and burn.

"Yes," Jake shook his head. "Well, the raid is tomorrow morning at 3:00 am and 4:00 am. We are going in, hopefully, quickly and quietly."

David and Amanda thanked Jake and Jenna. Jenna allowed David and Jake to shake hands, and she gently hugged Amanda. She whispered in her ear, "I will never forget you. You are a loving person. Nicci will have a family in you and David."

Jake waited until Jenna was done hugging Amanda, and then he went in for his hug.

"You're amazing, and this man loves you. I want the best for you guys. Stay in touch. If there is anything I can ever do for you, call me."

"Jake, you saved my life. You've done so much already. Just make sure Dallas doesn't follow us home."

"Done." Jake nodded in assurance, and Jenna and he led David and

Amanda to an officer waiting to take them back to the house rental in an unmarked car.

CHAPTER 31

After Amanda ate a dinner salad, David led her to the master bedroom they shared that morning. He helped her with her clothes and put her in the bed. As he held her, he watched her sleep until he couldn't keep his eyes open anymore. He dreamed of them on the beach; him chasing her, picking her up in his arms, and dodging waves. The thought of her in the tangerine-colored bikini, her hair wet, and her pure smile never left him.

He could hear her laughter and giggles over the waves. The boys were building sandcastles just feet away from them. Matthew and Mason were happy and laughing. Then it was time to go home.

Amanda entered the outdoor shower, rinsing off while the boys splashed each other and then hit each other with their beach towels. David told them to stop and load up the SUV. But it was not their SUV, and the drive home was unfamiliar.

David's dream now switched to him with his bare feet in the grass at their home in Brookview. He was shouting for Amanda; he was looking for her, but his feet were still. There was glass in the yard and fire. He was startled awake, saying, "We have to go. We have to go."

David sat straight up in bed with the morning light shining through the covered window next to the bed. Amanda said his name with her eyes still closed.

"Did I wake you? I'm sorry." David was trying to get himself into the present.

"It's okay. Are you alright?" Amanda asked and slowly sat up. She was glad she wasn't dizzy or nauseated, but her head hurt. David could tell she was in pain.

"Honey, let me get some water." He was eager to help her, and she ignored him, finally opening her eyes.

"What's wrong?" Amanda could hear that David's breathing was fast.

"Bad dream. Well, it didn't start out that way. It's okay; I'm fine." He looked at her. She noticed his face of sympathy.

"Please tell me my face is not purple," she pouted.

"No, not your entire face." David bit his lip.

Amanda slowly got out of bed and went to the bathroom to see herself in the mirror. David closed his eyes and pressed his lips together when he heard, "Oh my word!"

David got out of bed, put on a pair of athletic shorts, and saw Amanda in the mirror examining her left cheek. He kissed her shoulder and looked at her in the mirror.

"Honey, at least the swelling has gone down." David was trying to encourage her.

Amanda leaned into the mirror. Her whole left cheek was bruised—red, blue, and purple. She touched it slowly; it was painful to touch. She turned and faced her husband. "I'm not pretty. What should I say to the family?"

David laughed and then smiled. "Amanda Nicole Lloyd, you are beyond pretty. These bruises will fade; you glow from the inside out." He took her hand and pulled her close.

"I heard you yesterday, and I read between the lines as you explained what you think happened to Stacy. I was a fool to leave you, abandon you, and think we couldn't talk about race, our lovemaking, or our stresses. Please don't feel stupid for loving me right back home. You are a strong woman of God, and I'm so grateful for you."

David decided he wasn't going to take this time with his wife for granted. "Now, what does the gracious warrior want for breakfast?"

Amanda's eyes widened. "How do you know that name?"

"Leslie is my sister in Christ, too. Now, let me care for you. You need to eat."

"Okay. I need to call Norah and Nathan," Amanda said quickly and waited for the pushback from him.

"Okay." David was indifferent to her surprise. "First, let's check our phones," David thought. "The raid was early this morning."

They both looked at each other and went to the kitchen where they placed their phones on the island to charge.

David got the text:

> Grocery man,
>
> It all went according to plan. Snowflake Ranch is gone. Ryan was arrested. Nicci is fine.
>
> We will check in soon; lots of evidence to tag, witnesses, etc. Take care of the princess.
>
> Jake.

Amanda sighed and looked at her phone. Her text was from Nathan, then Norah. He wanted her to call him. Norah wanted to know if she was good; she was worried. Regina and Leslie checked in and hoped she and David were having fun.

"What should I say to Regina and Leslie?" Amanda asked.

"Well, we promised no more secrets, but there is still an investigation and an upcoming trial. They can't know everything," David pointed out.

"True."

David saw his wife with her phone and in her t-shirt and pajama shorts. He thought she was cute, bruised cheek and all. He went to the living room, took the Afghan blanket off the back of the sectional, and put it around her. He took her hand and led her to the first bedroom with the office and a twin bed.

"I'll make breakfast. You call Nathan and Norah." David moved her hair away from her face so he could look in her eyes with intention.

"I'm fine with it. Please tell them you are taking leave. I'm sure there is a lot of HR paperwork for Nathan on the Lucas McCormick situation."

David barely kissed her; he knew her cheek was sensitive. He examined the back of her head; the bump was there. By her reaction, it was still very tender. Amanda wasn't dizzy, but she asked David to close the blinds in the office, and he insisted that she put her feet up.

Amanda settled herself on the twin bed with pillows positioned where she was comfortable. She prayed. David knocked on the door and brought her coffee and sunglasses to wear. She sipped the coffee but didn't like the sunglasses; they hurt due to the way the bridge rested across her nose. She decided to video conference with Nathan.

"Amanda..." Nathan's voice was soft and caring.

"Yeah, despite my face, it all ended well." Amanda was trying to act positive.

"I heard. Jake shared the video with me this morning. You were fearless. You're a good woman."

Amanda looked away from him for a moment. "Honestly, I feel like a slut; like I betrayed my husband all week because you had me feeling something. Ryan had me feeling something. I wanted David to feel my hurt, but then I realized I needed to do this because none of this can follow me home. I need to be a good wife and a good mom."

"Well, you are already those things," Nathan said. "Those feelings are just that—feelings. It's the quiver of compromise. You stand right there at the foot of the cliff and decide if you're gonna dive in. You seduced Ryan into saying some things he wouldn't normally say. You got close enough to see the tattoo. You helped tremendously. I trust Jake and his team, and I'll make sure this is over for you and your family."

"Thanks. Jake told me that," Amanda replied.

"Good; believe it." Nathan was ready to change the subject. "Listen, the CEO of Augusta Retail is making changes. He doesn't want a company scandal and wants to distance himself and the company from those directors and sales representatives involved in SFR. He recognizes this could've been a lot worse if I hadn't informed the FBI. I am to tell you to expect a call from him. He wants to extend an apology to you directly."

"You sound so official," Amanda said.

"Yes." Nathan gave her that polite smile. "I know you don't like to hear this, but you were set to be the collateral damage here. You and I are going about our lives. I get pulled into a world of human trafficking, and I decide to tell and not participate. Imagine my surprise when I return home and find that you are connected to this operation by sheer coincidence."

"You had no idea that inquiring about your friend, Stacy, twelve years ago, would follow you to your job. Before you knew it, Snowflake Ranch was created by Stacy's daughter. Naturally, it makes sense for this young girl to want your approval; you're the only healthy connection she has left in her world. But her father, Ryan, interferes because he killed Stacy years ago and has gotten away with it. He doesn't need you back in the picture, snooping around, causing problems."

"But you liked Snowflake Ranch and had no clue it was taken over by Ryan, who now used it as a front for human trafficking and prostitution. You recognized the logo from your childhood and thought coming to Dallas for work would be business as usual, with a reunion of sorts from the past, but it was nothing like that. Drugs, human trafficking, and swingers were taking over the hotel where Augusta Retail suggested you stay for our national corporate meeting."

Then to have a colleague assault you..." Nathan finished his synopsis. "When I told this story to the CEO, he asked me to extend his deepest apologies today and to tell you to take as much time as you need to heal and think about your next steps, if any, with Augusta."

Amanda was silent. The story did sound so unbelievable out loud. She sighed.

"Nathan, what would I have done without you looking out for me? Ryan was watching me; he knew about David, his affair, and my sons. You knew about my past, my rape, my abuse, and you still befriended me, helped me."

"Oh Amanda." Nathan now gave her a full-blown smile with teeth. Amanda felt the warmth of it and took it all in. She couldn't smile back; it was too painful, but her eyes said it all, and Nathan saw it.

"When Norah and I interviewed you, I was dazed that day. I'm sure you have heard this a million times in your life. It's your inner presence of beauty that makes your outside beauty shine. Those of us who really care about you couldn't care less about your past. Stop being afraid of your past; it's just a testimony of Jesus and what he has done in your life."

Amanda put her hands up to her lips and blew a kiss. "Thank you for the reminder of that." She was sincere.

"You're welcome," Nathan replied. "Norah, Vanessa, and I are all talking about our next steps. Vanessa wants to retire. Norah would like to be a liaison between Augusta and Hindley Corp. It will allow her to move closer to her family in Ohio. And me? I want to move to Colorado. Christopher wants to go there for college, so I can work in the Augusta office there."

"All of that sounds great for you all. Will the Brookview office close? What about your ex-wife? You need to have that coffee?" Amanda wanted to remind him.

"Well, don't worry about the office. Most of the sales representatives would like to work from home. You just work on getting better." Then Nathan chuckled. "Yes, I've spoken to Jill. How could I not share the beautiful letter you wrote?"

"And?" Amanda's eyes grew big.

"My honesty and love for God are overwhelming to her. But she appreciates it. Since Christopher has decided on Colorado, I can relocate there. It would make Christopher happy if the three of us lived in the same area."

"I love that!" Amanda was excited. "Your second chance is right in front of you."

"I suppose it is. I have you to thank for that," Nathan said.

"No, I just stated the obvious," Amanda said.

"What about you and David? It will be easier to start over. Augusta Retail is changing, I take it he won't be working with that Sam woman. David does love you," Nathan wanted to confirm.

"Yes, to starting over. Yes, to no longer work with Samantha. We've put some major stress on this relationship. We love each other, but staying in love, now that's a whole new thing I hadn't thought about until now."

"You both are still in love with each other. You will figure it out with God's help," Nathan said, and then began to pray over Amanda.

He prayed for God to fix the broken places in their hearts. He prayed for God to fix his doubt about a second chance with Jill. He reminded himself that God could do and has done the impossible. He prayed for God to help him to be faithful and hopeful. Next, he moved on to Amanda and David.

Nathan prayed for God to fix Amanda's and David's marriage. Amanda loved that he asked God to reconcile them to Him, the Holy One, and then to each other. As they ended the call, Amanda put the phone down and cried, although she wasn't sure why.

When David came in, she tried hard to wipe the tears so he would not notice. Then she realized it. The crying was because Nathan said all the right things. It is easy to move on from the prideful and arrogant people who don't see their wrongdoings, but Amanda realized this was an entirely different experience.

David knocked on the door. Amanda gave him permission to enter, and David found his wife on the twin bed, pillows around, phone down, and sunglasses on. She felt she could endure the discomfort of the sunglasses over David asking her about her tears.

He announced breakfast was ready and escorted her to the dining room. He thought about her, the curtains not open, but wild roses on the table from outside, and her pain relievers with water ready for her. The table was set for two—plates beautifully designed, layered with bacon, eggs, French toast with berries, and orange juice. Because she was already filled with such emotion, she hugged him for a while, let go, and they ate quietly.

For the first time in weeks, David thought about his time with Sam. He thought about how Dr. Nick helped him recognize his selfishness and pride and how he was able to go home and ask for forgiveness. David couldn't help but think what would've happened to Amanda if he were still with Sam.

She would've come to Dallas alone, knowing her husband was with another woman, and she would've been vulnerable and could've cleaved to Nathan. Danger awaited her; what if Ryan drugged her, or Lucas raped her? Would she even be here? He thanked God in silence for His timing and provision. Right there, David was reminded that God's mercies were new every morning, and God told him that *He was doing a new thing. Let it go.*

When breakfast was done, David cleared the dishes and stood in front of Amanda, taking off her sunglasses and holding her hands. In her eyes, he could tell she had been crying. He was certain it had something to do with her conversation with Nathan, her quietness at the table; he knew she wasn't ready to unpack all that was said. He pleasantly sighed.

"Have you ever had a food craving where you didn't know what you wanted exactly, so you ate a thing that looked good? It was good, but it didn't satisfy the craving. It's the craziest thing, and you're still hungry." David looked at her.

Amanda shook her head, agreeing. "You just described every woman's nightmare, David." She laughed. "...the calorie intake of the thing you ate was good, but it didn't satisfy you. I'm getting fat just thinking about it because the danger is to eat until you satisfy the craving."

"Right." David looked at her, loving her insight. "That was me with Sam." Amanda understood what David meant. She looked at him and waited for him to continue.

"Sam and I had this craving. I wanted a release from the stress, and I felt I couldn't ask you because you were busy at work yourself. Truthfully, I was bored with my life, the routine of our lives. Because I wasn't building my relationship with God, I had nothing to build you up with. I began to desire being single again, and Sam took full advantage of that."

Amanda was still.

"Sam was desperate, alone, and grieving—an awful combination. She knew I was married; I didn't lead her on or tell her I was going to leave you. It was quite the opposite, but I was hungry. I was an idiot to eat what was in front of me without thinking."

"Amanda, I am not going to lie to you. The first time with Sam was hot, passionate, and sweet." Amanda felt the insecurity sweep over her. Then David touched her unbruised cheek and saw into her brown eyes.

"But she never satisfied me," David told her. "The sweet in the end made me sick. An artificial sweetener. Nothing like my honey at home."

Amanda now looked bashful. David led her to the master bathroom.

"You are the real, pure, original sweet from God for me, my honey." He whispered in her ear, "All these years, you are my Sunday honey. Melanie Leaf was right; the Saturday sweet is artificial."

Amanda had a look of appreciation. He let go of her hand and leaned against the bathroom counter with his back to the mirror, and Amanda stood in front of him. He held her waist.

He suddenly got shy. He looked away from her and scratched his head.

"Do you fake it?" David asked her. "I mean, I deserved that after coming home after being with another woman. But the way you sounded with Ryan, he wasn't even touching you. When I touched you, were you faking the orgasm?"

Amanda lowered her head. "Babe, there have been nights when I just was too anxious to tell you no and too tired to get into the mood. I'm guilty." She felt like she was barely speaking.

David felt his heart fall flat. Amanda saw the sadness take over his face. "I'm sorry."

"No, I'm sorry," David said abruptly.

The room was still. Amanda looked at him and touched his chin with her index finger. "I haven't faked an orgasm in months, David. We've hooked up and had to do it quickly, like when the boys are on their way home. I've come to realize that I don't like sex as much. It's the flat, routine *I know he is gonna want it, he hasn't been home all week,* every Tuesday night kinda thing."

"But as soon as you kiss me, and the more foreplay we have, the better sex can be. But when we can make love, well, that's my favorite. Here lately, we have been making love, and I adore it."

He gave her that wink and smile, then turned serious. "Thank you for explaining, but I don't want you to ever fake it with me again. Tell me you don't want me tonight. Tell me I'm being a jerk, you're just not in the mood, whatever. Love yourself enough in that moment to tell me no."

Amanda appreciated his permission to be herself. It was a reminder of why David was her husband. He knew how to encourage and empower her. She embraced him fully. "I love you."

David spoke to her as her head was on his chest. "I love you too. You are my forever."

They held each other as if they were slow dancing. Amanda began to tell David about her conversation with Nathan. He continued to hold her close and stroke her hair.

David ended the embrace and wanted to be clear. "Don't hide your emotions from me. Just tell me you're not ready and I'll understand."

"It is time for us to let this all go. God is telling me He is starting something new in us. Can you feel it?"

"Yes," Amanda said truthfully.

"Honey," he said, looking at her in the mirror. "Teach me how to wash your hair."

Amanda didn't question him. God said He was doing a new thing. She undressed.

David started the shower. He left the lights out and found candles and a lighter in the linen closet. Amanda lit them and got in the shower. David undressed and followed her. She closed her eyes and turned with her back to the water, tilted her head back, and wet her hair completely. David stood in front of her with his hands on the shower wall in front of him, covering his wife and close enough to her to kiss her, but instead, he softly spoke to her. "I appreciate all your long-suffering and patience with me."

Amanda opened her eyes and felt the tears start to come. As she reached for the shampoo, David helped her and opened his hand. Amanda put a healthy amount in his hand and turned around. David gently put the white, creamy soap in her brown hair. He was careful not to put pressure on her head injury.

As he washed her hair, he told her how kind she had been to him and his family. He told her how, even though they were in the same profession, she had always been supportive and non-competitive, never sharing their personal, social, or financial affairs.

"You are beautiful, the way you think of others before yourself. Sarah's Farm, your care for them is helping the family, Amanda." David shared how Michael gets extra produce because of her generosity and the sales she brings to the family business. Amanda was full of tears as David told her he was pleased with her as his wife, because she is about her Heavenly Father's business.

David told her that her forgiveness washed over him like the washing of her hair, cleansing him and making him want to be a better man. As Amanda turned to face him and backed into the shower water, David saw her tears and kissed them, but he continued to encourage her.

"My mother and my brother are better, kinder people because of you," he shared. "Because of who you are, Amanda, you are changing generations. It's how you carry yourself in this world as a daughter of the King. I am proud you are a black woman."

"I love your culture. I promise to gain a deeper understanding of your people's history. We know God has called us to a higher standard than the world on the issue of race. I promise to use my privilege to help, be a peacemaker, a way maker, a godly husband to you, and a godly father to our sons."

Amanda reached for the conditioner, repeating the pattern. She quickly turned her back to him. She knew she couldn't look at him anymore without breaking down into a full-blown cry.

David put the conditioner on her hair. She told him, through tears, to just let it be for a minute; she wanted him to wash her body. He took the blue loofah sponge, and she put body wash on it. David started rubbing the sponge on her right shoulder until suds appeared.

"Amanda, never once have you raised your voice to me where I felt disrespected in my house. I may be the leader of the Lloyd house, but you make it a home and manage it with love and compassion. You have always been about what is good and what is true."

Amanda finally turned to face him. She was crying, her chest rising and falling. David's hand guided the loofah across her chest and breasts. She rinsed out the conditioner and turned to put David in the stream of water.

"Thank you for always protecting our family through prayer. You have changed. I should've been the encouragement of that change. I should've told you all about my cravings instead of going outside the house. What I needed was right here the whole time. God worked it all out for us; no more sin, guilt, or shame, just us and our God."

Amanda kissed David. To form her mouth to pucker hurt, so she couldn't kiss him like she wanted.

"It's okay." David realized her physical pain and stopped her. "Honey, you need to feel it all. You love me in every way."

"The love I feel from you right now..." She couldn't finish her thought. Quietly, she said, "Just hold me."

He let her cry, and he held her as the water cleansed them both.

THE END

EPILOGUE

"Honey, what did the doctor say?" David asked Amanda as he sat in his office, glancing at the speakerphone and then his computer.

"I got a clean bill of health," Amanda said, smiling, as she sat on the edge of their bed in her silk robe.

"How is the Acuff Academy President and Director of Training and Development doing?" Amanda asked proudly.

David laughed, feeling flattered. "Good. I know I've been at work for just five hours and twenty minutes, but I'm missing my beautiful wife and wondering if she is looking forward to our date tonight."

"Absolutely." Amanda looked up from her phone as Vicki was exiting Amanda's walk-in closet with two blouses in her hand.

"Vicki is here helping me find an outfit to wear for my late afternoon lunch with Alice. I'll let you know how that goes."

David was happy about that. He picked up the phone, took it off speaker, and told Amanda, "Honey, I know we have to get back to our routine, but I loved our beach vacation with the boys, and thinking of you in that string bikini is distracting me this morning."

"Oh babe." Amanda smiled and blushed while Vicki rolled her eyes. "I loved our family long weekend in Wisconsin. I want to let you know you don't have to shave every day. That five o'clock shadow made me weak."

"I'm gonna remind the two of you of these mushy moments when one of you leaves wet clothes in the washing machine for days or traps farts under the covers."

"I hear Vicki," David said, chuckling. "Tell her I promise to finish up my proposal. She did leave me locked up in here and put everything on do not disturb."

Amanda gave Vicki the message and ended her phone conversation with David.

"The two of you are precious. With David being happy, it makes my job easier." Vicki smiled at Amanda. "You, my dear, are so good for him. You two make me miss my Max."

Amanda looked at Vicki sweetly. "Come to dinner tomorrow, please. You can talk to Michael."

Vicki glanced at Amanda and then back to the outfits. "I think you should wear white jeans and this long top with the ruffles and small flowers."

"Okay." Amanda took the outfit out of Vicki's hand. "I'm not trying to play matchmaker. I want Michael to know he made a difference in his son's life. I feel he gets depressed sometimes."

Vicki took a deep breath and let out one. She watched Amanda enter her walk-in closet to change and then said, "Can you keep a secret? While you and David were gone, Michael and I connected."

Amanda was grinning on the other side of the door. "What?! Vicki, you are just now telling me?!"

"Yes." Vicki was now sitting on the edge of the bed, letting Amanda get dressed. "I wasn't sure if I wanted to tell you. David would lose it."

"What happened?" Amanda was excited and slid into her jeans. "Did you call him? Tell me!"

Vicki smiled in remembrance. "I went by the restaurant. He didn't recognize me at first, but then, when I started talking and mentioned high school, he remembered everything."

"Oh Vicki." Amanda came out into the master bedroom, buttoning her blouse. "I'm sure he was grateful for what you have done for David and me, and that you being David's executive assistant was a divine appointment."

"Yes," Vicki said politely. "He caught that right away and thanked me. We talked for two hours, but it seemed like forty-five minutes. I watched him close the restaurant, and he cooked us dinner. It was beef tenderloin, a bottle of wine, and a kiss."

Amanda's eyes widened, and Vicki looked at her daughter's friend. "Not a word to David. It was a soft, simple *thank you* kiss."

Amanda sat on the bed next to Vicki, wanting to understand. "Wait; how do you know it was a thank you kiss, or a thank God for you kiss? How do you know what he felt?"

Vicki took Amanda's hand. "Sweet Amanda, I know when a man is being polite and when he wants something more. Michael was being polite, and he told me he was in love with someone."

Amanda had a surprised look on her face. "What?! Did he say who?"

Amanda searched her mind and her father-in-law's movements. She hadn't heard of another woman nor seen another woman around.

"He hasn't mentioned anyone to us."

"Well then, he doesn't want you to know." Vicki patted Amanda on the leg. "Now, not a word of this conversation to anyone, but..."

"But what? Don't keep me in suspense!"

"Well, Alice has been admiring you from afar," Vicki told her. "Barbara, Gerald's executive assistant, came to my desk when you were in David's office that day in just the raincoat."

"Oh my." Amanda realized the subject had changed and went to her vanity table to do her makeup. "Did I get David in trouble?"

"Oh, hardly, darlin'," Vicki replied. "You are the wife. Not that anyone really knew David was with Samantha, but you made it known that you take care of your husband in all ways."

Amanda laughed and quietly thanked the Holy Spirit for the counsel.

"Alice and I had a conversation about Samantha. Sorry, I told her and David how you put Samantha in her place. When David went to Gerald and told him everything, of course, he told his wife, and here we are... David being blessed for his humility and repentance, and now you're... both of you in a ministry of sorts."

Amanda didn't completely understand what Vicki was saying, but felt she would find out from Alice herself soon enough. "I bought her a gift. Small, a teacup with gourmet teas. Simple."

"Perfect," Vicki said.

Amanda turned around to show her face, and Vicki smiled. "You look great. You're a natural beauty."

Vicki stood up. "I have to get back to the office. I hope you won't run into Cherish Acuff; she is a piece of work."

"Don't I know it," Amanda agreed with contempt. "That woman! What does Scott see in her?" Amanda went to the master bathroom mirror, pinned her hair up, and then turned around to hug Vicki. "She is more than a handful."

Vicki followed Amanda out of the master bedroom. Amanda, with her white slingback heels in her hand, turned out the lights and shut the bedroom door.

"Remember, follow Alice's lead. She doesn't invite just anyone to the house." Vicki traveled down the stairs and went out the front door with a *see you later.*

~

After dropping off the boys with Meri and Bill at the farm, Amanda arrived at the Acuff estate on time. The private blacktop-paved driveway was outlined with tall pencil pine trees. The English Tudor house was large and majestic, and the driveway ended in a circle.

Amanda parked her SUV in view of the front door as it opened, and there stood Alice Acuff. She had a joyful look on her warm ivory face, wearing tailored pleated beige linen pants and a delicate white button-down blouse. Amanda thought she looked like 1940s vintage Hollywood, with her cranberry matte lipstick, manicured eyebrows, and her auburn hair barely resting on her shoulders with large soft curls. She was a beautiful, sixty-year-old woman.

Amanda got out of the SUV with a gift in hand, a clutch purse, and a pleasant smile. "Alice, it's so great to see you."

"Oh dear, yes." The two women embraced. Alice's body frame was thin and of average height. "You look so much better than on the airplane ride home," Alice said.

Amanda remembered and was somewhat embarrassed. "I'm sorry. I had no idea the turbulence, along with the concussion, would make me feel so awful."

"No worries." Alice led her from the covered entry into the foyer. "How terrible that you were assaulted. I'm so grateful David thought to go after you."

Amanda nodded and changed the subject. "Yes. I bought you a little something." Amanda handed her the gift, and Alice examined the pretty gift bag and smiled genuinely.

"Thank you." She laid it on the circular foyer table. "I appreciate the gesture."

Amanda stopped and faced Alice. "Really, Alice, thank you for all Gerald and you have done for David and me. I know the promotion incident was offensive, insulting, and embarrassing, but David and I are so grateful for your humility, support, and just loving us in our marriage."

"See, my dear, that heart right there." She closed her eyes for a moment and then touched Amanda's cheek like a mother would her child. "I just know you and I will work well together."

Amanda took in Alice's compliment and followed her through the foyer and out onto the terrace. There was a large, wrought-iron square table with a place setting for two covered with a deep red patio umbrella.

"Please sit, Amanda. Lunch out here on the terrace, okay?"

"Perfect," Amanda replied as she sat. Alice said the chef prepared one of Amanda's favorites, a Cobb salad. Amanda felt loved. Alice shared how she enjoyed the story of how David and Amanda met. Alice called it an *Acuff romance*.

Alice asked Amanda to share about David's affair with Samantha Coleman, if she felt comfortable. Amanda obliged.

"A happy ending for you. Not for so many corporate wives," Alice said. "What did you do that so many corporate wives don't?"

"I prayed," Amanda quickly said, then thought, "I really love David, and he really loves me. I didn't marry him for convenience, money, or any superficial thing. I knew he was stubborn and a leader who leaves his socks under the coffee table, half glasses of water everywhere around the house, and manages to burn microwave popcorn every time he makes it."

Alice laughed.

"Perhaps people don't marry true. David and I share a purpose—we want to do good and help people in their lives. We understand retail, so we do it well together. God has shown me what it really means to be a wife. I consider it a privilege."

Amanda could tell she said something right because Alice touched her hand.

"Amanda, you are a beautiful wife and not just on the outside."

Alice had to admit, "I am not Gerald's first wife. His first wife died in a tragic accident, highly publicized because here he was an heir to a major company. Gerald and Jacqueline were a good-looking young couple. A drunk driver hit them and ran them off the road. Gerald came out of the coma, and Jacqueline did not."

"Alice, I never knew." Amanda was interested in the story.

"Gerald would come to my work. I was a waitress at a local restaurant, a greasy spoon, on the edge of Carbondale. I was in graduate school. Here I was, this white girl, begging Ms. Nancy, this rotund African American woman, for a job. Oh, the dreams I had of owning my own hotel and restaurant," Alice shook her head.

"Gerald came in to hide. No one recognized him. It was there that I gave him peace of mind. He made my dreams come true."

"Alice, how sweet." Amanda loved the story and told her that Ms. Nancy and her family were dear friends of her mom, Janice.

As they ate their lunch, the women talked about men and women in relationships, why some worked and others didn't. Alice believed no one wants to work hard in relationships anymore, and Amanda agreed, but believed no one wants to be godly and do things in God's timing.

Cherish noticed them on the terrace as she looked at them through the sliding glass doors. They were laughing and smiling. Cherish pressed her lips tightly together, her nostrils flaring and air coming out. She opened the sliding glass door and walked through.

Amanda and Alice turned their heads toward the sound of the sliding glass door. There was Cherish; her gorgeous, perfectly tan body with not an ounce of fat anywhere. She wore a white bikini, sunglasses, and her long brunette hair covered partly by a large, brimmed hat. She put on a smile and headed towards the table in her high heels.

"Mom," Cherish said, acknowledging Alice.

"Mandy. How are you?" She said as Cherish sat next to Amanda.

"Cherish," Amanda said, empty. "It's Amanda." Amanda corrected her sharply. "I am well."

"I'm so glad. I heard about the assault that happened in Dallas." Cherish looked at Amanda over her sunglasses. "What a shame."

"Cherish, really?" Alice was firm. "What brings you out here?"

"Well, I'm getting in the pool this afternoon before I head to the spa. Scott and I will be leaving for the National Grocers Association meeting in Virginia next week. Was there a proposal Gerald wanted Scott to deliver?" She tried to sound professional.

Alice glared at Cherish. "The proposal has already been sent. You can carry on with your day."

"Right." Cherish smiled, rose from the table, and turned to Amanda again. "Tell that handsome husband of yours congratulations on the promotion. Quite the gig, huh?"

Amanda did not reply to Cherish in words, but the look of *leave* was all Cherish needed to walk down the stairs of the terrace and take her place by the pool.

"Amanda, I'm sorry," Alice said instantly.

"Not your fault," Amanda told her.

"C'mon." Alice noticed Amanda was finished with her salad; she placed her cloth napkin on the table.

Alice rose, and Amanda followed her lead. Alice told Amanda to take off her shoes and carry them. The women left the terrace and walked down the grassy trail on the property in their bare feet.

"Oh, how I wish my two daughters were in the grocery business. Heather and her husband, Roy, work at the University of Oregon, and Hannah leads a church with her husband, Tyler, in Tennessee. Scott is here doing well, but his wife is a complete disaster. Gerald and I know Cherish is the one who influences him to place value in things and not in people. It frustrates us."

"Alice, a wise woman builds her house, but a foolish one tears it down with her own hands." Amanda looked at Alice, knowing, and continued to walk on the path, enjoying the soft coolness of the grass on her feet.

"Amanda, what do you know?" Alice saw the knowing in Amanda's eyes.

Amanda hesitated, then spoke. "In January, David took me to the housewares show with him in Chicago. It was in the hotel women's lounge where I heard Gina McCallister confront Cherish to stay away from her husband. Cherish was rude as usual and pretty much stated that she gives Carl what Gina cannot. Gina slapped her, and Cherish slapped her back."

Alice tilted her head in surprise.

"Cherish noticed me as I made myself known coming out from the bathroom sinks and into the lounge. Gina was embarrassed and hurt. Cherish said, 'and here comes the mulatto to defend the prude.'"

"My word," Alice said, offended. "This is where I want you to start."

"What?" Amanda was trying to understand.

"I need you to help me with the corporate wives, starting with Gina," Alice blurted it out.

"How do I do that?" Amanda sounded anxious at first. "I knew what to do in my marriage because it's mine."

Alice took her hand and led her to a bench. The women sat down and looked out at the pond.

"Amanda, you underestimate yourself. By your example, do you know you are changing the way the Acuff corporate wife is viewed? It started with Vicki, the way you don't talk down to her. She is your partner, like a member of the family to you."

"I see you. I heard about you. You came to the office several times, not just to have sex with your husband, but to encourage him. You shared retail management information you did not have to share, and you stroked David's ego. Important for a man."

Amanda now saw it.

"These women, whether they know it or not, want what you have. I'm inspired. Because of you, Gerald and I in our Bibles and realizing the gift of sex in the evening of our lives."

Alice's face got warm and flushed.

"And if you think Samantha isn't going to try to seduce your husband again, you're wrong. Could there be another Nathan?"

Amanda looked at Alice, surprised.

"Oh Amanda, you don't have to worry about any of it. David is ready for her. His righteous anger, if or when she does try anything, she might lose everything. You're in love. Keep it that way."

"Alice, what does this *helping the corporate wives* look like?" Amanda asked.

"Whatever it takes that won't get you in trouble with God or get you arrested."

She laughed, and Amanda did too. "I'm gonna pay you to encourage Gina. Perhaps it's lunch, a spa day, or trips."

Immediately, the Holy Spirit inside of Amanda hooked on the word *encouragement*. God allowed Amanda to feel Gina's sadness and tiredness.

"Monday, go to Barbara; she will have your first check. Keep your receipts and encourage and inspire Gina. I want you to take care of yourself, and there is a young man, Willis, a marketing intern. He will contact you, too. Our social media accounts need some branding."

Amanda said yes to Alice. God told her that she would, but she didn't know she would be excited, nervous, and yet comfortable all at the same time.

"We both will get together right here." Alice rose and pointed towards a small house just 50 feet away.

"To pray, touch base. Once we get Gina loving God and herself—praying we can save her marriage—she can help us help other corporate wives."

Amanda smiled. She liked the idea and realized quickly it was more than that; this was ministry.

"I want to help corporate wives to be consumed with encouraging their husbands and to lead godly lives," Alice said. "Amanda, you inspired me. I know together we can inspire others."

The two women embraced and continued their walk. Alice showed Amanda the mother-in-law cottage and shared that they could meet there to do ministry. She explained Gerald and David know about this endeavor, and they would seek their husbands' guidance and counsel when needed.

Amanda drove home full of inspiration and purpose. She couldn't turn on the radio; she drove in silence and thought how God had made everything right.

With her time at Augusta Retail now in the rearview mirror of her life, here she was in a full-time ministry of sorts, working alongside her husband, using her gifts, and tears came. *Thank you, Dad, for blessing me*, she thought in the silence, and then she spoke. "You are so good to me."

When Amanda made it back home, David's sedan was in the garage. It was after five o'clock. She smiled as she opened the door to the smell of bleach and air freshener. David had cleaned the garage entry, mudroom, and kitchen. She was proud. He always cleaned like their home was the grocery store, using more product than really needed, but she never complained. She was just grateful that he saw the need. As she took a sigh to enjoy the peace, she heard several footsteps traveling down the stairs.

"Hey, Mom!" Matthew said first.

Amanda frowned and then saw her sons with David following behind them. She gave Matthew and Mason a hug and couldn't help but say what she was thinking. "What are you guys doing here? Where is Momma Meri and Bill?"

"Well," David began to explain. "A main water pipe broke at the clinic. Mom had to go in, and of course, Bill wasn't gonna let her handle that alone. Even though the city maintenance is taking care of it, Meri and Bill went in to make sure medical files were secure and the computer system wasn't affected."

"I understand."

"Mom, we are sorry we've interrupted your date time," Mason said politely.

"It's called romantic time." Matthew corrected Mason and then looked at his parents with his eyebrows raised.

David and Amanda chuckled.

"So I took the boys to the movie theater, and we got a sleeve of their good popcorn...," David started.

"... Because we all know Dad cannot make popcorn," Matthew interjected, and Amanda laughed.

"Okay, you didn't have to rub that in, Matthew. I know Momma Meri and Bill gave you guys a new video game, so head downstairs to play that. Your mom and I need a moment, and then we will order dinner, eat, have popcorn, and watch a movie, okay?"

"Sounds like a plan." Mason said and smiled so purely that his dimple showed. Amanda touched his cheek and kissed it.

Matthew kissed Amanda on the cheek and then headed downstairs. Mason grabbed the new video game and followed Matthew.

David stood in the kitchen, now facing his wife. He admired Amanda's white outfit and how it complemented her skin tone.

"You look great."

"Aww, thanks babe." She took his hand. "Not the night we planned, but I'm happy. Today was a wonderful day."

"Come here," David said and kissed her. "Tell me about it." David led her to the den and shut the French doors.

Amanda sat on the sectional, and David sat next to her, their knees together as he sat up straight on the couch, and she sat on the chaise lounge part of the sectional. They held hands.

"How was your time with Alice? The corporate wife's ministry a go?"

"Yes." Amanda noticed her smile again. "Babe, I cannot stop smiling. The joy, gratitude, and love that I feel are overwhelming."

"Good." David looked into her brown eyes lovingly. "Today, I thought about us, and it will be 12 years ago this Fall that I laid eyes on you and said you were worthy of happiness."

"Yeah," Amanda remembered.

David looked away for a moment, trying to figure out a way to soften the blow of what he had to say. "I got a yellow heart from Jake and Jenna today."

David felt Amanda tense up as he held her hands. He stroked her cheek to calm her. They both knew a yellow heart meant there was information.

"What happened?" Amanda asked.

"Ryan, out on bail, was shot and killed in a drive-by shooting in front of a nightclub in downtown Dallas. It was meant for him; no one else was hurt. He was shot straight in the chest and neck," David said, delivering the news.

Amanda went flat. "I don't know what to say."

"You don't have to say anything. Lucas McCormick is in rehab out East. Ryan is dead now. We have the autopsy on Stacy, and in my opinion, Ryan was guilty. His DNA matched the DNA under her nails; he drugged her and suffocated her to death. I didn't want to hear about a trial, now I don't have to. It's over."

Amanda hated that her best friend died so tragically. "Yes, but it doesn't feel like it's over."

"Amanda, honey, we have to move," David said, putting his hands on her shoulders for a moment.

Amanda closed her eyes; she felt it too.

"Remember the dream I had in Dallas? I had another dream two weeks ago; black smoke surrounded the house. The Holy Spirit is warning me."

Amanda agreed. "David, I've had dreams too. I didn't want to scare you, but two nights ago, I saw black smoke in the driveway. My dad is in front of me, and I was holding Matthew's hand."

"Honey, I told Bruce to start getting a crew on our Kingland home. It's time. Something is coming, and we need to be prepared and move now."

"Yes," Amanda said. "I know it is God's plan."

There was silence for a few seconds, and Amanda looked down at their hands, took a deep breath, and said, "I heard from Ian Gustafson, CEO of Augusta Retail."

"Yes?" David wanted to know more.

"We spoke on a video conference. He apologized and accepted my resignation. He said he understood. Because Nathan made it clear to them that I wasn't interested in suing the company and Augusta had terminated all parties involved with Snowflake Ranch, Ian said he wanted to make things right. He emailed me his proposed compensation package."

"Really?" David was surprised.

"Yes." Amanda now moved closer to her husband and leaned her head on his shoulder, staring at their hands together. "I need to sign it and send it back certified and notarized. Augusta has agreed to pay for all my medical bills regarding the head injury for the next 18 months. I might not have symptoms now, but if some develop in that timeframe, they agree to pay for them."

David loved the smell of Amanda's hair and held her gently. "Honey, that's fair and kind of the company."

"Yes, and Ian said that if Nathan hadn't been involved, the damages to his company would have been catastrophic. My cooperation with the authorities on behalf of the company was invaluable. They noted the pain and suffering caused by revisiting my past, but also took into consideration that Lucas assaulted me at a company gathering. Ian showed integrity and, of course, didn't want any of that publicized."

"I can only imagine."

"God is amazing, David. We both work diligently in our careers, loving what we do and not caring about how the world thinks. Our main concern is living right before God, and He is blessing us and showing us favor." Amanda raised her head and then whispered, "I want you to read this compensation package. Augusta Retail compensating me 1.2 million dollars."

David turned to Amanda and looked her in the eyes. "Seriously?!"

Amanda smiled back at him. "Yes. God did it. Don't you see? The money you gave away to the trainees, God multiplied it and gave it back to us."

David hugged and kissed her. "I'm so in love with you! And not just because you're a millionaire now."

They laughed, and then David began to pray and praise God. He thanked God for His loving care—from bringing them home as a family from Dallas to restoring their marriage, allowing family vacations, and their health. He praised God for His provisions, giving them favor, and showering their lives with good, godly success and heavenly prosperity. He thanked God for Amanda's heart and humility. She reminded the family consistently that every good thing comes from Him, their heavenly Father.

"That is why I love you. You point me to God and our Lord and Savior Jesus Christ every time," David told Amanda.

"I love you, David Jonathan Lloyd. Thank you for loving God and loving me."

"Honey, you make it easy, and whatever you want you shall have. Whatever you want to do, we shall do it in Jesus' name."

David wanted to make his intentions clear. "I already know you want to help Nicci. Jake and Jenna said she is officially Nicole Marie Mitchell. She has decided to move to a small town called Dearwell in Iowa. She is in equine therapy now, in a place where horses help individuals deal with trauma. Jenna says she needs space and time, but wants to see us when we visit Acuff stores in Iowa."

Amanda was proud. "Okay." She knew David could feel her intent to make sure Nicole got everything she needed and wanted.

"Now, that compensation contract can keep until the morning, yes? Let's order dinner and enjoy our family."

David rose from the couch, and Amanda followed. He then took her by the waist.

"Then, when those boys are fast asleep, I'm gonna make sweet love to my millionaire wife."

Amanda kissed David passionately. "I love it. I look forward to the million kisses you'll be planting on me."

David and Amanda ordered pizza and watched a family comedy with Matthew and Mason. They all laughed and enjoyed telling stories about their favorite parts of the movie and how much they enjoyed their summer vacation so far. Matthew shared his love of zip-lining in Wisconsin. Mason recalled making sandcastles at the beach in Florida.

Amanda thought of her life without David. The lonely apartment in St. Louis, and the day she drove to the Galesboro store with no idea that the love of her life would be waiting for her. She thanked God and acknowledged to herself that God was right: even with all the twists and turns, David was hers and would be hers forever.

When David put his sons to bed that night, his heart was full. Matthew told him that he kept his promise: he was present, the phone was gone, and David looked him in the eye more often.

Mason didn't say anything. It was what he was doing that David enjoyed. Mason no longer hid who he was; he spoke his mind. To him, it didn't matter if the rest of the family didn't understand; he knew he was loved and he felt appreciated. David and he would sing a song together when David tucked him in, and David could tell Mason loved that tender moment.

By the time David got to the master bedroom, Amanda was in bed waiting for him. They made love the way Amanda had dreamed when she was crying herself to sleep just a few months ago. Afterwards, David drifted off to sleep, grateful that God was restoring and refining his life.

Hours later, David sat straight up in bed seconds before he heard the sound of shattering glass downstairs. He woke Amanda and heard the sliding glass door open and the alarm. He dressed and put on tennis shoes quickly, grabbed his gun from the nightstand, and his cell phone.

Amanda knew what to do. She ran and put her sweatshirt over her gown, shoes on, and stood behind her husband, cell phone in hand; the alarm company was calling as the phone was on silent. David was ready to open the master bedroom door when they both heard another shattering of glass from the living room. Amanda knew exactly what it was. The living room picture window was shattered.

"Yes," Amanda whispered, answering the phone. "There is someone in the house."

When David opened the master bedroom door, Amanda went straight for Matthew's room. She went in and shut the door. "Matthew," she whispered firmly and woke him.

David at the top of the stairs, gun ready, but saw no one. There was a fire in the front yard. He shouted, "Amanda, stay on your bike."

Amanda and Matthew heard the code. Matthew got out of bed quickly, put on his shoes, and traveled through the Jack and Jill bathroom to get Mason out of bed. Seconds later, Matthew and Mason were next to Amanda, ready.

David went down the stairs and straight to the sliding glass doors. When she turned on the outdoor lights, she saw no one.

"Now!" David told them and continued outside to the left.

Amanda and the boys traveled down the stairs and went through the broken sliding glass door. Amanda saw the boys disappear into their hiding spot outside. She heard sirens in the distance and saw the glow of the fire behind her. She didn't see David, but she knew she had to go to the left as they practiced. She heard the gunshot and the sound of a car's engine screeching down the street.

"David!" she screamed, running to the front of the house.

When Amanda made it to the front yard, she was relieved. There was David with his hands on his knees, catching his breath. He had thrown his gun in the yard. Amanda turned and saw the cross burning in the grass. She quickly went to the side of the porch, turned on the outside faucet, and pulled the water hose.

David finally said, "There was a man in black clothes sprinting down the street. I shot at him, but he jumped into a black SUV, and they drove away."

Amanda had tears on her face, her hands shaking as she put the fire out. The police and a fire truck were on the street.

David and Amanda both looked at the now burnt grass in the yard, the shape of a black cross in the yard, shattered glass around them, and they both turned to the closed garage and saw the spray-painted message on the garage door with three swastikas: NIGGER LOVER.

"Dear God," Amanda spoke.

David looked at Amanda. "This is far from over."

ABOUT THE AUTHOR

Toni asks, "If your life were a house, how would you design it?"

Toni Jackson Lampley is an experienced house designer, life designer, and advocate for building strong relationships with God, self, and family. As the former director of a women's business center, Toni has taught many people the fundamentals of entrepreneurship.

She is also a state program director who promotes and supports mentoring programs for young people. A proud graduate of Iowa State University, Toni holds a Master's degree in higher education. She enjoys creating processes, curriculum, and instruction to help others build, restore, remodel, and renovate their lives. *Broken* is her first novel in the upcoming series.

CONTINUE THE CONVERSATION

Read the story. Then redesign what you believe about love.

Broken isn't just a novel—it's a mirror.

Amanda's world is shattered by betrayal and forced into the kind of pain that doesn't stay private. When heartbreak collides with public cruelty, *Broken* asks the questions most people avoid:

- What do you do when the person you trusted becomes the source of your deepest wound?
- How do you protect your children when your life is on fire— emotionally and literally?
- Can forgiveness exist without self-betrayal?
- And how do you rebuild when the damage is visible to everyone?

As a relationship guide and human-centered design coach, **Toni Jackson Lampley** writes emotionally intelligent stories that explore love after betrayal, identity under pressure, and the brave work of becoming whole. Her work is rooted in compassion, lived experience, and hope-centered tools that help people move forward with clarity and intention.

Ready to go deeper than the story?

This book is part of a bigger conversation—one designed to help readers, groups, and organizations explore relationship truths that change lives.

Continue the journey with Toni:

- **Download the complimentary Designing Self workbook** (guided prompts + reflection exercises rooted in human-centered design and the Science of Hope).
- **Join the community conversation** and explore resources created to help you heal, reflect, and design with love.

Bring "Broken" to your organization, group, or event

Toni is available for **Toni Talks, workshops, trainings, retreats, and facilitated book discussions** for:

- Women's conferences and retreats
- Counseling centers and support groups
- Faith communities and leadership spaces
- Colleges, learning circles, and community organizations
- Book clubs seeking deeper, guided discussion

To arrange a session or book Toni for your next gathering, visit her website and select **Get Started / Learn More**.

https://www.tonidesigncoach.com

www.ingramcontent.com/pod-product-compliance
Lightning Source LLC
Chambersburg PA
CBHW040511170726
48295CB00012B/164